The Devil Laughs Again

Also by Régine Deforges

The Blue Bicycle
Léa

The Devil Laughs Again

Régine Deforges

Translated from the French by Elizabeth Fairley Mueller

Lyle Stuart Inc.   Secaucus, New Jersey

Published by Lyle Stuart, Inc.
120 Enterprise Ave., Secaucus, N.J. 07094
Published simultaneously in Canada by
Musson Book Company,
A division of General Publishing Co. Limited
Don Mills, Ontario

Address queries regarding rights and permissions
to Lyle Stuart, Inc., 120 Enterprise Ave.,
Secaucus, N.J. 07094

Manufactured in the United States of America

Library of Congress Cataloging-in-Publication Data

Deforges, Regine.

   The devil laughs again.

   (The blue bicycle; bk. 3)

   Translation of : Le diable en rit encore.

   I. Title. II. Series: Deforges, Regine. Bicyclette bleue.
English ; bk. 3.

ISBN 0-8184-0473-6

To my father and to my son, Franck

Wo wir sind, da ist immer vorn
Und der Teufel der lacht nur dazu.
Ha, Ha, Ha, Ha, Ha, Ha, Ha!

We're always the Vanguard, Ha, Ha!
Wherever we are, Ha, Ha!
Devil's laughter is with us, Ha, Ha!
Never too far, Ha! Ha!

Voici que le temps fait son
oeuvre. Un jour, les larmes seront
taries, les fureurs éteintes, les
tombes effacées. Mais il restera
la France.

—Charles de Gaulle, *Mémoires de*
  Guerre. Le Salut

And so, with the passage of time,
our tears will be dried, our anger
appeased, and our graves overgrown,
but France will remain.

—Charles de Gaulle, *War Memoirs, Salvation*

Acknowledgments

The author would like to thank the following for their collaboration, often unknowingly given: Jean-Pierre Abel, Paul Allard, Henri Amouroux, Robert Antelme, Louis Aragon, Robert Aron, Alix Auboineau, Lucie Aubrac, Michel Audiard, Colette Audry, Marc Augier, Claude Aveline, Marcel Aymé, François Barazet de Lanurien, Maurice Bardèche, Georges Beau et Léopold Gaubusseau, Pierre Bécamps, Suzanne Bellenger, Jacques Benoist-Méchin, Christian Bernadac, Georges Bernanos, Pierre Bertaux, Nicholas Bethell, Maxime Blocq-Mascart, Georges Blond, M. R. Bordes, Jean-Louis Bory, Alphonse Boudard, Pierre Bourdan, P.-A. Bourget, Robert Brasillach, Georges Buis, Calvo, Raymond Cartier, Louis-Ferdinand Céline, Jacques Chaban-Delmas, Marguerite Chabay, René Chambe, Richard Chapon, Jean-François Chegneau, Bertrande Chezal, Winston Churchill, Maurice Clavel, René Clément, Guy Cohen, Colette, Larry Collins, Arthur Conte, E. H. Cookridge, Lucien Corosi, Gaston Courty, Jean-Louis Crémieux-Brilhac, Croix-Rouge française, Jean-Louis Curtis, Adrien Dansette, Jacques Debû-Bridel, Marcel Degliame-Fouché, Jacques Delarue, Jacques Delperrié de Bayac, Abbé Desgranges, Maja Destrem, David Diamant, Jean-Pierre Diehl, *la Documentation française,* Friedrich-Wilhelm Dohse, Jacques Doriot, Paul Dreyfus, Raymond Dronne, Claude Ducloux, Ferdinand Dupuy, Jean Dutourd, Georgette Elgey, Dr Epagneul, Jean Eparvier, Robert Escarpit, Raymond Escholier, Hélène Escoffier, Marc-André Fabre, Mistou Fabre, Yves Farge, J.-N. Faure-Biguet, Henri Fenet, Richard de Filippi, Marie-Madeleine Fourcade, Ania Francos, Jacky Fray, Henri Frenay, André Frossard, Lilianne et Fred Luncken, Jean-Louis Funk-Brentano, Jean Galtier-Boissière, Paul Garcin, Romain Gary, Charles de Gaulle, André Girard, Jean Giraudoux, Alice Giroud, Léon Groc, Richard Grossmann, Georges A. Groussard, Gilbert Builleminault, Georges Guingouin, André Halimi, Hervé Hamon, Robert Hanocq, René Hardy, Max Hastings,

Philippe Henriot, Jean Hérold-Paquis, Rudolph Hoess, Sabine Hoisne, Hoover Institute, Raymond Huguetot, Bernard Irelin, Jacques Isorni, Jeanine Ivoy, capitaine Jacques, Claude Jamet, maréchal Juin, Bernard Karsenty, Joseph Kessel, Jacques Kim, Serge Klarsfeld, Karl Koller, Maurice Kriegel-Valrimont, Jean Lacouture, Jean Lafourcade, Christian Laigret, Christian de La Mazière, Henri Dandemer, Roger Landes, Dominique Lapierre, Jean de Lattre de Tassigny, Jacques Laurent, Eric Lefebvre, Roger Lemesle, Alain Le Ray, Jean Mabire, Grégoire Madjarian, René Maisonnas, Franz Masereel, Pierre Masfrand, Micheline Maurel, Claude Mauriac, François Mauriac, William Peter McGivern, Léon Mercadet, Edouard et François Michaut, Henri Michel, Edmond Michelet, Margaret Mitchell, François Mitterand, Jean Moulin, André Mutter, Jean Nocher, Henri Noguères, Pierre Nord, Jacques Oberlé, Albert Ouzoulias, Guy Pauchou, Jean-Jacques Pauvert, Robert O. Paxton, Gilles Perrault, Philippe Pétain, Jacques Peuchmaurd, Eric Picquet-Wicks, L. G. Planes et R. Dufourg, Theodor Pliever, Edouard de Pomiane, Roland de Pury, *Sélection du Reader's Digest*, Lucien Rebatet, P. R. Reid, colonel Rémy, Jean Renald, Françoise Renaudot, Ludwig Renn, André Reybaz, Patrick Rotman, David Rousset, Claude Roy, Raymond Ruffin, Cornelius Ryan, Maurice Sachs, Georges Sadoul, Saint-Bonnet, Antoine de Saint-Exupéry, Saint-Loup, Saint-Paulien, Henri Sanciaume, Jean-Paul Sartre, Régine Saux, Simone Savariaud, Lily Sergueiev, *Service d'Information des crimes de guerre*, William L. Shirer, Jacques Sigot, Knut Singer, Sisley-Huddleston, Michel Slitinsky, A. Soulier, Philip John Stead, Lucien Steinberg, Pierre Taittinger, Guy Tassigny, Elisabeth Terrenoire, Geneviève Thieuleu, Edith Thomas, Charles Tillon, H. R. Trevor-Roper, Pierre Uteau, Jan Valtin, Pierre Veilletet, Dominique Venner, Jean Vidalenc, Camille Villain, Gérard Walter, Pierre Wiazemsky, Princess Wiazemsky, Prince Yvan Wiazemsky, Karl Wilhelm, Olga Wormser.

10

The Devil
Laughs Again

Chapter One

For Léa, there began a long wait.

The weather, which had been warm and wet in the new year, suddenly became colder on the morning of February 14. The temperature dropped below freezing, and for the next two weeks, snow fell, accompanied by a bitter north wind. Finally, in mid-March, the air lost its chill, announcing that spring was on its way. At Montillac, Fayard watched the sky anxiously; there was not a single cloud and it had not rained for some time. The drought was of great concern to farmers in the region, who needed to feed their livestock and were counting on the next harvest.

Relations between Fayard and those "up at the house" had been extremely strained since the day an accountant was brought in to go through the estate's books. The vintner had been forced to admit that he was selling Montillac's wine to the Occupying Forces, in spite of the fact that Léa and her father before her had expressly forbidden him to do so. Fayard countered that every other château in the region was selling its wine to the Germans and had done so long before the war broke out. He added that most of the German officers posted in the region were major wine merchants back home. Many had been dealing with local merchants for over twenty years; some had ties with families in the region that went way back. Surely Mademoiselle Léa remembered that friend of Monsieur d'Argilat's who paid them a visit during harvest of 1940?

Léa did indeed remember. She also remembered that her father and Monsieur d'Argilat had asked the man, a fine up-standing wine merchant from Munich who had become an officer in the *Wehrmacht*, not to come back until after the war. Fayard admitted he had been putting the proceeds of the sales "to one side," knowing how Mademoiselle would react if she knew, but claimed that he had always intended to give the money back. Hadn't he used some of it for repairs and upkeep? Mademoiselle did not realize how expensive even the smallest barrel had become!

Léa knew only too well how much things cost. The old bank manager in Bordeaux had been relieved to see the check from François Tavernier. (He had been wondering how he could possibly go after the daughter of an old school chum for over-drafts and unpaid bills.) But now, the roof tiles on the north wing of the house had lifted during a bad storm, draining the accounts once again. The contractor that François had sent to assess the damage had advanced Léa some money, thinking that he would be repaid in short order, but neither he nor Léa had heard from François since mid-January. And soon it would be April.

When he had completed his examination of the accounts, the accountant recommended that, under the circumstances, Léa should either come to some sort of agreement with Fayard or have him charged with embezzlement. Léa would do nei-ther.

Had it not been for Camille's son, Charles, Montillac would have been a very dreary place. And yet they all put up a brave front. Bernadette Bouchardeau would sometimes break down, and a tear would trickle down her cheek. Camille d'Argilat lived for the messages broadcast by the BBC, hoping for some sign that her husband, Laurent, was still alive. As for Sidonie, her health had deteriorated badly since the death of Doctor Blanchard. She spent her days in a chair by the front door of her cottage. From there, she could see the entire es-tate and, beyond, smoke rising from the chimneys of Saint-Macaire and Langon. Trains crossing the Garonne marked the solitary and otherwise silent hours. She had preferred to return home to Bellevue. Ruth brought over her meals, and Léa, Camille, and Bernadette took turns visiting. She grumbled that they were wasting their time, that they had better things to do than to look after a sickly old woman, but they all knew that their visits were what kept Sidonie alive. Even Ruth, normally so even-keeled, was beginning to feel the tension and anxiety; for the first time since the beginning of the war, she began to have doubts and would lie awake at night, imagining what would happen if the Gestapo or the collaborationist French militia arrived on the doorstep.

To make the time pass, Léa would spend long hours turning the earth in the vegetable garden and weeding the vines. When this was not enough to tire her out, she would cycle for miles through the rolling countryside. She would come home and curl up on the couch in her father's study, falling into a restless sleep. When she awoke, Camille would be there with a glass of milk or a bowl of soup. They would exchange a smile and watch the fire burning in the hearth. If the silence became too oppressive, one of them would try to get the BBC on the huge radio that sat on the commode near the couch. Jamming was making it increasingly difficult to understand the voices of the announcers who spoke to them of freedom.

"Honor and Country. François Morland, an escapee from a German prison camp and a member of the executive commit-tee of the Rassemblement des Prisonniers de guerre en France *will now speak:*
"First of all, for those prisoners of war who have been repa-triated or who have escaped, and for my comrades in the Re-sistance, I would like to repeat the good news. ..."

His words were drowned out by the static.

"It never fails," exclaimed Léa, pounding the radio with her fist. "We never get to hear the good news!"

"You know that won't help," said Camille, gently pushing her aside.

She turned the radio on and off several times, and was about to give up when they heard Morland's voice again:

"Speaking on behalf of all of you, I told General de Gaulle

15

that our faith is giving us the strength to fight. I told Commis-
sioner Frenay, an escapee like us, what keeps us alive. But
these men who have always believed in our future already
knew the hope we feel . . ."

The static drowned out all but the odd word. Then, suddenly, it stopped.

". . . but they want more, much more. They learned to recog-
nize one another in the prisoner-of-war camps and in the Re-
sistance, and so they want a country that shows no telltale
signs of fatigue or age. They were reunited, and so they want a
country where distinctions of class and race and rank do not
exist, a country where justice is stronger than charity. In exile,
they lived in the same misery as men of all races, men of all
nationalities, and so they want to share what the future has to
bring.

"Yes, comrades! We are fighting for all of mankind. We have
taken up arms for all of these reasons. Let us remember what
they told us when we left our loved ones behind. They said,
'This above all: Do not betray us. Tell France to come out to
meet us holding her head high.'

"The time has come for all men—escapees, repatriated pris-
oners, commandos—to keep this promise."

"Another idealist!" exclaimed Léa. "Morland should come
and have a look at France. It's a sight for sore eyes, a mask of
fear and hatred and envy, with deceitful eyes and a wagging,
treacherous tongue."

"Calm down, Léa! You know that not everyone in France is
like that. There are also men and women like Laurent,
François, Lucien, and Madame Lafourcade. . . ."

"I don't care!" cried Léa. "They're going to die if they're not
already dead and then who will be left?"

Camille became pale.

"Be quiet, don't say things like that!"

"Ssshh! Here come the messages."

Léa and Camille leaned so close to the radio that their fore-
heads touched the varnished wood.

"Johnny drank a cup of tea. I repeat: Johnny drank a cup of
tea. Marie's ducks arrived safely. I repeat: Marie's ducks

arrived safely. Barbara's dog is expecting a litter of three. Laurent drank his milk. I repeat. ..."

"Did you hear that?"

"... Laurent drank his milk."

"He's alive! Laurent is alive!"

Laughing and crying, Léa and Camille threw their arms around each other. That night, they both slept soundly.

One week after Easter, the butcher from Saint-Macaire, who had helped Léa's uncle, Father Adrien, to escape from Camp Mérignac, paid them a visit in his little van. Equipped with a gasogene, a device to produce gas for fuel, the van made such a racket that when it turned into the lane, Camille and Léa were already standing at the kitchen door.

Albert stepped out, smiling broadly, and handed them a package wrapped in a tea towel.

"Good Morning, Madame Camille. Good morning, Léa."

"Albert, what a pleasant surprise! We haven't seen you in nearly a month."

"We can't exactly come and go as we please nowadays, Madame Camille. May I come in? I've brought you a nice roast of beef and some liver for Charles. Mireille added a pâté. I'm sure you'll like it."

"Thank you, Albert. If it weren't for you, we wouldn't eat meat very often. How is your son?"

"He's fine, Madame Camille, just fine. He says it's rough and his chilblains were giving him a lot of trouble, but he's fine now.'

"Albert, will you stay and have a cup of coffee?"

"Hello, Mademoiselle Ruth. I'd love a cup. Is it real coffee?"

"Almost," said the housekeeper, taking the coffeepot from the corner of the stove.

"You're right, it's almost the real thing," said the butcher, putting the bowl back on the table and wiping his mouth with the back of his hand. "Now, gather round everyone, I have some important news. First of all, I received a message from Father Adrien yesterday. We may be seeing him again before too long ..."

"When?"

"I don't know. The second piece of news is that we helped the Lefèvre brothers escape from the hospital."

"How are they?"

"They're being looked after by a doctor near Dax. As soon as they're back on their feet, they'll join Dédé le Basque's group. Do you remember Stanislas?

"Stanislas?" asked Léa.

"You probably remember him as Aristide."

"Yes, of course."

"Well, he's back in the region to form a new network and punish the traitors who turned some of our men over to the Germans."[1]

"Are you with Aristide?"

"No, I'm with the Underground in La Réole, but because we're right on the boundary between the two sectors, I'm the liaison between Aristide and Hilaire. One of you should contact Madame Lefèvre to tell her that her boys are all right."

"I'll go," said Léa. "I'm so happy for them. Was it hard getting them out?"

"No, we have people on the inside and the police guarding the hospital work with Lancelot. Did you hear the message from Monsieur Laurent last night on the BBC?"

"Yes, it seems that after so many sleepless nights, all the good news is coming at once."

"Yes, well, good news for some, bad news for others. I can't help thinking about the seventeen lads from Maurice Bourgeois's group who were shot on January 27."

The headlines of *La Petite Gironde* on February 20 had read: TERRORISTS EXECUTED IN BORDEAUX.

"Did you know them?" asked Camille, her voice trembling.

"Some of them. Every once in a while we helped each other out, even though they're Communists and we support de

[1]Aristide was an officer of the Special Operations Executive (S.O.E.), a British organization that encouraged, directed, and supplied the Resistance. The S.O.E. set up and maintained communication with *maquis* groups in France, parachuting agents into the country beginning in the spring of 1941, and dropping such supplies as explosives, weapons, flashlights, and radios. In 1942, it parachuted seventeen radio operators and thirty-six other agents into France.—Tr.

Gaulle. There was one in particular I remember—Serge Arnaud—same age as my son. It's terrible to die at nineteen."

"When will it all end?" sighed Ruth, wiping her eyes.

"Soon, I hope! It's just that there aren't very many of us. The Gestapo is really clever. Ever since they stepped up the arrests, deportations, and executions in the Gironde, Aristide and the others have had a terrible time finding recruits."

Just then, they heard a bicycle bell. The door opened and Armand, the mailman, entered.

"Morning, everyone. I have a letter for you, Mademoiselle Léa. I hope you enjoy it more than Fayard enjoyed the one I delivered to his door this morning."

"Another letter from the bank," said Léa, sighing.

"Guess what was inside!" continued Armand. "No, don't even try, you'll never guess. A *coffin*."

"A coffin!" said the others in unison.

"Yes, indeed. A little black coffin cut out of cardboard. I think it had Fayard's name on it."

"Why?"asked Camille, astonished.

"They're sent to people who get too friendly with the Germans to let them know that when the war is over . . ." he drew his index finger across his neck from ear to ear.

"All for a few bottles of wine," muttered Camille.

"There's more to it than that, Madame Camille," said the butcher.

"What do you mean?" asked Léa.

"We don't know for sure, but Fayard has been seen leaving the *Kommandantur* in Langon on at least two occasions."

"But we've all been there at one time or another."

"I know, Madame Camille, but we've been hearing things. Then there's his son. When I think that I knew that kid when he was knee-high to a grasshopper. I can still see him and Léa chasing each other through the vineyards, stuffing their mouths with grapes. Do you remember, Léa?"

"Yes . . . It seems so long ago . . ."

"Well, this won't improve Fayard's mood any," said Ruth, pouring the mailman a glass of wine.

"That's for darn sure. First he went bright red, then, when

19

he saw what was in the envelope, he went white as a sheet. I didn't wait to see what happened next, I took off!"

He emptied his glass.

"Well, here I am, talking away and I haven't finished my rounds. So long, everyone."

" 'Bye, Armand. See you soon."

"I'd better be going, too," said Albert.

Léa walked with him to the van.

"They'll be parachuting in more weapons soon. Could you check to see whether the cache at the Calvary has been disturbed? There should be a case of clips and a case of grenades."

"I'll go tomorrow."

"If all is well, put a white chalk cross on the iron grating around the stone angel in the little square."

"Okay."

"Be careful, Léa. Your uncle would never forgive me if anything happened to you. And watch out for old man Fayard."

Everything appeared to be intact when Léa entered the chapel at the seventh station of the cross. The cases had not been touched. In spite of the fine weather, the Calvary was deserted.

During the night of April 15, the rain had carved deep furrows into the sloping paths, depositing little mounds of gravel here and there that were slippery underfoot. On her way back, Léa went through the cemetery, stopping at her parents' graves to pull out a few weeds that Ruth had missed. The square was deserted. She could hear children's voices. It must be recess, she thought, pushing open the door of the basilica. The cold and damp made her shiver. Three old women turned to look at her as she entered. Léa did not know what had brought her to the basilica. In her reliquary, Saint Exupérance appeared to be no more than a large wax doll in dusty robes. The awe she had inspired in Léa as a child was now gone. What had happened to the wonderful image of the little saint whose name Léa had taken for her work in the Underground? It all seemed so absurd, so dangerous! Léa felt a great emptiness, an overwhelming desire to drop everything and to seek refuge on Boulevard Saint-Michel or the Champs-Élysées with her sister, Laure, and her friends, drinking cocktails with strange names and stranger hues, going to illegal dances, and listening to banned American music, instead of delivering messages and grenades on her bicycle, poring over the ledgers, and waiting by the radio for news from Laurent or François, or the unlikely news that the Allies had finally landed. She was tired of living with the fear that the Gestapo or the French militia would come for her, or that Mathias would return, or that they would not be able to make ends meet. François had not written. He must be dead. The very thought made Léa feel faint.

"Dear God, say it isn't true!"

Overcome with grief, Léa left the church.

Her legs ached, as though the wooden soles of her shoes had turned to lead. Hungry-looking dogs barked and followed her beyond the outskirts of the village, finally turning back. At the little square with the stone angel, she looked around to make sure that no one was watching, then placed a chalk mark on the iron grating. The clock in Verdelais struck six. Heavy clouds began to fill the sky.

Perhaps it was the sky that made her apprehensive. She found herself climbing the path to Sidonie's cottage, so small and insignificant against the surrounding countryside. Léa understood why the old woman had wanted to come back to Bellevue. Here, one could travel in one's mind's eye to Les Landes or the ocean or beyond. Léa always felt a sense of well-being at Bellevue, a yearning for rest, reflection, and meditation, as Uncle Adrien would say.

Sidonie's dog, Belle, interrupted her reverie. The animal pawed at the door, whining. Léa stretched out her hand, but the dog recoiled, growling.

"Don't you remember me?"

Upon hearing Léa's familiar voice, Belle sat down at her feet and began to whine again. Suddenly uneasy, she opened the door of the cottage and went in. The room looked as though it had been torn apart by a hurricane; furniture, papers, and linen were scattered everywhere. When Léa saw the upturned mattress, she knew that Sidonie's home had been searched by experts. Who could possibly think that this modest dwelling had anything to hide? Léa knew the answer, but refused to believe it.

"Sidonie . . . Sidonie . . ."

The dog had worked its way under the bed and was now whimpering. Pinned between the wall and the bedframe lay Sidonie, unconscious. With great difficulty, Léa managed to pull her on to the mattress. Her face was a ghastly gray. Blood trickled from her right nostril and the left side of her face was swollen and blue. Léa bent down. The old woman's breathing was shallow and uneven. Under her white cotton nightgown, Léa could see ugly red marks around her neck.

She gazed down, stunned. This was the old woman who had always come to Léa's rescue, consoling her with candies when Ruth or her mother scolded her. The memory of evenings spent curled up with Sidonie in the big chair by the fire in the kitchen was more than she could bear.

"Donie!" she sobbed, "Donie, talk to me!"

The old woman struggled to open her eyes. Léa bent closer. "Sidonie, please say something . . ."

Sidonie slowly placed a hand on Léa's head. Her lips opened and closed without a sound.

"Please, Sidonie . . . try to tell me who it was . . ."

The hand felt heavier. Léa bent down to catch her words.

". . . away . . . you must get away . . ."

Léa felt the hand become heavier still. Gently, she raised her head to look at Sidonie.

"What do you mean?"

As if reluctantly, the hand slipped out of Léa's thick hair, landing with a thud against the frame of the bed.

Belle began howling.

Léa stopped crying. Incredulous, she stared at the old woman's face, suddenly strange and hostile.

It couldn't be. Only a moment ago, she had felt her warm breath against her cheek, and now, there was a corpse, barely covered by a cotton nightgown.

Angrily, Léa pulled the nightgown down.

Why wouldn't the dog stop howling!

She heard a sound behind her and spun around to see a man standing in the doorway. She stood frozen with fear. What was he doing here? Sidonie had died only moments before. Suddenly her outrage yielded to abject fear.

"Please! Please don't hurt me!"

It was Mathias Fayard who entered, but his gaze fell beyond Léa. He rushed past her, fists clenched.

"How dare they!"

Ever so tenderly, he brought Sidonie's hands together on her chest and closed her eyes. "Maman Sidonie," he had called her. She had provided refuge from his father's temper, too. He knelt down, not to pray—he had forgotten how to do that long ago—but because his legs would not hold him. Léa watched apprehensively, but when he turned, she saw that he was crying and rushed into his arms. They clung to each other and wept. When Sidonie died, what little was left of their childhood died too. Shivering, Belle climbed on to the mattress and licked her mistress's feet.

"You can't stay here, Léa," said Mathias at last, collecting himself.

She seemed not to have heard him. He took a crumpled handkerchief from his pocket and wiped her face, then his own. Léa sat dumbly. He tried to rouse her, gently at first, then almost brutally.

"Listen to me, Léa. You must leave Montillac. You and Camille have been denounced to the Gestapo."

"Good God!" he cried, tempted to slap her. "Don't you hear what I'm saying? Dohse's men and the Militia are going to come here and arrest you."

Léa finally grasped his words. Her expression of grief and despair gradually changed to incredulous horror.

"And I'm hearing it from your lips!"

Mathias looked down.

"I heard Denon giving orders to Fiaux, Guilbeau, and Lacouture."

"I thought you worked for them," she said, her disdain for him returning.

"I do—sometimes. You can think whatever you like, Léa, but I don't want them to touch you."

"I guess you know all about their methods!"

"I thought I did," said Mathias standing up and looking at the body on the mattress.

Léa followed his gaze, then stood up.

"Why Sidonie?" she asked, her eyes filling with tears.

"I heard Fiaux say that someone had written a letter accusing Sidonie of hiding your cousin, Lucien, and knowing the whereabouts of the Lefèvre brothers, but I never thought that they would interrogate her. I only thought about you, about warning you. What I don't understand is, why didn't they go up to the house after—"

"Maybe they did."

"No, I came through the vineyard. I would have seen their cars or heard them. Unless they hid in the pine woods."

"I didn't notice anything. I came through the woods on my way back from Verdelais."

"Let's get out of here."

"We can't leave Sidonie like this!"

"There's nothing more we can do for her. After dark, I'll go for the priest. Come on, hurry!"

Léa kissed Sidonie's soft cheek, now cold, and left Belle, still howling, by her side.

Outside, the sky was dark and threatening.

Below the terrace, Mathias touched Léa's arm.

"Wait here. I'll go ahead to make sure it's all right."

"No, I'm coming with you."

Mathias shrugged and offered her a hand up the incline. All was still. It was now so dark that they could barely make out the walls of the house.

Mathias stayed closed to the arbor where the buds of the trees were barely opened, avoiding the farm buildings. He doesn't want his parents to know he's here, thought Léa.

A little light filtered through the French doors on to the

courtyard. Camille must have been waiting just inside, for when the door opened, she was standing there in her navy blue coat, ready to go out.

"There you are!"

Léa bumped into Camille as she entered the room.

"Sidonie is dead."

"What?"

"His friends came to 'ask her a few questions.' "

Camille stared in disbelief at Mathias.

"Don't look at me like that, Madame Camille. We aren't sure what happened."

"Listen to him! Do you think that we're complete idiots, Mathias? We know exactly what happened. Do you need me to spell it out for you?"

"You don't have to and it won't change anything. There are more important things right now. You have to leave Montillac."

"How do we know that this isn't a trap, that you're not going to hand us over to your friends in the Gestapo?"

Mathias took a step forward, his face menacing, his fist raised.

"Go ahead, hit me, Mathias. You can get a head start on them. I know how much you enjoy it."

"Madame Camille, make her stop. We're wasting time!"

"How do we know that we can trust you, Mathias?"

"You don't, but I know how much you love your husband. Would you believe me if I swore to you that I love Léa and that in spite of the distance between us now, in spite of anything I might have done, I'm ready to die for her?"

Camille put her hand on the young man's sleeve.

"Yes, I believe you. But why are you trying to save me?"

"If you are arrested, Léa will never forgive me."

Ruth entered, carrying a knapsack which she handed to Léa.

"I've packed some warm clothing, a flashlight, and two jars of preserves. Now, off you go!"

"Go! Go!" mimicked Charles, his hat pulled down over his ears

"Hurry!" said Ruth, herding them out the door.

"Aren't you coming with us?"

"No, someone has to stay and answer their questions."

"I don't want you to stay alone, not after what they did to Sidonie!"

"Sidonie?"

"They tortured her. She's dead."

"Oh, my God!" cried the housekeeper, crossing herself.

"Make up your mind quickly, Mademoiselle Ruth, are you coming or not?"

"I'm staying. I can't abandon Monsieur Pierre's home. Don't worry, I'll know what to say. There's only one thing that matters."

"With both of us here, it will be easier to make them believe that you have gone to Paris," said Bernadette Bouchardeau, who had just entered the room.

"Your aunt is right, the fact that she and Mademoiselle Ruth are still here will make your absence seem more natural."

"But they could be killed!"

"No more than if you stay here."

"Mathias is right," added Ruth. "Off you go. It's dark now. You'll take good care of them, won't you, Mathias?"

"Have I ever lied to you?"

"Where are you going to take them?" asked Ruth.

"To Albert's, so that he can hide them."

"Why Albert's?" asked Léa, trying to make her voice sound as natural as possible.

"Because he's in the Resistance and he'll know what to do."

"Who told you that?"

"Come on, Léa. I've known for ages that he hides English flyers. He also knows where the drop sites are for weapons parachuted in from England, and he helped the Lefèvre brothers escape."

"And you didn't turn him in!"

"I don't turn people in."

"Your boss mustn't think very highly of you, Mathias."

"That's enough, you two!" said Camille firmly. "You can settle your differences some other time. Right now, what matters is being somewhere else when they show up here. Ruth? Madame Bouchardeau? Are you sure that you don't want to come with us?"

"Absolutely, dear. I want to be here in case Lucien or my brother needs me. I'm too old to sleep out under the stars, but you should leave Charles with us. We'll take good care of him."

"Thank you, but I'll worry less if he's with me."

"I'll go over to my parents' to make sure they don't see you leaving," said Mathias. "I left the car in Montonoire. We'll meet there in fifteen minutes."

Léa, Camille, and Charles drank a bowl of soup, put on their coats, and kissed Ruth and Aunt Bernadette goodbye.

They had been hiding near the large black car for nearly twenty minutes.

"He's not going to show up. I just know he isn't!"

"Yes, he will. Ssshh! Listen! There's someone on the road."

Camille crouched down, holding Charles closely.

"It's me, Léa."

It was so dark that they could barely make out Mathias's silhouette against the sky.

"You took your sweet time!"

"When I told my parents about Sidonie, they were so upset that I had a hard time tearing myself away. Get in."

Laughing and clutching Léa's old teddy bear, which Ruth had patched up for him, Charles climbed up on to the car seat. He was the only one to find the situation amusing.

The ancient streets of Saint-Macaire had never seemed so dark or narrow. What little light came from the headlights, camouflaged with blue paint, was not enough to show the way. At last, they pulled up in front of the butcher shop. Mathias turned off the motor. There was not a light, not a sound. The silence was oppressive. Inside the car, they all held their breath, listening and waiting, even Charles, who buried his face in his mother's neck. Léa jumped as Mathias loaded his gun.

"You'd better go," he whispered to Léa.

She slid off the seat and went to the door. Finally, after five knocks, she heard a faint voice:

"Who is it?"

"It's me, Léa."

"Who?"

"Léa Delmas."

Mireille, the butcher's wife, opened the door in her nightgown, a shawl thrown over her shoulders.

"You scared the living daylights out of me! I thought something had happened to Albert. Come inside quickly."

"Do you mean Albert isn't here?"

"No, he's gone to Saint-Jean de Blaignac for . . . why are you here?"

"The Gestapo. Camille d'Argilat and her little boy, Charles, are with me. Mathias Fayard brought us. . . ."

"Mathias Fayard! Oh, my God, we're done for!"

Pushing Camille and Charles ahead of him, Mathias entered the kitchen and closed the door.

"You've nothing to fear, Mireille. If I had wanted to denounce you, I would have done it long ago. All I ask is that Albert and his friends hide them—I don't want to know where—until I've found some other solution."

"I don't trust you. Everybody knows that you work for them."

"I don't care what you know. We're not talking about me right now, we're talking about Madame Camille and Léa. If Albert's worried, he can take my parents as hostages."

"*Qué Chibani*,"[2] exclaimed Mireille, disgustedly.

Mathias shrugged his shoulders.

"I couldn't care less what you think. I just don't want the Gestapo to arrest Madame Camille and Léa. If Albert wants to talk, he can leave a message for me at the *Lion d'Or* in Langon. I'll meet him wherever he wants. Now I have to go."

He was about to kiss Léa goodbye, but she turned away. Seeing his pained expression, Camille took pity on him.

"Thank you, Mathias."

[2]What an idiot!

The three women stood silently at the kitchen door listening to the sound of the car's engine fade away. Charles had fallen asleep on a chair by the fire, now cold, still clutching his teddy bear.

It was three o'clock in the morning when Albert returned from the drop site, accompanied by Riri, a *gendarme*, Dupeyron, a mechanic, and Cazenave, a road repairman. Each had a submachine gun slung over his shoulder.

"Léa! Madame Camille! What are you doing here?"

"The Gestapo are looking for them," said Mireille.

The men stopped in their tracks.

"And that's not the worst of it," she continued, her voice breaking. "They killed Sidonie and it was Fayard's boy, Mathias, who brought them here so you could hide them."

The mechanic swore under his breath.

"He's gonna rat on us," stammered the *gendarme*.

"No, I don't think he will," replied the butcher, pensive.

"Would you believe? He said if we didn't trust him, we could take his parents hostage!" exclaimed Mireille.

Camille felt that she had to say something.

"I'm sure he won't betray any of us."

"Maybe, maybe not, Madame Camille, but we can't take any chances. Mireille, we're going to have to take to the woods and join the *maquis*."

"Don't even think of it! What about our customers! What if our son has to get in touch with us, what if he needs us! Go if you want to. I'm staying here."

"But Mi—"

"Don't waste your breath, Albert. My mind's made up."

"Well, in that case, I'm staying too."

The big woman threw her arms around her husband's neck. He held her tight, trying not to let his emotion show.

"Well, I'm glad that's settled," said one of the other men. "Do you see me chasing after Lecuyer's steer with a butcher's knife?"

They smiled.

"What about them?" asked the *gendarme*, gesturing to Camille and Léa.

Albert led the other men to the far end of the room. They talked in low voices for a few moments, then Riri and Dupeyron went out.

"If all goes well, we'll leave as soon as they get back. We're going to take you to some friends whom we know we can trust. You can stay there for a few days. After that, we'll have to see. A lot will depend on what Mathias tells me when I see him."

He turned to his wife.

"Mireille, prepare a basket of food."

"That's all right," said Camille, "we've brought everything we'll need."

"No, we insist. You have no idea how long you'll have to stay in hiding."

"The coast is clear," said the mechanic, re-entering the room. "Riri is keeping an eye on the road."

"All right then, let's go. Mireille, don't worry if I'm not back by morning. I'll take the little fellah here and Cazenave, you take the basket. Say your goodbye's, everyone."

The ride was anything but smooth; the van bounced hard as Albert tried to navigate the ruts in the road.

"Do we still have a long way to go?" grumbled Léa.

"No, it's just this side of Villandraut. You'll be safe there. The leaders of the *maquis* in the region are friends of ours. Your uncle knows them well."

"Do you think we'll have to stay there long?"

"No idea. It all depends on what happens when I see Mathias. Ah, here we are."

Albert turned off the road and drove past a group of low-lying buildings, stopping in front of a building that was set apart from the others. A dog began to bark, then the door opened, and a man carrying a rifle emerged.

"That you, Albert?" he enquired in a low voice.

"Yes, I'm bringing you some friends who are in trouble."

"You could have warned me."

"There wasn't time, do you have any room right now?"

"You're in luck. The English cleared out last night. How long will they be staying?"

"We don't know."

"Two women! And a kid! I don't like the looks of that," muttered the man. "Where there's women, there's trouble."

"Great!" said Léa under her breath.

"Don't pay any attention," said Albert. "Old man Léon never stops complaining, but he's the best shot in Les Landes and you won't find anyone braver."

"Well, don't stand around outside," said Léon. "The neighbors we can trust, but these days it's easy for the wolf to slip in with the sheep."

They stepped into a long room, with a low ceiling and a dirt floor. There were three tall beds, each surrounded by a red curtain suspended from the beams in the ceiling, and heavy, carved blanket boxes. On a long table was a clutter of traps, red and blue shells, a dismantled sub-machine gun on sheets of newspaper, dirty dishes, and old rags. Near the stove, black with use, were chairs that been stripped of all but their seats and legs. On the mantle were mortar shells from the Great War and over the stone sink, old calendars, yellowed with age and speckled with fly droppings. The calendar for 1944, with a picture of kittens in garish colors, seemed totally out of place. The room was bathed in the soft, amber light of a gas lamp; the farm still did not have electricity.

The rustic decor, combined with the pungent odor of the tobacco hanging in sheaves from the ceiling, made Léa and Camille hesitate.

"I wasn't expecting new guests just yet," said Léon, taking some sheets out of one of the blanket boxes. "So I haven't had time to make up the beds."

"Is this the only room?" Léa whispered in Albert's ear.

"I'm afraid so!" replied their host, who was not at all hard of hearing. "This is all I have to offer, young lady. Here, give me a

31

hand with the beds. I think you'll sleep well. Real goose feathers in those comforters. Once you're in bed, you'll never want to get up."

The sheets were rough to the touch but smelled sweet and clean.

"When nature calls—behind the house. There's all the room you'll need," he added mischievously.

"What about for washing?"

"There's a basin outside and a well not far."

Léa must have made quite a face; in spite of her fatigue, it was all Camille could do to keep from laughing.

"You'll see, Léa, we'll be just fine. Let me give you a hand."

Charles did not wake up, even when his mother undressed him and slipped him under the covers.

Chapter Two

Camille and Léa had not slept so soundly for many weeks. Even Charles, usually the first to wake up, was still asleep in spite of the fact that the sun was already high. Filtering through the red curtains, the light was soft and pink, hinting at fine weather outside. The door must have been ajar, for they could hear the reassuring sounds of the farm. Hens cackling, the chain and bucket hitting the coping of the well, turtle-doves cooing, a horse whinnying in the distance. It seemed as though nothing could disturb the peace. Someone entered the room and put coal in the stove. The smell of real coffee filled the room. Camille and Léa, roused by the wonderful aroma, poked their heads out of the curtains. Seeing their tousled heads, Léon let out a grunt bordering on a laugh.

"Rise and shine! To think I had to resort to pure Columbian beans to get you two out of bed!"

Forgetting how high her bed was, Léa nearly fell as she reached out to take the bowl of coffee from Léon. She brought it close to her nose, inhaling deeply.

"I put in two lumps. Hope that's not too much."

"Two lumps of sugar! Did you hear that, Camille?"

"I did indeed," said Camille, so frail in her long white nightgown that she looked like an invalid.

Léon handed her a bowl, delighted at their expressions.

"Where did you get this stuff?"

"The English flyers gave me a package when they left. And that's not all."

Out of one of the blanket boxes, which did double duty as a food locker, he pulled a large round loaf of bread.

"You're going to love this. Pure white bread! Real brioche!"

From his pocket he pulled a knife, which he opened slowly, carving three thick slices from the loaf. Léa buried her nose in the fluffy, white bread, as though afraid the fragrant aroma would disappear forever. Camille looked at her slice of bread with the same intensity that she brought to all things.

"Bread ... bread ..."

Charles was standing on the bed, holding out his tiny arms. Léon swept him up and sat him on his knee, cutting another slice.

"That's far too much for him, Monsieur," exclaimed his mother. "He'll never be able to eat all that!"

"I'd be very surprised, he's a stocky little fellow. Now drink up or your coffee will get cold."

The old man was right. Charles ate every last crumb.

And so they spent three blissful days. On the evening of April 21, Albert returned. He had met Mathias in Langon, and Mathias had agreed to be driven in the trunk of a car, blind-folded and hands tied behind his back, to the *maquis* near Mauriac. There, he answered their questions without any reticence. Satisfied, Albert dropped him off near the train station in La Réole later that night.

"Has the Gestapo come to the house?" asked Léa.

"No, but Commissioner Penot's men did."

"Was Maurice Fiaux with them?"

"No."

"What happened? How are Ruth and Aunt Bernadette?"

"They're fine. The men were polite enough, according to Ruth, but didn't seem interested in their answers."

"What did they want?"

"They wanted to know if Ruth or Madame Bouchardeau had heard from Father Adrien. Not a word about you or Madame d'Argilat."

"That's strange! Why did Sidonie tell me to go, just before she died, and why did Mathias think that we were going to be arrested?"

"He told us that he had come upon Fiaux and one of the leaders of the Militia saying that you probably knew all about the Lefèvre brothers and the whereabouts of Father Adrien and your cousin, Lucien."

"So, why did they go to Sidonie's first?"

"Someone wrote a letter denouncing her, saying that she was hiding members of the Resistance. I think I know who it was."

"Why didn't Mathias warn us earlier?"

"Apparently, Denan detained Mathias in his office for several hours."

"Who is this Denan?"

"A real bastard, Lucien Denan! He arrived in Bordeaux just after the Great Flight from Paris. Up until 1942, he was a clerk in dry goods and notions at *Dames de France*. After work, he would go to the headquarters of the M.S.R. where he kept a card file with information on the staff of the store. He quickly became the M.S.R.'s top intelligence officer. He quit his job at *Dames de France* and was made associate inspector of Jewish Affairs and, shortly after that, was put in charge of the entire region. When the Bordeaux Militia was created, he was made Chief of the Second Division. Apparently, he also works for the Germans and goes by the name of "Monsieur Henri". That, in a nutshell, is Lucien Denan. Anyway, to get back to Mathias Fayard, as soon as he was able to get away, he took one of the cars. Unfortunately for Sidonie, he arrived too late. The funeral was this morning. There weren't very many of us there to pay our last respects."

Léa was unable to hold back her tears.

"Ruth made all the arrangements," Albert went on. "I've taken Belle home with me, but I'm afraid it won't be long before she joins her mistress."

"So are they or aren't they looking for us?" asked Camille.

35

"According to Mathias, no, at least not officially. But that doesn't mean anything. He thinks it would be a good idea if you stayed in hiding for a while longer."

"Does he know where we are?"

"Of course not. We don't trust him that far. We're going to meet at the train station in Bordeaux on the 24th. I'll try to come by the day after. Until then, keep a low profile."

The weather was sunny and warm, although the early morning air was quite cool. The smell of the pine forest was intoxicating. Léa and Camille, feeling as though they were on holiday, were lulled into a state of lethargy which neither tried to resist. They went for walks in the forest, picnicking under the trees, napping in little hollows in the sandy ground, and playing hide-and-seek with Charles.

The bubble suddenly burst when a member of the *maquis* came to tell Léon that Albert and his wife had been arrested. Mireille had been taken to Fort du Hâ and Albert, to 197 Route de Médoc (renamed Avenue du Maréchal Pétain) where he was to be interrogated.

Camille blanched upon hearing the news, remembering her stay in the basement of that sinister place listening to the screams of prisoners being tortured.

"When was he arrested?"

"He was on his way to meet young Fayard at the train station."

"Mathias ratted on him!"

"It doesn't look that way. As a safety precaution, we had alerted Aristide. Two of his men were watching the station and another was waiting for Fayard near the rendezvous point. Everything seemed normal. I arrived with Albert and Riri five minutes after the appointed time. When the train from Paris arrived, we got separated. Riri and I saw Fayard coming; he seemed to be alone. We turned around, and about ten yards behind us, we saw Albert surrounded by a German officer, two German soldiers, and three French civilians. We heard him say, 'You must be mistaken.'

"The crowd started moving away and I think that's when

36

Fayard realized what was going on. He went pale, started walking toward them, then stopped. I was near him. 'You bastard!' I said. 'We'll get you for this!'

"He looked at me like he didn't understand.

" 'I had nothing to do with it,' he said. 'I don't understand. This is just a coincidence.'

" 'Well,' I said. 'You're going to pay for it.'

" 'Cut it out,' he said. 'No one except me knew I was supposed to meet him here.'

" 'Yea, so how do you explain what just happened?'

" 'You can think whatever you like. Let's follow them, I want to know where they take him. Come on.'

" 'Yea! So they can arrest me too!'

" 'Here, take my gun. All you have to do is shoot me if you think I'm going to squeal on you.'

"So he handed me his gun. Just like that. Right out in the open where everybody could see. I grabbed it from him.

" 'Are you crazy?' I said.

"I checked to make sure it was loaded and stuck it in my pocket. We headed for the exit. Riri joined up with us. He looked like he wanted to shoot Fayard on the spot.

" 'Tell him,' Fayard says to me in a calm voice, heading for a car parked in front of the steps.

"Meanwhile, just a few yards away, they were shoving Albert into a Citroën with German licence plates. I got in beside Mathias, but Riri started walking away.

" 'Isn't he coming?' Fayard asked me.

" 'He doesn't trust you. He'll follow us with some friends we've got nearby.'

" 'Well, they'd better get the lead out,' he says, heading after the car with Albert in it.

"I pulled out the gun and pointed it at Fayard. By now, I was ready to kill him. I looked back several times wondering how Riri and the others were going to keep up. The car up front was really moving.

"Then Fayard starts to swear: 'They're not going to the Cours du Chapeau-Rouge.'

" 'What's that?' I asked.

" 'One of Poinsot's offices.'

" 'So?'

" 'So that means they're handing him over to the Germans. It's a lot harder to get someone away from them than it is to get someone away from the French police.'

"When we reached the Cours Aristide-Briand, we turned toward the Cours d'Albret. I said to myself, they're taking him to Fort du Hâ. But they kept right on going. We went past the prison. At the Rue de l'Abbé-de-l'Épée, Fayard asked me if I could see my friends behind us. Aside from a few bicycles and a German army truck the road was empty. When we got to the Rue de la Croix-de-Seguey, I figured out where they're going. Some German soldiers stopped us at the Médoc roadblock. I put the gun back in my pocket. I was shaking in my boots. Fayard showed them a card and they waved us through. The streets of Le Bouscat were practically deserted. Not another car in sight. Mathias slowed down to put a little distance between us. Still no sign of my friends. When the Germans stopped, we pulled over too, about a hundred yards behind. We saw them shoving Albert into the Gestapo headquarters. There was nothing we could do! I looked over at Mathias. He was still white and the veins on his hands were popping out. I felt like killing him then and there. He must have read my thoughts.

" 'That wouldn't do any good,' he says to me. 'You'd just get yourself arrested, too. We have to warn his wife and the others. I swear to God, I didn't rat on anyone. It's your guys you should be watching.'

"I let him start the car and we drove past number 224 real slow. That's the mansion where Kommandant Luther lives, almost opposite number 197. Everything was quiet."

He drained the glass of wine Léon handed him.

"And then?" asked Léa.

"Then we went back to the train station, to see if the others were still there. After checking out the station, Mathias says: 'We can't stay here. We're going to draw attention to ourselves. Let's go to Saint-Macaire to warn Mireille.'

38

"We took the right bank of the Garonne. Just before we got to Rions, we were stopped by the Militia. They were looking for the guys who did the sabotage operation the day before. As we were leaving Saint-Maixant, there was another road block, this time, the Germans. By the time we got Saint-Macaire, Albert had been in custody for three hours.

" 'We'd better go through the port,' said Mathias.

"He stopped the car below the ruins of the old castle, in a cave where they store home brew. We scrambled up the hill and came out behind the church.

" 'Don't make a sound,' he says. He didn't seem to notice I still had his gun trained on him.

"The street was completely deserted. All the shutters were closed, in spite of the fact it was broad daylight. Then we heard two shots.

" 'That sounded like it came from Albert's place!' Mathias says.

"We hid in a doorway. We saw Mireille being forced into a car by a German N.C.O. Then, in front of the butcher shop, we saw a dog, bleeding to death. A soldier kicked the dog and started laughing. The dog landed close to where we were hiding. I heard Mathias say: 'Belle. They killed Belle.' "

"Sidonie's dog!" exclaimed Léa.

"Then what did you do?" asked Léon.

"I made him go back to the car and drive me to a place near Bazas where I handed him over to Georges's men until we decide what to do."

"How did you find out where they took Mireille?"

"When we got to Georges's, a friend who is a policeman in Bordeaux had just arrived to tell us that both Albert and Mireille had been arrested. He knew where they were taken."

There was a long silence. At last, Léon turned to Léa and Camille, who held Charles tightly as he looked anxiously at Léa, then his mother.

"You aren't safe here anymore."

"What do you mean?" snapped Léa. "Albert would never denounce us."

"He'll hold out as long as he can, I've no doubt about that, but we can't take any chances. Don't forget that they also arrested his wife. If they torture her in front of him, he'll talk."

"Who could blame him?"

Just then, Léon grabbed his rifle which he normally kept hidden by his bed and aimed it at the door. They heard the latch turn, and the door was opened by a man wearing a bomber jacket.

"I say, old chap, don't you recognize me?"

Léon lowered his rifle.

"Aristide," he mumbled, "You took a mighty big risk showing up at the door like that."

"You're absolutely right. Hello, Léa. Do you remember me?"

"Yes, I do. It's nice to see you again."

"And you must be Madame d'Argilat," he said, turning to Camille.

"Yes, how do you do?"

"I have good news for you. Your husband has left Morocco with the armoured division that trained under General Leclerc for the Allied landing. He arrived in England on April 21 by way of Swansea, a port in south Wales. The General himself came out to meet them."

Camille's face shone with joy. How beautiful she is! thought Léa. In a spontaneous gesture of affection, she kissed Camille. The time when Léa had hated Camille for marrying the man she loved, and who had been her lover for one brief night in the underground passages of Toulouse, seemed so far away now. Léa felt only happiness for Camille. They had become friends.

"Thank you," Camille murmured. "Thank you for the good news."

"And I think that it would not be out of place to tell you that you may be receiving more good news shortly. However, in the meantime, I'm afraid that you can't stay here. I would take you to a friend of mine in Souprosses, but I have a feeling that she's being watched by Grand-Clément's men, who are looking for me."

"Couldn't we go back to Montillac since they aren't looking for us?"

"We don't know that for sure. We can't take that risk."

"We could stay in the dovecote for a few days," suggested Léon. "It's deep in the forest. They'd never find us there. It's not very comfortable, but ..."

"Staying alive is more important than being comfortable," said Aristide. "Pack enough clothing and food to last you for a few days. We must leave right away. Are there blankets?"

"I think so, but I'll take a clean one for the kid just in case."

"What about Mathias?" Léa asked the English agent.

"Twenty years hard labor, if I have anything to do with it," muttered Léon.

"It's not that easy. We shall have to interrogate him. I don't trust anyone, yet I have a feeling that he had nothing to do with the arrests."

"He still works for the Germans."

"He and many others, I'm afraid. But until we have proof to the contrary, I would say that he hasn't killed anyone."

"We're ready," said Camille, holding a small kit bag.

Colonel Claude Bonnier, a regional military officer whose code name was Hypoténuse, was sent to France by the *Bureau central de renseignement et d'action* (B.C.R.A.)[3] in November 1943 with orders to rebuild the Resistance in Aquitaine after Grand-Clément sold out to the Germans.

He was taken prisoner by the Gestapo in February 1944 while trying to send a message to London. (His radio operator in the Rue de Galard in Bordeaux had been denounced to the police and arrested. He, in turn, identified Hypoténuse who was arrested by Lieutenant Kunesch as he arrived at the operator's home.)

Taken to 197 Route de Médoc in Le Bouscat, Hypoténuse was interrogated that evening by Dohse himself. He steadfastly refused to admit that he had been sent from London and that his name was Claude Bonnier alias Bordin, in spite of the fact

[3]Headquarters established by the French in London to organize, direct, and supply Resistance units and, later, to amalgamate autonomous Resistance groups.–Tr.

that Toussaint, the Lespine brothers, Durand, and Grolleau had all fingered him. He also denied ordering the execution of Colonel Camplan, whom the Resistance had accused of treason.[4]

After about twenty minutes, Dohse lost patience, and ordered Hypoténuse locked in a basement cell, still handcuffed, saying that he would resume the interrogation after dinner. Late that night, Dohse was fetched from the officers' mess: strange things were happening in Hypoténuse's cell. When Dohse arrived, he was writhing on the floor, foaming at the mouth, his face and lips covered in dust, moaning softly. The guard, who was bending over his body, stood up.

"Er hat sich mit Zyankali vergiftet."

"Das seh' ich auch, Dummkopf! Haben Sie ihn nicht durch sucht?"

"Selbstverständlich, Herr Leutnant, aber die Kapsel muss in seinem Jackenfutter versteckt gewesen sein."

"Wie hat er das fertiggebracht, mit gefesselten Händen?"

"Er muss die Kapsel mit den Zähnen erwischt haben, aber dann ist sie ihm entfallen. Die Flüssigkeit hat sich auf dem Fussboden ausgebreitet und er hat sie aufgeleckt. Daher stammt auch der Staub in seinem Gesicht, und deshalb war er auch nicht sofort tot."

"Rufen Sie schnell einen Arzt!"

"Zu Befehl, Herr Leutnant!"[5]

[4]A hero of World War I, Eugène Camplan joined the French Resistance early on. As leader of the southern division of B2 Region, he was ordered by Colonel Touny in October 1943 to coordinate the activities of the *Forces françaises de l'intérieur* in the region of Bordeaux, which included five departments. Suspected of treason by Bonnier after it was discovered that he had met with Dohse and Grand-Clément, Camplan was executed by Bonnier's men in January 1944 in the Bois des Linaux near Ruffec. After the war, there was a lengthy inquiry and Colonel Camplan, the "victim of a tragic misunderstanding" was officially declared to have "died for France."

[5]"He's poisoned himself with cyanide."
"I can see that, you idiot. Didn't you search him?"
"Of course we did, sir. The capsule must have been sewn into his jacket."
"And how did he manage to get it out with his hands tied?
"He must have pulled it out with his teeth, but it dropped and broke. He lay down and licked the cyanide off the floor, which explains why he has dust on his face—and why he didn't die instantly."
"Quick! Call a doctor!"
"Yes, sir!"

The soldier ran upstairs, shouting:

"Einen Arzt, schnell einen Arzt!"[6]

The prisoners in the other cells plugged their ears so they wouldn't have to hear the moaning, but felt no remorse over the slow death of the man they had denounced. Twenty years old, manipulated by Dohse, they thought it was only fair that the man who had ordered the death of their leader, Colonel Camplan, should pay with his own life.

At dawn, Hypoténuse died without talking.

Impressed, Dohse was heard to say:

"The ones from London aren't like the rest."

Paradoxically, Bonnier's horrible death, which ought to have had a paralysing effect on the Resistance movement, gave it new strength, galvanizing it into action.

The same was true when Albert died.

The butcher was not like the rest either.

He had joined the Resistance out of a profound belief that the Germans had no business being in France and that he and men like him had to do whatever they could to get their country of the Occupant if they ever wanted to look their children in the face again. Albert's father had fought at Verdun and later died of his war wounds, and Albert had adopted one of his favorite sayings. Whenever he went for a walk in the hills of Pian, he would stop and gaze over the countryside, saying in a soft voice:

"France is worth dying for."

Albert did not have a cyanide capsule and his torturers had been given free rein. The methods they used included a new refinement—a butcher's knife.

At first, Albert tried to keep his morale up by telling himself that the good Lord was punishing him for having slaughtered so many animals.

They slashed his skin, laughing as they pushed slices of garlic into the slits.

"Doesn't he just look like an Easter leg of lamb!"

They put salt and pepper on the muscles of his chest,

[6]"A doctor! Quick, a doctor!"

43

stripped raw. They trussed him up "like a roast" and when they had had enough of "dressing the carcass" without managing to extract a single word, they rolled him down the basement stairs and locked him in the cell that had been Bonnier's. He regained consciousness in time to hear his torturers laugh and say:

"If he doesn't talk tomorrow, we'll dress his wife's carcass right in front of his eyes."

"I'll talk," Albert said to himself.

The slightest movement caused him such excruciating pain that he could not stifle his cries. For hours, he chewed on the rope pinning his upper arms. In spite of the damp cold of the cell, he was soon drenched in sweat. Just before dawn, the rope gave way, but he passed out from the exertion. When he regained consciousness, the sun was rising. He began removing the ropes binding the rest of his body, but they had become stuck in his wounds. At one point, the pain was so great that he broke down, crying as he had not cried since the death of his father when he was nine years old. A big, strong man, he lay on the filthy floor of the cell, sobbing loudly. Had his torturers returned at that moment, he probably would have talked. His tears mingled with the dust on the floor. He clenched the dampened earth in his fist. "The earth . . ." It was this thought that gave him the strength and the rage he needed to finish tearing off the ropes. A little light forced its way through a small window that had not been completely blocked off. Near the opening was a thick ring that was within his reach. A pipe ran the full length of the wall. Albert climbed up on the pipe and attached one end of the rope to the ring. With the other, he made a noose which he slipped over his head. As he stepped off the pipe, his feet fluttered back and forth. Instinctively, he tried to climb back on to the pipe, but the thin rope closed around his neck, slowly crushing his larynx. After several long minutes, he died.

In the next cell, two members from the *Franc tireurs et partisans* Resistance unit in Sainte-Foy-la-Grande began to sing, their voices breaking at first, then growing stronger and stronger:

. . . Ami, si tu tombes,
Un ami sort de l'ombre
A ta place.

Demain du sang noir
Séchera au grand soleil
Sur les routes.

Sifflez, compagnons . . .
Dans la nuit, la liberté
Nous écoute.[7]

Albert's wife and friends learned the details of his horrible
death only after the liberation of Bordeaux.

[7]Friend, should you fall,
Another will step out of the shadows
To take your place.

Tomorrow,
Blood will dry black in the noonday sun
Along the road.

Whistle, comrades!
In the dark of night,
Freedom hears our call.

Le Chant des partisans, lyrics by Maurice Druon and Joseph Kessel, musical
arrangement by Anna Marly, was broadcast for the first time over the BBC on February 9, 1944; it was read by Jacques Duchesne under the title, *Chant de la Libération*, then sung to Anna Marly's arrangement in April and August of 1944. Written in
London, this poem was first published in *Cahiers de la Libération*, an underground
paper founded in Occupied France by Emmanuel d'Astier de la Vigerie in September 1943.

Chapter Three

Dear Léa,

I don't know how things are at Montillac but Paris is absolutely crazy. Everyone here is waiting for the Landing. Parisians hate the English and Americans more than ever since they began bombing Paris. The night of April 20 was one of the worst. I was staying with friends who live on the top floor of a building in the Place du Panthéon. For over an hour, we drank champagne and whiskey and watched the bombs fall. Better than fireworks on the Fourteenth of July! There wasn't a single stained-glass window left in Sacré Coeur. Over six hundred people died. Aunt Lisa and Aunt Albertine were in a terrible state. I couldn't help feeling bad too, but I prefer not to think about it. Otherwise, I'll end up like them, spending my life praying in the basement or in a subway station or a movie theatre, all of which stay open until 6:00 a.m. as bomb shelters. The sirens go off almost every night and even during the day. It's really getting ridiculous.

It's a good thing I have connections, otherwise we'd starve at the Rue de l'Université. I'm sure things are easier at Montillac. Everybody here is talking about Doctor Petiot and the Rue Lesueur incidents. It's giving me nightmares. Aunt Lisa cuts out every newspaper article she can find on the subject. Apparently, the English dropped exploding cookie tins over Charentes. Did you hear anything about that? We think that it's propaganda, but some people say they're perfectly capable of doing something like that. We were graced with a visit from my former heart throb, Marshal Pétain, who put in a personal appearance at the *Place de l'Hôtel-de-Ville*. It was all Aunt Albertine and I could do to keep Aunt Lisa from attending.

I see Sabine and her baby every now and then. Otto got a 48-hour leave last week. He still hasn't got permission to marry Sabine. I think it's very hard on her, but she hasn't said anything to me about it. She pretends that she's having a good time with women she thinks are in the same situation as her when, in fact, they're just tarts. I suggested she should go back to Montillac until the war is over, but she told me that it was out of the question. You should write to her. Otto has gone back to the Eastern front. I'll try to get some cigarettes for you and some nice blue material for a dress.

I know you'll laugh, but I've started reading. A friend lent me this book that came out before the war, I think. It's about a family and their estate, sort of like ours only the story takes place in the southern United States around the time of the American Civil War. It's called *Gone with the Wind*. You'd really like it. You should get a copy at Mollat's in Bordeaux.

How are Camille, Charles, Ruth, and Aunt Bernadette? Give them a kiss for me. And don't forget Sidonie. Have you heard from Laurent? Have you seen your mystery man, François Tavernier, recently? Are Uncle Luc and our charming cousin still pro-German? And what about Mathias? I still find it hard to believe he's working for the Gestapo. Are his parents still robbing us blind? I wasn't able to get the money you asked for. I talked to Sabine and Aunt Albertine and Aunt Lisa, but you know what their financial situation is. They can barely make ends meet. When Sabine told Otto, he was really sorry he couldn't do anything to help. Ever since his father cut him off, he's had to live on his soldier's pay. Maybe you should consider Fayard's proposal. What does Camille think? I know you're going to kill me for suggesting we sell Montillac or even part of it. Well, I'll say goodbye for now. Some friends are picking me up so we can see a movie. We're going to the Helder to see *Le Voyageur sans bagages*.

Write soon!

Hugs and kisses,
Laure

p.s. Ignore the raids and come to Paris. You need a change. I'll take you to a basement cafe in the Latin Quarter to listen to some jazz!

Léa smiled as she finished reading the letter. My little sister is really out of it, she thought. She unfolded a third sheet of notepaper, written in an elegant script.

Dearest Léa,

I thought I should add a short note to your sister's letter to tell you how often I think of you and the dear home into which you and your sisters were born. Your father and mother did love it so. Your situation is a source of great concern for Lisa and me. We have checked and re-checked our own situation, and are on the brink of financial ruin. Apart from our apartment in the Rue de l'Université, we have nothing. We have had to sell our mother's most beautiful jewelry at ridiculously low prices just in order to eat. The few pieces that remain have only sentimental value. The investments we made before the war have been a complete disaster and our banker has disappeared with the gold that we entrusted to him. This is my way of telling you that short of selling our apartment, we cannot offer you any assistance. Lisa and I really do not know what to suggest. Have you tried asking your Uncle Luc for advice? I know that the two of you are not on the best of terms, but I am sure that out of respect for the memory of his brother, he would do whatever he could to help you. There are too many dishonest people out there just waiting to take advantage of women made vulnerable by the war. Soon it will be over. If only you could hang on a little longer!

Laure is quite a handful, constantly out, coming home at all hours, buying and selling goodness knows what. She's almost as much worry as her sister, Sabine; it seems as though her marriage is not to be. What will become of her after the war?

Do write us more often, Léa, and tell us about yourself and dear Camille. We are so thankful that she is with you. Please give my warmest regards to your aunt, Madame Bouchardeau, and to Ruth.

Dear child, please forgive us for not coming to your assis-

48

tance. Lisa and I pray for you every day and send you our bless-
ings.

Your loving aunt,
Albertine

Léa crumpled the letter and threw it on the floor. She felt so
despairing, so alone, yet there must be something she could
do.

After only two nights at the dovecote, Léa was awakened on
the third morning by a familiar voice. Still half-asleep, she
couldn't quite place it.

"She's sleeping like a log!"

"Father Adrien!" exclaimed Camille. "How wonderful to see
you again!"

"Uncle Adrien!" cried Léa, now wide awake.

"Hello, Sleeping Beauty!"

Kneeling on her blanket, Léa held her uncle's hand firmly
and gazed at him with a mixture of joy and disbelief.

"I thought I wouldn't see you again until after the war."

"It's almost over."

"When did you get here?"

"I was parachuted in last night, not far from here. Aristide
was waiting for me. He told me about Albert and Mireille. . . ."

"We have to do something."

"Aristide and his men are working on a plan, together with
the group in La Réole. For now, there's nothing we can do."

"I can't stop thinking that it's because of us that they were
arrested," said Camille.

"I don't think so. Sometimes the Gestapo find documents
when people are arrested. Other times, someone breaks
down under torture and provides names. While I was in
London, I found out the name of the young man who has
Poinsot's full confidence; I immediately feared for you, and for
Albert and Mireille. This person has known for a long time
that Albert is in the Resistance."

"Why didn't he show himself earlier?"

"He is a very perverse individual. He wants to round up the leaders of the *maquis* in the region singlehandedly so he can take full credit."

"If you know who he is, why hasn't he been eliminated?"

The priest's gaunt face, now hidden under a thick mustache dyed black, was sombre. Léa saw his body tense. Poor Uncle Adrien, she thought, in spite of the war, he's still a priest. Killing someone, even a traitor, means breaking the First Commandment. If only she were a man. . . .

"I think I know to whom you are referring," said Camille, articulating Léa's thoughts. "I'm only a woman, but I'll kill him if you tell me to."

Léa looked at her friend, dumbfounded. Camille, whom she had always thought of as a weakling, would never cease to amaze her! Léa remembered her shooting the man who had attacked them at Orléans.

"This is not a job for someone like you," said Father Adrien, looking at Camille tenderly. "This person has bodyguards who are just as ruthless as he is."

"Yes, but he wouldn't suspect me!"

"Please, I do not wish to discuss it any further."

"I think we should discuss it, Uncle Adrien. Camille is right, he wouldn't suspect us."

"You don't know what you're talking about. These people are dangerous, very dangerous. We have experienced men who can do the job, if it comes to that."

"But . . ."

"Camille, please . . ."

Father Adrien's tone did not call for a reply, but he smiled and went on:

"I have a surprise for you. Would you like to guess what it is?"

"You . . . you've seen Laurent?"

"Yes, when I went to see General Leclerc."

"How is he?"

"As well as can be expected. I agreed to bring you a letter, even though it's expressly forbidden. Here it is."

Hesitating, she took the crumpled envelope.

"Whatever you do, destroy the letter as soon as you have read it. Come, Léa, let's go for a walk."

Camille turned the unmarked envelope over again and again. At last, she tore it open with uncharacteristic force, pulling out two sheets of lined scribbler paper.

My darling wife,

What I am doing is incredibly dangerous both for us and for our friend, but I can't bear the silence any longer. Not a night goes by when I don't dream of you and our child. I see you both in my father's house at last. This is the moment that I am fighting for. These past months in Africa as one of many determined men training under a leader whom many respect but few like has given me new hope for the future.

Our camp is on the grounds of a magnificent estate. The staff headquarters are in the castle and we are very comfortably lodged in barracks generously donated by the British Government. We have close to a thousand acres for training purposes. I always think of you when I go to see the General. His office is in the library. Half of the books are French works published in the eighteenth century. The craftsmanship is superb. The library has tall windows that look out on to a lawn with stately trees on either side. The foliage is a green the likes of which I have never seen in France.

Since arriving here, the General has made a habit of dining with his officers, which means that every meal is consumed in gloomy silence. He is a man of few words. There is another, dubious honor here—that of being chosen to accompany the General on his walks. A short walk is nearly two miles, which can double or triple depending on his mood. The hapless idiot chosen as his walking companion is treated to long silences, punctuated with reminiscences about Chad or Ksar-Rhilane, or the two occasions on which he escaped from prison, or his trip across France on a bicycle. The other evening, he asked me to tell him about my son. It is so unusual for him to express any interest in the families of his men that, for a moment, I didn't say anything. He took offence: "Why aren't you answering my question? You're just like the others, you hate these walks and you hate my monologues about my military exploits. Well, I'm capable of showing interest in something other than war." I'm sure this is true, but we all have a hard time believing it. So I talked to him about you and our son, and the region and the people who live there. He didn't interrupt me once. When we arrived back at the castle, he tapped me on the shoulder and smiled in a way that makes his eyes almost disappear: "You see? I'm a very good listener. Good night."

Our days start before dawn and end well after dark. We are all over-trained and rather on edge. Tomorrow evening, there is a concert at the cathedral. We will hear Brahms' *Requiem* and Beethoven's *Fifth Symphony*. You will be in my heart and in my thoughts more than ever.

Darling, take care of yourself and our son. Tell our dear friend that knowing that she is with you is a great comfort to me. Give her my regards. I pray that God will reunite us soon. Talk to our son about me sometimes, so that he recognizes me when I take him in my arms. There won't be another opportunity to write to you, my darling. Please don't keep this letter. I want to kiss your sweet face and your beautiful hands.

Love,
Laurent

Tears of joy flowed down Camille's cheeks. For as long as she had known Laurent, even when he was far away, he had always been a loving presence. If only the war were over....

A shot rang out. Lost in her thoughts, Camille jumped up and ran to the clearing. Léon and three young men wearing large berets were using their submachine guns to push along a young man who held one hand bleeding to his chest. With one strong push, he fell at the feet of Léa and her uncle.

"He's a spy," said one of the *maquisards*.

"That's a lie!"

"Bastard! Why were you hiding?"

"And the gun? I suppose you were out rabbit hunting, were you?"

"It isn't safe around here without a gun."

"I'll say it isn't!"

The butt of a rifle came down on his wounded hand. He screamed and Camille bounded to his side.

52

"Stop it! Can't you see he's wounded?"

"Speak up, son. What are you doing in these parts?"

"I was trying to join the *maquis*."

"Liar! He's a spy, I tell you."

"Let us handle this, we'll make him talk."

"Please, Father, tell them to stop . . ."

Sitting on a stump, his beret pushed back, Léon watched the scene and sucked on a cigarette butt. He stood up at last, almost reluctantly.

"He's bleeding like a dog. Madame Camille, find some rags to bandage him up. You can stop crying now, lad, we're going to have a little talk."

Charles, whom everyone had forgotten, clung to Léa's skirt.

"Why are they hurting that man?"

Camille came back with a clean towel, which she wrapped around the mutilated hand.

"That'll do," said Léon. "The rest of you, back to your stations. Father, I think it's time to move on."

"I agree with you."

"Sit still, lad."

The prisoner, who was now standing, dropped to his knees on the sandy forest floor, trembling.

Without taking his eyes off the prisoner, Léon walked over to the priest and said in a low voice:

"Do you know the Ciron Gorges?"

"Yes."

"We have men there. Do you need a guide?"

"Only to get out of the forest. After that, I know the way."

"At Bourideys, go to the house with the blue shutters. The man's a friend of mine. Tell him, 'Léon is tending his mushrooms'. He'll hitch up his cart, send word to Aristide, and take you to the grottos."

"It's not very far. It's walking distance."

"Not for the women and the kid."

"You're right. What are you going to do with *him*?"

"Interrogate him, of course."

"You know very well what I mean."

"That's not your problem, Father. This is my sector. I have to know who he is. Too many of our men have been taken lately."

"I know, Aristide has received orders from London to execute Grand-Clément."

"He's not the only one who's collaborating with the Germans."

"That's why I'm here. Grand-Clément and the men he took with him when he went over to the other side have done all the harm they can do. I have to believe that there was more to his relationship with Dohse...."

"What there was, Father, was the betrayal of good patriots, the betrayal of Communist comrades, and the loss of tons of weapons from the British. As far as I'm concerned, that's all the evidence we need. A man like that should be shot down like a rabid dog."

The priest shrugged his shoulders wearily and went over to the prisoner.

"Speak, son, it will be better for everyone if you do."

"Especially for you!" jeered Léon, prodding the prisoner with his submachine gun.

Camille and Léa returned with their belongings. Léa had tied hers into a big blue handkerchief which she stuck on the end of Léon's hunting rifle. With her flowered dress, straw hat, and espadrilles, she looked like a peasant girl taking a meal to the workers in the fields.

"Jeannot," called Léon.

A young man with a beard emerged from behind a pine tree.

"Take them as far as the road. Keep your eyes and your ears open. He may not have been alone."

"Okay, chief."

"Good-bye and thanks for everything."

"You're most welcome. Now, off you go!"

The emotion that Camille felt as she looked at the old man, the dovecote, and the forest took her by surprise. Normally reserved, she kissed Léon warmly on both cheeks, her eyes filling with tears.

54

"I'll never forget my stay here. I hope I come back one day. Good-bye!"

The little clearing suddenly seemed chilly to Léa. She shivered.

"Shall we go?" she said, taking Charles by the hand.

They walked through the woods for about an hour, Uncle Adrien carrying Charles on his shoulders. The road to Bourideys was clear and before long, they arrived at the house Léon had described and found the man who was to take them in a cart to the grottos. The horse pulling the cart seemed to resent the heavy load. He whinnied, shaking his mane with an enthusiasm that was lacking in his step. In spite of the beast's ill humor, they arrived shortly in Préchac. As they entered the village, they were stopped by two *gendarmes.*

"Oh! It's you, Dumas."

"Hi Renault, hi Laffont. What's going on?"

"Who are these people?" asked Laffont warily.

"It's all right. They're friends. I'm taking them to the grottos. Léon sent them to me. But you didn't answer my question. What's going on?"

"You can't go to the grottos."

"Why not?"

"The Germans and the Militia are combing the area."

"Apparently, some big shot from London was parachuted into the region recently."

Camille hugged Charles harder. Léa twirled a lock of hair around her finger distractedly. Adrien stroked his conspicuously black mustache.

"Have they arrested any of our men?" asked Dumas.

"Not yet, but they sure know what they're doing, the bastards. If it weren't for some kid from Marimbault who was going fishing at dawn and who ran to Gillets to sound the alarm, we would all have been rounded up. They almost got Lancelot and Dédé le Basque."

"Damn! What am I going to do with this lot?"

Laffont gestured to Dumas that he wanted to talk to him in private.

"Are you sure we can trust the man with the mustache?"

"Of course! Otherwise, Léon wouldn't have sent him to us. I have a sneaking suspicion he's the one they parachuted in."

"In that case, we'll help. We'll take them from here in the car from the *gendarmerie*. You should go straight home, it's not safe around here. Everybody, out of the cart! Do you have somewhere to go?"

"Yes, we're going to Brouqueyran, near Auros. Do you know where it is?"

"We sure do! If you go to La Sifflette's, say hello for me. She's my cousin, a good woman. . . ."

"Give us a break with your family history, will you? Come on, let's get going."

"Okay, okay, you get the car. The rest of you, come on."

"Bye!" cried Charles, waving to the cart as it circled and headed home.

Not one word was spoken on the four-mile trip from Préchac to Captieux. Charles fell asleep on his mother's lap. As they approached the town, Dumas, who was sergeant at the *gendarmerie*, turned to Father Adrien.

"Do you have identity papers?"

"Yes."

"And what about you ladies?"

"Yes, why?" asked Léa.

"If we get pulled over by a German patrol, you're to say that you're on your way to spend a few days with the relatives in Grignols—people by the name of Puch."

"Who are they?" asked Father Adrien.

"Good people who have saved more than one life already."

Fortunately, the road was clear and they arrived in Brouqueyran safely. Sure enough, their destination was the general store and cafe run by the sergeant's cousin, La Sifflette.

She owed her nickname to her habit of whistling as she poured the customers' drinks and because she also enjoyed "whistling back" the odd glass behind the counter.

"Well, hello cousin! I see you've brought me some people."

"As usual."

Léa quickly glanced around the store. Behind the old wooden counter stood shelves that had once been filled with canned goods but were now vacant save for a few dusty tins. Against the wall stood a solitary bag of seed and a roll of wire. In the centre of the room, there was a long table with benches on either side. The tiles, worn smooth with years of coming and going, were covered with a fine layer of sawdust.

"May I speak to you alone?" Father Adrien asked the proprietress.

"Let's go into the courtyard where we won't be disturbed. Make yourselves at home. Laffont, serve them something to drink. And a lemonade for the little cherub."

They were not gone long. When they returned, Charles was sipping a lemonade, Laffont's kepi pushed down over his ears. When she saw him, La Sifflette burst out laughing.

"If all our recruits were like him, the war would be over in no time!"

"We have to go. Back at the *gendarmerie*, they'll be wondering where we are. So long, kid. Can I have my hat back?"

"No! I want to keep it!"

"Now, Charles, you must give him back his hat," said Camille, trying to coax the kepi out of Charles' grip. "It's much too big for you."

"No! No!" the little boy screamed.

"Give me that!" scolded Léa grabbing the kepi, which she restored to its owner.

The screams got louder.

"If someone doesn't shut that kid up, I'm going to punch his lights out!" yelled Léa, twisting his arm.

Charles was so surprised at the tone of Léa's voice that he forgot to feel pain and shut up.

"You shouldn't talk to him that way, Mademoiselle. He doesn't know any better," said La Sifflette, taking Charles in her arms.

Laffont put the kepi on his head and left with Renault.

As soon as they were gone, Father Adrien, who had been

carrying a heavy suitcase when he arrived at the dovecote, asked La Sifflette if there were a room where he could be alone.

"There's a room over the barn that we use for storing old clothes and furniture. You can use that, it has two doors."

Charles and Léa glared at each other. Camille couldn't help laughing.

"I wonder which of you two is more childish. He's only four years old, you know Léa."

"So what! That's no reason for him to throw a temper tantrum."

"Meanie! Meanie! I don't like you anymore. You're not my friend anymore. And when I grow up, I'm not going to marry you, so there!"

"I couldn't care less. I'll find someone more handsome than you."

"No you won't! I'm the most handsome, aren't I, Maman?"

"Yes, sweetie pie, you're the most handsome and I'm sure Léa thinks so too."

"No, she's not saying anything. See! She doesn't love me anymore."

This was more than Charles could bear and he burst into tears.

"Hey! I was only kidding. I still love you. I love you more than anything else in the whole wide world," said Léa, taking Charles from his mother and covering him with kisses.

"You do?"

"Of course I do, you big baby."

"Then why did you twist my arm?"

"I'm sorry. I was tired and upset. I promise I'll never do it again. Now, give me a kiss."

Camille looked on tenderly as Charles and Léa giggled, exchanging little hugs and kisses.

"Have you two love birds made up?" asked La Sifflette going over to the counter and whistling as she poured herself a little glass.

"You must be hungry," she remarked, knocking her drink

back. "I'm going to make you an omelette with wild mush-rooms and greens fresh from the garden. I even have a little leftover *pastis*.[8] How does that sound?"

"Just fine, Madame, thank you. May I give you a hand?" asked Camille.

"That's all right, just keep an eye on the little one. You can get settled in your room. It's at the top of the stairs, second door on the right."

"Thank you for everything."

"Basta! You can thank me some other time. Ssshh! Some-one's coming."

Three old men in black cotton jackets worn by men throughout the region of Bazas entered the store.

"Morning, everyone."

"Looks like you've got company, La Sifflette. More rela-tives?" said one of the men in a mock-serious tone.

"Leave her alone, Loubrie, her family is her business."

"You're right, Ducloux, especially these days."

"What'll it be, gentlemen?" asked La Sifflette.

"Got any of that white you served up yesterday?"

"It's too pricey for you old skinflints. Yesterday was on the house. Wouldn't want you to think I made a habit of it."

"Just give us a drink and stop your complaining, woman!"

La Sifflette brought over three glasses and a bottle of rosé.

"Did you hear the latest?" said the one named Loubrie. "The place is crawling with Germans."

"So I hear. My cousin from the *gendarmerie* was by earlier and he mentioned something about it."

"Who are they looking for?"

"Ask them," shot back La Sifflette.

"You think I'm crazy? I don't want them to take me for one of them terrorists."

"No danger of that happening," retorted La Sifflette. "They'd see right through your blather."

Loubrie's friends guffawed.

---

[8]*pastis*, a cake from the region of Bazas.

59

"You can't put nothin' over on La Sifflette."

"Yea, she knows you too well for that, you dirty old man."

"Watch your filthy mouth!" snapped Loubrie, cursing. "All's I can say is, she'd do well to stop running a hotel out of this here store. People are starting to talk."

"If you think your stupid little stories are making me nervous, they're not!"

"Just trying to help. Just trying to help. The Germans are the ones who are getting nervous. They can hear the English planes too, you know."

"Yea, and even if they couldn't, there'd be some tricky bastard ready to tell them anything they needed to know."

Loubrie drained his glass so quickly that the wine ran down his stubbly chin and he started choking. Ducloux thumped him on the back.

"Easy Loubrie!" said La Sifflette, laughing. "If you've got a clear conscience, you've nothing to worry about. The *maquisards* are just a bunch of nice, young kids from everything I've heard. Here, let me give your collar a wipe otherwise your old lady will be giving you no end of trouble."

Loubrie pushed away her hand and stood up, grumbling.

"Stop fussing over me like I was a baby."

La Sifflette laughed heartily as the three old men shuffled out. She locked the door behind them.

"That way, we won't be disturbed. I don't trust those busybodies. Tonight, I'll see what I can find out. . . . What a cute kid. Where's your daddy, honey? Gone to war, like the others. . . ."

As she talked, she began preparing the omelette. In a frying pan, perched on a corner of the stove that was black with years of use, goose fat began to sizzle.

"Would you set the table?" she asked Léa. "You'll find the plates on the sideboard, the omelette will be ready any minute now."

"Mmm! That reminds me of the omelettes with wild mushrooms and ham that Sidonie used to make us when I was a child," said Father Adrien, entering the room. "Madame la Sifflette, tonight you must tell the networks in Auros and Bazas to be on their guard. I'll go to Villandraut and Saint-

Symphorien, and Léa will go to Langon and Saint-Macaire. I've just learned that Poinsot and his men know the location of every cache of weapons and every hiding place in the region. The search that the Germans have undertaken in the Ciron gorges is just to divert attention. Maurice Fiaux has been put in charge of rounding up all resisters with Lieutenant Kunesch's help. Dohse and the Militia will do everything they can to prevent Aristide from rebuilding his networks. They're trying to work through Grand-Clément, but even the most gullible of our men are suspicious. London has reissued the order to execute Grand-Clément and Fiaux. . . . Well, let's eat. It's going to be a long night."

"Father Adrien, I want to help, too."

"No, Camille,"

"Why not?"

"Your first responsibility is Charles, he can't stay here alone."

"Yes, of course," said Camille, looking down and sighing. "You're right."

"Come on, everyone. The omelette's going to be cold. Is it good sweetie? Here, La Sifflette is going to make you some bread fingers. Father Adrien, how do you like it?"

"It's awful!" he teased.

Chapter Four

The night sky was magnificent. Before crossing the Garonne at Langon, Léa stopped in front of the church and got off the ancient bicycle that La Sifflette had loaned her; it must have seen service in the Great War. She had delivered her uncle's message to the chef at the Nouvel-Hôtel without a hitch.

"Tell him that I understand. You're very brave, Mademoiselle Léa, your father would be proud of you."

His words filled her with feelings of sadness and happiness. How quiet it was! How difficult to imagine that close by, perhaps just around the next corner, there were men hidden, just waiting for orders to kill. Instead of turning right toward Saint-Macaire when she arrived at the crossroads, Léa turned left, passing under the viaduct. She couldn't help herself. She had to see Montillac again.

The bicycle began to show its age, groaning and creaking as it climbed the long hill. Léa stopped for a moment. The heavy, dark Cross of Borde still stood high above the Domaine de la Prioulette. Léa had been standing under this cross when she accepted her first mission from her uncle. It seemed so long ago! Her heart beat faster as the dark trees of the estate came into view. It wasn't far now. At the gate she stopped, fighting the urge to run down the lane and seek refuge in the arms of the old housekeeper, Ruth. A dog barked, and then another. A light went on at Fayard's place. Léa could hear the vintner calling to his dogs to be quiet. It wasn't safe to linger. She climbed on the old bicycle and turned back in the direction of Langon.

It was one o'clock in the morning when she lifted the gate at the level crossing in Saint-Macaire. The guard dog leapt at her, barking and clanking its chain. She stifled a scream. Hurrying across the tracks, she mounted the bicycle again and headed down a street leading to the Porte de Benauge. When she arrived at the Cours-de-la-République, she stopped outside Dupeyron's garage. Riri, the *gendarme*, opened the door. When he saw who it was, he pulled her inside.

"Mademoiselle Léa, what brings you here?"

"I have an important message for you," she said, repeating the coded message she had given to the chef at the Nouvel-Hôtel.

"Jesus! We'll have to alert everyone in the region."

"I've been to Langon. By now, everyone in Villandraut, Saint-Symphorien, Bazas, and Auros will know."

"Good. Dupeyron, call Cazenave. I'm going back to the *gendarmerie*."

"You mean you're not coming with us?"

"I can't ask the other guys to cover for me. We have enough problems as it is."

"Have you heard anything about Albert or Mireille?"

"No, Mademoiselle. We think that Mireille is probably all right—she was taken to Boudet Barracks. But we don't know about Albert. Mathias Fayard and René were the last to see him. Since then, not a word. No one has seen him leaving the house in Le Bouscat. You probably haven't heard yet, but Mathias managed to run away last night, which means that the Mauriac group has had to take cover."

"Do you think he will denounce them?"

"I have no idea. I don't understand young people anymore. They seem to be going crazy. I used to know Mathias pretty well. We played soccer together, we went partridge hunting together, we were sort of friends, even though I was older. He's not a bad kid, but when he came back from Germany, he'd changed completely. He started talking politics! Politics are no good, especially now. Somehow, I don't think he's much of a threat, but Maurice Fiaux is a different story. That boy is evil through and through. Not only that, he knows the region like the back of his hand. . . . Well, good-bye, Mademoiselle. Tell whoever sent you that we'll do what we have to do. If they need to get in touch with me, they know where I am. Wait, I'll check the street. . . . You can go now. Good-bye and good luck!"

Now there was a cold, biting wind that slowed Léa's progress. In spite of this, she was drenched in sweat by the time she reached the woods at Constantin. Her hands, numb with the cold, gripped the rusted handlebars. At a place called Le Chapitre, one of the old tires finally ruptured and the bicycle went flying. Her hands and knees scraped and bleeding, Léa lay on the dirt road, too weak to get up, listening to the rusted wheel turning between its forks.

Finally, the cold forced her to stir. She could feel blood from the cuts trickling down her legs. Her knees hurt terribly, but her hands were worse. She righted the bicycle, only to find that both wheels were badly bent. Angrily, she pushed it off the road and carried on, limping.

Just before reaching Brouqueyran, the sound of car engines sent Léa into the ditch. A few feet away, three cars sped past in the direction of Brouqueyran. Friend or foe? There was no way of telling.

Before the dust had settled, Léa heard car doors slamming, then voices.

They must have stopped in Brouqueyran, thought Léa, running toward the village. I hope Uncle Adrien isn't back yet.

"Break the door down!"

At the sound of that voice, Léa froze. She knew that she had to get away, but her knees buckled under her and she sank to the ground, not noticing the pain that her knees were causing her. Some of the men began pushing in the door of the tiny cafe, while others began searching the grounds. Léa's first thought was for the transmitter. Then she remembered that Camille and Charles were alone in the house, and began running in full view of the men. Camille's screams stopped her in her tracks.

"No! No! Don't hurt him!"

A man came out of the cafe, carrying Charles, flailing his arms and screaming. Camille tugged at the man, but he kicked her.

"Maman! Maman!"

Hidden by the wall of the town hall, Léa peered through the darkness for a weapon.

A flame leapt from the house, lighting up the street. None of the men were wearing uniforms. Two had Militia arm bands. As the fire spread, Léa could make out their smooth young faces and their submachine guns which they held like toys. She could hear bottles being loaded into the car trunks. Laughter. French voices, insulting and mocking.

"Are you going to tell us where the others are, you bitch!"

"What about La Sifflette? I suppose you don't know her either, eh?"

"Albert, Mireille. Lucien. Aristide. And that goddamn priest. Those names mean anything to you?"

"I don't know what you're talking about. Give me back my son!"

"We'll give him back to you when you tell us where they are."

"Leave her alone, Jérôme, give her the kid. We'll make her talk when we get back. Your idea of setting the place on fire was brilliant. Now every *maquis* for miles around will be on to us."

"Take it easy, Maurice! We're ready for them."

"Maman!"

"Give her the kid, for chrissakes. Get in!"

Holding Charles tightly, Camille got into one of the cars. Maurice Fiaux sat in the driver's seat.

"We're going to La Réole!" he called to the others.

Léa, still pressed against the wall, watched as the cars drove off toward Auros.

Father Adrien found his niece, trembling from the cold and from a fever, by the light of the burning cafe.

"Where are Camille and Charles?"

"Fiaux ... Maurice Fiaux."

She shook her head, her teeth chattering, unable to utter another word.

He lifted her up gently and carried her, bewildered, toward the cafe. La Sifflette emerged from the flames like a spirit.

"Lord, oh Lord! Where's the kid? Where's his mother?"

"I don't know, apparently Maurice Fiaux and his thugs were here,"

"What have they done! Father, she's hurt!"

"Yes, I know. Did they leave anyone here?"

"If I know them, they took off like bats out of hell. Look what they're done! To think that people like you risk your lives for creeps like that!"

"Please! You are risking your life too. You've lost everything. Is the church open?"

"No, but I know where the priest hides the key. Look! The fire hasn't spread to the barn yet. Maybe your transmitter...."

Very gently, he laid Léa's inert body against the wall of the little cemetery and ran toward the barn, calling:

"Camille ... Charles ..."

La Sifflette took the key from a crevice in the wall and opened the door. Without too much difficulty, she managed to drag Leá into the church. In front of the altar lay a carpet that had been a gift from Mirail Manor. The magnificent carpet was now threadbare, but it was warmer than the stone floor. She laid Léa on it and, groping behind the lectern, found a box of matches. After many tries, she managed to light the candles on either side of the tabernacle. Taking one, she began searching the sacristy for something to protect Léa from the damp. All that she could find was the sheet with the white cross that was used to cover a coffin during funeral services.

As she left the church, she automatically made the sign of the cross.

The fire seemed to be burning less fiercely now, and they

could hear the siren of the fire truck coming from Bazas. This comforting sound brought only a shrug from the proprietress of the Brouqueyran's general store and cafe.

"You were right, the transmitter was in the barn," said Father Adrien, gesturing to the heavy suitcase. "Here come the firemen, I'd better hide this."

"You'd better hide with it. Take the key to the church and lock yourself inside. If anyone asks me for it, I'll say it's been lost."

"Any news?"

"I was just going to ask you the same thing. They must have taken them to Bordeaux."

"Somehow, I don't think that's good news."

"Father, you mustn't say things like that. Even people like that wouldn't touch a kid!"

"God is your witness."

But La Sifflette had not heard the priest's last comment. She was running toward the firemen, yelling and screaming.

When Léa regained consciousness, she was so numb from the cold that she had stopped trembling. She propped herself up on one elbow. The flickering candles, the altar, the shroud. For a moment, she thought that she was dead. With a wave of panic, she sprang to her feet, tearing off the shroud. Had the village priest entered the church at that moment he would have sworn he had just seen the Virgin Mary. Instead, Léa's uncle entered. What an amazing child, he thought as he locked the door behind him, straight out of a Gothic novel!

"Who are you?"

"Don't be afraid, it's me."

"Oh! Uncle Adrien!"

He put down his suitcase and made Léa sit on the steps of the altar. Wrapping her once again in the shroud, he put his arms around her.

"Now tell me what happened."

In a low but firm voice, Léa told him what she had seen.

He bowed his head, grief-stricken, blaming himself for not returning in time to save them. They could hear the voices of the firemen working to put out the fire.

"Are you sure Maurice Fiaux said he was going to La Réole?"

"Yes"

"Why La Réole? That's what I don't understand. He should have taken them to Bordeaux."

"How did they find out where we were?"

"The usual way: Someone denounced you. They thought they were going to find all of us here. Are you sure there weren't any Germans with them?"

"I don't think so. They all spoke French and none of them wore a uniform."

"This just proves what we heard in London: the Gestapo isn't fully aware of the activities of Fiaux and his thugs. They're acting on their own. That makes them all the more dangerous and unpredictable."

"Why would they do that? Without orders?"

"As always, there are many answers . . ."

"But you know Maurice Fiaux well!"

"Yes . . . that's why I'm so worried. He has a huge chip on his shoulder. He wants people to fear him, to respect him. He has also proved that he likes to kill and torture and maim."

"We must get Camille and Charles away from him."

Just then, someone knocked at the door.

"It's me, La Sifflette. Open up!"

Gun in hand, Father Adrien unlocked the door.

La Sifflette entered, pushing ahead of her a young man wearing a fireman's helmet that was too big for him.

"We're lucky old man Déon broke his arm. His son Claude here is filling in for him. I know him, he's with Léon's group over in Les Landes. He's going to try to contact Léon. I told him about the kid and his mother."

"Good, Léa tells me they were taken to La Réole."

"La Réole! I hope you're wrong. There's a rumor going around that the Gestapo is letting the Militia use rooms in the basement of the college to interrogate Communist *maquisards*."

"Is there any proof?"

"No, it's just what people are saying."

"I forgot to tell you, Uncle Adrien, Mathias got away."

"Then maybe there's hope ..."

"I have to go, sir, the other men will be wondering where I am."

"Yes, of course. Let me know what happens through the priest in Auros. Ask for Alphonse Duparc. Do you understand?"

"Yes, sir. You'll hear tomorrow."

The door closed behind La Sifflette and the young fireman.

"Uncle Adrien, what did you mean about Mathias?"

"Try to rest, Léa. I need time to think."

"Rise and shine! Laffont and Dumas are here."

Léa was barely able to open her eyes.

"Drink this, it's hot," said La Sifflette, handing Léa a mug filled with a coffee-colored liquid. Léa took a sip and nearly spat it out.

"What is this? It has alcohol in it."

"It's spiked to hide the taste of the oats. Come on, drink up. Otherwise, you'll catch your death of cold in here."

Revolted by the smell and taste, Léa forced herself to drink it down. Quickly she began to feel better. Without too much discomfort, she straightened her legs. Her scraped knees felt painful and tight.

The sun was already high. The charred ruins of the cafe were still smoldering. The two *gendarmes* were leaning against their car, their faces grim.

Father Adrien was checking a map.

"Where are we going, Uncle Adrien?"

"La Réole."

Léa looked at him, not understanding.

"We'll cross the Garonne at Castets. It'll be safer. Then we'll take the back roads to the farm above La Réole."

"Why La Réole?"

"The entire region is blocked off, there aren't any safe places for us to hide. From the farm, I'll be able to contact Hilaire without any problem."

"I haven't been back to La Réole since the Debray's died ..."

Taking a pitchfork, La Sifflette began searching the ruins, hoping to salvage some of her belongings. She hadn't uttered a single sigh, not a word of reproach. But her grief was evident as she sifted through the still glowing coals. A life of labor and toil gone, up in smoke. She had only the clothes on her back!

"Come on, La Sifflette, time to go," said Laffont, gently placing a hand on the handle of the fork.

"You're right, what's done is done."

She dropped the fork, and without so much as a backward glance, got into the car. Not one neighbor had come out.

From the farm you could always see who was coming, Jean Callède liked to say. Welcomed with open arms, La Sifflette gave Madame Callède a hand in the kitchen. Her grilled sausages, washed down with local wine, were well known to the *maquisards* in the region.

There was no time for Léa and La Sifflette to enjoy the Callède's hospitality: the day before their arrival, there had been a message from London, indicating that supplies were to be airlifted into the region that night. The two women wanted to take part. At Father Adrien's insistence, the men finally gave in. "Women!" they muttered. "Hiding guns and 'chutes in the pots and pans is about all they're good for!" Father Adrien would not take part. He was meeting with Father Dieuzaide from the Jade-Amicol group, Aristide, Dédé le Basque, Lancelot, and Georges in order to come up with a plan to rescue Camille and Charles and eliminate Maurice Fiaux.

A dozen people, including Léa and La Sifflette, took up posts at regular intervals around the field. They crouched in the dark, flashlights at the ready. Others were posted along the road in either direction. After what seemed like a very long time, they heard the faint drone of a plane engine.

"That's him" whispered Callède, "On your marks, everyone!"

The drone became louder and louder. Then a whistle was blown and in almost perfect synchrony, the flashlights were turned on for the count of five, then off, then on again. The drone became a roar as the plane circled back over the field and levelled out. A black shape dropped from the plane then, with a snapping sound, a parachute opened. Others followed and soon the metal containers began hitting the ground with a thud. The plane began its return voyage, but the last two parachutes had caught on the cabin door and unfurled, like two immense white flags, over La Réole. It would be a miracle if the Gestapo and the *gendarmerie* didn't see them! They quickly went to work to remove all traces of the airlift. La Sifflette and Léa removed the parachutes, which they folded and stowed in an ox-drawn cart. The containers were loaded into three vans to be taken to the Bienvenue sawmill, where some of the weapons were hidden in piles of sawdust. Others were hidden in barns and tobacco drying sheds. In La Réole, all was quiet. La Sifflette took the reins of the cart. She and Léa hid the parachutes in a barn, under the straw. The countryside was still once again, but they lay awake, seeing the white flags in the sky over the Garonne and the old town.

The next morning at dawn, Depeyre came to the farm on a bicycle.

"The Germans are out in full force," he gasped, trying to catch his breath. "Rigoulet came to warn us. Make sure that the weapons are well hidden and get the women out of here."

"Where am I supposed to take them? Rosier's place?"

"No, that's too close. Take them over to Tore's, in Morizès."

Shortly after they left, the Germans troops arrived and began searching the farm, pushing and shoving Callède and his wife. The farmer trembled from head to foot. In the panic, he had forgotten two parachutes from a previous drop that he had rolled up in old canvas sheets, as well as bullets for Stens hidden in packages of sugar. Finding nothing, the Germans took Callède, Loue, Depeyre, Bienvenue, Charlot, and Chianson to the Gestapo headquarters in La Réole for interrogation.

As luck would have it, the mayor of Gironde-sur-Dropt was standing in front of the college when the convoy pulled up.

71

He knew all of the men but had no inkling of their clandestine activities. He asked to see the *Kommandant* and vouched for them. All were released, except Pierre Chianson. No doubt, he had been denounced for the drop in Saint-Félix-de-Foncaude.

Léa had only the clothes she had been wearing on the night the cafe burned down. Like La Sifflette, all of her belongings had been destroyed in the fire. Without consulting anyone, she decided to go to Montillac and when everyone was asleep, she liberated a bicycle.

It was a clear night and quite mild. Just before Sainte-Foy-la-Longue, Léa stopped to look down at the Garonne winding its way across the vast plain. And, as always when she came upon a familiar setting, she was deeply moved. There was a feeling of astonishment and wonder, tranquility, the conviction that here, she could come to no harm. The earth radiated a sense of well-being as it lay sleeping. Everything would work out. Uncle Adrien would find a way to rescue Camille and Charles. ... The thought of the little boy who wanted to marry her brought a pang of anguish. The countryside became blurred. Her heart sinking, she climbed back on the bicycle. At Saint-André-du-Bois, she nearly collided with a man relieving himself in the middle of the road, and hurried off under a torrent of insults.

She hid the bicycle in the grass at the base of the cross, opposite the gates, then entered the field, avoiding the gravel along the lane. She could see a light through the shutters of her father's study. Ruth must be doing the accounts, she thought. As she neared the house, she heard voices, but she couldn't quite place them. Then there was the sound of laughter. No longer worried about being heard, she rounded the house. The heavy shutters were ajar. Navigating the dark living room, she opened the study door.

"Léa!"

Charles ran into her arms.

"Oh, my darling little lamb! I'm so happy to see you! When did you come home?"

"Tonight, Mathias brought me home."

"Mathias?"

"We played hide-and-seek. Maman didn't want to play . . . but now that you're home, we'll go and get her, won't we, Léa?"

"'Yes, yes . . .'"

And there was Mathias. He was even thinner than before and his hair dishevelled, but he was impeccably groomed and dressed.

"Ruth . . ."

Still holding Charles, Léa embraced the old woman whose cheeks were wet with tears.

"I'm so happy to see you, Léa. I thought I'd never see you again. So much has happened. Is it safe for you to come back here?"

"Probably not, but I don't have any clothes. Mathias, how did you find Charles? Why didn't you rescue Camille too?"

"I could only take one of them. Camille was too weak. She told me to take Charles."

"I don't believe you!"

"Well, it's true. She also told me to tell you that if anything happened to her, you were to look after Charles."

"I don't want her to die!"

"I'm going to do everything I can to save her. I had to really work on Fiaux to let me take Charles. He wanted to keep him to force Camille to talk. When he interrogated her, all she would say was, 'I don't know anything.' If he had beaten the kid as planned, she would have talked."

"That man was really mean," whimpered Charles, "He pulled my hair and kicked Maman in the tummy . . . even when . . . she wasn't moving anymore. I kissed her for a long time and then she woke up. Then I wasn't scared anymore. It was so dark! So Maman sang me a song. . . ."

Léa's rage was choking her. She could feel the little boy she had helped to bring into the world trembling and sobbing. She held back a long string of insults aimed at Mathias, her childhood friend. She had thoughts of murder. She wanted to destroy him, to eliminate him and the others. Gradually, she was aware of a new force within her, the desire to fight and to kill.

"I know what you're thinking, but it won't change anything. We have to rescue Camille."

"How? Do you have any ideas?"

"Yes, I'm going to try to get her transferred, but we don't have much time. She's very weak. If I succeed, I'll contact you. Where are you hiding?"

"I can't tell you."

"You must."

"No one knows where I am."

Mathias looked at her disdainfully.

"With that kind of attitude, it's no wonder your friends are caught all the time."

"They wouldn't get caught if they weren't denounced."

"As if the Germans needed to be told where to find you! All they have to do is eavesdrop in any cafe."

"They get the French to do it for them!"

"Not always, you screw up so often, they'd have to be blind not to know what's going on!"

Ruth stepped in.

"Please, children, stop arguing. Listen to me, Léa. I think we can trust Mathias."

"Maybe, but I can't tell him where I'm staying and he knows I can't."

"All right, then. Tell your uncle and Aristide or Hilaire's men that as soon as I can get Camille transferred to Bordeaux, I'll give you a description of the convoy, the number of men—I don't think there'll be many of them—the time they're leaving, and the route they'll be taking. Your friends will have to intercept the convoy and rescue Camille."

Charles had fallen asleep in Léa's arms.

"Do you think it can be done?" she whispered.

"Yes."

"Can I ask you a question? How come you're still with Fiaux and his gang? Do you do it for the money?"

Mathias shrugged his shoulders.

74

"Even if I told you, you wouldn't believe me."

"Try me."

"I do it because it's easier to make sure you're all right that way."

"You're right, I don't believe you."

"See!" Mathias shrugged his shoulders and grinned ingenuously.

"What are we going to do about Charles? Wasn't it dangerous to bring him here?"

"No, as long as Fiaux knows he's here. I asked my father to keep an eye on him."

"And he agreed?"

"He didn't have much choice."

Léa laid Charles gently on the couch and dropped into one of the armchairs by the fireplace.

"Ruth, I'm hungry and I'm cold. Is there anything to eat?"

"Of course, dear. I'll light the fire."

"Let me do it, Mademoiselle Ruth."

"Thank you, Mathias."

A flame shot up, and for a few moments, there was only the crackling of the vine shoots. This joyous sound, combined with the glow of the fire and the familiar setting, softened the animosity between them ever so briefly. As they watched the fire, their eyes met. In his gaze, there was boundless love and adoration. In hers, infinite weariness and bewilderment.

He wanted to take her in his arms, but he knew she would push him away. And she would have loved to blot out the memory of their night in the sordid hotel in Bordeaux. She wanted to bury her face to his chest, and unburden herself the way she had done when they were children, hiding in the playroom or the hayloft.

Without realizing it, they both sighed. It was a sigh heavy with inconsolable grief.

Ruth returned carrying a tray with two bowls of soup, homemade pâté, bread, and a bottle of Montillac's red wine, which they devoured with youthful gusto. As always when she enjoyed her food, Léa forgot the danger she was in.

75

"Your pâté is incredible," said Léa, between mouthfuls.

"Incredible," echoed Mathias.

They finished eating in silence, savoring this moment of peace. When the last glass of wine had been drunk, Léa turned to Ruth.

"I've lost all my clothing. Could you prepare a knapsack for me with two or three dresses about Aunt Bernadette's size? How is she anyway?"

"Not very well. She's worried because she hasn't heard from Lucien and her rheumatism is giving her a lot of trouble."

"Poor thing. Could you find me those dresses and put some woolens in as well?"

"Let me see what I can find."

Charles stirred in his sleep. Léa wrapped him in the tartan blanket that her father used to put around his shoulders when he worked at his desk during the winter months.

"We have to decide on a place to meet."

"How about the church in La Réole?"

"No, that's too dangerous for you. Fiaux and the others know about you, they might arrest you."

"Where do you suggest we meet?"

"Do you know the cemetery in Saint-André-du-Bois?"

"Of course!"

"Do you remember the tomb of the Roy de Saint-Arnaud family on the right as you go in?"

"Yes."

"There's a hole in the trunk of the last cypress on the left. I'll leave messages for you there. Check every day. If there's anything you need to tell me, you can leave a message, too. Do you understand?"

"I'm not stupid! What if they won't let me go?"

"Find a way. Camille's life is at stake."

Ruth returned, carrying a heavy sack.

"That's too big!"

"I'll attach it to your bike rack," offered Mathias. "Where is it?"

76

"Behind the cross."

"Okay. Ruth, do you have any rope?"

"Yes, I brought some just in case."

While Mathias secured the sack on the back of the bicycle, Léa stayed with Charles, stroking his fair hair.

"Take good care of him ..."

"I'll do my best. We're just about out of money. Your aunt has put her pine woods up for sale, but in the meantime..."

"I know, Ruth, what can I say? Sell the furniture if you can find a taker. I have nothing."

A tear fell on the child's cheek, and he made a little gurgling sound.

"Forgive me, dear. I shouldn't be bringing it up at a time like this. We'll manage somehow."

"I'll never be able to thank you for all you've done for us, Ruth."

"Go on with you! It'll be a fine day when I expect thanks! By the way, a few letters have come for you. I put them in the sack."

"Whenever you're ready, Léa" said Mathias, entering the room. "The sack is tied on tight. You could cycle across France and it wouldn't come off!"

"Good-bye, Ruth. Give Aunt Bernadette my love."

"Good-bye, dear. God be with you. Now Mathias, I'm counting on you to take care of her."

"Don't worry, Mademoiselle Ruth. Everything will be fine."

When they reached the bicycle, Mathias righted it.

"Are you sure you don't want me to go back with you?" he asked.

"You know that's impossible. Let me go."

Reluctantly, he let go of the handlebars. They stood for a moment, silent and miserable. Léa shivered.

"You'd better get going. You probably have miles to go and I don't like to think of you alone on the road at night."

"Mathias, I don't get it. What's happened to us?"

"What do you mean?"

"You and me ... hiding ... enemies ... and yet ..."

"And yet what?"

There was such hope in his voice! He'd better not think that she had forgiven him.

"Oh, nothing. It's just that the world is upside down. We don't know who to trust anymore. Even the people we love most turn out to be traitors."

Mathias blocked out the hardness in Léa's voice, hearing only "the people we love most." He was sure that she was referring to him. It didn't matter that she thought of him as a traitor. What mattered was that he would never betray *her*. The rest was just politics and that had nothing to do with his feelings for Léa.

He made a little gesture with his hand as if to say goodbye and turned away. Léa watched, disconcerted, as he walked toward the house.

Chapter Five

When Léa got back to Morizès, everyone was in bed. Alone in the kitchen where a cot had been set up for her, Léa watched the fire die down and smoked a cigarette made with tobacco pilfered by Callède. The strong, pungent smoke irritated her throat and made her eyes water but helped to relieve her anxiety over Camille, whom she knew was very ill. The Gestapo must have decided to take her to Saint-Jean Hospital in La Réole. No one had been able to get anywhere near her.

Father Adrien had met with Mathias and accepted his offer of help. Aristide and his men had agreed to help too. Maurice Fiaux and his entourage had gone back to Bordeaux. There was nothing to do but wait.

Getting up from a low chair by the fire, Léa tried the radio. Jamming had completely blocked out the BBC broadcasts for the past several days. After several tries, she heard the familiar voice of Jean Oberlé, barely audible over the static:

"Poet Max Jacob has died in the camp at Drancy. He was taken there because he was a Jew, yet he converted to Catholicism over thirty years ago. His entire work after that moment reflected the depth and intensity of his faith in the Church. But do the Germans care about such things?

"They mark their victims with yellow stars. They think of this as the supreme dishonor; for them, the only honorable badge is the swastika. "Catholic" and "Jew" mean nothing to them; Hitler is their God. And what does the death of Max Jacob

mean to the guards at Drancy? It means one less Jew on the face of the earth!

"He was a small man, balding, monocled, ironical. He was a deeply spiritual man with the most wonderful stories to tell, some learned, some invented.

"At the age of fifty, he was "discovered" and left Montmartre, where he had lived among painters and poets, for the salons. These in turn he abandoned for the Monastery of Saint-Benoît-sur-Loire, where, in peaceful reclusion, he wrote and painted. When friends came to visit from Paris or beyond, he would take them on a tour of the basilica. When the bell called the order to prayer, he would put down his pen or his brush.

"He was nearly seventy years old when he died. Jean Cocteau and André Salmon, two friends of Jacob's who are also poets, went to Drancy in the hope of obtaining his release. They were told he was dead.

"And so, the enemy that has brutalized our country for four years shows no more mercy for a poet than it does for a young patriot. For the Germans, it is very simple: one is a Jew and the other is a Communist. What need have we of poets when we have the prose of Henriot and Déat?

"Admirers of Max Jacob around the world, those who read and reread his poems and his prose, those who have his drawings and watercolors, will remember him. His friends will never forget what a remarkable man he was. Nor will they forget that he died, like so many others, at the hands of the German butchers, in a concentration camp. . . ."

Even poets, thought Léa, turning off the radio.

Undressing in the darkened room, she remembered Uncle Adrien's story about meeting Max Jacob at Saint-Benoît during a stay there and about his fervent convert's faith. Now Jacob was dead, as were Raphaël Mahl and perhaps Sarah, all Jews. Léa felt ashamed of associating someone as despicable as Raphaël with a heroine and a poet, even in death, but she had always been moved by his despair. In spite of all the trouble he had gone to, to be hated, he had never entirely succeeded, and his horrible fate absolved him for all time. She missed him, just as she now missed having someone with whom to share her thoughts.

She slid between the coarse sheets, still a bit damp. The faint glow from the coals gave the room a soothing, eerie quality. Through half-closed eyes, she saw the embers of another fire in another room. The eiderdown reminded her of a mohair blanket. Through her nightgown, the roughness of the sheets chafed her nipples. She turned to the wall to avoid seeing the fire. Anything not the think about him, his caresses, the feel of his lips on her body, desires she couldn't suppress. She sat bolt upright, furious at herself for an irrepressible desire to make love. She tore off her nightgown and quickly brought on her own pleasure.

The following day, Father Adrien arrived at Morizès, accompanied by Lieutenant Pierre Vincent, otherwise known as Grand-Pierre and leader of the *maquis* in Puy near Monségur, and three of his men. They talked animatedly about a gasoline depot at Saint-Martin-de-Sescas that fourteen of their men had destroyed in broad daylight on May 5. The *maquisards* and the priest could barely contain their excitement. Léa listened with envy; at least they were doing something!

After they left, Father Adrien spoke to his niece.

"Thanks to Abbé Chaillou, the chaplain at the hospital, I have seen Camille. She's much better. She has tremendous courage, not a single word of complaint. Her only concern is for you and Charles."

"Will I be able to see her?"

"That would be difficult and would put both of you at risk. The Gestapo has posted a twenty-four hour watch outside her door. However, one of the guards has a weakness for Sauternes."

"Let's get him drunk!"

Father Adrien smiled.

"We'll see. Other things are more important right now. We must get her out of there."

"What does Aristide say?"

"Right now, he has his hands full finding recruits, staying clear of Grand-Clément and his men and keeping the peace between the different factions, but as soon as we need him, he'll send us the men we need."

"Have you heard from Mathias?"

"No, not since he told us that Camille had been transferred."

"It's my turn to go to Saint-André-du-Bois."

"Don't forget that if anything goes wrong while you're there, you can ask Jules Coiffard for help. He lives in the big house on the road. He and his neighbors often act as couriers. This afternoon, I'll be in Chapelle-de-Lorette. The Militia and the Gestapo have stepped up their activities in the region since the American flying fortress over Cours-Monségur. The destruction of the depot in Saint-Martin-de-Sescas hasn't helped either. The Gestapo now have a dozen agents in the region. One of them, a man by the name of Coubeau, used to run a grocery store in the Rue de la Croix-Blanche. Disguised as a Canadian officer, he helped the *gendarmes* arrest Captain Lévy. They turned him over to the Gestapo in Toulouse."

"Was he tortured before they killed him?"

"I don't know, but it's very likely."

"When will it all end!"

"God—"

"Don't talk to me about God! You don't believe in God any more than I do!"

"That's enough!" he cried, gripping her shoulder.

What had happened to her affable, mild-mannered uncle? Léa looked at his emaciated face and feverish eyes, his gaunt cheeks and lips shut tight as though hiding a burning secret, his strong hands now rough and clenched as though suppressing the urge to strike. Could this be the same man whose voice had moved thousands of Christians throughout the world, whose faith had long dominated the lackluster Diocese of Bordeaux, and whose fatherly affection had so often helped Léa and her sisters?

"Stop! You're hurting me!"

Letting go, he pressed his forehead against the mantel, his shoulders hunched, suddenly old. He seemed so lost, so alone. That was it. He was alone, desperately alone with himself and a group of men whose ideas he was often at odds with. This was the person with whom Léa had felt the strongest bond since the death of her parents. Consciously or unconsciously, she listened to what he said. He was a mentor, someone not to be disappointed, an ideal to be strived for. If doubt, fear, and hatred made their home in his heart, an entire world based on reason, intelligence, and goodness would crumble. She could not bear for that to happen. Mute anger brought beads of perspiration to her brow and her heart began pounding.

After what seemed like a very long time, he turned to look at her. They were calmer now.

"I'm sorry. I'm probably just tired. Right now, everything gets me going. Do you forgive me?"

"Yes, Uncle Adrien," said Léa, still trembling as she laid her head on his chest.

But she felt in her heart that a wall had just been thrown up between them.

The arrival of Léa's two childhood admirers, Jean and Raoul Lefèvre, brought a brief moment of happiness. Léa had not seen them since the day that they and Doctor Blanchard were arrested and Marie killed in the square in Verdelais.

They hugged each other over and over, thrilled to be together once again.

The evening meal was very gay. Wedged between Jean and Raoul, her eyes shining partly from pleasure, partly from Callède's white wine, Léa leaned now on one shoulder, now on the other, touching their hands under the table, rubbing up against them. She laughed and talked about anything and everything, feeling happier than she had felt in months, her face shining.

"It's so nice to see you like this, Léa. The wife and I were starting to wonder whether you knew how to laugh," said their host.

"You haven't changed a bit," said Jean, kissing her neck.

"You're even more beautiful," said Raoul, kissing her too.

They had been sent by Léon in Les Landes to join Dédé le Basque and make plans to sabotage the train station in La Réole. They learned that Léa was in Morizès while in Chapelle-de-Lorette. They told her about their escape, saying how brave and cunning Albert and the others were. There was a moment of silence at the mention of the butcher from Saint-Macaire, who had not been heard from in some time, but the thought of his joviality helped restore their good humor. Callède brought out another bottle of wine just in case.

It was late when they rose from the table. It had been decided that Raoul and Jean would stay the night. They were given a blanket and a place before the hearth.

Jean, Raoul, and Léa stayed up long after the others had gone to bed, talking, smoking and drinking, putting off the moment when they would have to say good night.

Lying between them on her narrow bed, Léa let the warmth of their presence wash over her. Her fingers played with locks of their hair, as they drank in the smell of her skin, planting little kisses here and there. Their only desire was to be together, to frolic and play like young animals, but in their happiness at seeing one another again, they forgot that they were now adults, albeit young adults, whom the war had deprived of normal affection. Without forethought, the young men's kisses became more tender, their hands more eager as they explored her body. Léa only laughed the deep, husky laugh that had haunted them throughout their adolescence. Their hands opened new, light-filled spaces, banishing her sadness and anxiety. No more fear, no more war, no more death. As Jean entered her, she muffled her first cry against Raoul's lips.

At dawn, they awoke, naked and shivering. The brothers gazed at Léa and then, in horror, at each other, their eyes filling with tears.

"I'm cold," Léa murmured.

Raoul put a bundle of vine shoots on the fire which was still warm. Soon, the room was filled with light.

Jean began sobbing.

"Forgive us," he pleaded, hiding his face in her hair.

Without answering, Léa solemnly traced the long scar on his chest and stomach with her finger.

"Come over here," she said to Raoul, who had just finished putting on his clothes. Contrite, he sat on the bed.

"We mustn't regret what happened last night. We have always loved each other, we grew up together, and you two have always shared everything."

"But not you!"

His heartfelt cry made Léa laugh. In spite of the war, Jean had not changed. He was still exclusive in his relationships, a little boy torn between his love for her and his love for his twin brother.

"Don't laugh," said Raoul. "It's horrible."

"Don't say that," replied Léa suddenly serious, her voice hard. "It's our circumstances that are horrible, not us. Tomorrow, we could all be dead. Why shouldn't we try to live in the few moments we have? I am not ashamed of making love with you and I don't feel any remorse. My only regret is not doing it more often."

"Don't say that. You're immoral."

"And you're stupid. Morality doesn't exist any more."

"If morality doesn't exist, why did you side with the Resistance, instead of collaborating? You could be living in Paris, hanging out in tea rooms with your sister, Sabine—"

"Raoul!" cried Jean.

"—or selling wine to the Germans, instead of carrying messages and hiding weapons at the risk of being arrested and tortured. So, tell us why you're fighting with us, if morality doesn't exist any more!"

"Leave her alone!"

"It's okay, Jean, Let me try to answer. It's not a question of morality—at least not for me. Do you remember before the war? I used to think that all that stuff about the Germans and

85

the Allies and the Maginot Line and Poland was boring. Then you and Jean and Laurent and the others started leaving. France surrendered. Camille and I had to flee Paris, with people dying all around us. I saw Josette, riddled with bullets, bleeding to death. Then there was the man who attacked us. And Madame Le Ménestrel and her two kids. Maman dying during the bombing. And Papa. Even that wasn't enough to make me see that you and Uncle Adrien were right. But when I saw the Germans at Montillac, in my home, on my terrace, in my vineyards, I felt dispossessed and humiliated. I felt they had no right being there. That was when I understood what surrendering and being occupied really meant. And *that* I could not accept. You see, for me there was no noble oath of allegiance."

"Maybe not, but not everyone is doing what you're doing."

"They probably don't feel the same sense of attachment to the earth, or having been born of the earth, or belonging to it."

"You're just like your father, he loved Montillac, too," said Jean, hugging her. "You're right, let's think of last night as a wonderful moment that helped us forget morality and war."

"Come on, Raoul, give us a smile! We didn't do anything wrong."

Raoul looked at the two people he loved most in the world with true sadness. His love for Léa had made him jealous of his brother, something he would never have believed possible before. He forced himself to smile.

After a bowl of hot milk and a piece of bread, Jean and Raoul left for Chapelle-de-Lorette.

On May 11, the two brothers joined Grand-Pierre's group. During a skirmish between the Germans and the *maquisards* at Sauveterre-de-Guyenne, Jean was wounded. Raoul took him to Château de Madaillan then, when the château was no longer safe, to the priest in Blasimon, Abbé Maurice Gréciet, who agreed to hide him. Raoul and the others hid for a while in the woods at Colonne, near Château de Villepreux, before returning to their camp at Puy.

It was a boy sent by Callède, not Léa, who found Mathias's note saying that Camille would be transferred to the Boudet Barracks on the 15th at one in the afternoon. The day before the transfer was to take place, there was a celebration in honor of Joan of Arc, and the hospital had to manage with a skeleton staff. Dressed as a nurse and accompanied by Abbé Chaillou, Léa went to see Camille. The German soldier on duty was enjoying a glass of Sauternes in the company of a generously-endowed nurse. She had instructions to keep the guard occupied for approximately twenty minutes while one sister of Saint-Vincent-de-Paul watched the main entrance to the hospital and another, the chapel.

Léa, who had prepared herself to find Camille tired and thin, was horrified by her condition. She was completely emaciated and there were large dark circles around her eyes, sunken in their sockets. Léa managed a smile, kissed Camille, and burst into tears.

"Come, come, I can't be that ugly! You look lovely in that outfit. Please, don't cry. I'm really much better, aren't I, Father?"

"Yes, yes, you are," said the priest, looking away.

Léa fought back her panic and tried to smile again.

"Hurry, we haven't much time," said the priest. "I'll see how the guard is doing."

Once alone, the women held hands, too moved to speak.

"He's right, we haven't much time," said Camille at last. "How is Charles? Is he all right? Have you heard from Laurent?"

"Charles is just fine. We haven't heard from Laurent recently, but as long as he's in England, there's no reason to worry."

"What about François Tavernier?"

"No news," said Léa, feeling a pang.

"I'm sure you'll hear from him soon. He's not the sort of man to let himself get caught. Trust him. And how are you doing?"

"You only think of others," said Léa, laughing joylessly. "What about you?"

"I'm all right."

"We're going to try to get you out of here tomorrow. Do you think you're strong enough?"

"Yes, I want to see my son."

"Then listen carefully."

Quickly, she told Camille about the plan to ambush the ambulance during the transfer.

When Léa got back to Morizès, she told her uncle and the five men sent by Aristide that the plan had to be abandoned because Camille was too weak; however, she and Abbé Chaillou had thought of an alternative.

Chapter Six

The rain so anxiously awaited by the *vignerons* began to fall at last.

A car waited opposite the hospital in the Rue Perdue, its headlights turned off. Rigoulet and La Sifflette waited in a van at Place Saint-Michel. In the back of the van was a young *maquisard*, gripping the butt of his Sten and holding his breath. Two men were posted in the Rue des Écoles and a third, opposite the Maison du Prince Noir.

"Look out! Here they come!" said Father Adrien, as Léa began running down the Rue Saint-Nicolas. Not far behind was Mathias, carrying Camille.

The rear doors of the car were flung open and the driver flashed his headlights twice. The van flashed its lights in response and both vehicles started their engines.

"She's fainted," said Mathias, placing Camille on the car seat.

"Hurry up, it won't be long before they realize she's gone!"

"Thank you, my son. What you have just done redeems your past errors. Please join us, you will be welcome."

"I'm not so sure about that, Father. Besides, it's too late."

"What are you going to do now?"

"I'll keep watch. You'd better hurry. Good-bye, Léa."

"Good-bye, Mathias . . . and thank you."

As they drove off, with the van close behind, the hospital's lights went on, one by one. A whistle blew and people began shouting. Just before reaching the ancient town of Bazas, they turned left off the road and stopped in Saint-Aignan at a safe house. Camille, still unconscious, was carried inside. After making sure that everything was all right, Rigoulet set off alone for La Réole and the car carried on to Bazas.

It was Father Adrien who had arranged for Camille to be hidden at Saint-Aignan and convinced the other partisans that the Germans would not think of looking for her at such close range. They also needed time to find a chain of safe houses so that Camille could be smuggled into Switzerland. It was decided that Léa, La Sifflette, and two of the *maquisards* would stay with her.

Camille's escape, together with the destruction of the gas depot, the skirmish at Sauveterre, and numerous sabotage operations and attacks, put the Germans and the Militia in a state of full alert. Towns and villages watched as the khaki and navy blue uniforms ransacked their houses, barns, and churches. Saint-Pierre-d'Aurillac, Frontenac, Sauveterre, Rauzan, Blasimon, Mauriac, Pellegrue, Monségur, and La Réole were all searched. Between May 17 and May 20, scores of partisans were arrested: Jean Lafourcade, Albert Rigoulet, Jean Laulan, Georges Loubière, Arnault Benquet, Noël Ducos, Jean Gallissaire, Pierre Espagnet, Gabriel Darcos, seventeen in all from the Buckmaster unit. Some were tortured, some killed, and some deported. Fourteen never came home.

On May 19, La Sifflettte and Léa, wearing a large head scarf, hid Camille in a hay rick and took her to Morizès. Her condition had stabilized.

The next day, the Rosiers family with whom they had been hiding returned home from a shopping trip to La Réole. Madame Rosiers and her daughter were preparing the noonday meal and Monsieur Rosiers, the mailman, and his helper, Manuel, were enjoying an apéritif when they suddenly heard an engine and ran outside to see the black top of a car coming up the road below the farm. Ten days earlier, the Rosier's had left the farm in the middle of the night after being tipped off by friends, but this time it was far more serious. With no time to gather up their belongings, they fled over the fields and through the woods to Morizés, where Tore took them in. The mailman fled as well. No one was arrested, but the Germans found seven tons of weapons in the tobacco drying shed.

Léa realized that Camille's health would not improve as long as she was separated from her son. So, with the help of Madame Rosiers and La Sifflette, she decided to fetch Charles from Montillac. The two women accompanied Léa as far as Saint-André-du-Bois and it was agreed that La Sifflette would come out to meet Léa in two hours' time.

Léa arrived at Montillac to find a flurry of activity by the wine cellars, where Fayard and three men whom Léa did not know were loading crates of wine into a van. When he saw Léa, the vintner nearly dropped the crate he was carrying.

"Hello, Fayard. Business as usual?"

He set the crate down and took off his beret.

"Mademoiselle Léa," he stuttered, the color draining from his face. "Have you come home?"

"Don't worry, Fayard, I'm just passing through, but you'll be hearing from friends of mine before long."

The words were out of her mouth before she realized it. The look of fear on his face had brought to mind the *maquis* attack on a black marketeer in Lot-et-Garonne suspected of denouncing resistance fighters. She felt a rush of evil joy as his calloused hands began to tremble. His love of the land and his greed had driven him to do commerce with the Occupying Forces, to the point of denouncing his countrymen. To think that he might take Montillac away from her!

She turned abruptly and headed toward the house.

Although the air was heavy and warm, the old house had not shaken off the last of the winter chill. Inside, all was calm and quiet. The smell of wax floated in the air, mixed with the scent of white roses from the south wall of the wine cellar, the first of the season. Léa's mother, Isabelle, had planted these early-blooming, climbing roses. There was a bouquet on the round table by the door. If I close my eyes, Maman will enter . . .

"Léa!"

Charles ran towards her, tiny arms outstretched.

"You're back! Where's Maman? I want to see Maman."

"Yes my pet. You'll see Maman soon. I came to get you."

"To get Charles!" exclaimed Ruth. "Don't even think of it!"

"I have to. Otherwise, Camille will never get better."

"It's far too dangerous!"

"Please, I don't have much time. Could you put together some of his things?"

"Léa, I have something to tell you. Charles, go see Aunt Bernadette."

"No, I want to say with Auntie Léa."

"Do as Ruth says. If you're good, I'll take you to see Maman."

"Promise?"

"Cross my heart!"

The little boy ran out of the room, calling for Bernadette.

As she placed his things in a sack, Ruth told Léa about the visit from her uncle Luc and cousin Philippe.

"They were by last week to tell you that Fayard's lawyer had come to see them about selling Montillac."

"What business is it of Uncle Luc's?"

"Apparently, Fayard got Sabine to agree."

"What!"

"I said 'apparently'. That's what his lawyer said. Since Laure is under age and your Uncle Luc is her guardian, and since you've gone off to join the terrorists and are, *de facto*, outside the law, it's up to your uncle to decide whether or not Montillac should be sold."

"But that's ridiculous!"

"Maybe, but your uncle and your cousin are lawyers and they said it's perfectly legal, especially given your absence."

"It would make things a lot easier for them if I got myself arrested and disappeared for good!"

"No doubt Fayard thinks that way, but not your uncle. You are his brother's daughter, after all, and he wants you to keep the property. He's changed a lot, you know, since Pierrot disappeared..."

"That would surprise me. The last I heard, he was still collaborating with the Germans."

"I don't think so. He supports Pétain, but that's the extent of it."

"He let his daughter marry a German."

"That's true, but he was a good man."

"And we know how many good ones there are. Fayard, I can understand. He wants the land. For him, the war is simply a means of achieving his ends, of getting rich. French or German, he doesn't care. He'll collaborate with whomever he thinks will help him take over the estate. He doesn't even realize he's betraying his country and yet he's a veteran of the First World War! But for Uncle Luc, it's different. He's an intellectual. He knows the power of words and their effect on people. His reverence for order and bourgeois values and the legal profession mean that he will always bow down to whomever is in power. For him, Pétain is the legitimate head of the French state and Pétain has asked the French to collaborate with the Germans. He must be totally lacking in imagination, otherwise he would understand that, sooner or later, Germany is going to be defeated and today's 'terrorists' will be in power."

"But that's just what he wants to prevent, Léa. He says that if the Americans land and de Gaulle takes power, France will fall into the hands of the Communists and the Russians will take over. He thinks that only Germany can protect Europe from the threat of Communism. He's absolutely convinced of it."

"Needless to say, my dear cousin agrees."

"Worse. He's talking about joining the L.V.F.!"

"I'd be very surprised if he did that. Phillippe has never been known for his bravery."

"At any rate, your uncle thinks that the only way to prevent the sale from going through is for you to write a letter of refusal. He's not sure it will work, but it will buy him more time."

"I'm going to talk to Uncle Adrien and Camille."

"Don't wait too long. Let's have a look at you . . . you don't look well at all!"

"I do between twenty and twenty-five miles a day on that

bicycle, and around here, it's always uphill. If the war doesn't end soon, I'm going to have calf measurements like Le Guevel or Van Vliet. I'll be able to enter the Grand Prix de Bordeaux. What really worries me is Camille..."

"Poor dear! She has suffered so. Did they ... you know ..."

"Torture her? No, not really, not the way people like Denan use the word 'torture'. Did you know that those bastards in the Militia have come up with a new word for torture? Something more elegant and refined? Now, they call it 'touyagage.' "

"Touyagage?"

"Yes, after a chartered accountant by the name of Pierre Touyaga who was arrested by the Militia after someone denounced him. He was burned and beaten with a club. They tore off his skin and his nails. They burned his feet and his genitals. Marcel Fourquey of the Second Division of the Bordeaux Militia was so pleased with himself and his assistants, Guilbeau and Beyrand, that he coined a new phrase. It isn't torture anymore, it's touyagage."

"That's horrible!"

"Camille got off easy—mild touyagage—slaps, kicks, and punches. It was her frailty that saved her. They couldn't have continued without killing her, but she isn't getting any better and that's why I thought that having Charles with her might help."

"With the life you lead, that could be dangerous."

"I don't think so, the *maquis* have the region under constant surveillance and after the last wave of arrests, the Germans seem to have eased up. The greatest threat is men like Fiaux and Denan. I know for a fact that Aristide has received orders to eliminate them and that's why Uncle Adrien is here. Hopefully, by then, Camille and Charles will be in Switzerland. Is there any hot water, Ruth? I'm dying to wash my hair. I'll never get used to cold water."

After having a bath and washing her hair, Léa felt like a new woman. In spite of notices about hygiene from the leaders of the *maquis* and the BBC, the camps and safe farms were far from clean. Some of the leaders tried to enforce military discipline—saluting the flag, physical exercise, weapons handling, clean outfits, respect for rank, cleanliness and tidiness—but that was only possible in the larger groups like those in the Limousin, Vercors, and Brittany.

In early 1944, the groups in Aquitaine were still very small; however, by May the situation was quite different, and Aristide was able to send London a detailed report on the recruiting effort. Bordeaux and Bordeaux-Saint-Augustin, 500 men; Mérignac, 45 men; the submarine base, 15 men; the Lormont network, 40 men; Pessac, 20 men; the Le Bouscat commando, five men; the Bègles network, 25 men; Les Landes, 500 men; the rail workers, 145 men; and Arcachon, 300 men. A total of 1,595 men who knew what their mission was and were determined to carry it out. By D Day, their ranks would swell to 15,000 men. But even now, Colonel Buckmaster seemed satisfied.

Léa was happy to jettison the old bicycle that the Tore's had lent her in favor of her own blue bicycle with its rack, to which she attached Charles's little wicker seat. She had to act quickly. Fayard might already have alerted the Gestapo in Langon.

Ruth and Bernadette were very upset to see Charles go. For a brief time, the little boy, now laughing and waving from his wicker seat, had brought joy into their lives.

"Sit still or we're going to fall down."

La Sifflette was waiting for them just over the hill at La Bernille.

Camille and Charles's joy at being reunited again defused Father Adrien's anger at the three women for the risk they had run. La Sifflette took full responsibility, saying that she was the oldest. The priest made a pretense of believing her.

Chapter Seven

Maurice Fiaux and his thugs were still fuming over Camille's disappearance from Saint-Jean Hospital. Father Adrien was aware that the Militia and the Gestapo had infiltrated a number of the *maquis* groups, not only the O.C.M., but also *Libé-Nord* and the *Francs-Tireurs et Partisans*. Not that this would have presented any insurmountable difficulties: the young *maquisards* were often as gullible as they were self-assured. All it took was a glass of wine, a pretty face, or a favorable comment about the Resistance or General de Gaulle mentioned in passing for a banal conversation to yield information enabling Dohse and Robert Franc to make arrests. There was even talk that one of Grand-Clément's men had infiltrated commandos recruited by Aristide. The leaders of the Resistance were starting to see traitors around every corner. Fresh orders to execute Grand-Clément arrived from London. Up until then, the former leader of the O.C.M. had managed to elude Aristide, but he was determined to finish with Grand-Clément and his followers once and for all. One of Grand-Clément's henchmen, André Basilio, had been gunned down on May 22. They would have to act quickly because Grand-Clément knew that Aristide had returned to the region. The day before Basilio's execution, the British agent had bumped into André Noël in Bordeaux. Noël was a former member of Aristide's network who had gone over to the other side after succumbing to the theories of Dohse—and the man he still considered his leader—on the Bolshevik menace threatening France. Orders

96

were given to kill Grand-Clément and Noël, but they were nowhere to be found. Dohse's efforts to locate Aristide were no more successful.

Father Adrien and Aristide knew that it was only a matter of time before the Allies landed. In April, Aristide had received orders to begin listening for messages concerning the landing during the B.B.C. French broadcast at 7:00 p.m. on the first, second, fifteenth, and sixteenth day of every month. It was of the utmost importance that everything be in place and that preparations be carried out in complete secrecy. This was, of course, not the case. Early in the year small groups, some well-armed, some not, had begun harassing the Occupying Forces, sabotaging installations, attacking sentinels, and liberating prisoners. This forced the Germans and the Militia into a state of constant alert, seriously endangering the safety of the *maquis* in Aquitaine.

It was in this atmosphere of tension and restlessness that a message from Mathias Fayard, addressed to Father Adrien, arrived at Aristide's headquarters at a farm at Blaye-Saint-Luce, in the marshlands at the mouth of the Garonne. There was a moment of panic as they all wondered how he had known the location of the farm. They were unable to extract any information from the "courier," the simple-minded son of a local fisherman, who had been imprisoned at Fort du Hâ for distributing underground newspapers some time before Aristide's return. They hung on to the lad, just in case.

The letter contained alarming news. According to Mathias, Maurice Fiaux knew the exact location of every *maquis* camp east of Bordeaux, including the names of the leaders, the number of men, and how well-armed they were. For reasons known only to himself, Fiaux had not passed this information on to either the Gestapo or the Militia.

"How does Fayard know all this?" asked Aristide.

"Here's what he says: 'As you know Father, I'm keeping an eye on Fiaux to protect Léa. I've been hiding in the attic of his house in Le Bouscat. His bedroom is right below, and the ceiling is a simple wood floor, so I can hear all of his conversations. Yesterday, I heard him talking to his two bodyguards.

97

Some of the things he said make me think he'll try to sell this information to the Chief of the Gestapo. He doesn't trust his friends in the Militia who "would take all the credit", as he says. I thought about killing him—I could have done it from the attic—but then I thought that if I missed him, he and the others would get me for sure and there would be no one to warn you and protect Léa. You must act quickly, you must prevent him from talking. I would do the job myself, but he doesn't trust me, and it would be hard for me to get near him. This letter is proof I'm not lying or trying to set a trap for you. If you want to talk, leave a message for me at my parents' place at Montillac or at the *Chapon-Fin*. Ask for René, he's the chef's helper. He'll be able to get in touch with me the same day. I want you to know that I am not doing this for the Resistance; I am doing it for Léa. Yours truly,' etcetera, etcetera."

"This is absolutely crazy," said Lancelot. "I don't trust the little creep."

"What do you think, Father?" asked Aristide.

"I think he's telling the truth."

"How can we be sure?"

"Yesterday, in Castillon-la-Bataille, we arrested a boy whom we suspected of working for both sides. When I interrogated him, he laughed and said that we were done for because the Militia knew where all the *maquis* camps were and was preparing to attack. Just then, there was a message on the radio for me to decode. When I returned, he was dead."

"Dead?"

"Yes, they started to hit him. One of them tried to intervene, perhaps with his gun—they wouldn't tell me exactly what had happened—a shot was fired and he died instantly."

"Don't tell me you feel sorry for him."

"The death of a man is always cause for sorrow."

"Yes, but this is a war. We kill and get killed. Sometimes one man has to die so that tens and perhaps hundreds of others can live."

"That's the argument that is always used to justify war. I saw so many people die in Spain on that pretext. . . ."

"Yes, Father, but we don't have any choice. The Allies will

be landing soon and we can't run the risk of having our *maquis* attacked and destroyed. We have to eliminate Maurice Fiaux, his body guards, and Mathias Fayard."

"Why Mathias?"

"Because unlike you, I don't trust him."

"I've known him since he was a boy. His love for my niece has made him do some very silly things."

"Do you call working for the Gestapo and the Militia 'silly'?" asked Lancelot.

"I propose that we put it to a vote," said Dédé le Basque, speaking for the first time.

"Fine," said Aristide. "All those in favor of killing all four?"

Every hand went up except Father Adrien's.

"Then it's decided. Lancelot, send some of your men to locate them and report back. I want to know where they live, what their movements are, and any weak links in their security within the next forty-eight hours. Is that clear?"

"Perfectly clear, chief. You should go to Jard-de-Bourdillas in Les Landes de Bussac until we've eliminated those bastards."

"I'll let you know what I decide to do. I don't think I risk much here. We have men in Saint-Ciers, Montendre, Saint-Savin, Saint-André-de-Cubzac, and Bourg. Our headquarters are well protected. Father, may I have a word with you?"

Aristide seemed even more diminutive and youthful beside the tall, gaunt priest.

"How is Madame d'Argilat?"

"Much better."

"I'm glad to hear it. Have you managed to arrange for her to get to Lausanne?"

"Not yet, many of the guides have been arrested, and it's not the easiest thing in the world to get a sick woman across the south of France."

"I contacted London to try to get a plane, but was told that it was too risky for the time being. However, if what Fayard says is true, she and your niece can't stay at Morizès. We could send them to the Luze *maquis* near Arcachon."

"I would prefer for them to remain within Daniel Faux and

Lieutenant Vincent's sectors. Léa knows the region well, and if she ran into difficulties she would know where to hide. Besides, I'm waiting for my contact for Switzerland in La Réole."

"As you wish. But in that case, I'd like them to be closer to Lorette."

"Fine, I'll arrange for them to move in the morning. Tomorrow is the Pentecost. Let's hope God shines a little light on us."

"We'll meet here at 6:00 p.m. on Monday to discuss Fiaux's execution. Father . . . may I be frank?"

"Of course."

"I think you should see a doctor. You're looking awfully tired."

"We'll see about that later." the priest replied, smiling faintly.

The next day, Father Adrien celebrated mass in the church at Chapelle-de-Lorette. Most of the *maquisards* attended, regardless of their beliefs, as did the Couthure group, Camille, and Léa. Charles was left in the care of Madame Faux who, with La Sifflette's help, prepared her famous lamb-and-beans, a big hit with famished young resistance fighters. Madame Carnélos, whose farm above Lorette served as a lookout and weapons depot, prepared a fish caught in the Garonne. Around the thick-walled buildings, trenches had been dug. Machine guns had been set up at openings in the attic and behind the wall around the Faux's well.

Many young men had joined the ranks of the Resistance since the death of Captain Lévy at the hands of the Toulouse Gestapo. His replacement, Colonel Becq-Guérin, was carrying on the work Lévy had begun, training the new recruits—deserters from the forced labor camps, farm workers, casual laborers, and students—in the use of weapons.

Coming out of the church, Léa was greeted by the wonderful aroma of lamb-and-beans, one of her favorite dishes.

"I'm starving," she said, rubbing her stomach unaffectedly.

"Me too," said Camille, who was beginning to get her color back.

"Léa looked at her with a mixture of surprise and joy.

"I haven't heard you say that in ages."

"I feel as though I've been reborn. It did me good to pray, gave me back my courage. I feel we're safe here."

As in the forest clearing at Les Landes, Léa shivered in spite of the midday sun.

"Look who's coming for lunch!"

"Raoul! Jean!"

The two brothers kissed their friend a little awkwardly. Léa brushed aside their embarrassment, laughing and hugging them. Jean let out a cry.

"Sorry! I forgot. Did I hurt you? Is it serious?"

"No, but it's still painful."

"Jean was lucky. Another inch and the bullet would have gone right through his heart. Camille, it's so nice to see you looking better. How is Charles?

"He's here with me."

They entered the courtyard at the Faux's farm, where tables and chairs had been set up. The *maquisards* were already seated, waiting impatiently to be served. They stood up to make room for the young women, but Léa preferred the shade of a big linden tree with Jean and Raoul. Camille sat next to Charles, whose plate was already heaped with beans.

The meal was a very happy one and much appreciated by the guests. The guards were relieved and devoured what remained of the lamb-and-beans. To make up for the smaller portions, Madame Faux gave them extra slices of *pastis*, a cake for which she was as well known as her lamb-and-beans. When it came time to wash up, Léa slipped away, heading for the barn and taking Raoul with her.

"Kiss me."

"But . . . what about Jean?"

"He's wounded. Just kiss me."

They rolled in the hay and, for few moments, thought only of the pleasure their bodies gave them.

That evening, the *maquisards* returned to their camps and Father Adrien set out for Bordeaux across the vine-covered hills on a motorbike requisitioned from a garage owner in Langon.

It was exceptionally hot for the end of May. The grapes

thrived in the suffocating heat, but every other crop now craved water. There had been lightning earlier and with it, the possibility of rain, but the storm had moved off.

The road dipped into a valley and crossed a small wood. Father Adrien was hit by the strong, pungent odor of moss and mint and the cold damp of the undergrowth. Even after so many years, the sudden transition from cultivated field to wooded hollow, shut away from the sun and the sky, with tangles and thorns, huge roots and shallow pools of water and scurrying night creatures, always took him by surprise. Such places seemed all the more wild for the contrast, and he felt a fleeting uneasiness. Even on the hottest day of the year, the shade of the dark hollow was uninviting. He couldn't remember ever stopping there. But on this evening, his heart and soul felt at one with the dark, dank place.

He cut the motor and applied the brakes. The heat from the motor was comforting and he lingered a moment before leaning the motorbike against a tree. Parting the branches and trailing vines, he entered the wood. The peat beneath his feet made a damp, spongy sound. A fallen oak tree lay across his path and he sat down on its rotting trunk, unable to fight back mounting despair. He had not shed a single tear since that morning in Spain when he had seen young men, still children really, being shot. At that moment, his faith in God suddenly went out of him. He had lost count of the nights spent calling out to God for help. God, in whom he no longer believed, yet to whom he still prayed, hoping that the familiar words would bring back the wonderment of faith. He had unburdened himself to one of his Spanish friends, also a Dominican priest, who had looked at him with great pity and put his arms around him.

"My heart goes out to you, but there's nothing I can do. I'm going through the same agony. I even thought of killing myself. The only thing that stopped me was the thought of the pain I would cause my mother."

They had parted, even more deeply distressed than before. Father Adrien never mentioned it again. He tried to lose himself in his work, but to no avail. His suffering was so great that he wished only to die. Perhaps the time had come to act. . . .

The death of others, even traitors and assassins, had always seemed unbearable to him. Yet here, in the wood, he resolved to kill Maurice Fiaux and prevent him from denouncing the *maquisards* in detention. Once he had made this terrible decision, this man, this priest, who had been a fierce opponent of the death penalty before the war, felt at peace for the first time in years.

Then he worked out a plan. He could get Maurice's address from his mother. The boy wouldn't suspect him; on the contrary, he would be too caught up in the idea of arresting a leader of the Resistance who had eluded both the German and the French police. After killing Maurice, there would be no time to escape and one of Maurice's bodyguards would kill him.

He left the wood.

The next day, Father Adrien volunteered for the job of killing Maurice Fiaux. Those who knew he was a priest looked at him with disbelief, then horror, and tried to dissuade him. He stood firm, saying that he was the only one who could get close enough to Maurice to kill him with a minimum of risk. When this was not enough to convince them, he pulled rank and mentioned something about orders from London. They finally gave in, with much regret and reluctance. He also convinced them not to execute Mathias Fayard just yet; instead, he was placed under constant surveillance.

The plan had to be postponed. On the evening of May 30, Fiaux left Bordeaux for Paris. His mother said that he would be back by June 6 at the latest. The trip to Paris and a meeting with Darnand were to reward Fiaux "for a job well done."

Chapter Eight

Alpha wants six bottles of Sauternes.

Aristide was so startled that the knob of the radio nearly came off in his hand. He had been turning it back and forth for several minutes, searching for what was to be the sixth and final stand-by broadcast on the BBC. The time was 7:00 p.m., the date, June 2, 1944.

I repeat: Alpha wants six bottles of Sauternes.

There could be no doubt now. This was message A for his region, announcing that the Allies were about to land and ordering Resistance groups into a state of readiness. Later on that evening, he called together his officers, Lancelot, François, Jacqueline, Dany, and Marcel, and announced a meeting of the group leaders at three o'clock the following day at 29 Rue Guynemer in Caudéran, on the outskirts of Bordeaux.

They arrived at the appointed time and Aristide received them one by one, giving them precise instructions. Capdepont, who led the railway workers, was ordered to sabotage all locomotives, switches, signalling devices, and tracks over a distance of one hundred and twenty-five miles. Pierre Roland, leader of Resistance activities in the port of Bordeaux, was instructed to destroy the electrical system controlling the mines placed along the docks by the Germans. Henri Mesmet told Aristide that Léon in Les Landes had five hundred men who were ready, willing, and able to fight, but that only half of them had weapons. The S.O.E. officer reassured him that three shipments of weapons would be parachuted in over the next two days. Captain Duchez, leader of the group in Arcachon, had no such problems: his men were well-armed and trained in the use of heavy weaponry—machine guns, mortars, and bazookas. The leaders of the groups in Lège, Andernos, Facture, and Arès each had between seventy and one hundred men who were adequately armed; Pierre Chatanet reported that after the recent wave of arrests, the Mérignac group had been reduced to twenty men. Their job would be to cut telephone lines. La Réole, Bègles, Pessac, Lermont, Bordeaux-Saint-Augustin, and Blaye were also represented. Dédé le Basque reported that his men were waiting impatiently to go into action. The operation as a whole consisted of slowing the movement of German troops stationed in southwest France toward the landing beaches in the north, as soon as these had been identified.

As they left Caudéran, these handfuls of men who had never accepted defeat felt a renewed sense of hope. Hope, but also impatience. After four years of German rule, the last few days of waiting seemed like an eternity.

After washing and dressing hastily, Léa pitched the soapy water in the blue enamel basin into the courtyard.

"Hey! Watch what you're doing!"

She froze.

"What's the matter? Have you turned into stone?"

Laughter roused her from her stupor. The wash basin slipped from her hands, chipping on the stones of the courtyard.

"François!"

At the sound of her husky cry, François felt his loins stir. She ran toward him and as he caught her, he let out a groan of pleasure.

She was in his arms, alive and warm, smelling of coarse soap and cherry blossoms, a smell that was hers alone. He sniffed her like an animal, biting and nuzzling, nipping at her tongue and lips. She rubbed up against him, moaning in a way that made him desire her even more. He held her at arm's length, lest he come, and devoured her with his eyes. My God! how he had missed her! The thought of her body had haunted him for nights on end, awakening him with painful erections that neither his hand nor the comely British auxiliaries could satisfy. At first, having these huge erections at the thought of Léa, impossible and absent, had amused him, but as the months passed, they put him in a frenzy that benefitted only young English women and London prostitutes. Her touch completely undid him. He wanted to rape her, no gentle touches, no preliminaries. He wanted to take her right there in the courtyard under the mocking, envious gaze of the *maquisards* who tried to concentrate on their weapons, going down a mental checklist of maneuvers to avoid becoming aroused:

> *To load, put tray on charger so that pivoted tongue (f) enters slit (g). Place left hand on lever (a) so that ring finger slips into hole (b) and index finger is on tip (c). Place little finger on lip (d) and lower, inserting cartridge into opening (e) with right hand. Lift lever with ring finger and push to insert new cartridge. Repeat until twenty-eight cartridges have been loaded . . .*

One of the men dropped his box of cartridges. Turning bright red, he stooped to pick them up, then walked away. Most of the others followed suit.

Standing on the steps of the farmhouse, her hands on her hips, La Sifflette gazed at the lovers approvingly. Those two were made for each other! It would take a big strong man like him to tame this beautiful, insolent girl who looked at men with a mixture of innocence and appetite. If she didn't leave for Switzerland with Madame Camille soon, the men would end up killing each other over her.

"Hey, you two lovebirds!" she called out. "This is no place for smooching. There's no shortage of hideaways here. Hey, did you hear what I said?"

"Excuse me, ma'am," said François, taking his gaze off Léa for a moment.

"No need to apologize. I was saying, if I were a young stud, I'd do the same. And I wouldn't just stand there looking at her either! I'd head up to the tobacco drying shed on the hill filled with hay cut just yesterday!"

"Thank you for that piece of information. Léa, do you know where it is?"

"Come!"

La Sifflette watched them scramble up the rocky path.

The hill above the farm seemed to climb forever. In their haste, they kept stumbling and twisting their ankles, cursing and laughing. François placed one arm around her waist. In the other, he carried a sack and a rifle. There was a rusted padlock on the door of the shed. Using the barrel of his rifle as a lever, he pried it off.

The heady odor of tobacco and freshly cut hay aroused their desire further still. François threw down his rifle and sack, tore off his jacket, and pushed Léa into the hay. Hungry and impatient, they pitched backward, landing with a jolt that drew cries from both sides. A wave of pleasure enveloped them, rising and falling, drawing them further and further away, then abandoning them in disarray.

"Take off your clothes."

Without missing a single gesture, François took off his clothes. Naked, magnificently erect, he went to jam the door shut with his rifle. He was going to take his time savoring her eager body and did not want to be disturbed.

When at last his hunger was appeased, the afternoon was spent. They had not exchanged a single word, except those worn smooth from having been repeated over and over in lovemaking.

Someone knocked on the door.

"Who is it?" said François, reaching for his rifle.

"It's me, Finot, sir. They told me you were here."

Tavernier put down the rifle and started getting dressed.
"What do you want?"

"We have to go, sir, your plane will be landing any minute now."

"What time is it?"

"Four o'clock, sir."

"Good God! Why didn't you come for me sooner?"

"No one knew where you were, sir."

Propping herself up on elbow, Léa watched François.

"You're going?"

"I came over on a mission and wanted to see you. No one at Montillac knew or would tell me where you were. Luckily, I remembered Madame Lafourcade and her sons. Maxime called and ... here I am."

"But you're going."

"Yes, but I'll come back."

"Sir!"

"I'll be there in a moment."

"François!"

"Ssshh! Don't say a word, don't cry. Everything will be all right, the war will be over soon."

"But...we didn't have a chance to talk!"

"I know, my love, we'll talk another time."

He lifted her up and held her, naked and fragile.

"Kiss me."

"Sir, we have to go!"

He turned away, his mouth was filled with salty tears. He didn't know whether they were her tears or his own.

Bumping into his driver, he scrambled down the hill to the old black Mercedes waiting in the courtyard. As the driver started the motor, he turned and looked at the farmhouse. In the doorway stood a young woman who looked like Camille d'Argilat. She was holding the hand of a little boy and waving excitedly.

Parachuted in the previous day to make preparations for the Allied landing, François boarded an R.A.F. Blenheim to return to London that night.

When Léa came down from the drying shed later that evening, her eyes were red and puffy. Camille, who had come out to meet her, kissed her tenderly.

"You're lucky," she said simply.

They walked back to the farmhouse, hand in hand.

Léa had become accustomed to living in hiding and without creature comforts, even if from time to time she complained about the crudeness and the lack of privacy. Camille, on the other hand, had never uttered a word of complaint but was now finding that their life was taking its toll on her. More than anything, she was afraid that the farm would be attacked. Her health had improved but she was still so weak that she sometimes had difficulty walking. Her faith and her love for her husband and son were what kept her going.

On the night of June 5, the BBC broadcast Message B, long awaited by Aristide and his men. It was one of three hundred such messages that the French section of the S.O.E. transmitted that night to its officers stationed in France. *Wear a rose behind your ear*. The Allies had at last landed in Normandy and a general mobilization of the French Resistance had been declared.

At dawn, weapons painstakingly stockpiled in barns, drying sheds, wine cellars, and caves were quickly distributed. Underground cables linking the headquarters of General von der Chevallerie, Commander of the First Army stationed in Bordeaux, to Camp Mérignac and the barracks were destroyed as were those linking the *Luftwaffe* to the artillery units at Chut. In the shunting yards at Pessac, Pierre Chatanet and his men blew up nine locomotives, delaying the departure of three thousand German troops for the Front by several days. The Lacanau-Saint-Louis line was blown up. George's group dynamited the line between Le Puy and Lonzac, the railway bridge between Montendre and Chartressac, the German Army telephone system at Souge, eight 150,000-volt pylons near Ychoux, and three 120,000-volt pylons at Boir. Not to be outdone, the rail workers under Fernand Schmaltz sent Aristide a report on their operations over a forty-eight hour period: German troop convoy derailed near Pons. Railway bridge near Fléac destroyed. German troop convoy derailed after colliding with oil tanker convoy near Bordeaux, causing enormous fire with heavy German casualties including one captain and one sergeant. Thirty-three ton crane dynamited, falling on steam locomotive and knocking out line. Crane and locomotive both disabled. Rail lines at Soulac cut. The list went on and on ... The group in Arcachon under Commander de Luze and Captain Duchez blew up two high tension pylons, shutting down the southern sector of the railway grid. Telephone and telegraph cables at the seaside resort were also cut, making communication impossible. Relentlessly, Dédé le Basque and Léon des Landes harassed German convoys attempting to reach the beaches of Normandy by way of secondary roads.

On the evening of June 6, everyone at the Carnélos's farm gathered around the radio, straining to hear the voice which, for the past four years, had symbolized France's honor:

"The supreme hour is at hand!

"After so many battles, after so much hardship and pain, the moment we have all been waiting for is finally here. By this I mean, of course, the Battle of France, the battle for France! It is the sacred duty of all sons of France, whoever they are, wherever they may be, to fight with the means at hand. We must destroy the oppressor. It must be brought to it knees! It will do everything in its power to avoid the inevitable. It will fight to hold on to our land for as long as it can. But now it is nothing more than a savage beast cowering in a corner....

"And as we fight to break the chains that bind us hand and foot in the face of an oppressor armed to the teeth, we must remember three ...

The jamming blotted out the three conditions, but cleared just as General de Gaulle was ending his speech:

"The Battle of France has begun. Our nation, our empire, and our armies have but one desire and one hope. The dark cloud, heavy with our blood and tears, shall part and the grandeur of France shall shine once again!

110

As the *Marseillaise* began playing, they all rose to their feet, some weeping openly. Then, after a member of the staff of the Supreme Commander of the Allied Expeditionary Force read out instructions for people living in the landing zone, Jacques Duchesne began his broadcast:

"Dear listeners, it is no accident that this evening's program does not begin with the words, 'Today is the 277th day of the invasion'. Nor did we forget to add the phrase 'the 1,444th day of the struggle of the French people for their liberation.' It has taken 1,444 days for liberation to come, but never again will you hear those words."

Everyone applauded at the words "never again." Just a little longer and then no more fear, no more hiding! A few more days, a few more weeks perhaps, and they would be able to go back to their vineyards and factories and offices. In short, they would be able to go home. In a month or two, the prisoners would return, in time for the harvest. That night, everyone at the Carnélos's farm slept soundly.

When the Germans attacked, they were taken completely off guard.

The air was heavy and the sky overcast on the afternoon of June 9, as Léa and Charles returned from the woods at Candale, famished after a long walk in search of wild strawberries. They had found a dozen barely ripe berries, which they had divided equally. The little boy adored Léa; she treated him as though he were a kid brother, taking all their games very seriously. They had eaten the snack provided by Madame Faux long ago, and were returning to the farm a little earlier than planned, in the hope of finding leftovers from lunch.

They could smell the lamb-and-beans, now a permanent feature on the menu. Even Léa, who was partial to lamb-and-beans, had begun to tire of them. Suddenly, they heard machine gun fire.

"They're playing," said Charles, authoritatively.

"I don't think so. Wait here and don't move. I'm going to see what's happening."

"No, I want to come with you."

There was another burst of fire, then another.

"It's coming from the farm! Promise me you won't move, I'm going to get your mother."

Léa scrambled down the slope, hiding behind the big cherry tree overhanging the outbuildings. Three hundred yards away, in the wheat field, grey-green helmets began to emerge. With the German soldiers were French militiamen in navy blue uniforms and black caps. One of them straightened up, then collapsed with a cry, crushing the tender green shoots beneath him. A round of ammunition was fired from the farm. From the second floor of the farmhouse, Daniel Faux's light machine guns swept the field. As the men began to fall, others came forward to replace them. Camille was posted at one of the windows on the ground floor with a rifle, praying that Charles was with Léa somewhere far away. A few *maquisards* ran past the cherry tree and Léa followed them into the woods. They threw a few grenades in the direction of the German troops.

"Léa! Léa!"

"Shit! The kid!"

Frightened by the noise and the shouting, Charles had begun running toward the house. Léa ran after him, but fear had given him wings. There was a quick exchange of fire.

"Charles!"

Oblivious to her cries, he bobbed along like a little elf, rounding the corner of the house passing out of view.

"Dear God, protect him!" she prayed.

"Maman! Maman!"

Hearing Charles's voice, Camille screamed, dropped her rifle, and ran toward the door. La Sifflette tried to hold her back, but she screamed again and wrenched herself free. Suddenly, the shooting stopped. As Léa rounded the corner, someone knocked her to the ground. Charles stood alone in the middle of the courtyard. Camille appeared in the doorway of the farmhouse, then began running, arms outstretched, toward the little boy. How beautiful they are, thought Léa. And how slowly they moved! Charles turned, a red flower blooming on his white shirt. He raised his arms slowly, then tripped. One of his canvas sandals fell off. His mouth opened but he didn't make a sound. Camille could see that he was calling her. Don't worry, Maman's here. Careful, you'll fall. Did you hurt yourself? You're bleeding. It's nothing. I can't see you, something hot is dripping from my forehead, on my lips, something salty. Where are you? Why are you lying on the ground? That's right, you fell, but you're all right. Maman will make it better. Such a brave boy, not even crying. I'm going to lift you up now . . . how heavy you are . . . still not very strong . . . call Léa . . . she'll . . .

Léa could make out her name on Camille's lips and struggled to respond to the mute cry, but Jean Lefèvre pressed against her with his full force.

"Let go of me! Camille needs me!"

"It's too late!"

The bullets flew around Camille and Charles, then suddenly her body crumpled, pinning the little boy to the ground. Léa wrenched herself free, reaching their bodies just as La Sifflette began dragging Camille toward the house. As La Sifflette was struck down, Léa picked up Charles and began running toward the woods, not daring to look at him. Her fingers were sticky with blood but she kept on running.

She did not stop until she reached Deymier. There, a woman whose son had been killed in 1940 took her in. Her arms and legs were scratched from the thorns. Her clothes were in tatters. Gently, the woman relieved her of her precious burden.

"He's alive."

In Lorette, the order to pull out came at around 6:00 p.m. The Germans had brought in heavy artillery, and after fighting off the attack for as long as possible, the partisans retreated into the woods, taking their wounded with them. Before abandoning the farm, they took off their caps and knelt by the bodies of Camille and La Sifflette. Moments later, the house was stormed. Booby-trapped with plastic bombs, the roof collapsed as the troops entered, killing forty-eight Germans soldiers and twenty-eight French militiamen. The *maquisards*, regrouped at Lamothe-Landerron, were able to evacuate fifteen of the wounded. Not all were that lucky.

In spite of René Faux's courageous attempt to hide Robert Liarcou, during which René himself was hit in the heel, Liarcou was found by the enemy. With one knee completely smashed, he was dragged into the open. An enemy nurse placed a handful of straw over the wounded knee, then bound it between two planks. Liarcou was thrown, unconscious, into the back of a truck along with chairs, foodstuffs, and bicycles. He was taken to the Gestapo headquarters in La Réole. Paul Gérard was already there, lying in a pool of blood, his limbs shattered. He had been found in the Faux's farmhouse, then beaten to a pulp. That night he died, stabbed repeatedly by a militiaman. His body was put in a sack and thrown into a common grave on the banks of the Garonne.

When they came for him at dawn, Liarcou was sure that he would be shot. He was taken to the Gestapo in Langon then to Fort du Hâ. He received no medical attention, only moral support from two other partisans, Laforesterie from Puisseguin and Marcel Guinot from Bergerac, who were also wounded. A few days later, his guards dragged him to the infirmary where Doctor Poinot was given permission to examine him. Given the gravity of his injuries, the doctor tried to persuade the commander to have the young man hospitalized. Finally, after five or six episodes of heavy bleeding, he gave his consent. Liarcou's leg was amputated at the hospital in Béquet on July 14, thirty-three days later. In August, he was taken back to Fort du Hâ.

He survived. Three of the others who had been detained in La Réole—Bolzan, Labory, and Zuanet—were deported, never to be seen again.

Charles had lost a lot of blood from the bullet wound in his shoulder but in spite of his frail appearance, he had a strong constitution and recovered quickly.

Chapter Nine

Maurice Fiaux was more surprised than suspicious when he saw Father Adrien Delmas on his doorstep, late in the afternoon on June 9. After glancing into the street, he ordered his bodyguards to leave him alone with the priest.

"Nothing can happen to me in the company of a priest, isn't that right, Father?" he said with a mocking smile. "What can I do for you?"

"Germany is losing the war and people like you will be rounded up and shot. You can help us—I've been ordered by London to make you an offer. If you accept, you can save yourself getting killed."

Fiaux looked at the priest warily.

"How do I know this isn't a trap?"

"You have my word," said Father Adrien disdainfully. "My mission is to save lives. Let's go for a walk. I can't risk having your bodyguards hear what I have to say."

Fiaux hesitated for a moment, then said:

"As you wish, but I'll have to have us followed."

"I wouldn't, if I were you."

"Is there any money in it?"

"Possibly," replied the priest, barely able to hide his disgust.

"All right then, let's go. Anyways, I'm big enough to look after myself," said Fiaux, touting an automatic pistol.

They passed two young men smoking cigarettes on the landing.

"If I'm not back in an hour, call Commissioner Poinsot,"

said Fiaux. "Tell him I had a rendezvous with someone high up in the Resistance—the guy who pooped the party at Mérignac. He'll know what I mean."

"Don't you want us to come with you?"

"No, it's okay."

The air outside was hot and heavy. People milled about in the Rue de la Porte-Dijeaux as offices closed for the day. Pale children played in the dirty water of the gutters.

"Where are we going?"

"To the docks where we won't be disturbed."

Fiaux hesitated.

"I gave you my word," said the priest bitterly.

"This must be pretty important for you to risk being spotted and arrested. By the way, have you seen your charming niece lately? Someone told me she was playing war games somewhere over by La Réole . . . the name of the place escapes me . . . oh yes, it was Lorette. Have I got it right? I would never have believed that a young woman from a good Bordeaux family would get mixed up with Commies. I also heard that Madame d'Argilat is a Commie and her little boy sings *The International*, but that was too much. The son of a hero of London! Mind you, you haven't exactly set a good example. Even 'way back when you came to visit my mother's employer you had Bolshevik ideas. Kind of strange for a Catholic priest. Good thing they're not all like you!"

"There are more of us that you think."

"We know who they are. Remember Father de Jabrun? He was a Jesuit, too. Was he a friend of yours?"

"Yes."

"Well, apparently he died last year in Buchenwald."

So Louis de Jabrun was dead, Louis de Jabrun with whom he had spent hours on end before the war discussing the writings of Eckhart, Jakob Boehme, and Saint Augustine. Another great man struck down!

"And if I was Father Dieuzaide or Abbé Lasserre, I'd start saying my prayers."

Maybe you should be saying yours, thought Father Adrien blackly.

They walked on in silence. Their route took them along the Quai de Richelieu and across the Cour d'Alsace-et-Lorraine. When Father Adrien turned into the Rue de la Porte-des-Portanets, Fiaux stopped, suddenly wary, and put his hand on his gun.

"Drop your hand, Fiaux. This may only be a French gun, but it works just the same."

"You're crazy! What do you want with me?"

"Get inside!"

He pushed Fiaux into the dark entranceway of a magnificent eighteenth century building, now badly in need of repair. A stone staircase, covered in filth, lead to the upper floors.

"Where are we going?"

"The third floor ... the door at the end of the hall ... and keep your hand away from your pocket."

The stairs seemed incredibly steep. Fiaux stepped gingerly, imagining that he was about to be shot in the back, yet not really believing it. Father Adrien found the climb so strenuous that he was drenched in sweat.

"It's not locked, go in."

In contrast to the rest of the building, the vast room seemed exceedingly clean. It contained only a cot, a canteen, and two chairs.

"Sit down," said Father Adrien, relieving Fiaux of his gun.

"No."

"Sit down," he repeated, sitting on one of the chairs.

Pale, but defiant, Fiaux sat down.

"What do you want from me?"

"I'm going to kill you."

Stupefied, Fiaux looked at Father Adrien, a trail of saliva falling from his open mouth to his chin. He gripped the seat of his chair, his legs suddenly weak, and began to tremble.

"You have no right."

"Did you have the right to kill and torture and betray?"

"I was following orders!"

"So am I."

"That's not true! You're just trying to protect your family."

"Be quiet. If you believe in God, commend your soul to Him now."

Maurice slid from his chair and kneeled.

"But you're a priest! You can't kill me!"

"Oh yes, I can. If this is a sin, I take it upon myself."

"No, please! You knew me when I was a kid. Think of my mother. What will you tell her?"

That's right, there was a mother. Quick, get it over with.

The figure on the floor was now a puddle of terror, giving off a foul odor. Poor kid, thought Father Adrien, pulling the trigger. The bullet entered Fiaux's left temple, killing him instantly.

He contemplated the body without apparent emotion, then turned it over and went through the pockets. In a crocodile skin wallet with gold corners, he found a list of Resistance groups in the Gironde and, in almost every instance, the name of the leader and the number of men. Lorette was circled in red with the number nine beside it. Libourne, Targon, Villandraut, and Podensac had a red dot beside them. If the Germans had this list, it was game over for the Resistance in the southwest. He had to get word to Aristide as quickly as possible.

As he went out, he turned and made the sign of the cross.

Late that night, Father Adrien found the headquarters of the English agent, which had been moved every day since the Landing, and was told of the attack at Lorette and the death of Camille and La Sifflette. They were unable to tell him anything about Léa or Charles, except that Charles had been wounded with his mother and that he and Léa had disappeared when the Germans moved in on the farm.

Despite every effort on Léon's part to break the news gently, it came as such a shock, that Father Adrien collapsed. Two men rushed over to support him, and as he straightened up, he asked himself why he hadn't killed the monster earlier. Because of him, because of his idiotic scruples, women and a child had been killed and others had been wounded and taken prisoner. Tomorrow or perhaps that very evening others might meet the same fate because he had waited too long to act.

In a monotone, the grief-stricken priest related the execution of Maurice Fiaux. There was a strained silence.

"I'm going to La Réole to see what I can find out about Léa and Charles. Are there any messages?"

They all knew it was pointless to try to dissuade him. Dédé le Basque and one of the young partisans accompanied him to the edge of the village, where a bicycle was found for him.

"Father, you should rest, you can leave later."

"No, I must go. Good-bye, my friends."

Dédé le Basque watched anxiously as he disappeared into the night.

The sun had been up for several hours when at last the rooftops of La Réole came into view. Father Adrien got off the bicycle and began walking through the steep streets of the little town. When he reached the Place Jean-Jaurès, he entered the Hôtel Terminus. Just above the hotel, commanding a view of the Garonne, was the college that served as headquarters for the Gestapo. The man who was to smuggle Camille and Charles in to Switzerland was to leave a message for him here.

He lowered himself into a chair at one of the tables in the restaurant, and without his asking, a waitress brought over some bread and pâté.

"Shall I bring you a glass of wine?"

"If you like."

She returned with an opened bottle and a glass. As she poured, he asked:

"Have you seen Hélène again?"

She flashed him a look of relief and replied:

"Yes, she'll be here soon."

This meant that everything was ready for Camille and Charles to leave.

"You're very pale. Are you sure you're feeling all right?"

"Yes, I'm fine . . . just a little tired. When will she be here?"

"I don't know yet. Very soon, I think."

The restaurant was deserted. Through the door to the kitchen, they could hear the sound of pots and pans.

"I have to finish setting the tables for dinner," she said. Lowering her voice, she added, "No one must know you're in town. Did you hear what happened yesterday?"

"Yes, how many were killed?"

"Two or three women and a little boy, they say."

"Any wounded?"

"About fifteen."

"Where are the others?"

"Germaine!" came a loud voice from the kitchen. "You're behind! Get those tables set!"

"Yes, ma'am. I'll be right there. They're somewhere between Mangauzy and Lamothe-Landerron."

"Germaine!"

"Coming! He's just paying the check."

"Here, keep the change."

"Thank you, sir."

Father Adrien left the restaurant. At the suspension bridge, he passed a German patrol. He got on the bicycle and began cycling toward Marmande. His legs ached from the thirty miles he had covered during the night and he knew that he wouldn't last much longer. Zigzagging along the road, he made it as far as Mongauzy. His face crimson, a red veil descending over his eyes, he stopped in front of the church. His head was spinning and his chest was racked with pain. As he fell to the ground, the face of the man he had killed, ugly with fear, flashed before him.

When he regained consciousness, he was lying on the parish priest's bed.

"You gave me quite a fright, sir."

"How long have I been here?"

"Three days."

"I must go."

120

"Don't even think of it! The doctor said it was serious. He's coming back today. Sir! Please! Lie down. You mustn't get up."

"I have to."

"I don't know why you're in such a hurry to leave and I don't want to know, but you're safe here and the doctor and the teacher who helped me to carry you inside are people you can trust."

Father Adrien looked at the faded robes with their buttons missing. A good man. A country priest. What would he have done if he had known?

"I see our patient's on the mend! Please don't speak, I'd like to examine you first. When did he regain consciousness, Father?"

"About fifteen minutes ago."

The doctor examined him carefully. He was very old and should have retired long ago. His long thin fingers palpated Father Adrien's thin body. At last, he put his stethoscope carefully back in his bag and began wiping his glasses.

"Well, doctor?" said the parish priest, when he couldn't wait any longer.

"Not too good, I'm afraid. How old are you, sir?"

"Fifty-five."

"My dear fellow, you have the heart of a man my age and twice as worn out. You absolutely must get some rest. I'm going to prescribe a few things and we'll hope that the pharmacist has them in stock. I'd give them to you myself, but I gave away whatever I had long ago, and the events of the other day completed depleted my reserves."

"Do you mean the attack on the *maquis*?"

"Yes, terrible injuries, just terrible."

"Were there any women?"

"Among the wounded, no, but two poor women were killed."

"And the child?"

"I didn't see a child, dead or alive."

Father Adrien closed his eyes, placing his hands on his chest.

121

"Don't talk anymore, you'll tire yourself out."

"Just one more thing, doctor. Have you heard any talk in the region about a young woman and a little boy who are in hiding?"

"No, but I treated a young man with head injuries who kept saying: "Don't go, Léa, don't go.""

"She's the one I'm looking for. A very pretty girl–twenty years old."

"I didn't see any pretty girls. Why, is she a relative?"

"Yes, she's my niece."

"Well, I'll see what I can find out. People know me around here. If they've heard anything, they'll tell me. But on one condition: I want you to stay absolutely still."

"I promise."

"Good, if I hear anything, I'll tell Father."

"Thank you," murmured the priest, losing consciousness again.

"Poor man, he won't last long. Pray for him, Father, he must have suffered terribly to have aged like that."

"Do you have any idea where the young girl and the child might be?"

"No, but I'll go over to Jaguenaux's. That's where they took the wounded. I'll come by this evening. Good-bye, Father."

"Good-bye, doctor."

"Keep a close eye on your visitor."

The doctor was not able to return until the next day. His face showed his grief.

"Nobody knows what happened to them. The last time they were seen alive was when the Germans moved in on the farm. The child was either wounded or killed. Some say the Germans threw them into the house after setting fire to it. The place is under guard and no one can get near it."

Father Adrien listened, unable to speak.

"Why would they do that?" wondered the parish priest aloud. "They're soldiers, not animals."

"They're worse than animals, Father! They're the unholy creature in your scriptures!"

"Doctor, you look terrible! Why are you so upset?"

"I'm afraid I have more bad news. They massacred an entire village in the Limousin."

"That's impossible!"

But the tears flowing down the doctor's wizened cheeks told him it was true.

The old priest crossed himself and placed a hand on the doctor's shoulder.

"God will forgive them."

The doctor stiffened.

"*Forgive them*? God—if there is such a thing—cannot forgive that. I've seen a lot of misery and a lot of horror in my time. Men with their legs blown off, lying in the trenches. People mutilated and maimed in the Great War. My best friends blown to pieces at Verdun. I've seen war and I've seen death. It's revolting but I accept it as man's fate. But women and *children*! That I cannot accept!"

"Calm yourself."

"No, I will not calm myself, sir! Do you know what they did last Saturday in Oradour-sur-Glane? Well, do you? People were lining up for their tobacco rations. School children were lining up to see the doctor. Refugees had arrived the day before, maybe two hundred of them. The soldiers arrived in trucks, right after the noonday meal. They kept their rifles aimed up at the windows. The Major, Otto Dickmann, called for the mayor and the policeman. With two SS, the policeman went around the village banging on a drum, calling "Atten - shun, atten - shun!", the way rural policemen all over France do. He ordered everyone, men, women and children, to go to the fairgrounds immediately for an identity check. Those who were too sick or weak to walk were pulled from their beds by the SS and dragged to the fairgrounds, as were people working in the fields, families from neighboring villages, fishermen, and little children. Soon, the entire town was gathered on the fairgrounds. Shots were fired at the other end of town and panic spread through the crowd. Soldiers with machine guns formed a circle around them. Women and children started crying and clinging to each other, clinging to their baby carriages. The women and the school children were marched to the church by ten SS. The priest had never seen so many people! The men were made to stand in three rows and were not allowed to speak. You could hear the bell of the streetcar in Limoges passing over the bridge. Then another shot rang out. In flawless French, one of the soldiers shouted that terrorists had hidden a stockpile of weapons and ammunition somewhere in the village and they had better tell him where it is or else. An old man told the soldier that he had an old hunting rifle, but the soldier wasn't interested. Then the men were divided into four groups of about forty or fifty men each and led to seven barns on the outskirts of the village. The soldiers kept their submachine guns and machine guns pointed at the men, and laughed and talked among themselves. Then, with a loud cry, they opened fire. The men started falling, one on top of the other. Bullets ricocheted off the walls. There were screams. The firing stopped, and the soldiers, using handguns now, moved among the bodies, finishing off the ones that were still moving. They brought in straw, hay, and kindling, a wheelbarrow and a ladder. They lit handfuls of hay, tossed it on to the dying men, and closed the doors. The same scene was re-enacted in all seven barns. In the church, four or maybe five hundred women and children watched as a group of soldiers dragged a heavy case into the church. The soldiers lit the wicks that protruded from the case and hurried out of the church. When it exploded, heavy black smoke filled the nave. Panic-stricken and gasping for air, the women and children ran every which way. Submachine guns fired on to the crowd through the open portal. Grenades exploded. The smell of dust and incense was gone, gone forever! Now there was the smell of blood and excrement and burning flesh. Young men, no more than twenty years old, began throwing kindling and straw on to the swarm. A flame-thrower spit forth flames. A woman crawled toward her daughter, who was already dead. Two little children, huddling in the confessional, were gunned down. Mothers and their children, clinging to one another, burned alive. Can you hear their screams, Father? Can you? Can you see the walls of the holy place splattered with their blood? The traces of their fingers, clawing at the stones? The featureless faces? The dismembered bodies? A baby screaming in its stroller before being engulfed in flames? CAN YOU SEE THEM?"

The parish priest could see them so well that he had fallen to his knees in prayer. The old doctor closed his eyes against the horror of it. Without a word, he walked out the door and into the night, carrying the sorrow of the world upon his shoulders.

Father Adrien, his mouth filling with a nauseating taste, stood up. Very gently, he lifted the old priest on to the bed, dressed, and checked to make sure that his gun was in working order. As he was about to leave, he turned to look at the old man.

He walked through the vines and fields without making any attempt to hide from view. The people he passed along the way stopped to greet him, but he did not respond. They turned, perplexed, thinking what strange people one met along the road these days. He stopped at a farm and asked for a glass of water, thanking the farmer and his wife, who watched him leave uneasily.

"You'd think he'd seen the devil himself," said the woman, crossing herself.

It was some time after his gaunt, dark figure disappeared before she went back inside.

At dusk, he stopped in a little wood, damp and overgrown with moss. He rested against a tree, stroking its bark lovingly as he had done as a child in Les Landes. The pine left bitter resin on his fingers, and its lingering odor brought memories flooding back. One by one, he blocked these sweet images out, until his mind was completely blank. Not a thought. Turning his face to the empty sky, he took out his gun.

Chapter Ten

The disappearance of Adrien Delmas was an additional worry for Aristide. No one had seen him since the meeting at which he announced that he had executed Maurice Fiaux. They feared that a trap had been laid for him by the Militia or the Gestapo; their spies were not able to uncover any clues as to his whereabouts. Although they were urged to do so, neither Aristide nor Dédé le Basque would move the dates set for meetings and Resistance operations; both were convinced that even if he were tortured, Father Adrien would not talk. Lancelot thought that this was folly.

Ever since the "pact" between Dohse and Grand-Clément which had resulted in heavy casualties for the Resistance in southwest France, most of the Resistance leaders lived in fear of being betrayed. Some saw traitors behind every tree. In the case of Renaudin, a representative of the National Liberation Movement who was responsible for regrouping the Resistance forces and who was said to control a network of three thousand men, their fears were surely founded. He had been seen far too often in the company of Grand-Clément or some of his men.

One day, as he got off the streetcar on his way to a meeting in Parc Bordelais with Lancelot, Dédé le Basque came face-to-face with Renaudin and André Noël, who was already on the Resistance hit list. Noël greeted them with a big smile:

"Well, hello, inspector! They tell me that you've been very busy since you left the police force."

"I'll show you how busy I've been!" replied Dédé le Basque, putting his hand in his pocket.

"Take it easy! Everything's changed since the Landing. I've got some important news for you. Meet me tomorrow at the Place de la Victoire at eleven o'clock. There's something I want to talk over with you."

The next day, Dédé le Basque went to the rendezvous accompanied by Marc, a partisan from Toulouse, and four armed men. No one showed up. For a moment, they thought they saw Renaudin at the corner of the Rue Elie-Gintrac. They waited for a while, then decided to go. Just then, six SS came out from under the half-open metal roll-up door of a clothing store and grabbed the four *maquisards* walking ahead of Dédé le Basque and Marc before they could reach for their guns. Dédé le Basque and Marc managed to escape as the Germans pulled the *maquisards* into the store. Three of the SS went off in search of Dédé le Basque and Marc, passing right in front of the doorway in which Dédé le Basque was hiding. As soon as they turned the corner, he ran back to the store and began firing. The *maquisards* threw themselves on the SS and took their weapons. They could not take the soldiers prisoner, so Dédé le Basque ordered them to scatter. The few passersby who had not taken refuge in neighboring buildings or dropped out of sight as the first shots were fired watched the scene impassively.

When they returned to Aristide's headquarters, Dédé le Basque and Marc reported what had happened. Aristide was now sure that Renaudin was a traitor. Had he needed it, the arrest of Pierre Roland was further proof. Roland's job was to sabotage the electrical system installed by the Germans to detonate mines that would destroy the port and part of the city; however, he was only able to sabotage a small part of the system. He suggested that Aristide radio Colonel Buckmaster to bomb the sector where the cables were laid. The day after the message was relayed, fifteen bombardiers of the United States Fifteenth Air Force neutralized the entire sector. Two days later, Roland was arrested and taken to 197 Route du Médoc in Le Bouscat. He died without talking.

Angry and grief-stricken, Aristide realized the danger they now faced. He appointed four men to trail Renaudin. Three days later, on June 29, Renaudin was gunned down at the corner of the Rue du Héron and the Rue Mouneyra. Taking the Resistance fighters for robbers, a policeman gave chase, wounding two of them, Mouchet and Langlade. From where he lay, Mouchet shot and killed the policeman, enabling Jules and Fabas to get away before the German soldiers and the French police arrived. The two men were tortured by the Gestapo. Mouchet was executed and Langlade died during interrogation.

On August 11, it was André Noël's turn; he walked into a trap laid for him by Triangle. Doubtless avenging their comrades who had died or been deported, the *maquisards* did not kill Noël outright. When at last they decided to finish him off, he had been beaten beyond recognition. His body was thrown into the Garonne.

Grand-Clément was nowhere to be found.

In Deymier, Léa was still grieving for Camille. She would wake up at night in tears, calling her name. Madame Larivierre, who was hiding Léa and Charles, would put her back to bed and comfort her. She would drift back to sleep, only to be visited by the same nightmare that had haunted her after the flight from Paris. Now, the ghoulish cast included horrible images of Camille, Charles, and La Sifflette.

Through Madame Larivierre, Léa learned that the *maquisards* had scattered and that some had regrouped at Blasimon and Mauriac. The good woman could not or would not say more, except that Camille and La Sifflette had been buried temporarily at La Réole. She agreed to have a letter sent to Ruth, asking her to provide the carrier with some money and clothing. The young boy returned sheepishly, with Ruth in hot pursuit. she had locked him up until he would tell her where the letter came from. Madame Larivierre flew into a rage, certain that the Germans would come to arrest them, and made them leave within the hour. Ruth paid through the nose for an old bicycle for Léa and put Charles on the back of her bicycle.

"I would have come by train," she explained to Léa, "but the lines are still cut because of the bombs."

Léa thanked Madame Rivierre, who watched them disappear with a sigh of immense relief.

Léa was so weak, and the narrow lanes so steep and winding, that it wasn't until late the next day that they arrived at Montillac. Ruth managed to spirit Léa and Charles into the house unseen by Fayard. Léa spent the next two days in bed with a high fever. Charles, forbidden to go outdoors, wandered from room to room, forlornly calling for his mother.

As soon as she was strong enough to talk, Léa told Ruth about the raid on the Roux's farm and about Camille.

"What happened to your uncle and the Lefèvre boys?"

"I don't know. Uncle Adrien didn't come back after Francois's visit. I thought that you might know where he was.
. . ."

"I haven't heard a word. Your aunt Bernadette received a postcard from Lucien, but that's all. Your uncle Luc is very worried about Pierrot; apparently he's in Paris. After you left, there was a letter from Laure. I took the liberty of reading it."

"What did it say?"

"Nothing important. there's hardly any food in Paris; the subway has stopped running because there's no electricity; the suburbs are being bombed almost daily; and the Germans are getting more and more nervous. Your great aunts are well."

"Didn't she say anything else?"

"Only that she is waiting for you to come to Paris."

"What about Sabine?"

"She didn't mention Sabine, but I received a letter from her. She hasn't heard from Otto in over three months. He's still fighting in Russia."

"He won't come back."

"Why do you say that?"

"We're all going to die, just like Camille," Léa replied, turning toward the wall and pulling the sheet over her head.

Ruth gazed down at Léa, her heart aching. She felt so old, so powerless. Shattered by Camille's death, she didn't know what to do about Léa. She couldn't stay at Montillac because Fayard might see her and denounce her at any moment. Ruth didn't know of any hiding places in the region, since all of the safe houses were being watched.

Seeing that Léa had not stirred, she decided to leave her alone in the nursery.

On the evening of July 15, Ruth and Léa closed all of the windows and shutters in spite of the oppressive heat and listened to the BBC as Jean Oberlé announced the execution of Georges Mandel by the Militia.

"After Philippe Henriot, he's the second deputy from the Gironde to be assassinated in the space of a few days," said Ruth, who was making a shirt for Charles out of an old dress.

"Aunt Lisa must be very sad. She loved Henriot's voice."

There was a scratching noise on the shutters.

"Did you hear that?" said Léa.

"Yes, turn off the radio."

Léa listened, her heart pounding. The scratching started again.

"Hide," said Ruth. "I'm going to open the window."

"Who's there?" she whispered.

"It's Jean Lefèvre," came a hushed voice. "We're wounded."

"Quick, open the door, Léa."

The sun had just disappeared behind the hills of Verdelais. For a few lingering moments, it bathed the countryside in the rosy glow that ushered in summer nights. And, for a moment, it obscured the faces of the two young men, covered in dust and blood, spreading out around them like a halo. Forgetting her fatigue, Léa went out by the window and, with Ruth's help, brought them inside. Raoul slid to the floor, unconscious.

"He's lost a lot of blood, we have to call a doctor," said Jean, as he collapsed.

Strong as she was, Ruth began sobbing.

"This is no time for tears. Go and get a doctor."

Ruth wiped her face with her hands.

"But will he come? They're afraid of the Gestapo."

"You don't have to tell him they're wounded. Just say . . . say that someone has injured himself with a scythe or an axe!"

"What happens when he sees them?"

"He's a doctor. One thing is certain: if we don't do something, they're going to die."

"You're right. I'll call him now."

"Is the telephone working?"

"Yes."

"All right, then, what are you waiting for? I'll get some towels."

Léa bumped into Aunt Bernadette coming into the dark living room.

"What is going on? I thought I heard a noise."

"Now that you're awake, you can help. It's Jean and Raoul Lefèvre—they're wounded."

"Oh, my lord. Poor things!"

"Go and get some towels and the first aid kit. And don't wake up Charles whatever you do."

In the study, Jean had regained consciousness.

"Yes, doctor. Montillac," Ruth was saying. "At the top of the hill on the left. Please hurry!" She replaced the receiver. "He's on his way. It's the new doctor over in Langon."

"Thank you, Ruth," said Jean. "How is Raoul?"

Neither Ruth nor Léa replied. Ruth slid a cushion under his head.

Bernadette entered the study, nearly fainting when she saw the extent of their injuries and bursting into tears.

"Stop it!" cried Léa, grabbing the towels from her aunt. "Bring me some boiling water."

By the time Doctor Jouvenel arrived, they had washed the men's hands and faces. The doctor was very young, fresh out of medical school and blanched when he saw the young men.

"Why did you say that it was an accident?"

"We weren't sure whether you would come if we told you the truth," said Léa.

"I am a doctor, Mademoiselle, I have to care for everyone, Resistance fighters and Germans."

"Well, these are Resistance fighters," said Léa softly.

Without wasting any more time, the doctor began to examine Raoul, who was still unconscious.

"Give me a pair of scissors."

He cut away Raoul's trousers which were stiff with blood. They gasped. His abdomen was a single gaping wound.

"He's a mess, I can't do anything for him here. We'll have to get him to a hospital. He's lost too much blood."

"That's impossible, doctor," said Jean who had dragged himself over to his brother. If the Gestapo get their hands on him, they'll torture him."

"I won't allow that."

"If you step in, they'll arrest you."

The doctor shrugged his shoulders.

"Jean ..."

"It's okay, Raoul, don't worry. We're safe. We're going to take you to the hospital."

"I heard ... don't bother ... it's too late. ..."

"You're crazy! You're going to be fine."

"Léa ... is that you?"

"Yes, Raoul."

"I'm glad you're here. ..."

"Don't talk," said the doctor, placing a makeshift dressing over the wound.

"Doctor, don't bother ... you know it won't ... Léa, are you still there?"

"Yes."

"Give me your hand ... it's all right, doctor ... look after my brother."

"There's nothing more I can do, I'm going to call an ambulance."

"Wait ... look after my brother."

"Do as he says," said Ruth.

Jean had a bullet lodged in his shoulder, another in his thigh, and his hand was badly wounded.

"I'm going to have to take you to the hospital, too. I don't have anything for extracting bullets."

"Never mind, just put some bandages on them."

"You could contract gangrene."

"Raoul," Léa pleaded softly.

"It's all right, Léa ... I'm happy ... you're by my side ..."

"Don't talk like that!"

"Jean, are you there?"

"Yes."

"Good ... I love you, Léa ... you too, Jean ... it's better this way ... after the war, you can get married. ..."

"After the war, she's going to marry you, dummy! She has always liked you better, haven't you, Léa?"

"Really?"

"Yes," she murmured, unable to lift her eyes from the haggard face and the feverish eyes of the young man who had been her lover for one wonderful night.

"Léa ..."

His head was suddenly so heavy. Sidonie's death flashed before her eyes. How handsome he was in spite of the stubble that darkened his features. He was smiling. Gently, she pressed her lips to his.

As she stood up, her head began to spin, and she leaned on the doctor's arm for support.

"Lie down."

Jean cradled his brother in his arms, sobbing. Aunt Bernadette and Ruth were also crying. Léa's grief was so great that tears would not come.

With Ruth's and Léa's help, the doctor dug a grave in the loose earth beside the wine cellar, behind a clump of shrubs and lilacs. Wrapped in a sheet, Raoul's body was laid in the grave and covered with earth. The clock in the basilica at Verdelais struck three.

Jean did not flinch when the doctor gave him an injection against tetanus. After being given a tranquilizer, he fell into a deep sleep.

Léa accompanied Doctor Jouvenel to the spot where he had left his bicycle. There was no need to hide anymore; the Fayard's must have seen him arrive.

"You must leave here immediately," he said.

"Where will I go?"

"Do you have relatives outside the region?"

"In Paris."

"It's not easy to get to Paris right now. There aren't many trains, but if I were you, I'd give it a try."

"I can't leave them here alone!"

"I'll see what I can do. If there's any way I can help, I will. I should be able to arrange a lift to Bordeaux."

"Thank you, doctor. I'll see. What about Jean? Will he be all right?"

"I think so. But he'll have to have those bullets removed soon. Good-bye, Mademoiselle."

"Good-bye, doctor."

Jean slept in Pierre Delmas's study until noon. He gulped down the bowl of ersatz coffee that Ruth brought him and ate a huge slice of *clafoutis*.

"You're awake," said Léa, entering the study. "Does it hurt?"

"No, I'm going to leave."

"Where will you go?"

"I don't know, I'll try to find the others—if they haven't all been taken prisoner or killed."

"What happened?"

"Have you got a cigarette?"

Out of the pocket of her flowered rayon dress, Léa took an old tobacco pouch and a package of papers which she handed to Jean.

"This is all I've got."

His hands trembled so badly that he was unable to keep the tobacco on the paper.

"Here, let me do it."

Léa deftly rolled the tobacco into the paper, licked and

sealed the gummed edge, and lit one end. Jean smoked in silence.

"It all started last Monday, on July 10," he began at last. "Raoul and I were with Grand-Pierre's group. We heard a message on the BBC. I can still hear the announcer's voice: *Wear white at night. I repeat: Wear white at night.* Maurice Blanchet turned to Maxime Lafourcade and said, 'It's tonight for sure. Make sure everyone knows.'

"I asked Maxime what it meant. 'They're going to parachute in supplies over at the Bry farm in Saint-Léger-de-Vignague and it's a good thing too. Ever since the fighting at Saint-Martin-du-Puy, we've been short of ammunition.' That night, at ten o'clock, there were twenty men posted around the field, with another five watching the road, and two in a van hidden in the woods. The rest of us just stood and waited for the flying fortress. Finally, after about half an hour, we heard the plane overhead and lit our flashlights. On the signal, four of us ran over to the first container; it had Stens and bandages. The second one had tobacco, equipment for sabotage operations, and grenades. We were just about to open the third container when we hear the whistle.

" 'Here they come!' cried the lookout.

"Maxime shouted to us to hurry up. We managed to load the contents of the fourth container into the van. Maxime gave the order to clear out just as the Germans started firing. All but four of us joined up with the Duras *maquis*, and the next day we heard what happened to the others. ...."

Jean puffed nervously, but his cigarette had gone out. Léa lit another one for him, and he went on:

"Maxime stayed behind with Roger Manieu, Jean Clavé, and Elie Juzanx to cover for us. They set up a machine gun between two of the containers and dipped into the supplies that had been flown in, spraying the field with fire. The Germans fired back but didn't show their faces. Four militiamen guided them to within one hundred and thirty feet of our men, in spite of the fire. All four partisans were wounded and tried to get away, but it was too late, so they used up their ammunition. The Germans bashed the partisans over the head with their rifle butts, then laughed as the Militia tortured them, tearing out their nails, stripping their muscles bare, scalping them.

"They had to dig their own graves!" said Jean, sobbing.

"Then what happened?" asked Léa, dry-eyed.

"They burned down Bry's farm and left for Mauriac, singing. We were hiding with the Duras *maquis*, about one hundred and sixty feet down the road to Blasimon. As they passed, we started firing and throwing grenades. The Germans and the Militia hit the ground and fired back. That's when Raoul was hit in the shoulder. I was hit in the leg. Two of our friends, Jean Koliosky and Guy Lozanos, died right before our eyes. We pulled back, knocking off a couple of their men with our machine guns. When we got to the cemetery at Mauriac, we were hit again. Abbé Gréciet took us in and cleaned us up. Because of Raoul's condition, he called Doctor Lecarer in La Réole, who is a member of our network. Unfortunately, there were roadblocks, so he had to leave us in Pian. From there, we walked to Montillac."

They fell silent, hands clasped tight. Suddenly Ruth entered.

"I'm worried. There's no one over at the Fayard's, their house is closed up. Hurry, you must leave."

"Where will we go?"

"To your aunts' in Paris."

"I can't," protested Jean. "I must see my mother in Verdelais."

"I'll tell her about Raoul, Jean."

"Thank you, Ruth, but I have to tell her myself."

"I understand ... Then what will you do?"

"I'll keep fighting. I'm sorry, Léa, but you'll have to go on your own."

"Take my bicycle, Jean. It will be faster."

"Thanks. If I can, I'll bring it back. Goodbye, Léa. You should go now, too."

Without answering, she kissed him. Aunt Bernadette and Ruth kissed him goodbye and told him to look after himself.

Chapter Eleven

Léa put a few articles of clothing for herself and Charles and a little box containing what was left of her mother's jewelry into a duffel bag which she could sling over her shoulder. Ruth added some sandwiches, wrapped in a tea towel, and a thermos of water.

"I've given Charles a bag with some cherries and the rest of the *clafoutis*," she said to Léa.

"Please come with us, Ruth."

"No, dear. Someone has to stay to look after your aunt and the house."

"I'm worried about leaving you here alone."

"What could possibly happen to two old women? There's no need for you to worry, Léa, we'll be fine."

"Still no sign of the Fayard's?"

"No."

"When is Doctor Jouvenel supposed to be here?"

"At three. The train is scheduled to leave at four—if they can clear the tracks."

"Do you think we'll be able to get tickets for Paris in Bordeaux?"

"Doctor Jouvenel said he'd contact a friend who works at the station."

"Léa, when are we going?" asked Charles, running into the nursery.

"Soon, sweetheart. We're just waiting for the doctor."

"Is he going to take us to see Maman?"

"I don't know . . . maybe. Run outside, I'll be along in a minute."

Léa pulled the duffel bag shut and looked around her. I'll never see this room again, she thought.

With a heavy heart, she closed the door of the room which for years had provided a haven from her worries and fears.

There was not a cloud in the sky. The midday sun beat down relentlessly. Here and there, the fields showed signs of scorching. Why would Fayard leave Montillac when there was so much work to be done?

"I'm going to take our things out to the road workers' hut by the road," said Léa. "That way, the doctor won't have to come up to the house."

"Whatever you like," replied Ruth. "Here's a bit of money for the trip, it's all I have."

"Thanks, Ruth, but what about you?"

"We don't need money. We can get enough to eat from the garden and the hens are laying. Besides, your aunt will be receiving her pension cheque next month. Hurry, lunch is almost ready. And put a hat on, the sun's bad for you."

Not wanting to contradict her, Léa went back inside for her straw hat. The cool, dark vestibule was a welcome change from the white heat outside. She liked this room where the inhabitants of the house came and went, leaving a hat or a toy here, a newspaper or some mending there. I'll have to have it repainted when the war is over, thought Léa, looking at the white walls on which hung ancient engravings of various monuments in Bordeaux and white and yellow *Directoire* plates, depicting scenes from mythology. She caught a glimpse of herself in the tall mirror, badly in need of resilvering. She was so thin! Francois wouldn't be too pleased; he liked his women on the cuddly side. What struck Léa, though, was the hard, flat expression that stared back out at her. She saw the glassy, lifeless eyes of Raoul and Camille, Sidonie, Doctor Blanchard and his housekeeper Marie, her mother and father, Monsieur and Madame Debray, Raphaël Mahl. So many dead. How many

138

more had died? Albert and Mireille? Uncle Adrien? Laurent? Lucien? Her dear, sweet cousin, Pierrot?

"Léa, why do you have your hat on?"

Charles's voice brought her back to the present.

"I'm going to take this bag outside and go for a little walk. Do you want to come with me?"

"Yes! Yes!" he cried, giving her a big hug.

They put the bag in the hut and went down the slope toward the fields, hand in hand. Despite the shortage of labor, the vines were well maintained.

"My sandal's come undone!"

Léa knelt down and did it up.

"Don't move!" she whispered suddenly, pulling the little boy to the ground.

On the path bordered by cypress trees, seven or eight men in navy blue uniforms crept along, submachine guns poised. When they arrived below the terrace, they stopped. Above them, a man was bending down. Léa stifled a scream. Behind the man, German soldiers were moving silently. Léa could only see their helmets. A German officer signalled to the militiamen to climb up the incline to the terrace.

"Let go!" said Charles, trying to squirm free. "You're hurting me!"

"Be quiet. The Germans are at Montillac."

His little body began to tremble.

"I'm scared. I want to see Maman."

"Be quiet, otherwise they'll come and get us."

Charles cried soundlessly, not noticing that he had wet his pants.

The sun beat down on the fields. There was not a sound. Léa wondered for an instant if she had not imagined the whole thing. She strained to hear, but there was only the drone of the cicadas. She prayed that Ruth and Aunt Bernadette had seen the soldiers coming and escaped. That hope was dashed by a blood-curdling scream. Without thinking, Léa straightened up and began running toward the terrace, dragging Charles and

139

cursing her brightly flowered dress. They hid behind a cypress tree. The Germans and the militiamen were milling about in the courtyard. Some began breaking down the doors of the wine cellars with their boots and rifle butts. Soon, all of the windows had been shot out. Furniture was thrown from the second floor. Why would they do that, wondered Léa. She was too far away to clearly hear or see what was happening; the square stone columns of the courtyard partially obscured her view. A van pulled up, scraping against one of the columns. The pillaging continued. The shouting and laughter and shots that were fired seemed unreal in the familiar, sunlit setting. Two militiamen began chasing the hens through the vegetable garden. Suddenly, a silhouette in flames ran screaming from the house, stopped, and collapsed on the gravel of the lane.

Léa clung to Charles, who had stopped squirming. Wide-eyed, she watched as the body of one of the women she had spoken to only moments before twisted and curled. Was it Ruth or Bernadette? The flames had worked so quickly that it was impossible to tell. The face was completely gone, melted. The black hole where the mouth had once been was now silent. All that was left was a burning black mass. One of the soldiers poked at it with the end of a long pipe connected to two tanks strapped to his back. Doubtless he was not satisfied that she was completely burned, for another long flame leapt from the pipe, accompanied by a sinister hissing sound. A blackened hand twisted in the heat, fingers reaching skyward as though seeking divine protection. This amused the soldier, who turned and entered the courtyard. The van was now loaded high with crates of wine. Léa was unable to lift her gaze from the smoldering body, its ghastly odor reaching her nostrils. In the middle of this nightmare, the clock in Saint-Maixant struck two, and a train crossed the viaduct. The tracks at Saint-Pierre-d'Aurillac had been cleared.

"Léa, you're squishing me ... I want to go now.... I'm scared."

Charles! She had been clinging to him so tightly that she

had almost forgotten he was there. Slowly, she turned away. When he saw her face, he began to cry.

"Be quiet!" she urged, clapping a hand over his mouth and shaking him. "They're going to find us."

There was such urgency in her voice that he stopped instantly but tears continued to roll down his face, wetting his cheeks and shirt. Glancing toward the house, Léa could see wine flowing down the men's chins. A militiaman careened out the courtyard, holding a bottle in one hand. He unbuttoned his pants and urinated on the smoking corpse, choking with laughter. Turning, he raised the bottle in a toast to the deceased. Léa began vomiting.

"Come on, let's get out of here" said Charles, tugging at her dress.

He was right, they had to act quickly. As Léa stood up, flames began leaping from the window of her parents' bedroom, then from Ruth's bedroom. She straightened up, but remained rooted to the ground, in full view of the house. Montillac, the centre of her universe, the centre of her father's universe, was engulfed in flames.

"Don't look, Léa. Come on!"

He pulled her with all his might. Somehow they managed to get to the road without being seen. Charles took their bags out of the hut and handed them to Léa, who took them dumbly. The flames were now so high that they could be seen clear across the sun-drenched hills. The siren in Saint-Macaire wailed. Léa turned away. Something inside her had just died. There was no point staying now. She adjusted the bag on her shoulder, threw her straw hat on the ground, grasped Charles's hand firmly, and walked down the road.

The Fayard's returned late the next day.

The firemen had been able to save the Fayard's house, the barns, the wine cellars, and the outbuildings, but all that remained of the house were charred walls. When the vintner and his wife arrived, the men were still sifting through the ashes. They stopped when they saw the couple, mouths gaping at the devastation. A middle-aged man, his hands and face covered in soot, walked over to them, contemplated them calmly for a moment, then spat.

"What did you do that for, Baudoin!" exclaimed Fayard, "What's wrong with you!"

"You know bloody well what's wrong, you son-of-a-bitch!" the man said, gesturing toward the house.

Fayard looked at him, not seeming to understand. Baudoin leapt at him, grabbing him by the lapels.

"Don't pretend you don't know, you goddamn bastard! Don't try to tell me you didn't lead them here! You mixed with them! You sold the Delmas's wine behind their backs, you piece of shit! Don't tell me it wasn't you!"

"I never wanted them to burn down the house!"

"That I can believe! You've had your eye on it for a long time. Well, it's going to cost you a small fortune to rebuild, Fayard."

"So, Mélanie," said another man, coming over to Madame Fayard. "You must be wondering what happened to the ladies up at the house. No need to be scared, we don't have flame throwers, just our fists!"

"Easy, Florent. Let's not get our hands dirty."

Under her black straw hat, Madame Fayard's eyes were rolling in every direction.

"I don't know what you talking about, I'm sure. We were visiting my sister over in Bazas."

"Tell your lies to someone else, you two-faced hypocrite. You left because you went to the Gestapo about Mademoiselle Léa and Madame d'Argilat . . ."

"That's not true!"

". . .and you didn't want to have to watch. Might have been a little upsetting to watch Monsieur Delmas's sister burn like a piece of toast. And Mademoiselle Ruth pissing blood. And Mademoiselle Léa and the kid. Maybe they're in there too! Better that way than to be taken away by the Germans or the scum that mixes with them."

"We didn't know Mademoiselle Léa and Charles were back."

"In that case, you're the only ones who didn't. We knew they came back after Madame d'Argilat was killed in Lorette and we're over in Saint-Macaire. You live right on the property! If there's any justice in the world, you should be burned too."

"Take it easy," said one of the other men. "The war's almost over and when it is, people like them will have to pay. They'll be tried and sentenced by a people's tribunal."

"They don't deserve to be tried."

"We swear it wasn't us! I have had my eye on the estate for years, it's true, and I have been selling wine to the Germans, but who hasn't? How else could I afford to look after the vines, eh? How else could I pay for the labor and the materials, tell me that!"

"Don't be a smart ass, Fayard. We know how much you've socked away."

"That's just rumors, that is. Jealous rumors."

"What about your son, Mathias. Don't tell me he doesn't have his eye on the girl *and* the property. And collaborating with the Germans in Bordeaux?"

"That's not my son you're talking about."

"Don't worry, we'll get him too," said the man, about to strike Fayard. "In the meantime . . ."

"Stop!"

Two *gendarmes* got off their bicycles.

"Fayard," said one of them, addressing the vintner. "You'll have to come the *gendarmerie* to swear a statement and identify the body."

"Which body?"

"We think it's Madame Bouchardeau."

"Dear Lord!" cried Madame Fayard, hiding her face in her handkerchief.

"I would like you both to come first thing tomorrow morning."

The *gendarme* turned to address Baudoin.

"Have you found any other casualites?"

"No, we went through everything, but I don't think we're going to find another body."

143

"Well, that's a relief. We were told that there was a young woman and a child in the house. What happened to them?"

Baudoin shrugged his shoulders impatiently.

"All right, that's fine."

"Did you notify the relatives in Bordeaux?"

"The mayor is looking after that. Monsieur Delmas will be arriving tomorrow."

"Maybe he's heard from his niece. What about the other uncle, the priest. Has he been notified?"

"Are you kidding? You know very well that the French police and Gestapo are looking all over for him. If you know where he is, turn him in. There's a bonus in it for you."

"Who do you take me for? I'm not one of them."

"Then you've got more scruples than most. There isn't a day goes by we don't get anonymous letters denouncing Jews, *masquisards*, people who hide English pilots or listen to the BBC. Pretty soon, they'll be turning in girls who fraternize and dance with the Germans at Saint-Macaire."

"Damn right," piped in a young man with a spotty complexion and a pronounced squint.

"Jealousy will get you nowhere, Romeo."

"Don't call me Romeo. Those girls are sluts. They don't just dance with the Germans, they screw them while their boy friends are off in prison or the *maquis* or the labor camps. Just wait 'til the war's over. We'll teach 'em for shacking up with the Krauts."

"I wouldn't like to be in their shoes when the likes of you gets your hands on them. All right, men, the party's over. Time to go home!"

Bernadette Bouchardeau was buried in the family vault on the morning of July 22. Léa's uncle Luc and her cousin Philippe attended. There were many other people, a number of whom had come simply to express their anger and outrage. A van from the *gendarmerie* was parked under the lime trees. Standing near the tomb of Toulouse-Lautrec, two plainclothes

144

policemen from Bordeaux made a mental note of every person who came to offer his condolences. The Fayard's stood off to one side, aware of the animosity that most of the people present felt toward them. Luc Delmas went over and shook hands in a show of cordiality that everyone felt was overdone. There were no incidents.

At the hospital in Langon, Ruth hovered between life and death.

Chapter Twelve

The rivalry which had divided the major factions of the Resistance in southwest France since early 1944 worked to the advantage of the Occupying Forces. The French Forces of the Interior (F.F.I.)[9] were under the command of General Koenig. General Delmas had replaced Bourgès-Maunoury. Triangle was also General Gaillard, military delegate for B Region. Aristide was acting commander of the Gironde for General Koenig. Gaston Cusin was Commissioner of the Republic. The Gaullists didn't trust the Communists and General Moraglia, who had been sent over by the Military Action Committee, the most important body within the National Resistance Council, had not been able to assert his authority. The complexity of these relationships was of little interest to the Germans. Then there were the anonymous letters, denunciations, and confessions extracted through torture and intimidation, not to mention collaboration, all of which made it possible for the Occupying Forces to carry out bloody reprisals against the population, rounding up the leaders of the Resistance and neutralizing the *maquis*.

It was a denunciation that led to the attack on the Richemont farm near Saucats by thirty German soldiers under

[9]With the blessing of the Allied leaders, General de Gaulle established a headquarters in London for the *Forces françaises de l'intérieur* (F.F.I.), which then became a component of the Allied armies under Eisenhower. To ensure close links between the Resistance and the Allied command, teams consisting of one French and one American or British officer plus a radio operator were parachuted into France in uniform shortly before D Day.—Tr.

Lieutenant Kunesch and thirty French militiamen under Lieutenant-Colonel Franc. Eighteen young Resistance fighters, college and high school students for the most part, had set up camp at the farm while awaiting another airlift of arms and ammunition. On the morning of July 14, fourteen of them were at the farm: Lucien Anère, Jean Bruneau, Guy Célèrier, Daniel Dieltin, Jacques Goltz, Christian Huault, Pogre Hurteau, François Mosse, Michel Picon, Jacques Rouin, Roger Sabate, and André Taillefer. They fought valiantly for three days with what few arms they had. All fourteen were killed. The oldest among them was twenty-two years of age, the youngest, seventeen.

And it was a denunciation that enabled the Germans to locate the *maquis* in Médoc under Jean Dufour on June 25. Aided by a special East Indian commando unit, the Germans and the militiamen attacked the camp in the woods at Vignes-Oudines at dawn. With a handful of men, Jean Dufour tried to hold them off, but he ran out of ammunition and was killed. The hunt for the *maquisards* lasted into the next day, wiping out the groups in Vignes-Oudines, Baleys, and Haut-Garnaut. One hundred Germans and seventeen partisans were killed. One of the wounded was put on display in the public square in Hourtin and died without receiving any help. As with the attack on Saucats, those taken prisoner were summarily executed, as were the wounded. The militiamen and the soldiers descended on the town of Liard and the Château de Nodris, killing several people. Many others were arrested and taken to Fort du Hâ, where they joined six partisans taken during the botched attempt to blow up the gunpowder factory in Sainte-Hélène on June 23. They were tortured, then either shot or deported.

Yet another denunciation resulted in the arrest of Lucien Nouaux, alias Marc, and his comrade, Jean Barraud. Once again, Dohse's threats and promises had lured a young partisan, denounced by two other partisans arrested by the German police in Pauillac, into setting a trap for Marc and Jean. Accompanied by a Gestapo agent named Roger, he arranged to meet Jean and Marc near the stadium. Marc watched them approach, but did not suspect anything. Then, suddenly, German soldiers appeared and seized them both. They were escorted to the Gestapo headquarters for interrogation. Before being taken to see Dohse, they were savagely beaten. As they entered his office, Marc pulled out a small gun that his captors had missed and fired, injuring two German soldiers before being shot by the Gestapo agent, Roger. Too badly wounded to be interrogated, he was thrown into a cell at Fort du Hâ where he was killed the following day, July 28, 1944.

It was a particularly somber day for the region of Bordeaux. The sky was heavy and overcast, with intermittent rain. At dawn, forty-eight men were taken in *Wehrmacht* trucks to the camp at Souges to be shot. Among them was a prize catch: Honoré (Robert Ducasse) who, under the name of Vergaville, had been the chief of the secret army and a driving force behind the unification of the Resistance in the region of Lyon.

Arrested in October 1943, he managed to escape in January 1944 and was sent by Kriegel-Valrimont to Bordeaux as regional chief of the F.F.I. Hiding with Protestant friends in Bordeaux, he contacted the regional committee for the liberation of France, where he met Gabriel Delaunay. On June 22, he left for Sauveterre-de-Guyenne, accompanied by his adjutants, two men and two women. They were to organize a sabotage operation and recover munitions hidden in the quarries at Daignac. Crossing the town of Créon, they cycled past the *gendarmerie*. Something about them aroused the suspicions of the *gendarmes*, who telephoned ahead to Targon. Shortly thereafter, they were arrested. Their identity papers did not appear to be in order, and the *gendarmerie* in Targon contacted the police in Bordeaux. One of the women was brutally tortured and revealed the reason for their presence in the region. They were taken to Fort du Hâ, then handed over to the Gestapo by Commissioner Penot. Lieutenant Kunesch carried out the interrogations.

And so it was that Honoré was shot on July 28, along with

his two adjutants, René Pezat and Jacques Froment, and forty-five others. One of the women escaped. The other was deported.

That same day, Grand-Clément, his wife, and one of their friends were executed.

Ever since the death of Noël and Renaudin, Grand-Clément had known that his days were numbered. He had asked Dohse for protection, and Dohse had offered him a villa in the resort town of Pyla, where he had been staying with his wife, Lucette, under an assumed name. It was here that Meirilhac, sent by Colonel Passy to investigate the death of Hypoténuse, came across Grand-Clément.

After informing Colonel Triangle of his mission, the B.C.R.A. agent contacted Jean Charlin, who still thought of Grand-Clément as the leader of the O.C.M. for the southwest. Charlin agreed to pass the message along to 'his' leader, and the two men met at the *Volant-doré* in the Rue du Hautoir, Bordeaux. There, Charlin told Grand-Clément that London wanted to hold a hearing to clear him of the accusations against him, and that a man by the name of Lysander would take him to England. Realizing that his back was against the wall, Grand-Clément agreed to meet with Meirilhac.

Lest Dohse's suspicions be aroused, it was agreed that they would stage a kidnapping at the home of his friend and bodyguard, Marc Duluguet. On July 24, Meirilhac and three members of a Resistance group under Georges, commander of the third company under Aristide, arrived at Duluguet's home. They overturned the furniture and fired shots in the air. Grand-Clément demanded that his wife and Duluguet accompany him. Madame Duluguet was instructed to wait for one hour before calling the German police.

They spent the night in Léognan and, the next morning, were handed over to Georges for questioning. At first, Grand-Clément refused to cooperate and demanded to be taken to London as agreed. Then, probably fearing immediate reprisals against his wife, Duluguet, and himself, he agreed to answer

Georges's questions. He acknowledged that he had handed over arms to the Germans, and that he was indirectly responsible for three thousand arrests and three hundred executions. A statement was drawn up and signed.

On July 28, the three prisoners were taken to the home of a partisan named Frank Cazenave, near Belin. A heavy guard was mounted around the house. At about one in the afternoon, Aristide, Dédé le Basque, and Lancelot arrived. When he saw the British agent, Grand-Clément knew that there was no hope. The members of the tribunal were seated around a table, and Grand-Clément responded to further questioning, adding that he had agreed to cooperate with Dohse to protect the lives of his wife and family. The prisoners were then led out of the room while the tribunal deliberated.

The decision to execute Grand-Clément was unanimous. After much debate, his wife and bodyguard were also sentenced to death.

Late that afternoon, the former Resistance member got into a car with Lancelot and two other men, while his wife and bodyguard took their places in another car with Aristide and two guards. At one point, they were stopped at a road block by the Militia. Lancelot got out of the car and gave the German salute. Thinking that they were Gestapo, the Militia waved the two cars through. Grand-Clément had not moved. The cars stopped in the wood near Muret, where Aristide told them that they had been sentenced to death.

It was all over very quickly. Dédé le Basque dragged Grand-Clément into a sheep pen and killed him. Lancelot executed Marc Duluguet, and Aristide did the job for which no one had volunteered.

The bodies were buried in the wood.

Aristide reported back to Colonel Buckmaster that justice had been done.

Chapter Thirteen

The paving stones along the banks of the Seine felt hard under the beach towel, but Léa closed her eyes and let her mind drift back to the sound of the waves on the beach at Biscarrosse, the gulls, and the happy cries of children. The warmth of the sun was mildly soporific; her body felt alive again. She stretched her limbs, vaguely guilty at such a sense of well-being after the horror of recent days. Something deep inside told her to block it out, to pretend that it had never happened, that it was only a bad dream from which she would awaken without any recollection.

She opened her eyes ever so slightly. A gull passed overhead in the clear blue sky. A child laughed and clapped its hands. Men in caps and straw hats sat motionless, watching the red, yellow, and white floats of their fishing lines bob up and down. The water lapped against the embankment. An amateur artist set up his easel. A boat with young women in pretty summer dresses floated past. Not far, an accordion played a popular tune. The scene was altogether peaceful. Léa rolled over on to her stomach and continued reading the book that her sister, Laure, had recommended so highly.

Now, they would all dance—except her and the old ladies. Now everyone would have a good time, except her. She saw Rhett Butler standing just below the doctor and, before she could change the expression of her face, he saw her and one corner of his mouth went down and one eyebrow went up. She jerked her chin up and turned away from him and suddenly she heard her own name called—called in an unmistakable Charleston voice that rang out above the hubbub of other names.

"Mrs. Charles Hamilton—one hundred and fifty dollars–in gold."

A sudden hush fell on the crowd both at the mention of the sum and at the name. Scarlett was so startled she could not even move. She remained sitting with her chin in her hands, her eyes wide with astonishment. Everybody turned to look at her. She saw the doctor lean down from the platform and whisper something to Rhett Butler. Probably telling him she was in mourning and it was impossible for her to appear on the floor. She saw Rhett's shoulders shrug lazily.

"Another one of our belles, perhaps?" questioned the doctor.

"No," said Rhett clearly, his eyes sweeping the crowd carelessly, "Mrs. Hamilton."

"I tell you it is impossible," said the doctor testily. "Mrs. Hamilton will not—"

Scarlett heard a voice which, at first, she did not recognize as her own.

"Yes, I will!"

Scarlett was absolutely impossible! But Rhett! What a man!

"How do you like it?" asked Léa's older sister, Sabine.

"Mmm . . ."

"Leave her alone, can't you see she's dancing with Rhett?" said Laure in a mock-serious tone. "Pass me *Silhouettes.*"

"Wait, I just want to look at the clothing for children. I wish I had a little girl to dress up."

"You say the most idiotic things now that you live in Paris and buy from the big fashion houses. What happened to the Sabine I knew at Montillac? You aren't anything like the prim and proper nurse from Langon whom I remember."

"That's not fair. What am I supposed to do? Lock myself in my apartment with the shades drawn until the war is over? Or move to Germany like some of the other women in my situation? Where would I go? To live with Otto's father? He'd shut

152

the door in my face. I don't even know whether he's still alive. And what about Otto? He may be dead or wounded ..."

"I'm sorry, I didn't mean to upset you. Look at Charles playing with Pierre. They're like brothers."

"Yes, they're so cute together. Here, take *Silhouettes*."

Sabine stood up, adjusting her bathing suit and going over to her son's stroller.

"Did you see the article by Lucien François, extolling the virtues of 'proper undergarments' for women? What a hoot! Listen to this:

"My critics will frown and shake their heads that anyone could be interested in such a frivolous topic as women's undergarments at a time like this. After listening to Mayol's "Froufrous", one would be tempted to agree with them; however, it seems less frivolous when we consider that since the introduction of the brassiere and panties—both of foreign origin—thousands of French women have lost their livelihood in the lace and lingerie industries both of which are, at bottom, French ...

"Can you believe it? *At bottom*, he says. He probably thinks the French lost the war because their wives started wearing English and American panties. Listen to the conclusion ...

"In order for a race to be survive, there must be truly feminine women and truly virile men. When the line between male and female becomes blurred—when androgynous females wearing panties begin consorting with young men in hot pink chemises—the race is headed for decline. But have no fear: in a real marriage, a wife wearing lace pantaloons will never wear the pants!

"Don't you find it incredible that they can talk about panties when there's no electricity, no gas, and no subway service from Saturday at one in the afternoon to Monday at the same time. Estelle has to line up at seven in the morning for a single can of peas, we've been eating salt herring for the last three days, and thousands of people are dying in the air raids. It's incredible, don't you think so, Léa?"

Léa, who had stopped reading to listen to her sister, shrugged her shoulders.

"No more incredible than tanning on the banks of the Seine or going to hear Edith Piaf at the Moulin Rouge when people are fighting in Normandy and Brittany and Russia and the Pacific. What's incredible is that the three of us are still alive. I'm starving. Sabine, can you pass me a sandwich?"

"You're going to start a riot if people see us eating real bread and cold cuts, right, Laure?"

"They can do like I do, but don't think for a moment that it's easy to find bread and cold cuts in Paris on August 5, 1944."

"I believe you," replied Léa, sinking her teeth into the sandwich that Sabine handed to her. "With your flair for business, you should have been the one to handle Monti—"

Léa went pale. She had vowed never to say that word again. Realizing what had happened, Laure put her arms around her sister's shoulders.

"You'll see, we'll rebuild Montillac."

"Never! You didn't see it burn. You didn't see Aunt Bernadette running out of the house in flames. She never hurt anyone. And Ruth . . ."

"You'll only upset yourself, Léa. There's no point in going back over it. Try to forget."

"That's easy for you to say. What do you know about war except wheeling and dealing on the black market."

"Stop it, you two. Everyone's looking at us. Come on, let's go," said Sabine, gathering up her things.

"You can go if you want to. I'm going to stay a little while longer. Take Charles with you."

"I want to stay with you, Léa."

"No, sweetheart, you be a good boy and go home with Auntie Sabine. I need to be by myself."

He looked at her inquiringly, then took her hand and squeezed it hard.

"Will you come home soon?"

"Yes, sweetheart, I promise."

"Be home by two thirty. The concert starts at three thirty and it'll take us at least half an hour to get to the Place Blanche by bicycle—it's all uphill."

"Don't worry, I'll be there."

154

Turning her thoughts from her sisters and the children, Léa lay down again and closed her eyes, but the images that flashed through her mind were so horrible that she quickly opened them again.

One of the sunbathers put down his newspaper and dove into the Seine, sending a shower of droplets on to the bank. Léa picked it up; it was Marcel Déat's *Oeuvre*. There was an article entitled "A Description of the Species *maquis*," a vitriolic attack on Communists, Gaullists, Socialists, and other "vermin." Léa read on. One hundred and ninety eight "American" bars had been closed at the request of the Militia which had expressed its outrage at the "immorality" of these establishments. At the *Grand Palais*, there was a new exhibition entitled the "Soul of the Camps." Doctor Goebbels had declared that "the German people must rise up as one to change the course of history." Using special matériel, the German navy had sunk thirteen Allied ships. A French brigade of the *Waffen* SS was now engaged in combat on the Eastern Front. There would be races at Vincennes today and at Auteuil tomorrow. Trading was brisk on the Paris stock market. The Fuehrer and Doctor Goebbels sent a telegram congratulating Knut Hamsun on his eighty-fifth birthday. The committee to select French volunteers for the *Waffen* SS would sit on Monday, August 7, at 9:00 a.m.; the committee for the *Légion des volontaires français contre le Bolchevisme* was to meet at the *Caserne de la Reine* in Versailles. A home for children was to be named after Philippe Henriot. Tomorrow, at 3:00 p.m., there would be a race from the Pont d'Austerlitz to the Pont Alexandre III. Elvire Popesco was at the Apollo in *Ma cousine de Varsovie*. Jane Sourza and Raymond Souplex were starring in *Sur le banc* at the Casino de Paris. At Luna Park, there was Georgius, Georgette Plana and much, much more . . .

Léa put down the newspaper and slipped her flowered rayon dress, a present from Sabine, over her two-piece red and white swim suit. Then she laced up her canvas sandals with their high, wooden heels, and ran up the stairs leading to the quays.

On August 11, they heard over the radio that Saint-Exupéry

had been shot down over the south of France during a night flight. The announcer deplored the fact that the writer had joined the enemy camp.

That same day, a letter from Laurent addressed to Camille care of the Misses de Montpleynet, appeared under the front door at the Rue de l'Université. Léa opened the letter, her hands trembling.

My dearest wife,

At last I am back on French soil! Words fail me to express our joy and emotion as we felt the beach in Normandy beneath our feet. The hardiest among us fell to his knees and kissed the ground, crying. Some filled their pockets with sand which the Allies had had the privilege of touching before us. We have waited for this day for so long. It seemed as though it would never come!

I spent the first night in a jeep. I was only asleep for four hours, but I have never felt so well-rested in my life. When I awoke, I said to myself, I'm on the same soil, I'm under the same blue sky, before long I'll be holding you and Charles in my arms. I was bursting with happiness.

We landed at Sainte-Mère-Église on a grey morning with Général Leclerc, who poked at the sand with an air of disbelief. I heard him murmur, "Strange, isn't it . . ." Then he looked up with a smile that crinkles his eyes and said, "This is wonderful, absolutely wonderful." We were jostled out of the way by military press photographers who wanted pictures of the American General Walker shaking hands with our General. Leclerc wasn't very gracious about the whole thing and refused to return to the jetty.

I accompanied him to the headquarters of the United States Third Army to which our Second Armored Division is attached. There we met General Patton. What a contrast! One is a whiskey-drinking, colt-toting cowboy. The other is an aristocrat with two stars on his cap (and a third that's been waiting for over a year to be sewn on), the belt of his trench coat pulled tight, puttees, and a satchel! Patton was in fine form. They had finally penetrated the German defences at Avranches, which we passed through on our way to Le Mans. It looked like the Apocalypse. Civilians wandering through the streets, rifling through the rubble, fields with hundreds of grim-faced prisoners, and everywhere, the bodies of Americans and Canadians and Englishmen and Germans all jumbled together. In the villages we passed through, little girls held out flowers and bread and bottles of wine and cider. We went from the joy of the liberated to the despair of those who had lost everything.

We went straight into battle on August 10. The fighting was hard and dirty. We lost twenty-three men, close to thirty wounded, and fourteen tanks destroyed or lost. The next day, at Champfleur, the General commanded the maneuvers from the turret of Le Tailly. Then, alternating between his jeep and his scout-car, he led us into battle, oblivious to the bullets and the shelling. By the end of the second day, he was satisfied. We had liberated thirty villages and advanced twenty-five miles. We fell asleep on the ground, completely exhausted, but at around 2:00 a.m., the Germans began shelling the field in which Leclerc's camp had been set up, destroying a light armored vehicle and killing two of Leclerc's footmen. We didn't sleep again that night. Between August 10 and August 12, the Second Armored Division killed eight hundred Germans, took more than a thousand prisoner, and destroyed fifteen Panzers. In the forest at Ecouves, enemy soldiers surrendered by the thousands.

On Friday, August 13, we attacked the village of Cercueil. The worst carnage of all came as we entered Ecouché. Our objective was to reach the national highway, *la Nationale 24 bis*. I was in the tank behind my friend, Georges Buis, who was leading the advance. Across fields bordered with tall hedges, we could see the road, with enemy vehicles as far as the eye could see. They appeared to be floating above the hedges. Then all hell broke out. Our tanks started firing and the air was thick with smoke and the sound of men screaming. One of our detachments took back roads around the incredible blockage of mutilated bodies and burning tanks to cross the highway and reach our target: the bridge over the Orne.

After tender messages for his wife and son, Laurent's letter stopped. Léa folded it carefully. Drieu la Rochelle's suicide attempt was just being announced on the radio. The telephone rang.

"Hello. Ruth! Is that you?"

"Yes, dear, it's me."

Léa, who had not shed a tear since the death of Camille, felt hot, salty tears flow down her cheeks at the sound of the soft but unmistakable voice of Ruth, whom she had believed dead.

"Oh, Ruth. It's you, Ruth," she repeated, over and over again.

Sabine and Laure both wanted to talk to her. Soon, not only Léa and her sisters were crying, but also their great aunts, Lisa and Albertine.

"This is the first piece of good news we've had in a long time," said Laure at last, drying her tears. "Let's celebrate!"

She ran to her "supply cupboard" to get a bottle of champagne.

"It won't be chilled, but never mind. Estelle, bring some glasses and come and drink a toast with us."

Even Charles was allowed to have "a smidgen," as Aunt Lisa called it.

"We didn't even ask Ruth about Montillac," said Laure, emptying her glass.

That's right, thought Léa. I was so happy to know that she was alive that I forgot about Montillac. It's better that way. As far as I am concerned, Montillac no longer exists. Who cares whether it can be salvaged? Too much blood has been shed. Fayard can have it.

"Just imagine, Madame Sabine, twenty francs for a pound of potatoes, and three hours waiting in line outside the Marché Saint-Germain for a measly four pounds! As for butter, there isn't any, and at a five hundred francs a pound, you'd have to be a millionaire to afford it," exclaimed Estelle.

"Don't worry," said Laure. "I'll have butter tomorrow. Some tobacco and soap came in, and I should be able to trade them for groceries."

The old housekeeper looked at Laure with bald admiration.

"I don't know how you do it, Mademoiselle Laure. If it

158

weren't for you, we'd have died of hunger ages ago. Thank goodness you don't listen to your Aunt Albertine."

"That's enough, Estelle, I should be firmer with Laure. I should refuse the things she buys on the ... on the ..."

"Go ahead, Aunt Albertine, say it. On the black market. It's true, I deal on the black market, I don't want to die of hunger while I wait for the Allies to liberate us. I'm not stealing; I'm just exchanging goods and taking a little commission. All my friends do it."

"That's no excuse, dear. There are so many hungry people who have to go without. I'm ashamed of our comfort."

Lisa, who had not spoken until then, gave a start. Her face flushed, she turned on her sister:

"Comfort! I do hope you aren't serious, Albertine. No tea, no coffee, no chocolate, no meat, no bread worth eating! And, this last winter, no heat! All because you don't want to eat or to be warm as long as there are people out there who are out of work or in prison or doing without. They're not going to be any better off just because we starve ourselves."

"I realize that, but we should show our solidarity," replied Albertine.

"Solidarity doesn't exist anymore," cried Lisa.

"How can you say that?" murmured Albertine, looking at her sister as a tear rolled down her wrinkled cheek, streaking her face powder.

Disarmed by Albertine's tears, Lisa begged her forgiveness. Arm in arm, they went to Albertine's bedroom.

"It always ends that way. If one of them cries, the other stops and comforts her," said Laure. "What are you doing this afternoon?"

"Who me?" asked Léa.

"Yes."

"I promised Charles I would take him to the Luxembourg Gardens for a ride on the carousel."

"What about you, Sabine?"

"I'm going home. A friend of Otto's is supposed to call to-night."

"You've got lots of time."

"Not really. Now that the subway isn't operating, I have to walk home. It takes me at least two hours. What about you?"

"I don't know. Ever since they closed the bars, we don't know what to do. I'm going to see if my friends are over at the Trocadéro."

"Shall we leave together?"

"No, you're walking. I prefer to take my bicycle."

"Okay, I'll call you this evening if I have any news of Otto."

Charles held Léa's hand firmly. Every once in a while, he would squeeze her fingers until she responded by squeezing back, as if to say, Don't worry, I'm right here. He found this reassuring; he was terrified that she, too, would disappear.

When they had run away from the big house in flames, not even looking back, he understood that there were certain things that he mustn't talk about to Léa. Maman was one of those things. He loved her as much as Maman had. Poor Maman! Why did she scream when he started running toward her that day when the Germans were shooting? He remembered something hurting, then his mother holding him tight, then her letting go . . .

Whenever he asked about her, he was told that she would come back soon, but he knew this wasn't true. She was far, far away, maybe even in heaven! He remembered her saying that people went to heaven when they died. Did that mean that Maman was dead?

Suddenly, he stopped in his tracks, his mouth parched, his body trembling and covered in sweat. They were standing in front of the building where Camille had lived on the Boulevard Raspail. Léa imagined Camille opening the door of her apartment and smiling sweetly out at her. Charles was still holding Léa's hand firmly. He looked up at her. Slowly, without letting go, she knelt down and gave him a big hug.

A German officer, followed by his orderly, stopped to look at them tenderly.

"I had a little boy the same age, but he wasn't as lucky as your son. His mother and sister were killed in an air raid," he said in correct, heavily-accented French, stroking Charles's hair.

Charles recoiled as though he had been slapped.

"Don't touch me, you filthy Kraut!"

Blanching, the German officer withdrew his hand. His orderly stepped forward.

"Are you insulting a German officer?"

"It's all right, Karl, it's only normal that they don't like us. Forgive me, Madame, I let my emotions get the better of me. For a moment, I forgot this dirty war that has done our two countries so much harm, but it will all be over soon. Good day."

He clicked his heels and marched toward the Hôtel Lutétia. The swatiska still flew above the entrance.

Chapter Fourteen

In the *Jardin du Luxembourg*, there was a huge crowd beneath the trees and around the pool with its little sailboats, rented from a stand nearby. People strolled back and forth in front of the Senate, ignoring the guards behind the sandbags and the barbed wire. Children lined up with their mothers to see the puppet show. The merry-go-round and the donkey and pony carts were filled. Although it was August 15, there were so many children that it could have been any Thursday afternoon or Sunday during the school year. Most had not gone away on holidays, partly because of the rail strikes, but chiefly because the fighting was moving closer and closer to the capital. War games were a favorite among the ten- to twelve-year-olds, but no one wanted to be the enemy. The leaders had to resort to a draw; those who lost fought the French, but only half-heartedly.

After going on the merry-go-round three times without managing to catch a ring with his wand, Charles wanted some ice cream. Near the gates on the Boulevard Saint-Michel, a vendor with a brightly colored cart was selling "strawberry ice." Léa bought two cones. On the bandstand, an orchestra in green uniforms played a Strauss waltz. Pinned to some of the trees were yellow and black notices from the city's new military governor, General Von Choltitz, calling on the population to remain calm and warning that "swift and brutal" measures would be taken in the event of disorderly conduct, sabotage, or attacks.

Most of the people who read these posters merely smiled. At noon, the radio had announced the Allied landing in Provence. Some were saying that the Americans were on the outskirts of Paris; they had heard the cannon. Others had just come from a ceremony commemorating the wish of Louis XIII at Notre-Dame Cathedral.

In spite of the fact that General Von Choltitz had expressly forbidden them to attend, Parisians had listened to their bishops and turned out in full force. There were so many people, in fact, that they spilled out of the doorways of the cathedral and filled the square, pressing forward to see the platform that had been erected at the main entrance to duplicate the ceremony inside. As the procession emerged from one side entrance and went in by the other, the crowd prayed fervently with the missionary standing on the platform. Saint Joan-of-Arc, Liberator of our Country, pray for us. Saint Geneviève, Protectress of Paris, pray for us. Holy Mary, Mother of God, Patron Saint of France, pray for us. Here, the missionary paused for a moment as a priest stepped forward and whispered something in his ear. Those standing beneath the platform could see his face light up. Many fell to their knees as he announced, in a trembling voice, "We have just learned that the Allies have landed in Provence. Dear brethren, let us pray that Marseilles and Toulon are spared. Our Father, who art in Heaven, hallowed be thy name . . ." The emotion reached fever pitch when Cardinal Suhard delivered an impromptu speech in which he talked about "the last battle to be won." The German soldiers standing in front of the Hotel-Dieu and the Prefecture had not moved. There was not a policeman in sight; that morning, the Parisian police force had struck in support of the police in Asnières and Saint-Denis who had been disarmed.

The day after the Assumption, *Je suis partout* reappeared on the newsstands, announcing that the next issue would appear on Friday, August 25. Truckloads of militiamen began leaving the capital, heading east. On the Avenue de l'Opéra, the Champs-Élysées, and the Boulevard Saint-Michel, German sol-

163

diers marched to military music under the mocking gaze of the Parisians. "It's the beginning of the end," they remarked to one another.

On August 17, Parisians could barely contain their joy as buses, trucks, ambulances, and cars filled with grim-faced soldiers filed past. Bringing up the rear was an eclectic assortment of carts, horse-drawn carriages, rickshaws, and even wheelbarrows filled with radios, typewriters, paintings, armchairs, beds, trunks, and suitcases. Perched on top were mattresses, reminding Parisians of their own exodus four years before.

What a pleasure it was to watch the dregs of the invincible army creep away! Where were the magnificent conquerors of June 1940? What had become of their impeccable uniforms? Were they beginning to show signs of wear after four years on the steppes of Russia and the deserts of Africa? Or in the wing chairs of the Hôtel Meurice, the Crillon, and the Intercontinental? People settled into chairs in the gardens bordering the Champs-Élysées smiling as they watched the motley motorcade, seeing who could count the highest number of cars and vans. They were still smiling as soldiers began to walk by, soldiers who now seemed too young or too old, wearing tunics too small or too large, unshaven, unkempt, limping along with a rifle or with armfuls of food and fabric that some eagerly sold to onlookers.

Laure and Léa cycled along the quays. In spite of the tension that reigned in some neighborhoods, the noise of engines and the cries, the smoke from the piles of police and government files burning in the streets, the panic of the fleeing soldiers, and the nine o'clock curfew, there was euphoria in the air. A long car overtook them. In it were two very elegant, very blond women clinging to a monocled general.

The banks of the Seine were lined with fishermen and bathers. Sailboats rocked gently at their berths in the white summer light. The entire city waited. Léa and Laure had to get off their bicycles to cross the Pont Royal, across which spirals of barbed wire had been stretched.

In the Rue de l'Université, Charles waited impatiently for Léa so that he could give her the drawing he had been working on all morning. Estelle moaned incessantly about her varicose veins (all that standing in line!). Aunt Lisa was very excited: at noon, there had been an announcement over the BBC that the Americans were in Rambouillet. Aunt Albertine seemed preoccupied.

Thanks to Laure's "supply cupboard," their dinner of sardines packed in oil and real gingerbread seemed like a veritable feast. The power was restored between 10:30 and midnight, and with it came a letdown for Lisa: the Americans were in Chartres and Dreux, not Rambouillet.

Shortly before the curfew, the SS began firing on the crowd watching German office workers moving files out of the Trianon-Hôtel in the Rue de Vaugirard. Many other onlookers were killed or wounded in similar incidents at the Place de la Sorbonne and on the Boulevard Saint-Michel.

Parisians were shaken in their beds as munitions depots were blown up.

"No papers this morning," said the man at the newsstand opposite *Les Deux Magots* on the Boulevard Saint-Germain. "Things are getting really nasty for the *collabos*. See the guy with the glasses? That's Robert Brasillach–has his coffee at *Le Flore*. The guy's never looked healthy, but for the last two days, I'd say he's been looking really ill. If I were him, I'd hitch a ride with the Krauts."

So that was Brasillach. Raphaël had spoken of him with such admiration. He looked like a sickly teenager.

Léa sat at a pedestal table not far away and ordered a coffee. An ancient waiter, wearing a long apron, told her that there were no hot drinks, because the gas had been cut off. She ordered a *diabolo-menthe* instead, but the mixture of mint cordial and soda was ghastly.

At the next table, a tall, dark man in his thirties with thick glasses was writing in a journal in tiny, even script. A thin, fair-haired man sat down beside him.

"Hi, Claude. Working already?"

"Hi, Claude. Sort of working. What's new?"

"Lots since last night. The Germans starting firing on the crowd in the Rue de Buci and on Boulevard Saint-Germain."

"Any casualties?"

"Lots. How's your father?"

"Fine. He's at Vémars. I'm going to see him tomorrow."

The sound of a faroff explosion prevented Léa from hearing what was said next.

"Must be the munitions depots," said one of the men.

"They set fire to several cafes and warehouses behind the Eiffel Tower. It won't be long now. The *collabos* are running like rats leaving a sinking ship. We'll never have to listen to Jean-Hérold Paquis's harangues again. Radio-Journal has been taken off the air. The likes of Luchaire, Rebatet, Bucard, Cousteau, and Bonnard-Gestapette are heading for Germany. He's the only one who's staying put," said the fair-haired young man, gesturing in the direction of Brasillach, "and I'd love to know why."

"Some misguided sense of honor, I suppose. I don't even hate him anymore, he's so pathetic."

"Why did you hate him?"

"Oh, it's an old story—an article he wrote about my father in '37."

"I remember! 'The Critical Age of Monsieur Mauriac.' "

"Yes, his insults really got to me. I wanted to punch his face in."

Léa put some change on the table and stood up. They watched as she left the cafe.

"Pretty girl!"

"Very pretty!"

Had it not been for the faroff thunder of the munitions depots, August 18, 1944, would have been like any other late summer morning. The air was hot and heavy. The streets were calm. What few people there were in the streets strolled like tourists. Young girls in pretty summer dresses cycled by, laughing and smiling. Outside the Church of Saint-Germain-des-Prés, a group of young people were engaged in a lively discussion. In the window of the Divan bookstore, a few well-thumbed copies of Martineau's journal collected dust. In the little square near the church, an old woman unfolded a newspaper containing food for stray cats, perhaps her own rations. She scattered it at the foot of a tree, calling:

"Here, kitty, kitty, kitty! Come on, kitty!"

At the Place Furstenberg, two drunks fought over the last drop of a bottle of wine. In the Rue de Seine, two *concierges* stood on their doorsteps, editorializing the events of the previous day. In the Rue de Buci, the green grocers' stands were painfully bare; this did not prevent housewives from lining up, just in case. The Rue Dauphine was deserted. In the Rue Saint-André-des-Arts, kids chased after one another with scraps of wood for guns, hiding in the nooks and crannies of the Cour de Rohan.

"Bam! Bam! Hands up or you're dead meat!"

Léa wandered aimlessly.

She found herself at the Place Saint-Michel, where a crowd had gathered around a plane tree. Léa made her way to the front of the crowd that was reading a small white poster. At the top were two small tricolor flags, staffs crossed.

Provisional Government of the Republic of France
The Allies are on the outskirts of Paris.
Prepare yourselves for the final battle to oust the oppressor.
The battle for Paris has already begun.
Wait for orders, by poster or by radio, before you act.
Fighting will begin one neighborhood at a time.

There was not a soul in Paris who did not know that it was only a matter of days or hours before Paris was either liberated or razed. Some had begun making preparations, but most had decided to sit tight and wait until the Germans left before celebrating.

Léa found herself swinging from hatred to fear, and from thoughts of vengeance to an overwhelming desire to forget.

167

These rapid swings left her jittery and exhausted. After many sleepless nights there were pale purple shadows around her eyes.

Léa realized that she had to take action, and contacted a Resistance network in Paris that the young doctor from Langon had told her about. On the day that Léa and Charles left Montillac, the doctor had found them wandering along the road and had taken them to the station just in time to catch one of the last trains leaving for Paris. The trip had taken two days. The lines were constantly cut and the train was bombed several times, forcing the people on the train to take refuge in nearby fields. Léa followed the other passengers, oblivious to the danger and to Charles who did not let go of her hand for an instant. Even the warm welcome from her aunts and sisters had not roused her from her lethargy. It was not until she heard Ruth's voice over the telephone that Léa responded. The tears she shed helped restore her desire to live, but the self-confidence that had been her strength was gone.

She wandered through the streets, tense with the waiting, until dusk. Finally, her hunger got the better of her and she returned to the Rue de l'Université just before the curfew. Dinner consisted of cold mashed potatoes and a wedge of chalky camembert cheese. Aunt Albertine was so relieved to see her that she didn't scold her for coming home so late. Charles, who had refused to go to bed until Léa came home, promptly fell asleep, holding her hand.

Nightmares kept Léa awake for part of the night. Finally, at dawn, she dropped off.

Chapter Fifteen

"Wake up, wake up!"

Léa sat up and stared, half-awake, at her sister.

"The French Forces of the Interior have taken over the Prefecture," said Laure breathlessly. "There's fighting everywhere, the Americans are coming, get your clothes on."

"What are you talking about?"

"The Gaullists are occupying the Prefecture and the police have joined them."

"Says who?"

"Franck, a friend of mine whom you haven't met. He lives in a hugh apartment on the Boulevard Saint-Michel which has windows facing the boulevard, the quays, and the Rue de la Huchette. He just called. Last night, he and some friends went dancing and drinking. It was after curfew, so they decided to sleep at his place. When they went to close the shutters at seven this morning, they noticed men crossing the Pont Saint-Michel and heading for Notre Dame Cathedral. They got dressed again and followed the men to the square in front of the cathedral. There were a thousand, maybe two thousand men standing and talking in low voices. Franck guessed from what they were saying that they were policemen in civilian clothing. A van pulled up and a few rifles and five or six submachine guns were distributed. They were given orders, then they headed for the main gates of the Prefecture without making a sound. Franck watched from a distance. The gate was opened and the crowd poured into the courtyard. A tall man

169

wearing a houndstooth check suit and a tricolor arm band climbed on to the hood of a car. "In the name of the Republic and General de Gaulle, I hereby take possession of the Prefecture of Police!" The guards on duty did not offer any resistance. They hoisted the flag and sang the *Marseillaise*. Franck told me that he had a lump in his throat and he's no sissy. Apparently, a new Prefect was appointed, Charles Lizet I think his name is. Come on, let's go! It'll be fun!"

"Fun? I don't think so, Laure. Interesting maybe," said Léa, getting out of bed.

"Do you sleep in the nude?"

"I forgot to pack a nightie when I left Montillac. I'm going to get dressed now."

"Hurry up, I'll wait for you in the kitchen."

"All right, but don't say anything to Aunt Lisa or Aunt Albertine."

"Of course I won't, I'm not crazy."

German soldiers wearing helmets and clutching rifles and submachine guns, waved and called out as they passed Laure and Léa on the Boulevard Saint-Germain at the Rue du Bac.

"They don't look too worried," said Léa, turning.

The boulevard before them was empty. Just as they reached the Rue du Dragon, a soldier pointed his gun at them.

"Abhauen oder ich schiesse."[1]

Half-empty cups and glasses waited on the pedestal tables at *les Deux-Magots* and *Le Flore* for customers who had taken refuge indoors. In the Rue de Rennes, people scattered in all directions. There was a burst of fire, and two of the people fell. At Mabillon, young men in white coats with Red Cross arm bands ran to rescue the wounded. At the Odéon, a tank blocked the street. Léa and Laure turned into the Rue de Buci. Most of the stores had their metal doors rolled down; cafe owners hurried to bring chairs and tables inside. Men wearing tricolor arm bands hurried past.

[1]Leave the area at once or I'll shoot.

170

"Go home!" one of them called out to Léa and Laure. "All hell is going to break loose!"

The Rue Saint-André-des-Arts was oddly quiet. A concierge swept the entrance to her building as she did every morning. At the cafe with the tobacco and stamp counter, the owner of the bookstore enjoyed a glass of white wine with the printer from the Rue Séguier. The candy vendor polished her jars filled with imitation candy. On the Boulevard Saint-Michel, a joyous crowd was looking in the direction of the Prefecture and Notre-Dame Cathedral where the tricolor flag now flew.

Laure and Léa were given a warm welcome as they entered Franck's apartment.

"I brought my sister, Léa. I told you about her."

"Hi, Léa. Is it true that you're a heroine of the Resistance?"

"Don't believe everything Laure tells you. She likes to exaggerate."

"I didn't have to exaggerate."

"I don't want to talk about it," said Léa firmly.

"Whatever you like. Anyways, welcome. Come and see."

The young man led her over to one of the tall French windows in the spacious living room.

"Look. We have front row seats. My mother's going to be really sorry she went to Touraine. She wouldn't have missed this for anything in the world. She probably would have invited all of her lady friends. It's pretty quiet right now. What do you think? Great view, eh?"

"Yes, great."

"Franck, is there anything to eat? We were in such a hurry that we didn't have time to eat."

"You know my motto: You can get anything you want at Franck's restaurant! Apart from the bread, which is a little stale, there's ham, cold cuts, pâté, cold roast chicken, pastries, wine, champagne, and whiskey. Just help yourself."

"Do you own a grocery store?" asked Léa dryly.

"I could, my dear, but I prefer silk stockings, perfume, and cigarettes. Do you smoke? Filter or plain, take your pick."

"Filter, but right now I'm hungry."

"Yes, ma'am! Food and wine for the princess! Would Her Royalness deign to drink a toast to our future liberators?"

Léa looked at the young man for the first time. He looked like the boy next door, the sort you would trust with your secrets but never think of as a man. He was not very tall and seemed lost in a suit with exaggerated shoulders and ultra-short pants to show off the white socks and triple crepe soles worn by every Parisian *zazou*. A long lock of blond hair fell in a perfect pompadour over his unprepossessing face. According to Laure, his talent for ferreting out any commodity was unequalled. Following in his parents' footsteps, he had made a fortune on the black market. He was also very generous and treated his friends, and the friends of his friends, regularly. Doubtless satisfied with what she saw, Léa smiled.

"Yes, let's drink to the liberation of Paris."

Sitting on the window ledge, she thought how odd it was to be drinking champagne in a city that was about to see heavy fighting.

Newly-formed "passive defense agents" crossed the Place Saint-Michel below, calling out that there would be a curfew at 2:00 p.m.

"That's not true," said a boy, entering the apartment. "I was just at the police station in my neighborhood, and they hadn't heard anything. The F.F.I. occupying the building hadn't heard anything either. . . . You're new. I'm Jacques."

"And I'm Léa. Where were you just now?"

"All over. Many of the city halls are in the hands of the Communists."

"How do you know that?"

"That's what I heard. They're the only ones who are sufficiently armed and organized. Red Cross stations have been set up on the Rue de Rivoli, the Rue du Louvre, at the Châtelet, the Place de la République, and the Avenue de la Grande-Armée. Everybody's scrambling around for weapons. Someone with a knife takes a German soldier's gun or rifle. With the rifle, he takes a submachine gun, and with that he takes a truckful of ammunition that he hands out to his friends.

172

"One man, one Kraut" is the order of the day for new recruits."

"Are you going to fight?"

"Why not? We'll be heroes . . . I'll think about it when I've had lunch."

The little group, five young men and three young women, sat down at the kitchen table which had been set by Laure and a pretty blonde girl named Muriel.

"Why don't we put on some music, for some atmosphere!"

"Okay, put on the Andrew Sisters," said Muriel.

"What do want to hear?"

" 'Pennsylvania Polka' or 'Sonny Boy'."

"Where did you get those records?" asked Léa "I thought American music was forbidden."

"We have connections, we'll tell you when the war is over."

The high, melodic voices of the Andrew sisters filled the apartment. The meal was very gay; everyone had a joke or a funny story to tell. They were so young, so carefree that Léa found herself laughing too. Franck looked on approvingly and poured her another glass of wine.

He went to wind up the phonograph again. Before the next record began, shots rang out.

"Quick, the Germans are attacking the Prefecture!"

They all ran to the window.

On the Boulevard du Palais, three *Wehrmacht* trucks were firing at the gates of the Prefecture. Three tanks headed toward Notre-Dame Cathedral. Shots were fired from the Palais de Justice and the Prefecture, killing some of the soldiers in the trucks, which disappeared toward the Châtelet. Mortars exploded. A few moments later, more *Wehrmacht* trucks were stopped on the Boulevard du Palais. From the window, they could see men in shirt sleeves with rifles and revolvers, hiding in the subway entrance and the *Café du Départ* where a machine gun had been set up.

A truck crossing the Pont Saint-Michel was their first target. A soldier, lying wounded on the hood, slid to the ground. The truck stopped, just as another crashed in the *Rôtisserie*

173

Périgourdine on the Quai des Grands-Augustins. Onlookers applauded loudly. Members of the F.F.I. ran to recover the bodies which they dragged to the steps leading down to the Seine. Sunbathers along the Quai des Orfèvres watched with interest. A column of black smoke rose from the Châtelet as a truck caught fire. A car painted with a "V" for victory and the cross of Lorraine, screeched to a halt at the Quai Saint-Michel, followed by an ambulance and a fire truck. From the square in front of Notre-Dame, three tanks prepared for an assault on the Prefecture.

"They'll never hold out," said Franck. "They have almost no ammunition and a few bags of sand aren't going to keep the shells out."

A group of teenagers ran along the quay, carrying an old submachine gun which Franck identified as a Hotchkiss. One of the kids had a string of cartridges around his neck. His name was Jeannot. He was fifteen years old and he didn't know that he was about to die on the Quai de Montebello, his neck torn open by an explosive bullet.

A fire bomb thrown from one of the windows of the Prefecture landed in the open turret of a tank which burst into flames instantly. The shouts of joy from the Prefecture could be heard on the other side of the Seine and were echoed by the residents of the Quai Saint-Michel. Oblivious to the danger, they leaned out of their windows so as not to miss any of the action in the street below. A group of German prisoners filed past with their arms in the air, escorted by members of the F.F.I. In the Place Saint-Michel, a passerby was struck down by a runaway bullet. A German soldier, covered in blood, fired into the air as he pirouetted and fell to the ground. Another bullet caught him in the head. For a few agonizing moments, he continued to crawl forward, before collapsing in the middle of the street. Léa was the only one who didn't look away.

The neighborhood was rocked by an explosion as a truck carrying gasoline crashed into the wall of Notre-Dame-Hôtel. Flames leapt up the facade. Members of the F.F.I. left their posts to try to move the truck and preserve the historic building. Thankfully, the sirens of fire trucks were soon heard.

There was a lull and one of the party decided to go downstairs and have a look. He returned an hour later, saying that a truce had been declared so that the dead and wounded could be recovered. This news called for yet another bottle of champagne, which quickly joined the others in one of the bathtubs.

The evening air was heavy and hot, and Parisians went out to reclaim their streets. They strolled along the boulevards, stopping from time to time to contemplate a pool of drying blood and falling silent.

"Darn! We forgot to call Aunt Lisa and Aunt Albertine," cried Laure, running over to the telephone.

Above the Pont Neuf, the sky became more and more menacing.

"Aunt Albertine wants us to come home right away. Charles has a high fever."

"Did she call the doctor?"

"There was no answer at old Doctor Leroy's and the others refuse to come."

"I'll go. Are you coming with me?"

"No, I'd rather stay here. If you need me, just call. Franck, can you give Léa your telephone number?"

"I'm going to accompany her home on your bike. I'll be back in less than an hour."

Chapter Sixteen

Léa spent the entire night watching over Charles, delirious from the high fever. The next morning, she wrapped him in a blanket, borrowed an ancient baby buggy from the concierge, and headed for the nearest hospital.

In spite of the storm overnight, the sky was still overcast. The smell of dust rose from the damp pavement. It was Sunday, yet the streets were completely deserted. The heavy silence made Léa uneasy.

At the *Hôpital Laënnec* in the Rue de Sèvres, the intern on duty took Charles from Léa. He was clearly unable to diagnose the problem, and suggested that she leave the child at the hospital until the doctor arrived. When she refused, he gave Charles some medication and led them to a room with two beds.

Much later that afternoon, Léa was awakened by the sound of voices.

"You're a very sound sleeper, young lady. Is the boy your child?"

"No."

"Where are his parents?"

"What's wrong with him, doctor?"

"He has acute laryngitis and the first signs of pulmonary congestion."

"Is it serious?"

"It can be. The best thing would have been for him to stay here."

"Isn't that possible?"

"We're very short-staffed. But you didn't answer my question: where are his parents?"

"His mother was killed by the Germans and his father is with General de Gaulle."

"Poor child."

"Léa ... Léa ..."

"It's alright, sweetie. I'm here."

Charles clung to Léa, shuddering. The doctor looked at them anxiously.

"I want you to take him home and do exactly as I say. Do you know how to give injections?"

"No."

"Well, I'm going to teach you."

"But ..."

"It's not very complicated."

Suddenly, the door was flung open.

"Doctor, some children have just been brought in!"

"Are they seriously wounded?"

"Stomach and legs."

"I'm on my way. Put them in the operating room. You see, mademoiselle, this is exactly what I was afraid would happen. There simply aren't enough of us."

The doctor finished filling out the prescription.

"Ask the nurse at the reception desk for the address of the all-night pharmacy and give her your address as well. I'll try to come by tomorrow morning or I'll send one of my colleagues."

"Doctor, he's not ..."

"No, he's a strong little boy. He'll be just fine. Give him the medication as directed and watch his temperature."

For the next three days, Léa slept only a few hours. She watched over Charles constantly, completely losing track of time. She found herself uttering prayers for his recovery.

177

Gradually, her hands became steadier as she gave him his injections. At dawn on August 23, the fever suddenly broke.

"I'm hungry," he said, in a thin little voice.

Léa smothered him with kisses and he smiled a tired, happy smile.

"What is it, Léa?" asked Albertine, entering the room.

"Charles is better! He asked for something to eat!"

"That's wonderful news! It's a good thing that Laure managed to find us some milk and cookies. I'll have Estelle prepare a little snack."

Charles nibbled on a cookie and drank half a glass of milk before falling asleep under the tender gaze of the four women, who tip-toed out of the room.

"Is there any water? I feel like a bath," said Léa.

"Yes, but it's cold as usual."

The water was indeed cold, but her relief that Charles would not slip away from her was so great that she seemed not to care. Her fear had clung to her like an extra layer of skin, but she had been determined not to let him die. Whenever his body seemed about to give up the fight, she had tried desperately to draw the illness out of his body with her hands. She sensed now that he was out of danger.

Her anxiety and fatigue dissolved into the icy water, leaving her covered in goose bumps. She scrubbed herself all over with the horsehair mitt, rubbing the mitt first on a bar of lily-of-the-valley soap from Laure. There was no shampoo, so she used the soap to wash her hair too, rinsing with vinegar to restore its sheen.

She examined herself in the huge gilt-framed mirror that gave the little white-tiled bathroom a look of luxury.

"There's nothing left but skin and bones," she said aloud.

She was much thinner, but she found the effect far from displeasing. She stroked her breasts, her nipples hard from the icy water, and arched her back. She could almost hear François murmuring admiringly:

"What a great ass!"

The thought of François brought the blood rushing to her

178

cheeks. She quickly put on a terry-towel robe and began rub-bing her hair dry. In the front hall, the telephone rang.

"Léa, it's Laure. She wants to talk to you," called Albertine through the door.

"Coming!"

She picked up the receiver breathlessly.

"Hello, Léa? Aunt Albertine says that Charles is better."

"Yes, his fever is gone and he had something to eat this morning. Could you get some more milk?"

"It's getting harder and harder with the General Strike. The truck drivers are refusing to leave Paris. It's just about impossi-ble to get anything except meat. The French Forces of the Interior—the F.F.I.—took over three thousand five hundred tons of meat that the Germans had been storing in refrigera-tors at Bercy and Vaugirard. I can get you some, but I'll need ration cards. They've clamped down on the black market."

"I'll bring them over."

"Be careful, things have changed since Saturday. There was heavy fighting yesterday and the day before yesterday in the Latin Quarter. There are barricades everywhere. The Militia and the Germans have snipers on the rooftops. The morgues are taking in hundreds of bodies every day, and with the heat, you can imagine what it's like over at Notre-Dame-des-Victoires. That's where they have the services and put the coffins until they can be taken to the *Cimetière de Pantin* for burial in the insurgents' plot. The Red Cross people are in-credible. Not only are they rescuing the wounded, they're filling in for the undertakers who are on strike. . . . Has anyone heard from Sabine?"

"No, I don't think so."

"I'm worried about her. Yesterday, at Place Saint-Michel, they lynched a collaborator. It was horrible. The women were the worst. They beat the man with anything they could get their hands on, screaming hysterically the whole time. Some-one told me that they gouged his eyes with a spindle from a broken chair. It was awful. You should have heard the screams! The worst part was the crowd. People just stood around, watching and laughing and preventing the F.F.I. from intervening. When they'd had enough, they took off, their clothes and their hands covered in blood. There was nothing but a bloody mess left on the sidewalk. .... Léa, are you still there?"

"Yes, Why are you telling me this? What has it got to do with Sabine?"

This time, there was silence at the other end of the line.
"Laure, did you hear what I said?"
"Yes, I heard you ..."
"Well?"
"They're also rounding up women who fraternized with the Germans."
"What are they doing to them?"
"Apparently, they're shaving their heads."
"*What!*"
"They've already started in some neighborhoods. They hang the hair from the wrought iron work and paint a swastika on their skulls. Most of women were the mistresses of German officers or prostitutes. Their neighbors turn them in."
"But Sabine isn't one of them!"
"I know that, but do you think they're going to stop to ask questions? I just hope she took my advice and left for Germany with Pierre."
"Have you tried calling her?"
"Of course, but there's no answer. The last time we spoke was Monday morning. She had just had a visit from a German officer who wanted to take her to a hotel where they're putting all of the women in her situation. She refused to go."
"What's the name of the hotel?"
"I don't know. I didn't make a note of it."
"We'll have to call every hotel in Paris."
"Do you have any idea how many there are?"
"No, but that doesn't matter. We can start with the ones in the Michelin Guide. Does Franck have a copy?"
"I think so."
"Start at the back while you're waiting for me. I'll have Aunt

180

Albertine and Aunt Lisa start at the front and call us if they find anything. I'll be right over."

"Be careful," said Laure, but Léa had already hung up.

Her great aunts were extremely distressed when she explained the situation, but Albertine quickly got a grip on herself and began telephoning.

"Hello, is this the Crillon?"

"Aunt Albertine, I doubt very much that Sabine is at the Crillon, the Majestic, the Meurice, the Continental or the Lutétia. They're already fully occupied by the German Army!"

The Rue de l'Université was completely deserted. In front of the Faculty of Medicine in the Rue des Saints-Pères, Léa passed the charred remains of a *Wehrmacht* truck, branded with the *Croix de Lorraine*. The Rue Jacob was also deserted. She was about to turn left, taking the Rue de Seine and the Rue Guénégaud toward the Seine, when she remembered Sarah Mulstein's arrest. She had not come this way since that terrible night. So she turned right along the Rue de Seine, then left along the Rue de Buci. A long line of housewives had been waiting since dawn outside the bakery. Léa remarked that in spite of their war-weariness and the shortages, people seemed happy for the first time in four years, as though the air of Paris were suddenly easier to breathe. In the Rue Dauphine, she was overtaken by a young man on a bicycle. He had a rifle slung across his shoulders and a bundle of newspapers under one arm.

"*L'Humanité!* Read all about it! *L'Humanité!* Would you like a paper, mademoiselle?" he asked, pulling up beside Léa.

"When did the newspapers start printing again?"

"On Monday. That's two francs. Stay away from the Pont Neuf, the Germans are firing on the barricade. Just a while ago, some bastards in the car marked 'F.F.I.' started firing on the partisans. Two of them were killed. The Germans are fleeing by way of the Rue Christine. Be careful!"

Léa stood in a doorway, glancing through the paper.

Rise up! The Commander of the French Forces of the Interior for the Greater Metropolitan Region calls on all Men, Women, and Children to Demonstrate their Courage and Support for the F.F.I.! Fortify the Streets and Buildings of Paris. Form your own Partisan Militias! Attack is the best Defence! Harass the Enemy! Don't let the Germans Leave Paris Alive! Battles Waged on Every Front. Non-stop Fighting in First, Fourth, Fifth, and Sixth Arrondissements. Partisans Gaining Ground. People Fight to Overthrow Oppressor. Communist Women Fight for Liberation of Paris. Young Woman Tortured by Militia. Join the Party of Those who gave Their Lives for France's Freedom.

At Place Saint-André-des-Arts, people were shouting and milling about, old men and women of all ages. They all wore the same expression of hatred and were hurling insults, mouths twisted in anger, bare arms raised, fingers like claws. Bastard! *Collabo*! Traitor! Assassin! In their midst, a tall fair-haired man, his face bloody from the clawing, was trying to defend himself.

"I'm Alsatian," he pleaded.

"Alsatian, my ass!" came a voice with a Parisian accent.

The crowd roared with laughter.

From the window of a nearby building occupied by the F.F.I., a man in a vaguely military outfit tried to make himself heard. A girl thumbed her nose at him and a woman with bleached blonde hair and dark roots screamed back:

"He's a filthy German. I know him, I'm sure of it. Kill him!"

She grabbed the man by the hair while one woman spat in his face and another tried to unbutton his pants.

"Let's see if he has any balls, the bastard!" she sniggered.

There was another roar of laughter, then:

"Off with his clothes! Off with his clothes!"

"I'm from Alsace!" the man kept repeating, over and over, as he tried to free himself.

By now, his nose and cheeks were streaming blood. One of his eyes had closed. He stumbled and blows rained down on

182

him. One caught him on the nose. He stood up. A young man wearing an F.F.I. arm band tried to intervene, but was gently lifted into the air by three men and set down beside Léa, who was unable to take her eyes off the spectacle. Without realizing it, she had begun to rock back and forth. The thoughts collided and shattered inside her head. From the bloodied hole that had been his mouth, he struggled again to say that he was French.

Overcome with nausea, Léa turned away. The young man with the arm band was still there, tears running down his pale cheeks. Their eyes met.

"Léa!"

"Pierrot!"

They put their arms around one another, trembling with fear and revulsion.

"They're going to kill him!" said Léa, straightening up.

"There's nothing we can do, there are too many of them."

"You're in the F.F.I. Go get help."

"They won't intervene, one of them almost got lynched yesterday when he tried to defend a collaborator."

"It's horrible."

"Don't look! Come on, we'll go over to Colonel Lizé's headquarters in the Rue Guénégaud."

"I don't want to go to the Rue Guénégaud," howled Léa.

Pierrot was startled by his cousin's vehemence.

"I have to, I'm the liaison between Lizé and Rol."

"Who's Rol?"

"Don't tell me you haven't heard of Colonel Rol!" he said, looking at her with amazement. "He's the leader of the insurrection, the leader of the French Forces of the Interior."

"And Lizé?"

"Colonel Lizé is also a leader. . . . I don't understand it completely myself. Some sort of political alliance. All I know is that Rol is a Communist."

"Wouldn't your father be proud," said Léa wryly.

"Don't talk about my father. He's a collaborator. As far as I'm concerned, he's dead and buried."

They entered the Rue Gîte-le-Coeur. Pierrot stopped in front of the dirty window of a small grocery store, climbed the three short steps, and knocked on the door.

"We're closed!" came a gruff voice.

"Open up. It's Pierrot—from Bordeaux."

The door opened a crack.

"Oh, it's you! Come in! Who's this?"

"This is my cousin Léa."

The grocery store was also a restaurant. Its walls were covered with prints, Épinal reproductions, engravings, and portraits bearing a questionable resemblance to Napoleon. These, in turn, were covered with a brown film. Dividing the room was a short wooden counter which did double duty as a bar and display case, and on which sat a few empty tin cans. On the other side of the counter were tables with red and white checked cloths and an enormous stove with shining copper utensils. On top of the stove there was an alcohol burner. The smell escaping from the simmering pot was vaguely like rabbit stew. It was almost too much for Léa.

"Whoa! Watch your cousin, she's about to pass out!" cried the women who had let them in.

Pierrot helped Léa to sit down and to take a tiny glass of *eau-de-vie*. The color started returning to her cheeks and the room stopped spinning.

"Feeling better? Here, have some more."

"No, thanks."

The room looked as though it had not been touched since the turn of the century. It must have served good food before the war—the stove was lovingly maintained. Léa found this reassuring. The place couldn't be all bad.

"You must be hungry," said the woman, heading over to the stove.

"Starving!" exclaimed Pierrot. He hadn't eaten a square meal in several days.

"No, thank you," replied Léa. "I'll just have a glass of water."

"You don't know what you're missing, Léa. Madame Laetitia's food is excellent, in spite of the shortages."

He sat down and was at once serve a steaming dish of stew of an unidentifiable color.

"I don't know how you can eat," said Léa sharply.

Beneath the dirt on his face, Pierrot blushed violently. His spoon stopped in mid-air and he looked at her with such sadness that she wished she had held her tongue.

"I'm sorry. Tell me what's happened to you since I last saw you."

Between mouthfuls, Pierrot told his story.

"When I found out that my father wanted to stick me in a Jesuit college with orders not to let me out, I decided to join the *maquis*. I'll spare you the details of how I got there— hiding in freight cars, sleeping in ditches to avoid the police, robbing food from farmers' fields. At the train station in Limoges, I was chased by the Militia. Luckily, some railway workers helped me to avoid getting caught. For several days, they hid me in an old freight car on a siding. There were so many Germans and militiamen questioning passengers and employees that it was impossible for the workers to get me out. Then, one day, they hid me in a cattle car on a freight train heading for Eymoutiers."

"Eymoutiers. Is that in the Limousin?"

"Yes, why? Have you heard of it?"

"No, but I have a Jewish friend who was in hiding there for a while. Go on."

"At Eymoutiers, some other rail workers helped me out. They took me to their leader, Colonel Guingouin, also known as le Grand and Raoul. An incredible man! The Germans are scared stiff of him. The command post was in Châteauneuf Forest, but when it started getting cold, we had to abandon our camp at Trois-Chevaux. It's just as well because a few days later, three thousand men descended on the forest. The Germans were so afraid of ambushes that they called it 'Little Siberia'. They suffered heavy casualties. For the past six months, I've been the liaison between all of the *maquis* groups. I know every village and wood in the area. Thanks to Guingouin's leadership, we have food and clothing, and the population is on our side. I wanted to go with them on their sabotage operations and when they attacked convoys, but they said I was too young. At the beginning of August, they sent me here with a message for Colonel Rol. First, there was the General Strike, now the insurrection. I haven't been able to leave."

Léa looked at her cousin admiringly. The little boy who used to look her with puppy-love eyes had grown up!

"What about you? How long have you been in Paris?"

"Since the beginning of August."

"How's everyone at Montillac? Has Camille heard from Laurent? What about Aunt Bernadette? And Ruth? And Mathias? Léa, what's wrong?"

Léa looked down, rubbing her forehead.

"What's wrong?" he repeated anxiously.

"Camille and Aunt Bernadette are both dead. There is no more Montillac."

"What do you mean?"

"The Germans and the Militia killed them, then they burned the house."

For a long moment, neither spoke. It was only when a boisterous group of young people entered the restaurant that they looked up.

"There you are, Pierrot! We've been looking for you everywhere. We thought maybe they'd done to you what they did to that *collabo* who was trying to pass himself off as an Alsatian."

"Maybe he was Alsatian!"

The boy, barely older than Pierrot, spun around to face Léa. "Maybe, but people have suffered so much, it's only normal that they want revenge."

"Normal! Do you find that kind of butchery normal?"

"What about the Krauts? Aren't they behaving like butchers? Do you know how many comrades they killed in the Bois de Boulogne last week? I didn't think so! Thirty-five who were your age. Magisson, nineteen. Verdeaux, nineteen. Smet, twenty. Schlosser, twenty-two. Dudraisil, twenty-one. The Bernard brothers, twenty and twenty-one. Shall I go on?"

"I know just as well as you do what they're capable of, but that's no reason to be worse than they are!"

They glared at one another.

"Leave her alone," said Pierrot. "She's right."

"Maybe, but this isn't the time to say so."

"There will never be a right time."

"Be quiet, Léa. Are you coming to Lizé's headquarters with me?"

"No, I have to see Laure. We're staying with our aunts in the Rue de l'Université. Call me. I want to see you again to talk some more."

"As soon as I get a chance, I'll call or come by. Give Laure a kiss for me."

They parted outside the restaurant.

It took Léa almost an hour to cross Place Saint-Michel. Snipers on the rooftops were firing on anyone brave or foolish enough to venture across the square. Two people had already been gunned down.

Franck's huge apartment, now occupied by a dozen F.F.I., looked as though it had been hit by a cyclone. Of the original group, only Laure, Muriel, and Franck remained. They were very happy to see her.

"Did you locate Sabine?" she asked.

"No, not yet. We've called about twenty hotels, but with no luck."

"We have to keep looking. I bumped into Pierrot in the street."

"Pierrot?"

"Yes, our cousin."

"Uncle Luc's son?"

"Yes."

"That's great! What's he doing here?"

"He has an arm band and a big revolver."

In the kitchen, two young people were busy making fire-bombs, following Frédéric Joliot-Curie's recipe which Colonel

Rol had distributed. They filled bottles with gasoline and sulfuric acid in a ratio of three to one, then corked the bottles and attached a seal soaked in potassium chlorate. Upon impact, the bottles would break, causing the potassium chlorate to come into contact with the fluid inside and igniting it.

There was a massive explosion in the street; they all ran to the window. The people manning the barricade in the Rue de la Huchette climbed to the top to see what had happened.

"The Krauts are blowing up Paris!" screamed the baker's wife.

Her pronouncement spread like wildfire through the neighborhood, and there was a moment of panic. Far off, over the Champs-Élysées, thick black smoke rose in a tall column. Everyone crouched down, waiting for the next explosion. There were sporadic bursts of fire from the *Jardin du Luxembourg*. Then all was quiet.

Gradually, street fighters and onlookers alike went back about their business, gesturing at a group of German prisoners in tattered uniforms, their hands on their heads, who were being taken to the courtyard of the Prefecture by three F.F.I. Just then, a motorcycle with a sidecar appeared from the Quai des Grands-Augustins and headed straight for them. The soldier in the sidecar shot and killed one of the F.F.I. A cry went up on the other side of the barricade. A young boy clambered to the top and threw a firebomb in the direction of the motorcycle. He did not live to see the bomb reach its target. He was struck down and collapsed on the makeshift barrier of bicycles and bedsprings. As the bottle landed, a huge flame leapt up in front of the motorcycle. In an instant, the driver and his passenger were engulfed in flames. The motorcycle zigzagged on before finally crashing into the parapet near a bookseller's stand. For a few moments, no one moved. A hand rose out of the flames, reaching skyward.

Gripping the window ledge, Léa relived the final moments of her aunt's life with the same agonizing powerlessness. With her aunt, there had been the same gesture of supplication. Does such a death hasten the ascent to heaven, she wondered.

Then, from behind the barricade blocking the Place Saint-

André-des-Arts and neighboring side streets, the crowd descended on the prisoners. They had watched, in horror, as their compatriots died. The two surviving F.F.I.'s tried to intervene, but were swept aside. One of them ran toward the Prefecture for help. When he returned with a dozen policemen, three of the German soldiers were already dead. One had had his eyes plucked out, another had had his nose cut off. The third no longer had a face at all. The other prisoners, some wounded, crouched on the pavement. These courageous men, many of whom had fought on the Russian Front, cried like babies. The arrival of the police, some of whom were now in uniform, dampened the spirits of the crowd. It was no doubt a crowd of ordinary people, most of whom walked away, exhilarated from the carnage, and promptly put the incident out of their minds. Onlookers who had stood by helplessly would never forget it.

In the apartment, no one spoke. The F.F.I., sitting on the floor, stared down at their rifles in their laps. Franck and the others stood staring at the wall. The arrival of a 'lieutenant' provided a welcome distraction.

"The Germans set fire to the *Grand Palais!*"

"So that was what we heard!"

"There was a circus in there!"

"Yes, the Houcke Circus. I don't know whether the rescue workers managed to save the animals or not. The horses escaped. One of them was killed at the Rond-Point des Champs-Élysées. You won't believe this, but I saw people run out with knives to strip the carcass, with bullets flying over their heads! Some of them even came with plates! By the time I left, there wasn't much left."

"You could have brought us some!"

"Are you crazy or what? They would have lynched me!"

His sardonic Parisian accent made them burst out laughing.

"I can just see them, sitting on the curb around the Rond-Point with spotless white napkins tucked into their collars, eating raw horse meat with their pinkies in the air, while lions on leashes held by Germans soldiers watch with hungry eyes!"

After the tension, it felt good to laugh and crack jokes.

In the street below and on the quay, the bodies of the soldiers and the insurgents were being carried away. The wounded were taken to the *Hôtel-Dieu*.

They spent the rest of the afternoon calling hotels, but to no avail. ("No, there's no Madame Delmas here with a child. No, we don't have any of *those* women staying here.") Léa and Laure were beginning to lose hope.

"Try one more, Laure," said Léa. "The Hôtel Régina, Opéra 74-02."

"Okay," said Laure. "Hello, is this the Hôtel Régina?"

"And then we'll call Aunt Albertine and Aunt Lisa to see whether they've had any luck—

"Yes, that's right. Please put her on the line. What do you mean you can't put her on the line! You have orders?"

Léa grabbed the receiver.

"I'd like to speak to Madame Delmas. I don't care what your orders are. I want to speak to her right now. Hello! Lieutenant who? Lieutenant, I'd like to speak to Madame Delmas. Yes, I'm her sister. She'll call me back? Are you positive? We're very worried about her. Thank you."

"Thank goodness, we found her!" said Laure.

"Yes, but we couldn't talk to her," answered Léa. "I hope that he wasn't lying and that he'll give her the message. I'm going back to the Rue de l'Université. Are you coming?"

"No, I think I'll stay here. Keep me posted."

One of the F.F.I.'s escorted Léa as far as the Clavreuil Bookstore on the other side of Place Saint-Michel.

In contrast to the Latin Quarter, the Rue Jacob and the Rue de l'Université were mercifully quiet. Charles, who had spent part of the day sleeping, greeted Léa with open arms. She responded with weary tenderness.

From Franck's, she had brought half a quart of milk, a few lumps of sugar, and some bread and meat which disappeared into the kitchen with Estelle.

They waited for Sabine to call.

When the telephone finally rang at around ten o'clock that

evening, Léa and her aunts had just heard over the BBC that Paris had been liberated. Just then, a burst of machine gun fire rocked the peaceful neighborhood. Albertine brought a long, thin hand to her forehead and commented, in her inimitable way:

"The gentlemen in London do not appear to have their information quite right."

"If they said it, it must be true," said Lisa, who believed every word she heard on the radio, whether from Jean Hérold-Paquis, Philippe Henriot, Maurice Schumann or Jean Oberlé.

Léa was about to say something nasty when the telephone rang.

"Hello, Sabine, is that you? Are you all right? Why didn't you come here? Hello! Can you hear me? You'll call tomorrow? Yes, I love you too. Talk to you tomorrow. 'Night."

Léa replaced the receiver, feeling distinctly uneasy. Sabine could not stay at the Hôtel Régina; it might be stormed at any moment. Léa resolved to go for her sister the next day.

In spite of her anxiety, she slept very soundly.

Chapter Seventeen

When Léa awoke, the sky above Paris was a dirty gray.

She watched Charles sleeping in his little cot beside her bed. His thin, delicate features were peaceful. He certainly looks like Camille, she thought, stroking his soft fair curls. She put on a blue cotton robe and went to the kitchen. By a stroke of luck, the gas was working, so she heated a little milk and drank half a bowl of Estelle's "coffee," which was still hot. She could hear the static from the radio in Lisa's room. Charles's sleepy head appeared in the doorway.

"Get back to bed! You're still sick, you know, you'll catch cold."

"No. I'm all better now. I want something to eat."

"All right, sit down. I'll give you some milk and cookies."

"Then can we go for a walk?"

"No, sweetie, it's too early. Besides, there's a war out there."

"I want to go out. I want to kill those mean soldiers who hurt Maman."

Sighing, Léa looked at the solemn little boy who talked about killing as he sipped his milk.

"Only grown-ups fight wars."

"Then why do they shoot children?"

Léa was at a loss to answer his question.

"Is my Papa fighting too?"

"Yes, with General de Gaulle."

"When is he coming back?"

"Very soon."

"He's been gone a long time!"

Charles was right, it had been a long time. Four long years. Four years of going through the motions of living so as not to despair altogether. Death everywhere. Nothing but hardship for four long years!

"Papa will be sad when he finds out Maman is dead."

So he knew! For the past two months, he had been pretending to believe her evasive answers.

"Yes, he will, but we'll be there to make him feel better. You'll have to love him very much."

"You'll be there, too, won't you Léa? You'll love him too, won't you?"

She could hear Camille's voice: "If anything happens to me, promise me you'll look after Charles . . . and Laurent." Laurent. She loved him like a brother now, like a dear friend, but not as a lover. She was amazed that her love for him had changed so radically. Love always dies before the loved one, as Raphaël Mahl would say, referring to Chateaubriand challenging the faint hope expressed by the man who loved Juliette Récamier: "Sometimes, in a very strong person, love lingers long enough to become a deep friendship, a duty. It then takes on the qualities of a virtue, shedding its inherent weaknesses and living by immortal principles."

Was he right?

"You will love my papa, won't you, Léa?"

It was raining. Léa covered her hair with an old Hermès scarf and pointed her bicycle in the direction of the Pont-Royal.

Having tried to get through to the Hôtel Régina with no success, she decided to go there without telling her aunts.

The streets of Paris were silent and deserted. Every now and then, she heard machine gun fire. On the bridge, young German sentinels let her pass. The *Jardin des Tuileries* had been reduced to a vast expanse of mud, pock-marked with huge craters dug around the tall trees. In the distance, the Obelisk and the Arc de Triomphe formed a cross against the dark sky. The Rue de Rivoli was completely blocked off, but an N.C.O. offered to go the hotel, which stood overlooking the statue of

Joan of Arc. When he returned, he told Léa that all of the women had left the hotel early that morning, and that no one knew where they were. Bewildered, Léa thanked him and set off again.

On the Quai Voltaire and the Quai de Conti, she passed Red Cross vehicles and carloads of F.F.I. singing the *Chant des Partisans*. Near the Rue Guénégaud, two young men wearing tricolor arm bands stepped into the path of her bicycle, grabbing the handlebars.

"Where d'ya think yer going?"

Léa found his familiarity irritating.

"None of your business!"

A slap sent her head flying backward.

"You'll answer nicely when I talk to you! Tougher chicks than you have smartened up after a trip to the barber."

"Let go of me."

"Watch it or we'll have to get nasty. You don't get through unless you show your pass," said a third man. "There are important leaders in the area. We have to keep a lookout for spies. So be a good girl and tell us where you're going."

Léa saw that it was useless to contradict them.

"I'm going to meet some friends who live at Place Saint-Michel."

"The barricade in the Rue de la Huchette?"

"Yes, the big apartment building on the corner."

"Léa, what are you doing here?"

"Pierrot, tell them to let me through."

"Leave her alone, she's my cousin."

"Okay, okay! We're just following orders."

"Come on, Léa. I want you to meet a friend of mine who's in charge of the barricade."

And what a barricade it was! Every folding bed in the neighborhood must have been requisitioned. Basements had been purged of old and useless objects; radiators and old bicycles, kiddy-cars and barrels, crates and bird cages, all held in place with sandbags. There was even an antique copper bathtub. A truck stripped of its doors and wheels formed the centerpiece of the barricade, which was fortified with fruit vendors' carts and dollies, providing convenient arm rests for the shooters. Léa and Pierrot hurried along a narrow path that had been cleared beside the parapet. Someone was firing from one of the buildings on the *Île de la Cité*.

"Everybody down!"

They took refuge in one of the rounded recesses of the bridge where two men were already crouching. Léa recognized the young man with the glasses from the *Café de Flore* and smiled. He recognized her and smiled back.

"It's coming from over there," he said, pointing in the direction of the City Hall.

"It's been like this since this morning," Pierrot told Léa. "But we think it's a lone sniper. Probably a militiaman. Hey, look, there are some friends over there on that roof!"

High above them, they saw the silhouettes of armed F.F.I. against the dark sky.

"Are you the one who lives at Place Dauphine?" demanded the man in charge of the barricade, addressing the friend of the young man with the glasses.

"Yes."

"What's your name?"

"Henri Berri."

"And yours?"

"Claude Mauriac."

Maybe he's the son of our neighbor back home, thought Léa. She didn't have time to enquire, for the man gestured to them that it was safe to go, and shouted to the F.F.I. to hold their fire.

The two young men ran toward Place Dauphine, and Léa and Pierrot went back behind the barricade. Pierrot was still pushing Léa's bicycle.

"You shouldn't be riding around like this, Léa. There are stray bullets everywhere. What did I tell you!"

On the Quai des Grands-Augustins, a woman had just been struck down. She dragged herself behind a tree for shelter. From the Rue des Grands-Augustins, two young men and a young woman in white came forward with a stretcher, waving the flag of the Red Cross. Taking no notice of the bullets, they lifted the woman on to the stretcher and hurried toward the makeshift infirmary that had been set up by Doctor Debré.

"Let's take the side streets. It's less dangerous."

The Rue de Savoie was quiet. A few F.F.I. stood guard outside an eighteenth-century hotel.

"The headquarters of one of the leaders of the Resistance," said Pierrot importantly.

"You have to help me find Sabine."

"That slut!"

His remark stopped Léa dead in her tracks.

"Do you realize what you're asking me to do?" Pierrot explained. "You're asking me to help a collaborator, someone who betrayed her country."

"Sabine is not a collaborator, nor is she a slut. She's a poor innocent girl who had the misfortune to fall in love with a German while our two countries were at war. That's not grounds for being shot."

"Maybe not shot, but she deserves to have her head shaved and to be put in prison."

"You're crazy! I'd rather die than have my head shaved."

"It grows back in," he sniggered, ducking a slap.

They heard laughter, applause, and shouts coming from the Rue Saint-André-des-Arts. A crowd was taunting a balding, middle-aged man whose pants had been torn off. He was a pitiful sight. His socks, one of which had a hole, were held up by garters, and he was carrying his pants and his shoes. Behind him was a round young woman in a flowered dress, sobbing, her head shaven and painted with a white swastika. Léa felt a wave of shame. Pierrot looked away. They stood silently, then Pierrot placed a hand on Léa's shoulder.

"Come on, let's go find her. We'll start at Colonel Rol's headquarters."

They never made it to the underground command post at Denfert-Rochereau.

Near the barricades at the intersection of the Boulevard Saint-Michel and the Boulevard Saint-Germain, which had been dubbed "Death Row," a grenade from a rooftop exploded at their feet. To Léa, who was walking slightly behind, it felt as though her head had been raked. Then, as though watching a film in slow motion, she saw Pierrot fly into the air and fall back to earth. As figures in white pressed around them, the sky and trees along the boulevard crashed down around her ears.

"There now, you'll be fine. You can go home."

Léa sat up, a little light-headed. A young doctor helped her down off the table. His features were pinched and drawn.

"Next!"

A man who had been wounded in the stomach was brought in.

"Where is my cousin?"

"I don't know," replied the doctor. "Ask at the front door."

Her dress stained with blood and her head wrapped in bandages, Léa wandered the corridors of the *Hôtel-Dieu* looking for Pierrot until after dark. No one knew what had become of him and the medics who had brought him to the hospital were nowhere to be found.

"Come back tomorrow," she was told.

Her heart heavy, she finally left. Taking pity on her, a policeman wearing an F.F.I. arm band guided her through the obstacle course in front of Notre-Dame Cathedral, taking his leave at the corner of the Rue Saint-Jacques and the Rue de la Huchette, where another member of the F.F.I. escorted her to the apartment on the Boulevard Saint-Michel.

Franck was alone in the apartment. Without a word, he took her to his room, drew a bath, and helped her to undress. While the bath was running, he made some tea which she drank, shivering, for the water was cold. After wrapping her in a big bathrobe, he put her to bed and held her hand until she fell asleep. They had not exchanged a single word.

"Bleed! Bleed! It's as good to bleed in August as it is in the month of May!"

The cry heard on August 24, 1572, Saint Bartholomew's Massacre, haunted Léa's dreams.

As she was preparing Charles's breakfast that morning, she

had looked up at the calendar and noticed that it was Saint Bartholomew's Day. This had brought to mind Brantôme's book on the life of Charles IX, which she had read after devouring *La Dame de Montsoreau*, *Les Quarante-Cinq*, and *La Reine Margot* by Alexandre Dumas. It was there that she first read the horrible reference to blood-letting. Now, as she slept, the medieval and modern-day massacres merged into one. There were Germans and assassins in the hire of Francois de Guise, women with shorn heads and Amiral de Coligny, the F.F.I. and the future King Henry IV, corpses floating in the Seine and bodies scorched by flame throwers. She even saw Charles IX standing at the window of his room in the *Palais du Louvre*, firing arrows from a crossbow.

"Wake up! Wake up!"

Her face nearly as white as her bandages, Léa opened her eyes.

"What is it?"

Franck had lost his usual composure and was twirling the knobs of the radio excitedly.

"Listen!"

"Parisians, it is with great joy ... that we announce the liberation of your city. ... General Jacques Philippe Leclerc's Second Armored Division has entered Paris. In a few moments, they will be at the Hôtel de Ville. *Please stay tuned. In a few moments, you will hear the voice you have all been waiting for. What great news! We are broadcasting live ... under very difficult conditions ... we have not eaten in three days. Some of our comrades have just come back from last-minute preparations for the arrival of Leclerc's troops. ... We may be drunk but if we are, we're drunk with joy! And happiness! It's so good to be home again!*

Léa got out of bed and went over to where Franck was standing. He embraced her passionately.

"I have just ... I've just been told that at 0915 this morning, at Poterne des Peupliers, a column of French, Spanish, and

Moroccan soldiers was sighted. Where is Poterne des Peupliers, anyway? Gentilly! No, Issy! Here they are! Here they come! Leading the troops ... two armored cars. ... They're stopping in front of the Hôtel de Ville. General de Gaulle must be in one of the cars. ... What we do know for sure is that the Allies are at the gates of Paris ... it is very likely that General de Gaulle is there. Open your windows wide. Hang out banners! I have just received a telephone call from the Secretary General of Communications. The Secretary General has asked me to ask all priests listening to the broadcast to please start ringing their bells. I repeat: this is Schaeffer broadcasting from the Radio of the French Nation; we have been broadcasting for the past four days under the German Occupation. I have been instructed by the Secretary General of Communications of the Provisional Government of the Republic to ask any priests who may be listening at this time, who can be notified immediately ... my instructions are ... to ask them to begin ringing their bells to announce the arrival of the Allies in Paris."

Franck and Léa embraced each other again, laughing and crying. Then they ran to the window. Around Place Saint-Michel, shutters were flung open and lights went on. The blackouts and the passive defence measures were over! Let there be light! People ran into the square from all directions, kissing and hugging one another. Then, over radios at full volume, came the *La Marseillaise*. Everyone in the square stood still and joined in.

In the western sky, a huge fire tinged the heavy clouds red.

Hearing the voices of the people in the square, Léa and Franck began to sing without realizing it, holding hands so tightly that they became numb.

Suddenly, a church bell began to ring, faintly at first, then stronger and stronger on this, the last day of the Occupation. Soon the bells of Saint-Séverin began chiming, joined by Saint-Julien-le-Pauvre, Saint-Germain-des-Prés, Sacré-Coeur, Saint-Étienne-du-Mont, Saint-Germain-l'Auxerrois, Saint-Sulpice, Sainte-Geneviève, and Saint-Eustache. Then, at last, came the thundering drone of Notre-Dame. Paris was in a state of delirium.

At 2122, Captain Raymond Dronne drew up in front of the *Hôtel de Ville* in his jeep nicknamed "Kill the Bastards" with fifteen half-tracks and three Sherman tanks, Montmirail, Champaubert, and Romilly. One hundred and thirty men set foot on the pavement of the capital for the first time in four years.

The radio announcer, overcome with emotion, began to quote from Victor Hugo:

Wake up! Wake up! Cast off your shame!
May France reclaim her former name!
May Paris know her former fame!

In the square, people danced around a huge bonfire. Suddenly, shots rang out. Everyone froze, then began screaming and running.

Letting go of each other's hands, Léa and Franck heard the announcer's voice, stammering now.

"We may have been a little hasty. . . . It's not over yet. . . . We suggest that you close your shutters. . . . Close your shutters. . . . We don't want anyone to get hurt. . . ."

One by one, windows darkened again, shutters closed, fear returned.

"We would remind you of the passive defence measures issued by Colonel Rol. We ask you to please show your happiness in some other way."

All of the bells ceased their chiming but one, which rang out in defiance of the cannon at Longchamp. Then it too stopped, as did the cannon and the shooting at the *Hôtel de Ville.*

It was dark. All around the *Palais du Luxembourg* and the *Odéon* dark figures, heavily laden, headed for shelter underground. The liberation of Paris was not over.

During the night, there was a violent storm. Léa stood by the window of the apartment, watching the clouds race across the sky and listening to the thunder, following by flashes of lightning. For a brief moment, the Pont-Neuf was visible. It looked like a toy bridge placed across the black ribbon of the Seine, its smooth surface now troubled by heavy drops of rain.

Chapter Eighteen

At eight o'clock the next morning, Laure rushed into the room where Léa lay sleeping.

"They're coming! They're coming!"

Léa sat up, trembling.

"Who?"

"General Leclerc's troops! They're in Paris! They're at the *Porte d'Orléans*. Get up. What's wrong? Are you hurt?"

"No, I'm fine. Have you heard from Pierrot or Sabine?"

"No, I thought you had."

Léa began to cry without making a sound.

"Don't cry. We'll find them. Come on, get up, let's go see."

A *fifi*, as members of the F.F.I. were now called, poked his head around the door.

"They're in the Rue Saint-Jacques!" he cried.

"Did you hear that? They're in the Rue Saint-Jacques. Hurry up!"

"He's dead, I just know it."

"Who are you talking about?"

"He's dead, I tell you."

"*Who* is dead?"

"Pierrot."

"Pierrot!"

Franck knocked on the door, which was ajar.

"Don't stand in front of the window," he said, pushing Laure into the middle of the room. "You could get hit by a stray bullet."

"Have you heard from Pierrot?" asked Léa, getting up.

"No. I went to several hospitals, but none of the wounded picked up in the Latin Quarter answers your cousin's description."

"Dead or alive, he's got to be somewhere."

"What happened?" asked Laure.

"Léa and your cousin were hit by a grenade yesterday on Death Row. Léa was taken to *Hôtel-Dieu*. We don't know where your cousin is."

They fell silent.

Franck had changed in recent days. He seemed older now, having lost whatever remained of his carefree innocence watching people his own age—friends and enemies—lose their lives.

"Don't worry, we'll find him."

None of them believed it for a moment.

"General Leclerc's troops are coming down the Rue Saint-Jacques," said Laure at last. "Let's go."

Léa washed quickly, taking off the dressing and leaving only a small bandage. Her dress was badly stained and torn. Franck went to find something for her to wear in his mother's cupboard and returned with an armful of multi-colored dresses.

"They're probably a bit too big for you, but they should be all right with a belt."

Léa chose a short-sleeved Jeanne Lafaurie dress with a small floral print in blue. She tied a blue scarf under her chin to hide the bandage and put on her white platform-soled sandals.

It was a beautiful day. From all directions, people began making their way toward the Rue Saint-Jacques, women wearing robes thrown over their nightgowns, men who had not taken the time to shave, young mothers carrying babies, children who ran back and forth between the adults' legs, veterans from the Great War wearing their medals, students, workers, store clerks. . . .

The Rue Saint-Jacques was an immense river of joy, completely engulfing Colonel Billotte's Sherman tanks, that were now decked with bouquets and flags. Hands reached out to touch the tanks. Young women climbed up and embraced the soldiers, taking no notice of their filthy condition. Laughing and crying, people waved and blew kisses, handing their children up to the soldiers.

"Bravo! Long live France! Thank you! Long live General de Gaulle! Bravo!"

Laure clambered on to an armored car and kissed the driver, who protested, laughing. Franck applauded wildly and called out to the soldiers.

Léa felt strangely detached, almost indifferent to the joyous tumult. She noted the names of the tanks as they filed past. Austerlitz, Verdun, Saint-Cyr, El Alamein, Mort-Homme, Exupérance. Exupérance? Standing in the turret, a grimy-faced officer was waving to the crowd. Léa caught a glimpse of his face.

"Laurent!"

Her cry was lost in the roar of the engines and the shouting. She tried to reach him, but was accidently struck in the head and fell back. A young F.F.I. saw what happened and managed to pull her away from the quickly-moving crowd.

She was taken to a little cafe in the Rue de la Huchette.

"Here, sweetheart, drink this. You'll feel better in no time. I've been saving it for the victory party!"

She was handed a tiny glass of amber liquid, which she drank all at once. It exploded in her mouth and, almost instantly, she felt better.

"Nothing like a shot of Armagnac to put the color back in your cheeks, I always say. A little more?"

So Laurent was in Paris! When she saw him, her heart had begun to pound as it had when she thought she was madly in love with him. Perhaps she still was. Perhaps it was the Armagnac. She felt as though she were in a pink fog. Then, suddenly, it lifted. Shots rang out.

"Everybody inside! Quick! Watch out for the snipers!"

As if by magic, the street was suddenly empty. Léa was clear-headed now. Laurent was in Paris, but Camille was dead. At the thought of having to break this news to him, her knees nearly gave way again. Someone else would have to tell him, she thought. Her cowardice made her feel ashamed and she blushed. No. She was the one to tell him. Camille would not have wanted it any other way.

Tanks had assembled in the square in front of Notre-Dame, but she did not see the one named Exupérance. A column of armored vehicles advanced along the quay. Parisians watched and commented.

"Will ya look at those machines? If we'd had them in '40, we never would've lost the war."

"You sure they're French? Look at their uniforms."

"Sure I'm sure! That's the American uniform. Better than puttees any day!"

"I don't ... I don't see any French uniforms."

"Who gives a shit what uniform they're wearing? English, American, Russian—same difference!—what counts is they're here! Long live de Gaulle! Long live France!"

Léa walked along the quay, oblivious to the jostling crowd, so tired that she could not put her thoughts in order. Laurent is alive, she thought, but where is Pierrot? I can't find Laure and Franck. I must tell Aunt Lisa and Aunt Albertine. Have they heard from Sabine? Did Charles get any milk today? Laurent is back! How do I tell him about Camille? Why are all these people clapping? Ah, yes, General Leclerc's troops have arrived. Laurent is with them. And François, where is he?

"Sorry!" A man with a camera on his shoulder had just backed into Léa.

She had arrived at Place Saint-Michel. She went upstairs to Franck's apartment, but neither he nor Laure were there. Fifteen *fifis* had taken over the apartment. Léa was unable to get their attention; in their excitement, they were oblivious to everything. The telephone, which had worked throughout the past few turbulent days, now seemed to be out of order, yet she had to leave some sort of message. Taking a tube of lipstick from Franck's mother's room, she wrote on every mirror in the apartment, "I've gone back to the Rue de l'Université. Laurent, Sabine, and Pierrot may be there."

The tanks were now at Place Saint-Michel. A wildly excited crowd greeted them with cries and applause. Léa made her way over to one of the tanks. Climbing up on one of the wheels, she pulled herself to the turret.

"Do you know where Lieutenant d'Argilat is?"

"No, I haven't seen Captain d'Argilat since *Porte d'Orléans*." In the middle of the tumult, an order was barked.

"Get down, we're going to attack the Senate."

"Please, if you see him, tell him that Exupérance–"

"That's the name of his tank!"

"Yes, I know. Tell him that Exupérance is in Paris, at her aunts'."

"Okay, but give me a kiss."

Léa obliged good-naturedly.

"You won't forget?"

"Is he your boyfriend? He's lucky to have someone like you. I promise I'll tell him. Unless, of course, I get killed."

How silly, thought Léa. Of course, if he gets killed. . . .

She jumped down and watched the tanks maneuver. To the sound of thunderous applause from the people lining the street, the tanks entered the narrow Rue Saint-André-des-Arts, passing shops with their metal doors rolled down. Across a few of the doors, someone had written in chalk, "Watch out! If you see F.F.I. Vehicle No 3, open fire. It is carrying four militiamen."

The column of tanks turned left toward the *Odéon*. Léa turned in to the Rue de Buci. It's only noon, she thought looking at a clock whose hands had stopped. Cafes began to open their doors again. She stopped and had a shandy at the bistro in the Rue Bourbon-le-Château where the regulars were discussing the morning's events. One of them claimed to have seen American tanks and trucks on the Pont Neuf.

A few people had hoisted tricolor flags at their windows. They stood on their doorsteps chatting, from time to time glancing anxiously up at the rooftops.

The door of the apartment in the Rue de l'Université was wide open. The front hall was in an uncustomary state of disorder. Oh, my God! Charles! thought Léa, running to her room. But he was sitting on her bed, calming turning the pages of a Bécassine album that had belonged to her mother. When he saw her, his tired little face lit up.

"You came back! I was afraid you wouldn't come back."

"How can you say that, darling. I would never leave you alone. Have you had lunch?"

"Yes, but I didn't like it. It's nice out. Can we go for a walk now?"

"Not today, sweetie pie. It's still wartime."

"I know. When you were gone, I heard guns and people shouting. Then Aunt Albertine went out. She was crying."

Pierrot's dead, thought Léa.

"I'll be right back. I'm going to see Aunt Lisa."

She found Lisa and Estelle crying in the kitchen.

"There you are!" cried her aunt.

"What's wrong? What happened?"

They began crying even harder. Their mouths opened but not a sound came out.

"Would one of you please tell me what's wrong?"

"Mademoiselle Sabine," Estelle managed to blurt out.

Léa suddenly felt a chill.

"What about Sabine? What happened?"

"She was ... arrested."

"When?"

Estelle shrugged her shoulders.

"The woman from the creamery in the Rue du Bac came to tell us," Lisa blurted out. "Albertine left right away, without even putting on a hat."

Under any other circumstances, Léa would have found this remark amusing, but the fact that her aunt had not taken the time to put on a hat meant that something was seriously wrong.

"Where did she go?"

"To the square in front of the church."

"Very long ago?"

"About half an hour ago."

"I'm going. Keep an eye on Charles."

"No, don't go!" cried Lisa, clinging to Léa's sleeve.

Without a word, she pried herself free and went out.

Chapter Nineteen

It was a beautiful day and there was a feeling of celebration in the air. Pretty girls in short summer dresses, their hair decorated with cockades and little tricolor flags, overtook Léa, laughing. The elegant women one normally saw at church on Sunday had donned less somber garb. Old ladies walked arm-in-arm with their companions, a new spring in their step. All were hurrying toward the square.

Although Léa expected to see curious onlookers, she stopped dead in her tracks when she reached the square: it was packed.

On the steps of the church, where other spectacles had been played out in other times, a melodrama was unfolding before an unruly, irreverent crowd, egging the players on with gestures and cries. The set could not have been simpler: a few benches, a chair with a straw seat and, affixed to the door of the church with a knife, a sign that read in large black letters: "FREE HAIRCUTS!" The action had already begun when Léa arrived, and the actors were throwing themselves into their parts. The master of ceremonies, a heavy-set man wearing an F.F.I. arm band, read out the crimes of the accused in a booming voice:

"Ladies and Gentlemen! Here we have the Michaud woman. She denounced her husband to the Gestapo. Does she deserve to be spared?"

"No! No!" screamed the spectators.

"Wellll?"

"Take it all off!"

A roar of laughter went up from the crowd.

On the makeshift stage, two members of the "people's tribunal" forced the woman into the chair. The "barber" leapt forward, brandishing a huge pair of tailor's shears which he twirled and snapped open and shut around the woman's head, launching into a parody of Maurice Chevalier:

> *"Avez-vous vu le noveau chapeau de Zozo,*
> *C'est un chapeau un chapeau rigolo."*

> (*"Well, have you seen Zozo's new hat?*
> *It's a brand new hat, just fancy that!"*)

Near Léa was a large woman wearing a white smock from a creamery or a butcher's shop. She was clinging to the arm of a fireman, choking with laughter.

"Jesus! I'm going to wet my pants if he doesn't stop! I'm going to wet them for sure! Ooops! What'd I tell ya'!"

Waves of laughter worked their way through the crowd, making Léa nauseous. Clumps of hair were tossed back and forth, like the tail or the ear of the bull in the arena. The cries of the crowd were no less bloodthirsty, as hands reached out to catch the wretched trophies.

The "barber" had finished cropping the woman's hair and was reaching for a razor.

Her face haggard, smeared with spit and tears, "the Michaud woman" was getting what she deserved for denouncing her husband to the Gestapo—or so the crowd thought. She claimed that he had joined the *maquis* in Corrèze to avoid the labor camps, but what did that matter? Hadn't a neighbor woman seen her talking to a German soldier who had asked for directions?

Léa could feel the cold metal of the razor on her scalp. Some of the women standing nearby had fallen silent. One wiped away a tear; perhaps she was now sympathetic to the poor, humiliated creature, her tiny head emerging from a flowered dress. Around her neck was a hand-made sign on which had been written, in crude lettering, THIS SLUT DENOUNCED HER HUSBAND.

Two men pulled her out of the chair and pushed her over to the bench to join those who had already been shaved. The women moved over to make room for her and she sat down beside a woman rocking a baby in her arms.

Léa searched the faces of the unshorn women for Sabine.

Next, it was the turn of a tall, elegant woman.

"Ladies and gentlemen, feast your eyes on this one! She looks so fine you'd trust her with your little brother! Well, let me tell you something. She'd spread her legs for the Krauts before she spread them for one of her own! Wellll?"

"Take it all off!"

It was a game, a farce, a spoof, a medieval mystery play presented for the edification of the flock; however, this was not the mystery put on Valenciennes in 1547, for which spectators paid two farthings or six pieces of silver. It was France on the morning of its liberation, absurd and magnificent, treacherous and magnanimous, courageous and idiotic, heroic and criminal.

The woman was not crying. She sat very erect, her face proud and pale. A lock of hair fell on to her hands which lay clasped in her lap. Her fingers closed over it. The crowd fell silent. It had expected cries and tears, but she smiled disdainfully. As her fingers released the lock of hair, a murmur of disappointment could be heard.

No doubt angered by her composure, the "barber" began to hack away at her hair, cutting her. Blood ran down her cheek. The crowd let out a long sigh.

Léa clenched her fists and looked away. Wasn't there anyone who would put an end to this abomination? Luckily, Sabine wasn't there, and yet. . . .

The woman on the bench who was holding a child lifted her head. She looked vaguely like Sabine emerging from the Garonne after a swim. Léa's heart beat furiously. That couldn't be her! Thank God, Maman and Papa didn't live to see this, she thought. It would have broken their hearts. Léa felt a hand on her arm. It was Albertine. The old woman's face showed her horror at the spectacle. Léa put her arms around her aunt's shoulders, surprised at her own adult gesture and her aunt's frailty.

When the razor stopped at last, the woman stood up with such a look of disdain that the crowd began grumbling and let loose a few insults. She sat down on the bench with the other women, ignoring the blood dripping on to her dress.

Another woman was dragged, screaming and crying, to the chair, where she fell to her knees.

"Please! Please! I won't do it again. Please don't do it!"

The scissors hovered menacingly over her head.

"Stop! That's enough!"

A young man wearing plus-fours and carrying a rifle marched up the steps. The "barber" must have known the man, for he grabbed a handful of hair defiantly and said:

"Let us do what we have to do."

With that, he cut off the hair.

The young man brought the barrel of his rifle down on the man's hand, making him drop the shears.

"You have no right to do this. If these women are guilty, they will be tried in a court of law. You must hand them over to the police."

Uniformed policemen finally emerged from the police station wedged between the church and an apartment building.

"All right! Break it up! You can go home now! Rest assured these women will receive the punishment they deserve."

Gradually, the crowd thinned and the policemen took the women into the police station. The members of the "people's tribunal" adjusted their arm bands, cartridge belts, and revolvers, sniggered, and walked off. Soon the square was deserted except for Léa and her aunt who had not moved. They marched across the square.

The tiny station was in a state of total confusion. The police had no idea what to do with the women, who were either crying or prostrate. The young man in the plus-fours was making a telephone call.

212

"The Prefecture is sending a van over to take them—"

"Where? The *Petite Roquette*?" asked one of the policemen.

"No, the *Vélodrôme d'Hiver*. The F.F.I. will guard them."

"That's funny!" said another one. "That's where they put the Jews!"

Léa remembered what Sarah Mulstein had said in her letter about the way in which people were rounded up at the *Vélodrôme d'Hiver*. She turned to stare at the man who thought this was "funny."

"Go home, ladies. You have no business here."

"I came to get my niece, sir."

The men turned to look at the white-haired woman who had spoken so firmly and calmly. She had a lot of nerve!

"I'm afraid that's impossible. These women have been accused of collaborating with the enemy. Their cases have to be heard by a competent authority."

"Sabine!"

One of the women lifted her head, blank-faced.

"Sabine, it's me, Léa! It's all over. We've come to take you home."

"You can't do that, young lady. This woman was arrested in the company of mistresses of German officers."

"I never went with a German," cried the Michaud woman. "We came across these women in the street. I was put with them by mistake."

"Shut up! The court will decide that. Please leave, ladies."

"Please, sir, this woman is my niece. I'll answer for her. I have known her ever since she was a small child."

"You must leave now."

"Surely you're not going to put her in prison with a child!"

Perplexed, the young man looked at Sabine and her son, then at Albertine.

"I don't know about the child. . . . I'll let you take him. . . . that is, if she agrees."

Pierre had recognized Léa and was holding out his little arms.

"Do you want him to come with us, Sabine?"

Without a word, Sabine handed her the child.

213

"Leave your names and addresses," said the oldest police-man.

"When may we see her?"

"I have no idea, ma'am. You'll have to wait. We'll let you know."

Sabine held out her hand.

"What do you want?" asked Léa.

Of course, I should have thought of it, Léa said to herself, taking off the blue scarf and knotting it ever so tenderly under her sister's chin.

Chapter Twenty

Léa accompanied Aunt Albertine and Sabine's son, Pierre, back to the Rue de l'Université, then hurried back outside. She wanted to be alone. She needed to sort through the things that had happened. Most of all, she wanted to find Laurent.

As far as the Church of Saint-Germain-des-Prés, Boulevard Saint-Germain was filled with people strolling back and forth, but once past the Rue Bonaparte, the mood changed. The strollers gave way to groups wearing arm bands and carrying rifles and young people in Red Cross uniforms. Housewives scurried along the Rue de Buci, hoping to find a green grocer that was still open. One woman stopped Léa, placing a hand on the handlebars of her bicycle.

"Don't take the Rue de Seine. The Krauts have been firing mortars from the Senate for the past three days. They go right down the Rue de Seine. Several people have been killed or wounded already."

"Thanks, I'm trying to get to Place Saint-Michel. What route do you suggest I take?"

"If I were you, I'd stay away. It's too dangerous. Leclerc's troops are preparing to attack the *Palais du Luxembourg.*"

As if on cue, a mortar exploded in front of the fish store in the Rue de Seine, breaking the few remaining windows and hitting three passersby in the face and legs.

Now walking her bicycle, Léa turned back. She stopped in a little square outside the former archdiocese. All of the benches were occupied by people sleeping. A group of kids sat in the sand box, passing around a bottle. Léa sat to one side, her back against a tree. She closed her eyes and tried to put her thoughts in order, but her mind was filled with horrible, violent images. As it to banish them, she shook her head then began banging it against the tree, unaware that she was crying.

"Stop! You'll hurt yourself!"

One of the kids put out a grubby little hand to stop her.

"Here, have a swig. You'll feel better."

Léa grabbed the bottle and drank so fast that the wine trickled down her neck.

"Not bad for a chick!" said the kid, who couldn't have been more than fifteen, as he reclaimed the nearly empty bottle. "Nothing like some red to make you feel good. It's burgundy. We ripped it off at Nicolas's. Want a cigarette?"

Léa nodded.

She inhaled deeply, again and again, feeling herself become slightly drunk.

"Feeling better? Good. Here's some water from the fountain. Wash your face."

She did as she was told.

"Why are you crying? Did you lose your boyfriend? Your father? You don't want to talk? Okay! Here, have another swig. . . . You're nice looking, you know that?"

The admiration in his voice made her smile.

"And you're even nicer looking when you smile! Right, guys?"

"Right!" his friends said in chorus, laughing and punching one another. The only girl in the group turned away.

"Your friend is jealous."

"Rita! Don't worry about her. What's your name?"

"Léa. What about you?"

"Marcel, but they call me Cécel. And these are my good buddies, Alphonse, Polo, Vonvon, Fanfan, and the fat one over there—"

"Hey, I'm not fat!"

They all laughed, including Léa.

"He doesn't like it when we call him fat. But he isn't thin either, even with the shortages. His name is Minou, and that's Rita over there."

Each of the kids shook hands except Rita, who nodded her head.

"We're all from the Thirteenth Arrondissement. We haven't been home since the 19th."

"What about your parents? They must be worried."

"Don't worry about them. They're not worried about us! Last we heard they were playing war games over by Place de la République. We've been working as couriers for Colonel Rol and Colonel Fabien."

"So you probably know my cousin, Pierrot Delmas. He's from Bordeaux," said Léa.

"Maybe. There's lots of us."

"He was wounded yesterday on Boulevard Saint-Michel. Since then, nobody has seen him."

"Hey, don't start crying again. We'll look for him, okay? What does he look like?"

"He's about my height, he has dark brown hair and blue eyes."

"What's he wearing?"

"Khaki pants, a blue and green plaid shirt, a cotton wind-breaker, an arm band. And he has a revolver."

"Vonvon, go down into the sewers and see what you can find out about this guy. We'll meet you-know-where tonight. Rita, you check all the hospitals on the Left Bank and Minou, you check the Right Bank. We'll meet same time, same place. Understood?"

"Okay, boss."

"Are you the boss?"

"You better believe it! Fanfan, I want you to go to the Rue de l'Abbé-de-l'Epée with Polo and see if Fabien needs us. While you're at it, say hello to my brother."

"I doubt if I'll see him. He's probably fighting over by the Senate."

"Is your brother a policeman?"

"No, he's a welder. They were going to send him to a labor

217

camp in Germany in '43, so he joined the *maquis* in Haute-Saône. That's where he met Fabien also known as Albert, also known as Captain Henri, and, after he escaped, Commandant Patrie. For a while, he distributed pamphlets, acted as a lookout, delivered messages. Starting in September, he took part in every sabotage operation in the region. With the Liberté group, he blew up the lock in Conflandey and attacked the German command post near Semondans. Three German soldiers were killed. He helped blow up railroads, bridges, locomotives—all on Fabien's orders. Fabien announced that he's going to take Luxembourg today. And he will, you'll see. Especially now that Leclerc's here to help him."

Cécel's chatter helped to distract Léa.

"I'm starving," said Alphonse. "Let's grab a bite."

"Good idea, are you coming with us?"

"I don't know."

"Don't think too hard, it's not good for you. Nothing like some grub for putting things in perspective."

"You're right. Where are we going?"

"Rue du Dragon. This friend of my dad's is a waitress in a bistro there. The lady who runs the place kinda likes me and the food's not too bad. Take your bike with you, otherwise it'll get ripped off."

Cécel's father's friend led them to a little table under a spiral staircase. She immediately brought them sausages covered with a thick puree of spit peas and a carafe of wine. After two mouthfuls, Léa put her fork down.

"Not hungry?"

"No," replied Léa, emptying her glass.

She drank three or four glasses of wine, watched closely by Cécel and Alphonse.

They continued drinking a lethal mixture of wine, liqueurs, and aperitifs. At approximately five o'clock, Fanfan rushed in.

"They surrendered. . . . It's over. . . . Choltitz signed the surrender terms . . ." he gasped, trying to catch his breath.

"Hurray!"

"So is the war over?"

"Tell us all about it! Who signed?"

"Get this! We signed too!"

"Give me a break!"

"I'm serious! As Commander of the French Forces of the Interior for the *Île de France*, Rol signed along with General Leclerc and General von Choltitz."

"Hey! Let's celebrate."

"Don't you think you've have enough to drink already?"

"You've never had enough when you're celebrating a victory."

"I wouldn't speak too soon. They're still fighting in the *Jardin du Luxembourg*, in the barracks at Place de la République, at the *Palais-Bourbon*, in some of the subway stations, and probably on the outskirts of the city."

"I'm not worried. Fabien's gonna cream them. What else did you find out?"

"Leclerc's tanks have control of the Rue de Vaugirard. The F.F.I. and the Moroccan Cavalry Corps have entered the *Jardin du Luxembourg* by way of the Rue Auguste-Comte. Cars with loudspeakers from the Prefecture are driving around the neighborhood announcing that the Allies are going to start bombing at 1900 if the Germans don't surrender. The curfew is at 1835, but I don't think they'll have to send planes in. Are you coming?"

"We can't just leave her like that."

"I'm coming with you," mumbled Léa, trying to stand up.

"Are you crazy? In your condition?"

"I want to fight with the tanks!"

"Come on you guys. You're not going to hang around for some chick who's drunk are you?"

"I'm not drunk," Léa mumbled, ". . . just had a few drinks to celebrate the arrival of our heroes."

"You go. I'll keep an eye on her," said the waitress. "Come on, honey, I'm going to put you to bed."

"Okay, but before I go, I'm going to have a little drink."

"Take good care of her, okay?"

"Trust me, Cécel. The way you're talking, you'd think you were in love with her. I can think of one person who's not going to be too happy about this!"

Shrugging his shoulders, he left the bistro.

With a great deal of difficulty, the waitress managed to get Léa up the stairs and into a little room that served as a staff room and storage area. As soon as her head hit the pillow, she fell asleep, snoring softly.

Chapter Twenty-One

Léa slept until evening. Through the half-open door, she could hear people talking and shouting in the bistro downstairs. She sat up, her head pounding with a migraine.

"What am I doing here?" she wondered aloud.

There were footsteps on the stairs. The door was thrown open, and Rita and Alphonse entered the room. Wild-eyed, Rita rushed at her.

"Why did you let him go? Why?" she screamed, raising a fist to hit Léa.

She tried to duck out of the way, but not fast enough. The blow made her head, still in bandages, pound even harder. Groaning, she tried to stand up, holding her head in her hands. The girl grabbed her by the hair and began slapping her.

"Stop!" said Alphonse.

"Get lost! I'm going to make this bitch pay!"

"Stop it! Cécel wouldn't have wanted you to do that," he continued, trying to restrain her.

Slowly, her hand released its grip on Léa's hair, and fell to her side. She looked at Léa, lying on the bed, then at Alphonse, as though trying to make sense of what was happening.

Awkwardly, Alphonse tried to console her.

"It's not her fault. Cécel went crazy when he saw his brother go down."

"I wish he'd stayed here and slept with her," she blubbered.
Léa sat up and looked at them, not understanding.
"What's going on?"
Alphonse blew his nose loudly.
"Cécel got killed in the Rue de Tournon."
"No!"
Rite looked her straight in the eyes.
"It's true and your cousin's dead, too!" she screamed.
"Shut up, Rita!"
"Why should I be the only one to suffer!"
"How do you know?"
"One of Colonel Rol's lieutenants told us," answered
Alphonse. "Your cousin was taken to Val-de-Grâce. That's
where they found him. You should go home."
"What happened to Cécel?"
"We had just arrived where they were fighting. In the Rue
Garancière, we ran across saw Cécel's brother, Clément. He
yelled at us to take cover, but Cécel didn't want to, so we followed them right up the Rue de Vaugirard. The fighting was
incredible. This Kraut came out from behind a tank in flames
and started firing in all directions. Clément got hit in the legs.
He started crawling away but the guy just took aim, emptied
his bullets into him, and headed for the Senate. Cécel went
crazy. I tried to hold him back, but he got away. He picked up
his brother's rifle and went after the soldier. The guy just
stopped and turned around. I think he was smiling. The both
took aim. Cécel got him in the face. He got Cécel everywhere.
And that's how it happened."

The three of them just stood there with their arms at their
sides, crying like little lost children for their fifteen-year-old
friend, the kid brother of Gavroche, who had just died on a
fine summer's day in 1944, the day that Paris was liberated.

Rita and Alphonse dried their tears, and without a word,
went out. Alone again, Léa lay on the bed sobbing. She saw
Pierrot's face, then Cécel's. She heard their laughter.

"They're dead! They're dead!" she sobbed, burying her face
in the pillow.

222

Laughing and drinking, Parisians began to dismantle the barricades. The air was fine and warm. On the Pont-Neuf, people began dancing to the music of an accordionist. Their hair upswept in elaborate hairdos or falling loosely on their shoulders, young women spun around and around in the arms of the F.F.I. and the Leclerc Division, out on late passes. The Rue Mazarine, the Rue Dauphine, and the Rue de l'Ancienne-Comédie were strewn with broken glass. All along the quays and at Place Saint-Michel were the charred remains of cars, trucks, and tanks, brutal reminders of the violent fighting that had taken place. Here and there, tiny bouquets had been placed on the ground, marking the spot where some man, woman or child had been struck down. Some knelt before the stains.

Léa made her way along the Quai des Grands-Augustins, trailing her fingers along the stone parapet and the wooden boxes of the booksellers, still warm from the sun. At Place Saint-Michel, tanks maneuvred to the delight of the crowd. Leaning against the parapet, she watched them go by, desperately unhappy. In the late afternoon sun, her hair was flaming red. The soldiers waved, beckoning to her to join the other girls on the tanks.

"Léa!"

In spite of the din, she heard her name called and looked around to see who it could be.

"Léa!"

A soldier was waving excitedly from one of the tanks.

"Laurent!"

She fought her way through the crowd. He had his driver stop the tank and held out his hand to help her up. Oblivious to the looks of the other men, he held her close, murmuring her name over and over. Léa could not quite believe it. What was she doing here, standing on a tank heading toward the *Hôtel de Ville*, before a magnificent sunset, in the arms of a soldier who smelled overpoweringly of gunpowder and oil and dirt and sweat. Laurent! He was telling her how happy he was to see her, how beautiful she was on this, the happiest of

all days, how happy he would be to see his wife and son. . . .
Léa wondered what on earth he was saying, why he was talking about such unpleasant things. They were alive, laughing
and crying in each other's arms. She felt a long wail rising to
her lips, like a wild animal trying to escape from a cage. How
do I tell him? I'll wait . . . I'll tell him tomorrow. . . .

At Châtelet, the American tanks joined Leclerc's tanks to the
cries and applause of the crowds.

"Long Live America!"

"*Vive la France!*"

"*Vive de Gaulle!*"

Léa found herself swept up in the enthusiasm of the crowd
and clung ever more tightly to Laurent.

The tank stopped near the Tour Saint-Jacques, where Captain Buis was standing.

"Well, well d'Argilat. I'm glad to see you're having a good
time!"

"It's not what you think it is, Buis."

"I'm not thinking anything, I'm just observing."

Laurent jumped down and held out his arms for Léa to slide
down.

All around them, couples were forming. Their laughter became shriller, their words softer, their gazes steadier, every
gesture more precise. They were thinking about celebrating
the liberation of Paris in the simplest and most natural way
imaginable—by making love.

Léa slowly looked up at Laurent.

"Camille is dead."

The world came crashing down around Laurent's ears.
Everything exploded then went dead. Cold, faint colors
outlined objects and figures that moved with unreal slowness.
It was as though a heavy frost had fallen over Paris, awakening
the dead. But they had not come to see the French soldier in
an American uniform standing under the Tour Saint-Jacques,
leaning against a tank bearing the name of a long-forgotten
saint and crying. They were simply passing by, roused, perhaps, by the music and the sighs that made Paris, that night,
the city of love.

Léa watched the man she had loved suffer. She felt great pity, but was unable to help him, so great was her own suffering and despair.

"Charles is all right."

That was all she could find to say.

"What's up, d'Argilat? Bad news?," asked Captain Buis, laying a hand on Laurent's shoulder.

Laurent straightened up, not trying to hide the tears that ran down his dirty face.

"I've just been told that my wife is dead."

"I'm very sorry. How did she die?"

"I don't know," he said, looking at Léa.

"She died when the Germans and the Militia attacked a farm occupied by the *maquis*."

They fell silent, cut off from the joyous celebrations around them. Buis was the first to speak.

"Come on, he's asking for you."

"I'm on my way. Léa, where is my son?"

"He's with me. We're staying at my aunts' in the Rue de l'Université."

"I'll try to get permission to come by tomorrow. Kiss him for me."

"Good-bye, mademoiselle. I'll take care of him."

Exhausted and grief-stricken, her head throbbing, Léa walked along the Rue Jacob, jostled by passersby drunk from the wine and the celebrating. She arrived in front of her aunts' building, went inside, and sat on the bottom step in the dark, too weak to climb the stairs. The light went on. "The power is back on," she thought, climbing the stairs and leaning against the bell.

"All right! All right! I'm coming! Mademoiselle Léa, it's you! Don't you have your key? What's wrong? Good grief! Mademoiselle Lisa! Mademoiselle Albertine!"

"What's wrong, Estelle?"

"Léa!" exclaimed Aunt Albertine. "Quick, Lisa and Laure, give me a hand."

They laid her on the sofa in the living room. Her pallor and ice-cold hands sent Lisa into a panic.

Albertine bathed her temples with cool water. Gradually, her features relaxed and she opened her eyes. What a terrible dream! Who was this child that Laure was holding? Why was she crying? Where was the baby's mother?

"Oh my God!"

At the sound of her cry, all four women jumped. The baby woke up and Charles came running into the room, sleepy-eyed. He climbed on to the sofa and hugged her.

"It's all right, Léa, I'm here."

"He's been crying and calling her name all day," Estelle whispered to Lisa, "and now he's comforting her. What a funny kid!"

Léa brought her hands to her forehead.

"Estelle, prepare some herbal tea for Mademoiselle Léa and bring the aspirin."

"Yes, mademoiselle."

"It's all right, dear. We were so concerned."

"Have you heard from Sabine?"

"No," replied Laure. "When Aunt Albertine called me to tell me what had happened, I came as fast as I could. Franck and one of his friends looked everywhere they thought Sabine might be, but they couldn't find her. We don't know where she is. Where were you?"

Léa didn't answer.

"I saw Laurent."

"Well, that's good news!"

"Pierrot is dead."

Laure said nothing. She already knew.

"Poor dear child," said Lisa. "I shall pray for his soul."

She did not see the look of hatred on Léa's face.

"Have you got a cigarette?" she asked her sister.

Laure handed Léa a green pack with a red circle on it.

"Lucky Strike," said Léa. "I've never seen these."

Estelle brought the aspirin and the herbal tea, sweetened with honey which she had unearthed in a little shop in the Rue de Seine.

Albertine carried Charles, now asleep, back to bed and Lisa carried Sabine's son, Pierre. Léa and Laure sat quietly sipping their tea and smoking.

Chapter Twenty-Two

Through the open windows, they could hear shouting and singing in the street below, transforming the quiet neighborhood. Laure went to turn on the radio.

"They're going to broadcast General de Gaulle's speech from the *Hôtel de Ville.*"

"Why should we hide the emotion that we all are feeling—men and women alike—here at home, in Paris, a city that has thrown off its chains with its own bare hands. No! We will not hide the very deep and sacred emotion that we feel at this time. This is a moment that transcends the lives of each and every one of us. . . .

"Paris has been dishonored, defeated, and humiliated. And now, Paris has been liberated! Liberated by Parisians with the help of the French Armies, and the support and cooperation of all France. France strong and free! The only France! The true France! France eternal! Now that the enemy that held Paris prisoner has capitulated, France is returning to Paris, returning home. Bloody and wounded, yes, but victorious. France is returning, having learned a hard lesson, but more convinced than ever of its duties and its rights."

Suddenly the power was cut off and with it the voice of the man who, for the past four years, had symbolized the hope of the French nation. At the Ministry of War, abandoned by the Germans only a few hours earlier, he now "governed France."

Laure lit the kerosene lamp on the table beside the sofa where Léa lay resting.

"I'm going to bed. I think you should too. We'll try to work everything out tomorrow."

"That's right. . . . We'll try. . . . Good night."

"'Night."

The lamp cast a warm glow over the room; its old-fashioned charm reminded Léa of Montillac. She sighed and lit another cigarette. Putting the pack of Lucky Strikes back on the table, she noticed a newspaper. FRENCH TROOPS ARRIVE AT CITY HALL YESTERDAY AT 2200 read the headline across six columns on the front page of *Le Figaro*. One of the articles, entitled "Our Leader," was by François Mauriac:

> *At France's darkest hour, the hope of our nation rested with one man. It was snuffed out by this man and by him alone. How many joined him in his solitude, those who understood in their own way what it meant 'to give oneself to France'?*

The words danced on the page.

> *The Fourth Republic is born of martyrs. Much blood has been spilled, but it is the blood of martyrs, the blood of Communists and Nationalists and Christians and Jews who have rebaptized us all at the same time. And in our midst, General de Gaulle is the living incarnation of this rebirth. . . . We have no illusions now. . . . How many times during these four long years did I ease the pain by remembering what Victor Hugo wrote:*

> *O France, rise up, free at last!*
> *O white robes, after the blast!*

The paper slid to the floor; Léa had fallen asleep.

Once again, the ghost of the man from Orléans pursued her, this time brandishing a huge pair of shears. Just as he was about to catch up with her, she awoke, drenched in sweat. She did not sleep again until just before dawn.

There was the smell of coffee. Could it be real coffee? Who could have brought this rare commodity? Strangely, in spite of a mild migraine, Léa felt good. Laure entered, carrying a tray.

"Coffee?" asked Léa.

"Sort of. Laurent brought it."

"He's here?"

"Yes, he's with Charles in your room."

Léa jumped up from the sofa.

"Wait, don't go. Charles is telling him how his mother died. Drink it while it's still hot."

"It tastes like real coffee. What is it?"

"It's a powder made from real coffee. You put it in a cup and pour hot water over it. It's from America, apparently."

"Still no word from Sabine?"

"No, but Franck called. He went to see a man who is in charge of rounding up collaborators—an old friend of his father's."

"I thought his father *was* a collaborator."

"He was, and so was this other man."

"I don't get it."

"It's simple. When the tide started to turn, lots of collaborators started slipping into the ranks of the F.F.I. Apparently, some of them even fought hard. When Franck bumped into this man, with a rifle and an F.F.I. arm band, he couldn't believe his eyes. The man recognized him and was afraid Franck would talk, so he agreed to help him find Sabine. If all goes well, we should know by this afternoon."

"What about Pierrot?"

"His body is at the morgue. I went to identify it yesterday."

"Yesterday? You didn't tell me."

"There was no point. We'll have to call Uncle Luc. Aunt Albertine promised me she would do it as soon as the lines between Paris and Bordeaux are re-established."

Someone knocked at the door.

"Come in."

It was Laurent, carrying Charles. Their eyes were red.

"Papa came back, Léa."

"Good morning, Léa. General Leclerc is waiting for me, so I

229

can't stay. I'll come by after the parade along the Champs-Élysées. Thanks for everything," he added, kissing her forehead. "See you tonight, Charles."

"I want to ride with you in your tank!"

"You can't, son. Maybe some other time."

Charles began to whimper.

"Don't cry," said Léa, giving him a hug. "We'll go to watch Papa in the parade in a little while."

"We will?"

"Yes."

After giving Charles one last kiss, Laurent went out.

He looks so unhappy, thought Léa.

A huge tricolor flag was flying under the Arc de Triomphe.

The sky was a brilliant blue, with not a single cloud. A crowd of over a million Parisians had gathered along the parade route, hoping to catch a glimpse of General de Gaulle, Generals Leclerc, Juin, and Koenig, and the leaders of the Resistance and the F.F.I. From the Place de l'Étoile to the Place de la Concorde, and all the way to Notre-Dame Cathedral, the sidewalks and the streets were jammed with people. A small American press corps plane circled overhead. Holding Charles firmly by the hand, Léa and Laure were gradually swept up in the euphoria of the crowd.

"Here they come! Here they come!"

Sitting on the low wall of the Tuileries overlooking the Place de la Concorde, they watched as a wall of flags and banners advanced toward them. At the head of the procession were four French tanks, Lauraguais, Limagne, Limousin and Vercelon. Then, the tall, stately figure of General de Gaulle. The procession paused as the Guard played the *Marseillaise* and the *Marche Lorraine*. All at once, everyone was singing and chanting:

"Vive de Gaulle! Vive la France!"

Years later, Charles de Gaulle would write in his memoirs:

It was like a human sea. A huge crowd had gathered on either side of the street, perhaps as many as two million people. The rooftops of the buildings along the street were also lined with people. At every window, there were more people and more flags. They hung in clusters from ladders and flagpoles and lampposts. As far as the eye could see, there was one enormous wave of humanity, in the sunshine, under the tricolor flag.

I walked. This was not the sort of occasion when one inspected the troops, spit and polish, and trumpets blowing. It was a day to restore dignity to the people, a day for a massive outpouring of joy, blotting out the memory of defeat and dispersion under the boot of the oppressor. And because for those gathered, Charles de Gaulle had become a refuge and a symbol of hope, it was important that they see the man on a human scale, familiar and fraternal. It was important that this spectacle further strengthen our national unity. . . .

It was a supreme moment in our national consciousness, one of those moments that, over the centuries, has shaped our history. There was only one thought, one cry, one feeling. Differences fell away, we become one. . . .

But there is no such thing as pure joy, even for those who are victorious. And in among the feelings of joy that I felt at that moment were many doubts. I knew that all of France wanted nothing so much as to be free. The same fervor that had surfaced in Rennes and Marseille the day before, that now held Paris, would reveal itself the next day in Lyon, Rouen, Lille, Dijon, Strasbourg, and Bordeaux tomorrow. I had only to look and to listen in order to know in my heart that France wanted to stand on its own two feet once again. But the war was not over. We were not yet victorious. And what, pray tell, would be the cost of victory? . . .

The General waved to the crowd, then got into the large black convertible Renault that had carried Marshal Pétain on his last visit through Paris. Just then, shots rang out.

"Snipers!"

"Get down, everyone!"

People threw themselves to the ground as parade marshals, revolvers in hand, herded women and children behind the tanks and half-tracks.

What a mess, thought Léa, looking around the huge square. It was now a sea of trembling bodies, fluttering skirts, upended bicycles, tangled barbed wire, jeeps, and tanks. Laure pulled Léa and Charles, who was enchanted by the spectacle, down behind the low wall. The F.F.I. fired in the direction of the Pavillon du Marsan. More shots could be heard coming from the Gare d'Orsay and the Rue de Rivoli. Then, as suddenly as it had started, the firing stopped. People stood up, sheepishly looking around. Léa and Laure began running across the Tuileries Gardens, now a parade ground, lifting Charles along by the arms.

"Are you tired?" asked Léa anxiously.

"No!" he laughed. "I want to see Papa on his tank."

They were about to cross Avenue Paul-Déroulède, across from the Arc du Carrousel, when the shooting broke out again. They threw themselves down on the grass. Panic-stricken onlookers fled in all directions. There was such confusion that the F.F.I. on the opposite bank of the Seine began firing on the Pavillon de Flore and the F.F.I. at the Tuileries, thinking that it was the Militia, started firing back.

"It would be too stupid to die here," said Léa, getting up after a volley of bullets sped past, a few feet away from them.

Near the ticket offices outside the Louvre, they met Franck, walking his bicycle. Laure put Charles on the baggage rack and they made their way toward Notre-Dame.

General de Gaulle had just alighted in the square in front of the cathedral. He was kissing two little girls in Alsatian costumes, who presented him with a red, white, and blue bouquet.

The tanks in the square were instantly engulfed. There had been sniper fire all along the parade route, and many people had been injured in the panic that ensued.

232

Exhausted from four years of deprivation, on edge from the street fighting that preceded the liberation, Parisians expressed their joy with shouts and applause.

"Vive de Gaulle!"

"Vive la France!"

"Vive Leclerc!"

As General de Gaulle advanced toward the portal of the Last Judgment, the shooting broke out again, this time at close range.

"They're firing from the towers!" someone screamed.

Almost everyone dropped to the ground. De Gaulle puffed calmly on a cigarette, surveying the scene with amusement. Leclerc's troops and the F.F.I. began firing at the towers, breaking pieces off the gargoyles that fell on the people standing below. Officers of the Second Armored Division hurried back and forth, trying to restore order.

"I see that your men are not accustomed to street fighting," Colonel Rol couldn't help remarking to Lieutenant Colonel Jacques de Guillebon of the Second Armored Division.

"No, but they will be before long," responded de Guillebon, eyeing Rol scornfully.

With his walking stick, General Leclerc began striking a soldier who had panicked and was firing indiscriminately. General de Gaulle dusted off his tunic impatiently and entered the cathedral. Colonel Peretti forged a path through the crowd. General de Gaulle had arrived thirty minutes earlier than expected, and the clergy were not there to greet him. The organ was silent and the choir sat in darkness; there was no electricity. No sooner had he entered, than firing broke out inside the cathedral. Chairs and kneeling benches were overturned as people scrambled for cover, frightening by the echo that amplified the noise.

"The Militia are firing from the Gallery of Kings!"

"No! Those men are from the Prefecture!"

Unperturbed, General de Gaulle walked up the two-hundred-foot-long nave. On either side, amid rows of upended chairs, the faithful crouched with their heads between their hands. Here and there, a face emerged long enough to shout:

"Vive de Gaulle!"

Walking behind General de Gaulle, La Trocquer was heard to say:

"There are more derrieres than faces."

When they reached the choir, General de Gaulle sat in a chair to the left of the Crossing, followed by Parodi, Peretti, and Le Trocquer. Bullets continued to whiz through the air. Monsignor Brot, archpriest of Notre-Dame, approached de Gaulle.

"General, His Eminence was to have received you, but he was not able to be here. He has asked me to convey to you a firm but respectful message of protest."

General de Gaulle was to have been met by Cardinal Suhard, but the Provisional Government had informed the cardinal that very morning that his presence was not welcome. Some criticized him for formally receiving Marshal Pétain at Notre-Dame, others for conducting the funeral service for Philippe Henriot, in spite of the fact that, at Henriot's funeral, he had refused the Germans' request that he speak.

The man's a Gaullist, the Militia had said.

Neither a Gaullist nor a collaborationist, Monsignor Brot must have thought to himself, just a man of God.

"Tell the organists to begin playing," ordered Le Trocquer.

"There's no electricity."

"Then get everyone singing."

Hesitant at first, the Magnificat rang out under the vaulted ceiling. General de Gaulle's voice could be heard above the others, encouraging everyone to join in. The shooting stopped for a moment, then resumed. Three people were wounded. Young priests gave them absolution. Then singing started up again, punctuated by gun fire.

Young people wearing white smocks recovered the wounded and those who had been trampled. The Magnificat faded and died. It had become too dangerous. There would be no Te Deum that day.

A verger in magnificent robes cleared a passage for General de Gaulle.

Outside, the crowd greeted him with thunderous cheering.

"Vive de Gaulle!"

"God save de Gaulle!"

"God save France!"

He waved to the crowd again and calmly got into his vehicle, driving away to more applause.

Charles was the happiest and the proudest of little boys. Standing in the turret of his father's tank, he was on top of the world.

Léa, Laure, and Charles had met Laurent, returning from the Place de la Concorde, at the *Hôtel de Ville*. He told them that he was leaving Paris in less than an hour.

"Even with the snipers, it's hard to believe they're still fighting north of Paris."

"Haven't the Germans surrendered?"

"It's valid for General von Choltitz's men, but not for the others—at least, that's what they say. They've dug their heels in at Le Bourget and Montmorency Forest. They have fresh troops who've just arrived by bicycle from Pas-de-Calais and the tanks of Major General Wahle's 47th Infantry Division."

"Papa, show me how it works."

Léa, who had climbed on to the tank, tapped Charles on the hand.

"Don't touch. You could blow us all up."

Laurent smiled wanly. He kissed his son, lifted him up and handed him, protesting, to Franck.

"Take good care of him, Léa. I'll come and see you as soon as I can. We'll talk about Camille, I want you to tell me exactly what happened."

Charles and the others watched the tank maneuver, then walked along behind as far as Boulevard de Sébastopol.

235

Franck accompanied them back to the Rue de l'Université, promising to return that evening with food and news of Sabine.

The outing had tired Charles, who complained that his head hurt. Estelle took his temperature; he had a fever of one hundred and two.

"I told you so," she grumbled. "He shouldn't have gone out, he's not well enough."

Léa put him to bed, watching over him and holding his little hand in hers until he fell asleep. She must have overestimated her own strength for before long she, too, was fast asleep.

She was awakened by a persistent droning sound, and looked at her watch. It was half past eleven! The room was pitch black. The droning became louder. Planes! There were planes flying over Paris—no doubt Allied planes on their way to the Front. Sirens began to wail. In tighter formation now, the planes flew over Paris again, this time very low. Léa ran to the window.

Not since Orléans had she seen so many of them at one time. They seemed not to notice the tracer bullets and the sporadic anti-aircraft fire. Suddenly, huge explosions near the *Hôtel de Ville* and *Les Halles* shook the neighborhood, lighting up the sky.

"Quickly!" Down to the basement!" cried Albertine, running into their room with Sabine's baby in her arms.

Lisa and Estelle ran past, their hair dishevelled.

"Go down without me, take Charles with you."

Half asleep, Charles clung to Léa.

"No! I don't want . . . I want to stay with you."

"Okay, you can stay with me."

Sitting in one of the wing chairs in the living room, he fell asleep in Léa's arms. She smoked a cigarette as the German bombs fell on the Marais, Rue Monge, and Hôpital Bichat, killing seven nurses. Part of the wine market was also destroyed, setting off a fire that lit up the sky like a fireworks display.

At around midnight, there were sirens, signalling that the raid was over. The bombs were replaced by the wail of fire engines and ambulances. Paris went back to bed, but not for long. There was a second raid at around three in the morning.

The next day, it was estimated that one hundred people had died and that five hundred had been wounded. For those who thought that the war was over, it was a rude awakening.

At dawn on the morning of August 27, 1944, the city began licking its wounds. At Notre-Dame Cathedral, a strange ceremony took place behind closed doors. Because the "blood of the crime" had been spilled in the cathedral, it had to be "reconciled" before the faithful could return. Accompanied by Canon Lenoble, Monsignor Brot blessed the inner and outer walls of the basilica with Gregorian water, an admixture of water, ashes, salt, and wine. After this ceremony, witnessed only by members of the clergy at Notre-Dame, services were resumed.

That Sunday morning, on a barricade on Boulevard Saint-Michel bedecked with flags, a mass was said by a chaplain of the F.F.I., a *maquis* priest from Haute-Savoie, attended by a large, solemn crowd.

Léa refused to attend high mass with her aunts at Saint-Germain-des-Prés.

After a number of attempts, Albertine was finally able to reach Pierrot's father, Luc Delmas, in Bordeaux. The connection was very bad and she had to scream into the mouthpiece in order to be heard.

"Hello! Hello! Can you hear me? This is Mademoiselle de Montpleynet. Léa and Laure's aunt. Yes, they're here with me. Yes, they're fine. I'm calling about your son. Pierrot, yes. No. No. He's been killed. I'm terribly sorry. By the Germans. Yes, I'm afraid it is possible. I went to identify the body yesterday. I don't really know. He was with Léa on Boulevard Saint-Michel. I'll see, she was wounded. One moment. . . . Léa, it's your uncle, he'd like to talk to you."

"I have nothing to say to him. It's his fault Pierrot is dead."

"Be reasonable, Léa. He's heartbroken."

"Serves him right."

"You have no right to talk like that. He's your father's brother, don't forget. If you can't speak to him out of Christian charity, do it for your parents' sake."

Why was Aunt Albertine talking about her parents? They were dead! Like Camille and Pierrot!

"Hello!" she shouted, grabbing the receiver from her aunt. "Yes, this is Léa. I met him by coincidence a few days ago. He had been in the Resistance—with the Communists—for a year. He came to Paris to act as liaison between various leaders of the Resistance. He was killed by a grenade. No, I don't know whether he suffered. I was wounded. We were taken to different hospitals. Hello! Hello! Don't hang up! Hello! Who is this? Philippe? Yes, it's awful. Paris has been liberated. What about Bordeaux? What? You hope the Germans will push the Americans back! I don't think you realize that it's all over for the Germans. People like you and your father could be shot. No, I won't be happy. I won't care one way or the other! Yes, Pierrot is dead. Yes I have changed! What do you want us to do about the funeral? Call me at my aunts'. Littré 35-25. Have you heard from Uncle Adrien?"

Léa replaced the receiver, suddenly pensive.

"Aunt Albertine, it was awful to hear him cry," she said in a tiny voice.

Chapter Twenty-Three

September 1944 was to be a month of important decisions for Léa.

It all began on the evening of August 30.

At eight o'clock, the telephone rang. Albertine answered.

"Hello! Yes, my niece is here. May I ask who's calling? I beg your pardon? Monsieur Tavernier. François Tavernier? Yes, hello. Where are you? In Paris! When did you arrive? With General de Gaulle! It's so nice to hear your voice. Yes, Léa is fine. Madame d'Argilat? I'm sorry, Madame d'Argilat is dead. Her little boy is here with us. We saw his father a few days ago. He's fighting north of Paris at the moment. One moment, I'll put Léa on. Léa, it's for you!"

"Who is it?"

"Monsieur Tavernier."

"Fran—"

"Yes, dear. What's wrong? Don't you feel well?"

Her heart was pounding so hard that her entire body ached.

"I'm all right," she replied weakly, sitting down before taking the receiver from her aunt.

Albertine gazed at her with tender concern. She would have given anything in the world to see the daughter of dear Isabelle happy at last.

"Aunt Albertine ... I'd like to be alone."

"Of course, dear, excuse me."

239

Léa was afraid to put the receiver to her ear, but the voice on the other end of the line became more and more persistent.

"Hello, François? Yes. Yes. No. No, I'm not crying. Of course, I'm all right. Where? The Ministry of War? Where is it? 14 Rue Saint-Dominique. I'll be there. Give me time to dry my hair. François? Okay, okay, I'll hurry."

Overcome with joy, laughing and crying, she replaced the receiver, ready to kneel down and give thanks that he was alive.

When Camille died, she had tried to put François out of her mind, protecting herself against the possible loss of another loved one. And when she saw Laurent again and realized how happy she was, she thought this strategy had worked. But the mere sound of François's voice sent shivers up and down her spine, as though he had reached out and touched her. She wanted to be in his arms, to forget the war, to forget death, to think only of pleasure. . . . Damn it, she thought, my hair still isn't dry. I'm going to look awful!

She ran to her room, rubbing her hair vigorously with a towel, rifling through her closet for something to wear. Whatever happened to that blue dress that looked so good on her? She couldn't find it anywhere and began going through the laundry hamper.

"Laure, Laure. . . ."

"Take it easy! Stop shouting!"

"Laure, lend me your red and green dress."

"But it's brand new!"

"Exactly. Please lend it to me. I promise I'll be careful."

"Okay, I'll lend it to you just this once. Where are you going?"

"I'm meeting François Tavernier."

"What! He's back?"

"Yes."

"Lucky you! Hurry up, don't make him wait. I'll get the dress."

When Laure returned, Léa was putting talc all over her naked body.

"You're so beautiful!"

"No more beautiful than you."

"Yes, you are. All my friends say so. Here, put it on. But be
careful, the material is very delicate."

Laure helped her into the chiffon crepe dress. It had a
plunging neckline, full short sleeves, and a tiny waistline ac-
centuated by a short gathered skirt.

"Wow! Jacques Fath!"

"I traded it for ten pounds of butter and five quarts of oil."

"That's not much."

"Oh yes it is. There is much more demand for butter than
haute couture dresses. With the liberation, these dresses will
be a dime a dozen. Every woman who fraternized with the
Germans has closets full of them."

"You're amazing, Laure. Who would have thought that a little girl from the provinces, whose hero used to be Marshal
Pétain, would end up a black marketeer."

"So? Anyone can make a mistake. I was mistaken about Marshal Pétain. You may be making a mistake over General de
Gaulle. And don't forget: if it weren't for the black market,
there would be days when you didn't have anything to eat."

"I'll be the first to agree with you. I'm just admiring your
flair for business. As for de Gaulle, it's a good thing he was
there. . . ."

"We'll see, he's a military man, just like the last one."

Léa shrugged her shoulders but said nothing.

"Still no word from Sabine?"

"No, Franck's still looking. Talk to François. He'll know what
to do. And what about Pierrot?"

"I don't know. Talk to Aunt Albertine."

"When will you be back?"

"I don't know. Just tell Aunt Albertine and Aunt Lisa that I'm
going out, and keep an eye on Charles."

"That's it, leave me with all the dirty work," said Laure in a mock-angry tone. "Anyways, have fun and be careful with the dress."

"I'll take care of it like it was my own—where would I get my hands on ten pounds of butter and five quarts of oil to pay you back?"

"Now it's worth double that!"

"Keep it up, Laure, and you'll be a rich woman one day."

"I sure hope so. You'd better go. I can hear Aunt Lisa. If she sees you going out, you'll have to spend an hour making excuses. Who? Where? When? Why?"

"'Bye! Thanks again!'"

Léa was in such a hurry that she missed the second last step and fell headlong on the marble floor of the entranceway, twisting her wrist.

"Shit!"

"Such an ugly word from such a pretty mouth!"

"Franck! Is that you? I can't see a damn thing in here with the power off. Help me up."

She let out a scream as he helped her to stand up.

"Did you hurt yourself?"

"I'm all right. . . . You're really loaded down. What's that?"

"Stuff for Laure. By the way, I found your sister."

"Why didn't you say so?"

"You didn't give me a chance."

"Well?"

"She's at the *Vélodrôme d'Hiver*. That's where the F.F.I. are taking collaborators."

"Is it easy to get in?"

"If you're bald it is."

"Very funny."

"Sorry. No, it's not easy. There's a crowd of rowdies permanently stationed at the front door. Every time someone is brought through, they shout insults and start hitting and scratching. Lawyers get the same treatment, even with an F.F.I. escort."

242

"Please try to find out what you can. I'm meeting a friend who's close to General de Gaulle. I'm going to talk to him about it."

"Ask him to use his clout to get her out of there. Apparently, the conditions inside are really awful. It's not safe to go out alone at night. Are you sure you don't want me to go with you?"

"No, thanks. I'm just going to the Rue Saint-Dominique. It's not far. Thanks for helping with Sabine. I'll call you tomorrow if I find out anything."

"Talk to you tomorrow. Have fun!"

Léa was already in the street.

No sooner had she given her name to the sergeant-at-arms at the Ministry of War, than she was escorted to a large sitting room on the second floor. The room still bore the traces of its previous occupants. A portrait of the Fuehrer lay discarded in a corner. Flags and papers with the swastika lay everywhere. There were boxes, half-filled with files and documents, all testifying to a hasty departure.

"I have informed the Commander that you are here. He asks that you kindly wait for a few moments. He is with the General. There are papers if you'd like something to read."

Newspapers from every corner of the country lay on one of the tables. *La Nation, Les Allobroges, Le Franc-Tireur, Libération, Combat, Défence de la France, La Marseillaise, L'Aisne Nouvelle, Lyon Libérée, L'Humanité, Le Patriote Niçois, Le Libre Poitou, La Petite Gironde.* Bordeaux had been liberated! The F.F.I. had entered the city at 0630. On the front page of *La Petite Gironde*, the Regional Council for the Liberation of the Southwest, represented by regional military delegate Triangle (also known as Colonel Gaillard) and War Office Major Roger Landes (also known as Aristide), had issued a statement to the F.F.I. Aristide was alive! thought Léa. Uncle Adrien must be with him. "Bordeaux Celebrates its Liberation" read the headlines of *Sud-Ouest*, a paper Léa did not recognize. It had the same address and the same crowing cock as the issue of *La Petite Gironde* dated Monday, August 28, but it was dated the 29th. . . .

Lost in her thoughts, Léa did not hear François enter. Before she knew it, she was in his arms.

"Let go. . . . François!"

"Léa. . . . Léa. . . ."

They careened around the room, clinging to one another, bumping into furniture, so drunk with delight that they did not notice that they were not alone.

"So this is the urgent appointment you were telling me about, is it, Tavernier?"

"Excuse me, sir, as you can see, it is of the greatest importance."

"Yes, so I see, so I see. Very charming indeed. Well, when your, er, meeting is over, come and see me—in an hour shall we say?"

"Yes, sir. Thank you, sir."

Dumbstruck, Léa watched the tall figure recede.

"Was that really him?" she whispered.

"Yes."

"I'm so ashamed!"

"Why? He's a man. . . ."

"That's what I mean."

"In the meantime, we have an hour to ourselves with his blessing."

"You mean?"

"Yes."

She blushed deeply. He burst out laughing.

"Don't laugh. It's not funny. What is he going to think of me?"

"Don't worry, he's already forgotten you. Come, I want you so badly."

Forgetting her shame, she followed him to the third floor.

"That's the General's office," he whispered, indicating a door where a young soldier stood guard.

After trying several doors, he found what he was looking for at the end of the hall.

It was a narrow broom closet with a skylight, containing carpets and wall hangings that had been carefully rolled up and folded. The tiny room was stifling and smelled strongly of dust and mothballs. François pushed Léa back on to a pile of Aubusson tapestries and followed her down.

"Wait. Kiss me first."

"Later, I've thought about you and your pretty little pussy for so long that I'm ready to burst. I can't wait any longer."

Feverishly, he tried to tear off her panties.

"Jesus, this stuff must be pre-war," he said, pulling harder and harder.

"Stop, you'll rip my dress."

"I'll buy you ten more. Ah!"

He penetrated her with such force that she let out a cry of pain and anger.

"You're hurting me! Let me. ..."

"I'd sooner die. ..."

She struggled, trying to pry herself free.

"Bastard!"

"Your first words. ..."

"Bastard! Bastard! Bas. ..."

His pleasure was gaining on her. Now they were like two animals, groaning and biting each other, mating furiously.

This brought only momentary relief. Without a pause, they began making love again, experiencing pleasure neither could remember having felt before. Exhausted and replete, they fell back on to the wine-colored carpets that seemed to envelope them.

They lay there, not speaking, feeling the waves of pleasure in their limbs. François raised himself up on one elbow and gazed at her. Rarely had he seen such abandon in lovemaking. As soon as he penetrated her, she gave herself without holding back. He brushed her swollen lips. Her eyelids were almost translucent. It was more than he could bear.

"Look at me."

When her beautiful eyes slowly opened, there were tears of sadness.

"Are you angry with me?"

She shook her tousled head. Large tears fell on the heavy, wine-colored carpet.

"I love you, Léa. Please don't cry."

"I was so afraid," she blurted out.

"It's all over now. I'm here."

She sat up, pushing him away.

"No, it's not all over! People are still killing each other and humiliating each other."

"I know, I know. We can tell me about that later. . . . I know about Camille."

"You do? Do you know about Pierrot? And Raoul? And Sabine?"

"Sabine?"

"She was arrested by the F.F.I. They shaved her head."

"How do you know that it was the F.F.I.?"

"They were wearing arm bands."

"A lot of very unsavory elements have infiltrated the F.F.I. The General is aware of the fact and everything will be done to re-establish order and bring them to justice."

"I don't know whether the Resistance has been infiltrated by 'unsavory elements' as you call them, but I can tell you that most of the people who came to watch my sister and other women have their heads shaved enjoyed it immensely and found it perfectly normal to punish them like that."

"You're so beautiful when you're angry!"

"François!"

"Sorry. What happened then?"

"She was taken to the *Vélodrôme d'Hiver.*"

"Well, she's in good company. That's where they took Sacha Guitry and Mary Marquet. Don't worry, we'll get her out of there. Good God! I have to go. The General must be waiting for me. I'll call you tomorrow morning. Be good."

He ran out, buttoning up his pants.

"François!"

"Yes?" he said, turning back.

"I'm glad you're back."

He lifted her up and held her close, kissing her with a tenderness that always took her by surprise.

Léa listened to his footsteps grow fainter. Strangely, she felt either very secure or as though she were in very grave danger when she was with him. She was not given to analyzing things but now, sitting in a broom closet at the Ministry of War, she tried to sort out her feelings. He frightens me, she thought, but that's ridiculous! Why should I be afraid? He's never done anything to make me feel this way. Am I afraid he doesn't love me anymore? Am I afraid he'll leave me? Of course I am, but that's not what's bothering me. It's almost physical. When he calls me his "angel," it sends shivers up and down my spine. I feel so strongly drawn to him that I would follow him anywhere, but how does he feel? He says he loves me, but whenever we see each other, he throws himself on me. All he ever says is, Come, I want you. Not that it doesn't excite me, but I also need words of tenderness. My soul wants to be made love to, as Raphaël Mahl and Balzac would say. And why does he make me so angry? When we were talking about Pierrot and Sabine, it was as though I somehow held him responsible for what had happened to them. I don't understand it. Maybe it's because his attitudes, his way of speaking, and his relationships are so confusing and unclear. I somehow hold men like him responsible for the war, but that's absurd. Camille would know. Dear God, how I miss her! This is exactly how I felt after Maman died, so abandoned, so alone. And when I think that I betrayed Camille! That I wanted to steal her husband! Forgive me, Camille. There are so many things that I didn't tell you. And so many that you didn't tell me. Now it's too late, it's all over. God, I'm crying again! Oh, what's the point of it all?"

Angrily, Léa tried to straighten her dress, but to no avail. Cheap, wartime fabric! How was she going to get past the sergeant-at-arms like this! She decided at last that she had to leave the closet. Opening the door a crack, she checked the hall, then ran to the staircase which she descended with all the dignity she could muster. The entranceway was full of young soldiers and F.F.I. They watched her go by, dishevelled and flushed, envying whoever it was that had put her in that state. She held her head high, ignoring the whistles of admiration that followed her outside. Once in the street, she began to run, hot with anger and shame.

When she arrived at the Rue de l'Université, Charles greeted her with cries of delight.

"Aren't you in bed yet?"

"Papa is here! Papa is here!"

Charles tried to drag her into the living room.

"Wait, I have to get changed."

"No. Come on."

"In a minute."

"Papa! Papa! Léa is here. She doesn't want to come in."

Laurent's tall, thin frame appeared in the doorway.

She kissed him. How tired he looked!

"Wait, I'm going to change."

But it was too late. Laure came into the hall.

"There you are! Look at my dress! Just look at it!"

"I'm sorry. I fell."

"You *fell?*"

Léa fled to her room. She didn't know what to tell her sister.

When she entered the living room, Aunt Albertine looked at her severely.

"You know I don't like it when you go out at night without telling us where you are going."

"I'm sorry. I went to see François Tavernier about Sabine. He's going to look after it. I saw General de Gaulle," she added, attempting to change the subject.

"What is he like?"

Léa described her brief encounter with the General, glossing over the exact circumstances. . . .

Tired out by all the excitement, Lisa and Albertine took their leave.

"Your room is ready, Monsieur d'Argilat."

"Thank you, thanks for everything."

248

"You're welcome. Good night, everyone."

Laure whispered in Léa's ear:

"I hope it was worth it, otherwise I'll never forgive you for ruining my dress."

The color of Léa's cheeks was all the confirmation Laure needed.

"I'm going to bed, too," said Laure. "I wasn't cut out to be a nursemaid. 'Night, Laurent. I hope you sleep well. Come on, Charles, time for bed."

"No, I want to stay with Papa."

Laurent lifted the little boy up and gave him a big hug.

"Papa, keep me with you!"

"I'll always keep you with me, but right now, you have to go to sleep. I'll come in and kiss you later."

"Léa too?"

"Léa too."

"Thanks, Laure. Good night."

"Good night."

Alone at last, Laurent and Léa sat smoking in silence. Laurent went over to the open window and looked out at the stars. Without turning around, he said:

"Tell me what happened."

Chapter Twenty-Four

"Mademoiselle Albertine, it's for you."

"Thank you, Estelle."

"Hello. Yes, this is Mademoiselle de Montpleynet. Hello. Yes, of course I'll be responsible for my niece. When? Today! How can I ever thank you, Monsieur Tavernier? By allowing Léa to have dinner with you? I really don't see how that's possible if her sister is coming home. Would you like to speak to her? She's still sleeping. She was up for part of the night talking to Monsieur d'Argilat. Fine. I'll tell her you'll call again this evening."

Albertine replaced the receiver and went to her room, closing the door softly. She sat in the old Voltaire chair that she was particularly fond of. Her heart was pounding. Her hands, now clammy, gripped the arms of the chair. Gradually the joy of seeing Sabine again yielded to mounting anxiety. How would the other occupants of the building react, or the neighborhood merchants or their friends, when they learned that her niece had had her head shaved because she was the mistress of a German soldier? Albertine had always lived in harmony with the people around her; now she felt marginalized. As the Occupation drew to a close, disparaging comments about Sabine's German "fiancé" and Laure's activities grew more frequent. Lisa, the more worldly of the two, suffered terribly from this situation, to the point where she had stopped going to their weekly bridge game.

Albertine blamed herself for not being stricter with Isabelle's girls; she had felt responsible for them since the death of their parents. She acknowledged that she felt totally out of her depth; her nieces were so unalike yet all so stubborn. I simply wasn't equal to the task, she thought. I failed to protect them. What would their mother say? And what will become of Sabine? Otto must surely be dead. She will be branded an "unwed mother," if not worse. What about her adorable little baby? Dear God, have pity on us! Give Sabine the strength to overcome her grief and shame. Forgive me. You gave me a mission and I have failed. Forgive me!

Albertine wept, holding her head in her hands. She was so absorbed in her thoughts that she did not hear the door open.

"Aunt Albertine! What's wrong?"

Kneeling at her feet, Léa tried to part her aunt's hands, spotted with age.

"Please, Aunt Albertine, please stop crying."

At last, Albertine looked up. The grief in her expression, normally somewhat distant and reserved, filled Léa with pity and anxiety. What! Even Albertine? So strong and reserved and dignified? Another part of Léa secure childhood had just fallen away. She felt lost. When she had seen Montillac burning, something inside her had died. It had isolated her in her grief, leaving her only enough strength to survive and to protect Camille's son. She had worn herself out trying to comfort Laurent. But is it possible to console someone else when one is inconsolable? What words could she find now to give this dear old woman courage? Camille would have known.

It was Albertine who spoke:

"Up you get, dear. I'm just a silly old woman. Just a little tired, that's all. I have no right to complain! There are so many who have suffered more than I."

She wiped her eyes slowly, then added:

"Monsieur Tavernier called. Sabine should be here this afternoon."

"Is that why you're crying?"

"Yes and no. Please don't misunderstand me, I'm very happy that she is being released—just a little worried."

"Did he say anything about me?"

"He wanted to invite you to dinner, but I told him that was impossible today."

"Why did you tell him that?"

Albertine stood up, looking at her niece severely.

"Your sister will need all the support we can give her. I thought it would be better if you were here."

Léa looked down, feeling suddenly very tired.

"At any rate, he is going to call back this evening. Please don't tell Lisa what happened, it would only upset her. You know how simple and straightforward she is. She's even more disturbed by what's happening than I am and it's starting to tell on her health. Promise you won't say anything?"

Léa kissed her aunt.

"I promise. Aunt Albertine, may I ask your advice about something?"

"Of course, dear. What is it?"

"Well, I—"

She stopped. Was there any point in raising the subject, when her own feelings were so unclear?

"What is it, dear? Is it that hard to say?"

"I have decided to join the Red Cross."

"The Red—"

Had Léa simply said "I would like to join the Red Cross," she might not have embarked, headlong, on such an adventure. But there she was, announcing her decision, her pride preventing her from retracting it.

"Yes, you heard me correctly. I've decided to join the Red Cross."

"But you're not a nurse!" her aunt exclaimed.

"I'm not signing up as a nurse. I'm signing up as a driver."

"Why, Léa, when you know that we all need you here? What about Montillac? Have you thought about that?"

"There's nothing left of Montillac!"

"It can be rebuilt!"

"With what? We don't have any money!"

"The lawyers ..."

"The estate is mortgaged up to its—"

"Léa!"

"Please, Aunt Albertine! Let's face the facts!"

"Have you thought of your sisters? And what about Charles? He loves you as though you were his mother."

"My sisters can manage very well without me, thank you very much. Laure has an excellent head for business. And Charles has his father."

"When did you decide—and why?"

"When? I really don't know. Last night, perhaps, seeing Laurent's grief, reliving Camille's death and Aunt Bernadette's and Sidonie's and Raoul Lefèvre's and Pierrot's and so many more. I want to follow General Leclerc's troops. I want to go to Germany with him. I wish I were a man so I could take up a gun and fight. I wish I could kill hundreds of them—"

"Léa, stop! You don't know what you're saying!"

Léa was beside herself, her face was hard and red, her eyes full of hatred, her mouth twisted.

"Maybe I don't, but I want to see them suffer. I want to be there when they surrender. I want to see them run when the bombs start to fall. I want to see them blown apart, their eyes gouged, their children burning alive. I want to see their towns and camps razed, their houses flattened. Most of all, I want to see them humiliated, the way they humiliated us. I want them to grovel, the way we grovelled. I want to see them begging on their knees. I want them to be wiped off the face of the earth!"

Léa's shrill voice had alerted Laurent, who listened in disbelief as the foul words spewed out of her mouth. She was almost hysterical.

"Ouch!"

A slap brought the outpouring to a halt. She looked at Laurent, stupefied. She would never have thought him capable of slapping a woman.

"Watch out! She's going to fall!" cried Albertine.

Laurent reach out to help her, but Léa had already straightened up.

"It's all right. I'm fine now."

"I'm sorry, Léa."

"It's all right. In your place, I would have done the same," she replied, going over to the window.

"Monsieur d'Argilat, do you know what Léa was telling me?"

"No."

"She has decided to join the Red Cross!"

Laurent forced her to turn around.

"Is that true?"

There was such anxiety in his voice!

"Yes."

He put his arms around her and held her very close.

"Maybe you're right, maybe you should ..."

Albertine left the room, shrugging her shoulders.

For a long moment, neither spoke.

Laurent gently lifted her chin. She tried to turn away.

"Why?"

She looked like a lost child! How he would have loved to chase away the horrible memories that haunted her, to give her back the lightheartedness that was part of her charm. But he was too caught up in his own grief to help. He knew that her decision was a response to her fear of the future, which she could only see as dark and difficult.

"Why?" he repeated.

"Because I want to die."

In any other circumstances, he would have thought this was hilariously melodramatic, but now ...

"Don't say things like that, you have your whole life ahead of you."

"You sound just like my aunts."

"It's common sense, Léa."

"What is? Do you know what common sense is? I don't! I haven't seen anything since the war broke out that made any sense at all. The entire war has been one absurdity after another. Is it common sense to lynch people and shave their heads?"

"I agree with you, but don't add to the absurdity with a decision that is so unlike you. Think, Léa! In a few short months, the war will be over. We can start rebuilding. We can start living again."

"Do you think you can do that? After what they did to Camille?"

A wave of pain washed over Laurent's face.

"I have to. I have Charles to think about."

"At least you have Charles. I don't have anyone."

"You have Montillac."

"I do not want to hear that word mentioned again. Too many people died there. I hate the place. I'll never go back."

"That's not what you said yesterday. I thought you were happy to see François Tavernier again. He's perfect for you."

"All he ever thinks about is—"

"What man wouldn't when he lays eyes on you?"

"You!"

For a moment, the memory of their one night in the underground passages of Toulouse was so vivid that they both blushed deep red.

"He loves you. Camille told me so. And she thought that you loved him."

"Well she was wrong."

"Camile was hardly ever wrong."

"I don't want to talk about her. She's gone—just like Montillac. I need to be alone, Laurent. Please."

He left the room, closing the door gently behind him.

Holding her head in her hands, Léa let out a long, mute cry that made her body tremble. She dropped to her knees against the Voltaire chair, biting the worn fabric of the cushion. The words came tumbling out of her mouth.

"I can't take it any more. I can't take it. They're all around me. They want to take me away! I didn't mean what I said to Laurent, I don't want to die! But every night, they call me. They try to catch me. I can feel their icy hands, covered in blood. And those fingers! Help! And the smell of burning flesh, the writhing, blackened body. The screams! Sarah! Your poor, cra-

255

tered cheeks. It's as though you were calling to me from Hell. Sidonie, your voice as sweet as the candies you used to make. I can't get the sight of your poor mutilated body out of my mind. Have pity! Be quiet! Raoul! I know you wish me well, I know you want me to live. When you died, you took our simple love with you. Aunt Bernadette! Please stop screaming. My God! The flames are engulfing your body. Raphaël! Go away! Have pity! I'm burning too. Forgive me, Aunt Bernadette. Forgive me. Maman, protect me. Send them away. They want to take me with them. Maman, tell Pierrot to leave me alone. It's not my fault that he died and I lived. La Sifflette! Monsieur and Madame Debray! Père Terrible. And the little children at Orléans and their mother. That man again. The man I killed. Help! Maman! He's grabbing me. Papa! Get him off me! Blood! Blood everywhere. There are so many of them. . . ."

"Léa! Léa, calm down! It's all right. Quick, call a doctor!"

François carried Léa, limp and drenched in sweat, to her room, while Laurent tried to reach a doctor.

"Call Doctor Prost at the Ministry of War. He's a friend of mine. Tell him to come right away."

François shooed Laure and Léa's aunts out of the room. Sick with worry, he looked at the woman he loved lying unconscious on the bed, her body shuddering from time to time. He covered her body with his and spoke in a soothing voice.

"There, there. It's all right. Don't be afraid. I'm here now. I'll protect you. There, there."

His words seemed to have a calming effect, so he quickly undressed her. He was moved by her beauty, so strong yet so fragile. It never failed to amaze him, each time he took possession of her. Even now, in her state of great confusion, she seemed moving and desirable. He had to get her away from Paris until she was herself again. Where the hell was Prost?

"D'Argilat!"

Laurent poked his head around the door.

"Yes."

"Were you able to reach Doctor Prost?"

"He's on his way. How is she?"

"She's a little calmer. Did anything unusual happen yester-day?"

"Not that I'm aware of. She told me about my wife's death."

"Yes, I'm very sorry. I wanted to tell you how much . . . your wife was a fine woman . . . a fine woman."

"Thank you. We can talk about it another time."

"I think the doctor's finally arrived."

"I didn't hear the bell downstairs."

"You're forgetting that we still don't have electricity. He knocked on the door on the landing."

They heard voices.

"This way, doctor."

A short stocky man with a thick neck and broad shoulders, wearing a captain's uniform, entered the room and went over to François.

"What's up, Tavernier?"

"None of your colleagues seem to be answering the tele-phone, so I called you."

"Are you ill?"

"It's not me, it's this young woman."

"Charming."

"Look, this is no time—"

"Okay, okay. Where can I wash up?"

"This way, doctor," said Albertine, showing him to the bath-room.

"Do stop pacing, Monsieur Tavernier, you're making me quite seasick."

"Forgive me, mademoiselle. It's the worry. He's been exam-ining her for over an hour."

"It's been more like ten minutes, Monsieur Tavernier."

"Ten minutes. An hour. Whatever. It's far too long."

The living room looked like a dentist's waiting room. Laure bounced Sabine's baby on her knees. Laurent stood, holding Charles, who kept asking in an anxious voice:

"She won't die, will she, Papa? Will she?"

Lisa fanned herself with a hankie, damp with tears, murmur-ing:

"Holy Mary, have pity on us."

Albertine sat very still, her eyes closed. From the way that her lips trembled, it was obvious that she was praying. At last, the door opened and the doctor beckoned to Albertine. François pushed her aside and entered the room ahead of her.

"Monsieur Tavernier!"

Ignoring her protests, he rushed over to the bed. Léa appeared to be sleeping. Relieved, he straightened up and turned to Prost.

"Well?"

The doctor turned instead to Albertine.

"Is she prone to fainting spells?"

"No, not as far as I know. She is my niece, doctor, but she has only been living with me for two months."

"When she was a child, was she subject to this sort of thing?"

"No. Yes! When her fiance died, she remained unconscious for several days."

"How many?"

"I don't remember. Two, or perhaps three."

"I see that she has sustained head injuries on two occasions. Have there been any sequelae?"

"Not as far as I know."

"Does she get migraines?"

"Rarely, but when she does, they're very severe, to the point where she has to lie down."

"That's all past history!" cried François. "What's wrong with her now?"

"She is in a coma vigil."

"A what?"

"A coma vigil."

"What does that mean?"

"It means that she is unconscious, but can still respond to certain stimuli—pain, for example. Mademoiselle, you mustn't worry if she cries out or becomes agitated. She is not completely unconscious."

"What must we do?"

"Nothing."

"Nothing?"

"That's right. We just wait and see."

"For how long?"

"It's hard to say. Two days ... four days ... a week ... perhaps longer. It depends."

"On what?" demanded François.

"On Mother Nature—or God—depending on your point of view," the doctor replied.

"I don't give a damn about God, Prost. You're a pretty mediocre physician if you can't even cure her!"

"Don't shout at me, Tavernier. She needs peace and quiet. The best medicine would be for you to drop out of her life!"

"Gentlemen, please!"

"I beg your pardon, mademoiselle. As I was saying, there's nothing we can do at this point except to wait and see. See that she gets lots to drink. Try to give her a little broth and keep a close watch on her temperature. Do you have a family physician?"

"Yes, but we don't know what's become of him."

"I'll come back tomorrow if I'm not able to rustle up one of my colleagues. I want someone to stay with her at all times. You will need a nurse."

"That won't be necessary, doctor. There are enough of us that we can take turns."

"Fine. Coming, Tavernier?"

"No, I think I'll stay for a while. I'll come by later."

"Don't forget that we have a meeting with the press in an hour."

"Damn the press!"

"You can tell the General that. Good-bye, mademoiselle. There is no need to worry. She has a strong constitution and she'll pull through."

"God is your witness."

Chapter Twenty-Five

When Léa opened her eyes in the darkened room, twelve days had gone by. The first person she saw, gazing down at her from beneath a fringe of hair emerging from an elegant turban, was her sister, Sabine. It did not even strike her as odd that Sabine's hair had grown in so quickly.

"Léa? Can you hear me?"

"Yes. I feel as though I've been asleep for a long, long time."

"You've been asleep for over a week," said Sabine, laughing and crying.

"What?"

"You've been in a coma for twelve days."

"Twelve days! Are you sure? What's happened? Tell me!"

"You mustn't tire yourself. I'm going to call the others to tell them that you're awake."

"No! Wait! I'm not tired. I don't really remember what happened. The last thing I remember was Aunt Albertine talking about you coming home and then . . . Twelve days! When did you come home?"

"That afternoon—the day you fell ill. François Tavernier came to get me at the *Vélodrôme d'Hiver*. An F.F.I. called to me. 'Hey, you slut,' he said. 'You're free to go!' I couldn't believe my ears. You should have seen the looks of joy on the faces of the other women. An actress who hadn't had her head shaved gave me a lock of her hair and slipped it under my scarf—"

260

"That's why . . ."

"—and kissed me. I was so touched that I burst into tears. I promised to give their families messages and letters. Luckily, they didn't have time to frisk me on the way out. François grabbed my bag from a pimply-faced 'colonel' who took great pleasure in humiliating the detainees. The document from the Ministry of War ordering my immediate release was covered in signatures and seals. The 'colonel' just stood there, turning it over and over. François took me to a chauffeur-driven limousine that had a tricolor pennant with the *Croix de Lorraine* on it, and said: 'Get in quickly, I'm afraid they'll notice that the papers aren't quite in order.' I was so shocked, I nearly fell over. Luckily, they didn't suspect anything and my name was struck from the purge list."

"What's that?"

"That's right, you wouldn't know. They're conducting a purge: arresting, interrogating, trying, and sentencing anyone who had anything to do with the Germans. Businessmen, politicians, writers, actresses, newspaper editors, hotel owners, prostitutes, stenographers, you name it."

"What are they doing to them?"

"Some are let go. Some are put in prison. Some are shot."

"Who have they arrested so far?"

"Among the names that would mean anything to you, Pierre Fresnay, Mary Marquet, Arletty, Ginette Leclerc, Sacha Guitry, Jérôme Carcopino, Brasillach. They're still looking for others— Céline, Rebatet, and Drieu la Rochelle, for example. They publish a list in *Le Figaro* every day."

"Most of them deserve it."

"True, but some innocent people have been arrested because a jealous co-worker or a nasty concierge denounced them, or simply because someone got a kick out of doing it."

Léa closed her eyes, not wanting to get involved in this topic with her sister.

"You're tired. We should stop talking. I'll go and—"

"No, wait! How is Charles?"

"He's fine. He hasn't stopped asking for you, especially since his father left."

Léa sat bolt upright.

"Laurent is gone?"

"Calm down, you mustn't excite yourself."

"Where is he?"

"With the Second Armored Division. They left for the East on the morning of the 8th."

"How was he when he left?"

"Not great. He felt terrible leaving you in your condition and abandoning his son."

"Did he leave anything for me?"

"Yes, there's a letter."

"Could you get it for me?"

"It's right here, in your desk."

Sabine opened a drawer and took out a letter which she handed to Léa. Her hands trembled so badly that she was not able to open the envelope.

"Open it and read it for me."

"Dear Léa,

If you are reading this letter, it means that you are well once again. I feel terrible leaving you like this, unable to help you or bring you back to life. I have asked your aunts and sisters to look after Charles, but now that you're better, I want you to look after him. Please say you will. He loves you like a mother and he needs you. I know that it's a great responsibility, but you are strong enough to take it on. You've already proved that. I hope you have reconsidered your crazy plan to join the Red Cross. Your place is with your family, with my son and your sisters. Go back to Montillac. I have written the lawyer who is looking after my father's affairs, asking him to try to sell some of the property so that you can rebuild Montillac. I feel happy and sad going to war again—happy because it helps me forget that I have lost Camille and sad because I have to leave you and Charles.

Love and kisses,
Laurent

P.S. I'll send a forwarding address as soon as I can.

"He's right, you're crazy to want to join the Red Cross."

"That's neither his business nor yours. I'll do as I like."

"Why?"

"I don't want to stay here. It doesn't feel right. I need to think things through."

Léa, you're awake! Doctor, I think my niece is on the mend."

"It certainly looks that way. So, you want to play Sleeping Beauty, do you? I'm sorry I can't be your Prince Charming. How are you feeling, Léa?"

"Fine, doctor."

Their old family doctor, whom they had finally managed to track down, examined Léa.

"Good. Good. Her blood pressure is normal. Her heart, too. In a few days, you'll be skipping through the woods on the arm of your Prince Charming. He was worried sick about you."

Léa looked inquiringly at her sister.

Sabine gave her a look that meant, "As if you didn't already know."

"I want to get up."

"Not until you get some of your strength back. Your poor legs won't support you. What you need is lots of good, healthy food."

"That's easier said than done," said Sabine bitterly.

"I know, madame. But you'll have to manage as best you can. Count on Prince Charming. He's very resourceful and what wouldn't he do for the family of his dearly beloved? Well, that's enough of that! I'd like you to make sure that she eats meat every day, as well as dairy products, fish, and eggs."

"All of which are impossible to find, doctor!"

"Monsieur Tavernier will help out in that department. Goodbye, Léa. And remember: let them fuss over you."

"I'll see you to the door, doctor," said Albertine.

After Albertine and the doctor left the room, Léa let out a little giggle. Hope springs eternal! she thought, watching Aunt Lisa's old beau take his leave.

"Did François come by often?"

"Are you kidding? Every day, several times a day, with phone calls in between to see how you were doing."

"I've been awake for at least an hour and the phone hasn't rung once!" pouted Léa.

"That's not fair. Whenever he could, he spent the night right here by your side, talking to you, stroking your face, not sleeping a wink. I'd bring him a cup of coffee in the morning, but it was so sad to see him leave, exhausted, unshaven, his eyes red. Sometimes, Charles waited for him outside your door and he would let him come in. They would sit on the end of your bed, talking. When they came out, they both looked better. Now Charles calls him 'my big friend' . . . You're lucky to be loved."

The sadness in Sabine's voice was not lost on Léa, who felt guilty that she had been so oblivious to her sister's problems. For the first time since returning to Paris, she looked intently at Sabine. How she had changed from her nursing days in Langon! She had worn her love for her German officer on her sleeve but now, the glow that had softened her rather plain features was gone. So was the carefree young woman in love, discovering the pleasures of Paris! Gone, too, the glow of a young mother proudly walking her baby along the banks of the Seine.

Léa looked at her sister, now a stranger, and noticed small lines on either side of her mouth. It was clamped shut as though hiding some dark secret. She noticed the rouge, accentuating her pallor, and her anxious eyes, darting back and forth. The turban with the ridiculous lock of air made her look like a silent movie star. Sabine clasped and unclasped her hands constantly. Perhaps it was her hands that made Léa realize the full extent of her sister's physical and mental suffering. She would have loved to hold Sabine in her arms, to beg her forgiveness for her selfishness, but suddenly she felt awkward. Her heart aching, she whispered:

"Have you heard from Otto?"

She stifled a cry: Sabine had undergone a brutal transformation. Her face was ashen grey, and her body limp, like an old doll. Slowly, she removed the turban, exposing her bald head in all its crudeness. Her eyes, wide open yet unseeing, filled with tears.

A wave of nausea pinned Léa to the pillow.

The two sisters lay silently on the bed. When the nausea lifted, Léa sat up and crawled over to her sister, stroking her tear-drenched face with a mixture of compassion and disgust. Not a single word of comfort came to her lips. Taking a corner of the sheet, she gently wiped away the streaks of mascara until the tears stopped.

"Thanks," said Sabine, putting the turban back on. "I'll get Aunt Albertine and Aunt Lisa ... No, I haven't heard from Otto."

Léa was suddenly very weary. She lay down and closed her eyes.

When Lisa and Albertine entered the room, she was fast asleep.

Chapter Twenty-Six

That evening, Léa found another face peering down into hers.

"François!"

All of the thoughts and feelings that they had been unable to express to one another went into their kiss, and when their lips parted, their desire to live had been restored and, with it, the strength to overcome even the greatest hardships.

"We're going to have to fatten you up. You know I don't care for skin and bones."

"With the shortages, that's not going to be easy."

"Don't worry about that, I'll take care of everything."

"How? Is it business as usual for your black market friends?"

"I'm glad to see that your illness hasn't dulled your wit! That's a good sign. My friends, as you call them, have disappeared into thin air. At this point in time, they are either staying in the stately homes of Baden-Baden or at inns in Spain. Others have taken their place, people who are just as clever and unscrupulous. Estelle is going to bring you some chicken broth, a soft-boiled egg, and some cream cheese, which I think you'll like. There's even an excellent Lafite-Rothschild to wash it down."

"That won't be enough to 'fatten me up.'"

"Remember, 'Too much haste was the finish of the serpent who wanted to swallow the sun.'"

"It's very flattering to be compared to a snake."

"You're the nicest little sidewinder I know," he said, stroking her hair. "Tomorrow, I'm going to have a hairdresser come by. Your hair feels like straw. In the meantime, you're going to have a bath."

The bath put François in a state to which they turned their immediate attention, first making sure that the door was locked. Afterward, François put Léa back to bed.

They devoured the meal prepared by Estelle and polished off the bottle of Lafite. The wine gave Léa back some of her color, making her eyes shine. François's eyes clearly indicated his intention to pick up where he had left off, but just then, someone knocked on the door.

"Open up! Open up!" cried Sabine.

François opened the door and Sabine rushed in, wild-eyed. "They found the bodies of Monsieur and Madame Fayard in a well!"

Laure, distraught, was close behind.

"They were killed and thrown into the well in the lower vineyard."

"Who told you that?"

"Ruth. She just called."

"Who did it?" asked Léa, although she knew the answer.

"The *maquisards*."

For a few moments, the only sound was Sabine, gasping.

"She said that terrible things are happening in Langon, Saint-Macaire, and La Réole. They're shaving women's heads and parading them through the streets so that people can humilate them and spit on them. People are being strung up from trees and tortured and killed."

"Dear God," cried Lisa, whom no one had heard entering the room.

"Why doesn't someone put a end to it?" cried Léa.

"General de Gaulle is trying to do just that, but don't forget that the Germans tortured women and children. I don't know whether you realize it, but France is on the brink of a revolution. General de Gaulle is going to have to use every ounce of his authority to prevent it from turning into the full-scale confrontation the Communists want it to be. That's why he established a national government representing all factions."

"Even the Communists?" Sabine retorted.

"They suffered too. It's only normal."

"I know. The party of the martyrs, as they call themselves."

"Don't complain! They fought the hardest and suffered the heaviest losses."

"Yes, but to go so far as to include them in the government," protested Lisa weakly.

"He had too. Don't you think it's normal for every faction of the Resistance to be represented? I wouldn't be at all surprised to see men as politically divergent as Jeanneney, Frenay, Bidault, Tillon, Capitan, Teitgen, Mendès France, and Pleven."

"Maybe you're right. We know so little about politics," said Laure.

"Have you heard from Uncle Luc or Philippe?"

"No, not really," replied Laure reluctantly.

"Why, what did Ruth say?"

"There are conflicting reports. Some say that Uncle Luc was arrested and taken to Fort du Hâ. Others say that he and Philippe were killed."

"How?"

"Nobody knows. According to some reports, they were hanged. Others say they were lynched or shot. Communication between Bordeaux and Langon still isn't very good."

"Has anyone heard from Uncle Adrien?"

"No. Nothing. But they found Albert."

"Alive?" cried Léa.

"No, dead. Tortured by the Gestapo."

"Poor Mireille. I wonder if the death of Fayard and his wife will avenge Albert's death. Taking one life doesn't bring back another and yet, when people we love die ..."

"Do you remember Maurice Fiaux?" Laure asked Léa.

"How could I forget him?"

"He was put to death on orders from the Resistance."

Laure, who once thought that she was in love with Fiaux, made this announcement without the slightest hint of emotion. More deaths! When would it all end?

"How is Ruth?"

"All right. She's gradually recovering, but the news of Albert's death, then the Fayard's, was a setback. All she could say was, 'It's crazy, completely crazy.' Apparently, the Fayard's death was awful. They were pushed and prodded with pitchforks and sticks, all the way through the vineyards to the well. Then they were tied together and thrown in. They let out one long scream."

"I can hear it!" gasped Léa. "I can hear them hitting the water. Oh, Mathias, I didn't want it to end this way!"

Drenched in sweat, her teeth chattering, Léa fell back on to the pillow.

"We shouldn't be talking like this in front of her. Please go, she needs to rest."

They filed silently out of the room.

François mopped her brow, murmuring words of comfort. Gradually, she became calmer. Then, at last, she fell asleep.

In spite of the disturbing news from Bordeaux, Léa made a speedy recovery. When General de Gaulle left Paris to visit General de Lattre de Tassigny at the Front on September 24, François took Léa on an outing to Marly-le-Roi Forest. Despite an atrocious meal at a well-known restaurant in Saint-Germain-en-Laye, they took full advantage of the fresh air and inviting moss of the forest floor.

That evening, at a luxurious restaurant on the Champs-Élysées where the food was excellent, François told Léa that he would be leaving soon.

"Where are you going?"

"On a mission for the General."

"What sort of mission?"

"I can't say, but I won't be gone more than a month or so."

"A month! Are you serious?"

"The war isn't over."

"Don't leave me, François!"

"I have no choice."

"I want to go with you."

He burst out laughing, drawing the attention of the other diners and a waiter, who hurried over.

"Did monsieur wish for something?"

"Yes, a bottle of your best champagne."

"What are we celebrating?" asked Léa crisply.

"You, my darling. Your beautiful eyes, your speedy recovery, life ..."

When Léa failed to smile, he went on:

"Don't worry, everything will be fine."

"I don't know why, but I'm more frightened now than during the four years of the Occupation."

"That's only normal. A new world is being born—better in some ways and worse in others. It's what you don't know that frightens you. But I know you can overcome that fear. Go back to Montillac. Start rebuilding. That's what I want you to do until I come back."

"I'm not going back to Montillac, at least not for a very, very long time. And who says that I'm going to spend my time waiting for you? I suppose you'd like me to start knitting socks for prisoners, making parcels for orphans, visiting the sick."

"Yes, I can see it now! Léa, bending down to comfort the wounded, consoling the grief-stricken widow, doing without so that others can have a few biscuits or a little toy. Ouch!"

Léa's foot had not missed its mark.

"That will teach you."

"You're such a brute, you'd never make it. You'll never be a real woman."

"How dare you say that!" she retorted, throwing her shoulders back, her nostrils flaring.

He could not resist the temptation to tease her. Never was she more desirable than when she was angry. She was a real woman all right, just the way he liked them, free and submissive, vain and unaffected, courageous and weak, gay and melancholy, sensual and modest. . . . Well, not really modest. Provocative was more like it. She didn't behave like a girl from a good French family. She was more like the heroine in an American movie, tantalizing, untouchable, yet capable of sit-

270

ting down in a way that revealed lots of leg and even more on top. Yes, that's what she was like. He knew how she loved to arouse men. When they looked at her, she blossomed. He wasn't jealous exactly, more annoyed and amused.

"I was just kidding, you know I was."

The waiter brought the champagne, providing a momentary distraction. They drank in silence, lost in their thoughts.

Léa was the first to speak.

"When are you leaving?"

"The day after tomorrow."

All at once, she grew pale, and her features became drawn. She emptied her glass.

"So soon!"

Two simple words, yet he nearly stood up and hugged her.

"Let's go!"

He paid the bill and rose to leave.

They ran across the Champs-Élysées, and as they entered the Rue Balzac, she asked:

"Where are we going?"

"To a hotel."

A wave of desire washed over her. She would have liked to protest, to be shocked at his audacity, to tell him that she would not be treated like a streetwalker, none of which was true. He behaved exactly as she hoped he would.

The hotel was done entirely in pink curtains, crystal chandeliers, thick, discreet carpets, and mirrors. Over each door was the name of a flower. The staff managed to look indifferent, yet jaded. The perfume of the previous occupant lingered in the room with its huge canopy bed. A comely chambermaid entered with an armful of thick, pink towels. On the wall, was Fragonard's *Le Verrou*. Léa smiled. The same print hung on the wall of her father's study at Montillac.

"Come!"

Just as impatient as François, she tore off her clothes and, without bothering to pull down the pink satin coverlet, lay back on the bed.

271

The light filtering through the silk lamp shades bathed their bodies in soft, pink light. They lay silently smoking. Her body seemed soft and fragile, his, raw and hard. She propped herself up on one elbow and traced the scar running from his heart to his groin.

"Have you been wounded again since Spain?"

"Not seriously. A bullet in the shoulder. Would you still love me if I were covered in saber scars?"

"It suits your image."

"And what, pray tell, is that?"

" 'One of those', as my Uncle Luc would say. She looks like *one of those* girls."

"He's absolutely right, you do."

Léa started pounding his chest, but soon found herself pinned beneath him.

"Now what are you going to do? You are at my mercy. Do you love me?"

"Let go of me! I won't answer until you—"

"Until I what?"

"François! Stop it! I have to go home!"

"There's still time."

"No! No! I'm afraid I'll get pregnant."

François suddenly stopped playing.

"Now you tell me!"

"I just remembered!"

When he burst out laughing, Léa started.

"You should have thought of that earlier. I'd love to have a child by you."

"You're crazy, François!"

"Crazy about you!"

"Let go of me! I don't want a baby!"

"Too late!"

She struggled at first, pretending to put up a fight, then yielded to the desire aroused in her by the man she loved but could not quite admit loving.

Later, this business about a baby began to worry François. He had meant what he said about wanting a child by her, but given the circumstances in which it was uttered, it was purely

272

symbolic. He had tried to raise the subject once or twice before, asking Léa whether he should take any precautions, but she had always evaded his questions. He had been all too happy not to have to bother, and now she was saying that she was afraid she would get pregnant! How careless! What would he do if it were true? He knew of a woman near the Cambronne subway station, but not for all the tea in China would he allow her to bring her filthy hands anywhere near Léa. The only solution would be to marry her.

For the longest time, nothing could have been further from his mind. He loved women and freedom too much for that! And yet he had already thought about marrying Léa. Would she accept? He wasn't entirely sure. She was different from other women; she had never looked for a husband, apart from a passing interest in Laurent d'Argilat which had been snuffed out by his engagement to Camille. What a wonderful woman she had become, but so strange, so unpredictable! She could be moved from laughter to tears and from temerity to the most abject fear in a matter of moments. He put this down to the trauma of the war, yet part of him was not entirely convinced . . .

"Help me join the Red Cross."

There she went again! Why on earth did she want to volunteer for mud, blood, and horror?

"The Red Cross doesn't need you. I know that many young women from good families have joined up, but it's not a tea party, you know."

"I know that. I'm serious, François. Please help me."

She did seem serious enough, he thought, his heart sinking. What if this were her way of putting distance between them? Or of being closer to Laurent?

"Why, Léa?"

"Would you start a bath for me?"

He went to the bathroom and stood gazing at his reflection in the mirror. Watch your step, old man, it seemed to be saying, you could lose her! Then again, you could find yourself tying the knot!

"Why?" he repeated, re-entering the room.

"I don't know for sure. I just know that I have to do it."

"Think hard, Léa, this isn't the sort of decision one makes lightly."

"I'm not, even if I don't know exactly why I'm doing it. I could give you a dozen reasons, each of them valid. I don't want to see my sisters, my aunts—"

"Laurent has asked you to look after Charles."

"That is the one thing that would have made me stay. But Sabine can do a better job of looking after him than I can."

"But he loves you!"

"I know. Please don't say anything! I want to go. I'm suffocating here. I don't have anything in common with people here."

"Even me?"

"With you, its . . . well . . . it's wonderful when I'm in your arms, but then . . . all of my fears come rushing back."

"Léa, those are only figments of your imagination."

"Perhaps, but that doesn't change anything. Please, if you love me, help me."

There was such distress and determination in her voice. He held her close, stroking her head aching with so many painful and conflicting emotions.

"I'll do whatever you ask. If you had a little patience and a little trust in me, I could make those fears disappear forever. It breaks my heart to see you like this and not be able to help you. But if you think that this is what is best for you, I'll do whatever you ask."

"Thanks. Darn, my bath!"

Chapter Twenty-Seven

The next day, François called to say that he had arranged a meeting with the woman in charge of screening Red Cross applicants and that, at his request, Monsieur de Bourbon-Busset had agreed to provide a recommendation.

"Who is he?"

"He's the man who created the commission for the repatriation of prisoners of war, deportees, and refugees in Paris last August 24. He's also the head of the French Red Cross. You couldn't have a better recommendation."

"Tell him how grateful I am. Tell him that he won't regret it."

"The meeting is at nine o'clock tomorrow morning at 21 rue Octave-Feuillet. That's in the Sixteenth Arrondissement. Don't forget to take your I.D. A Madame de Peyerimhoff will see you. And be on time: she's a real stickler for punctuality."

"Thanks, you're wonderful."

"Don't thank me. I'm not doing this for the pleasure of it. I just realize that you aren't going to back down. You're so bloody stubborn. I have to leave tomorrow—early. Please say you'll spend the evening with me."

"I'm going to have a hard time convincing my aunts to let me go."

"Leave that to me. I'll come by at seven. Put on your best dress."

Léa's heart was pounding as she replaced the receiver. She dreaded seeing François go. Her uneasiness now was much stronger than her concern for Laurent, who was actually fighting. The thought that something might happen to François completely undid her. Although she had not heard from Laurent, she told herself that if he were wounded—she refused to believe that anything worse could happen—they would be the first to know.

The flowers and chocolates worked their magic on Albertine and Lisa. Albertine managed to say that Léa probably should not stay out too late as she was just beginning to feel better. François gave them his word and whisked Léa away in a luxurious sedan confiscated from a prosperous black marketeer. He took her to a new restaurant that had just opened in Montparnasse. It reminded Léa of the little clandestine restaurant in the Rue Saint-Jacques.

"Whatever happened to Marthe and Marcel Andrieu? And their son René?"

"After René's arrest—"

"René was arrested?"

"Yes. He was tortured and deported. Marthe and Jeannette went back to the Lot region with the baby early last summer. Marcel stayed on. His concierge denounced him as a collaborator. The superintendent of police had been one of their best customers, so he cleared Marcel's name and declared that he had been a member of the Resistance."

"Wasn't he?"

"Yes and no. He helped members of the Resistance, even hid a few, but he had never wanted to join. René did though."

"Poor Marthe."

"Let's drink to her health. She'd like that."

The meal was delicious and Léa felt happier than she had in months. Once again, François marvelled at her vitality.

He announced that he had opened an account for her at the *Société nationale* on Boulevard Saint-Michel. She thanked him, but said no more. Now I can buy myself a new pair of shoes, she thought.

That evening they made love with unaccustomed slowness and attentiveness, savoring each other's bodies as never before. They let their pleasure build slowly, irrepressibly, until it drowned them in a sea of tenderness so painful that it brought tears to their eyes. She wrapped her legs around him, only releasing her grip when she felt him swell and grow hard again. Again, their pleasure brought oblivion.

They fell asleep in each other's arms. Léa awoke before François, and looked at him intently. Something told her that she would not see him again for a long time. She studied his face; in repose, he looked like a young boy. How old was he? She had never asked. How was it that she knew so little about him, yet they had known each other for years? What was it that had made her reluctant to know more? Now she wanted to know everything about him. His childhood, his youth. Did he have brothers and sisters? What were his parents like? Were they still alive? Why had he fought in Spain? Why had he gone there? How well did he know Uncle Adrien? What women had he loved? What had he done before the war? And what would he do when it was over? There were so many questions that would remain unanswered; tomorrow, he would be gone.

How handsome he was! Yes, handsome was the word. He had strong features and a pronounced jaw, softened by a magnificent mouth and full lips. His beetle brows could accentuate a hard look then, moments later, express tenderness or irony. His sarcasm had often hurt her, although it concealed a passionate interest in everything that concerned her. The memory of these looks was almost more than she could bear.

Her fingers caressed his strong shoulders, playing with the hair on his chest. As they slid down his belly, a hand reached out and grabbed her by the wrist.

"Caught you! Depriving a poor man of his sleep!"

Through half-closed eyes, he looked at her with an intensity quite unlike his playful tone. She tried to withdraw her hand.

"No, don't stop. I like the way you touch me."

Her fingers resumed their downward journey, finally closing around his sleeping penis. Deftly, she began to stroke it until it stood stiff and erect between her fingers. Placing her legs on either side of his, she lowered herself slowly on to him. She made love to him, controlling the pace of his pleasure, slowing when she sensed that he was about to burst, watching the effect this produced on his face.

"You are mine," she said defiantly.

Clinging to one another, they gazed into each other's eyes, baring themselves to one another, letting go completely, their faces disfigured by pleasure. As her body shook with spasms of pleasure, he held her at arm's length, drinking in this image of her, then it was his turn.

After the briefest or perhaps the longest of pauses, she collapsed with a cry, clinging to him. He rocked her as the spasms continued.

As last, she was quiet and quite motionless. With a damp towel, he sponged her forehead and temples, and began wiping her stomach and thighs.

"That's cold," she murmured, pushing him away.

He put her clothes on her as if dressing a little child, not attempting to brush out her tangled hair. She was as limp as a ragdoll.

He carried her to the car, then up the stairs to her room. When he laid her naked on her bed, she was already asleep, smiling sweetly like a baby.

He tore himself away from his contemplation of her, now unbearable, and left the apartment as quickly as he could.

Chapter Twenty-Eight

Bordeaux, Tuesday, August 22, 1944

Dear Léa

I don't know whether this letter will ever reach you. I may rip it up before finishing it or it may get lost in the mail.

Those of us who collaborated with the Germans, worked with the Militia or the Gestapo or signed up to fight in Germany are trying to get out of Bordeaux as fast as we can. Remember the guys who used to strut up and down the Quai des Quinconces and the Rue Sainte-Catherine and at the Régent? You should see them now! Many are trying to join the *maquis*, but the guys in the Resistance are suspicious of anyone trying to join up at the last minute. Ever since the Allies landed, they've been falling all over themselves to get in. You'll see. When the war is over, the F.F.I.'s biggest heroes will be *collabos* who changed hats. They're really disgusting! If the tide turns again, they'll come running back to Marshal Pétain. I've decided to go against the current. I'm joining the side that's losing. I'm going to be the underdog, just like in the stories we used to read. Remember the dark knights who made pacts with the devil? They were our favorites. Of course, they always lost, but they took a few down with them!

I guess this is my way of saying that I didn't sign up with the *Waffen SS* for some political ideal. It's just that there's nothing left for me here. No future. When the war is over, the guys on top of the heap will only have one desire: revenge. I'm not going to be a lamb waiting to go to slaughter. There is only one

279

thing that worries me: what if they take it out on my parents. My father has received many threats. They're blaming him for the death of your aunt and the destruction of Montillac, but they're wrong. They found Maurice Fiaux's body. He was executed by the Resistance. Aristide also had Grand-Clément and his wife executed, too. Now they control the region. I saw your cousin Philippe last week. I told him to go into hiding. He said his father refused because he has nothing to hide. Not everyone in Bordeaux thinks that way. Everybody's following the events in Paris closely. You're probably on the barricades, making last minute preparations for the Allies. It wouldn't have taken much for me to be there with you.

This letter may be my last. I want you to know that I'm sorry about the way I behaved. I was crazy about you. I know that's no excuse, but I want you to know anyway. Also, I hope you will cherish the happy memories of our childhood. I'll remember chasing you through the vineyards, playing hide-and- seek in the chapels of the calvary at Verdelais, swimming in the Garonne, and playing in the hay.

Think of me from time to time. Remember that you are the only woman I have ever loved or will ever love. You will always be in my heart.

Your friend,
Mathias

P.S. In a few hours, a trainload of German rail workers will be leaving Bordeaux for Germany. There's a coach for us.

Mathias!

Where was he now? Was he dead or alive? His letter had taken nearly three months to reach her. The mails were still irregular. She had not heard from Laurent or François, but was too busy to be worried; her Red Cross training had begun.

On the day François left Paris, Léa went to her interview in the Rue Octave-Feuillet. She had slept in, and barely had time to dress. The subway, packed as always, seemed to move at a snail's pace. DUBO ... DUBON ... DUBONNET. The billboards along the platforms were almost legible. At Pompe Station, she elbowed her way through the crowd on the platform and bounded up the stairs. It was ten past nine.

Madame de Peyerimhoff, impeccable in a well-cut blue uniform, greeted her coolly.

"You're late."

"Yes, Madame. I apologize."

"You have been recommended by our president. Do you know him?"

"No."

"I see," said Madame de Peyerimhoff, eyeing her scornfully. She looked down.

"Do you always wear your hair like that?"

Léa blushed violently, as though she had been caught with her hand in the cookie jar.

"Is that the latest style? I'm sure some people find it attractive. However, if you are accepted, I suggest you find something a little more compatible with our uniform. Do you know how to drive?"

"Yes, Madame."

"Do you know how to change a tire? Or to repair an engine?"

"No."

"I see. We'll have to teach you everything. I don't suppose you know how to administer first aid either, do you?"

Léa was growing impatient. This woman was beginning to get on her nerves with her airs.

"No, Madame."

"Why are you signing up?"

"To serve my country."

Phew! She had remembered François's instructions. This seemed to satisfy Madame de Peyerimhoff who continued in a friendlier tone:

"Very good. If you are accepted, you will undergo six weeks of training, during which time you will learn basic automobile mechanics and first aid. Then, you will be sent wherever you are most badly needed."

"When will I know whether or not I have been accepted?"

"Later this week. We have many applicants and we only want those who are most capable. If you are accepted, you will be notified."

A strong handshake and the interview was over.

Five days later, Léa sat down to her first meal with the new recruits in the Rue François-Ier. She quickly showed an aptitude for removing wheels, cleaning plugs, and minor engine repairs. Alix Auboineau, in charge of the ambulance pool in the Rue de Passy, complimented her in front of the other women, one of whom remarked, with a knowing air:

"The Chief has taken a shine to you."

"Why do you call her 'the Chief'?"

"Claire Mauriac gave her the nickname."

"You mean the daughter of ...?"

"Yes. She's been posted in Béziers, she's doing an excellent job. I hope she'll be back soon."

No doubt, the friendship of the other women and the training which Léa enjoyed helped her to overcome the fear and terror conveyed by Ruth's letter, which arrived on October 7. Léa read it aloud to her sisters and aunts.

Verdelais, October 2, 1944

Dear Léa and Laure,

For the past two weeks, I have been putting off the moment when I had to sit down and write this letter. What I have to say is so horrible that I can barely hold my pen, which explains why my writing is so illegible. My darling little ones, you will need to be very brave when you read what follows. Albert is dead. His body was found buried in the garden of the villa occupied by the Gestapo in Le Bouscat. The autopsy revealed that he probably committed suicide by hanging himself after being tortured. Mireille has been extremely courageous. Not a single tear, and yet, she still has not heard from her son. Albert was laid to rest in the cemetery at Saint-Macaire. The mayor of Bordeaux and several members of the Resistance were there. The event sparked some rather shameful behavior, I am afraid to say. Collaborators—or supposed collaborators—were beaten up and insulted. Ever since the death of Madame Bouchardeau and the Fayard's, the slightest sign of violence sets me to a trembling that lasts for hours. The doctor said that it would pass with time.

Your uncle, Monsieur Delmas, and his son, Philippe, were lynched by a crowd in Bordeaux ...

"Oh, my God!"
Lisa de Montpleynet lurched toward the bathroom. The others sat in stunned silence. When Lisa returned, pale and trembling, her hair wet, they had not moved. The old woman placed a hand on her sister's sleeve. This tender gesture roused Albertine from her stupor.
"Continue, Léa," she said, her voice faltering.
Léa made several false starts before continuing.

... their bodies were paraded through the streets of Bordeaux, then left on the Quai de la Monnaie. The apartment and office were ransacked. It was horrible! Their housekeeper, Madame Dupuis, came to see me at the hospital. She said that Monsieur Delmas hadn't been the same since hearing about Pierrot. In a few days, he aged ten years. She and Philippe and Monsieur Giraud, the firm's oldest employee, tried to convince him to leave Bordeaux and go into hiding. He refused, but told Philippe to go. Philippe refused to leave his father alone. Madame Dupuis is convinced that your uncle stayed on so that he would die. My dears, I know that this is hard news. Please forgive me. The worst is yet to come ...

"No, not him," cried Léa, who had broken off her reading several times.
"Who?" asked Sabine.
"You read it," said Léa, handing her the letter.

—the *gendarmes* sent for me to identify a body. Three other people had been summoned, a rather short man in a uniform and two members of the F.F.I. They looked at the body and, one by one, made a positive identification. When it was my turn, I began to feel poorly, but the commander of the *gendarmerie* insisted, saying that I was the only member of the family left in the region. So I looked. Part of his face had been eaten away but it was, unmistakably, your Uncle Adrien—

Léa collapsed on the floor, sobbing:

"I knew it. I knew it."

Albertine and Laure helped her to the sofa.

"Lisa, call the doctor!"

"How did he die?" Léa gasped, pushing them away.

"Sabine will finish reading the letter. You know the worst now. Why torment yourself?" asked Albertine.

"No! Finish the letter."

The coroner said it was a suicide.

"A suicide?" they cried in unison.

"But he was a priest. That's impossible!" exclaimed Albertine, crossing herself.

Overcome with grief, Léa lay curled up, her teeth chattering. I knew it, she thought. I should have understood what was happening when he let me see that he had lost his faith. Why did he do it? He was courageous. His work in the Resistance was important. It was so unlike him. She tried desperately to dismiss the idea that her uncle had taken his own life, but something told her that it was true.

Kneeling, hands clasped, Albertine and Lisa prayed. For these devout Catholics, there was no greater crime. Knowing that this man, whose words of love and peace had filled Notre-Dame Cathedral, who had guided them better than their own confessor, would burn in Hell for all eternity not only caused them immense grief, it shook the very foundations of his teachings. By this heinous act, he had refuted the very existence of a Christian God. Nothing could be clearer.

Laure picked up the letter which had fallen from Sabine's hands and continued reading:

None of us wanted to believe it, but we were forced to face the truth, given what the commander of the *gendarmerie* and the coroner had said. Your poor uncle was laid to rest in the family tomb at Verdelais, beside your aunt and parents. There was neither mass nor benediction. Had there not been so many flowers, it would have been the funeral of a total outcast.

I'm at my friend Simone's in Verdelais and will stay on here until I'm back on my feet. Then, if it's all right with you, I'd like to come to Paris. The harvest started two days ago. It will be a good one, but the wine will be mediocre. I have had to hire German prisoners to help with the picking. They are so afraid of the *maquis* that they are working very hard. Some decisions will have to be made about the future of the estate and the house. I started going through Fayard's papers, but found it too confusing. Our lawyer is dead. We will have to find someone to replace him. Give it some thought.

My dears, please forgive me for being the bearer of so much bad news.

Ever faithful,
Ruth

That's right! thought Léa. It's harvest time. I had completely forgotten.

They spent the day shut in their rooms. Charles and Pierre sought refuge in the kitchen with Estelle.

Léa missed her class on topography. Albertine called Madame de Peyerimhoff to explain, in part, why Léa was absent.

In the days that followed, Léa experienced a closeness with the women in her course that she had not known existed.

During practice runs on impassable roads in Marly-le-Roi Forest, she showed herself to be an excellent driver and mechanic. The Chief said that after the war she would have no trouble finding employment in a garage. Where first aid concerned, however, she seemed to be all thumbs.

"Watch it!" shouted the doctor teaching the course, "if you lift someone with stomach injuries like that, you'll spill his guts. This man has spinal cord injuries and you're lifting him like a sack of spuds. God help me if you ever have to give me first aid."

Léa spent her evenings with Laure and her friends, busy trading cigarettes, whisky, gasoline, and stockings with American soldiers. Sometimes, she and Laure would stay out dancing until one in the morning, driven by the desire to live and to live fast that most young people their age felt. The soldiers that had come to liberate Paris were attracted to Léa, but she

285

spurned their advances. She flirted and drank with them, but remained strangely distant, present yet somehow in a world of her own. In the arms of these eager young men, she seemed ready and willing only for as long as it took to dance one dance until one day, a tall black sergeant who didn't appreciate her teasing slapped her.

On November 7, she received a letter from Laurent. It was dated October 28.

Dear Léa,

François Tavernier, who came here briefly with a message for General Leclerc, told me that you were better. I was so happy I didn't know what to say. He also told me that you were determined to join the Red Cross. You know that I don't entirely approve, but each of us is the master of his own destiny. Please tell you aunts how grateful I am for everything they're doing for Charles. Tell them to talk to him about me, and when you are with him, talk to him about his mother.

We have been living in a mud-colored world since September 22. The public buses that brought the battalions of Parisian F.F.I.'s joining the Second Armored Division went in right up to their axles. We had to abandon two of them before crossing the Meurthe. The others were pulled out with Sherman tanks. When they see it, the young recruits from Paris say it's like being in Panama. You should see these poor young kids in their sandals and street shoes, ankle-deep in the mud, with no uniforms or helmets and one rifle for every two men. They patrol the woods. They complain all the time, but never back down. We are constantly being shelled by the Germans. They aren't short of ammunition, as was the case in August. We're expecting a real offensive any day now, but the armored division is getting edgy. We have lost two of our best officers just sitting here; I first met Dubuy and Geoffroy in Africa and we became friends. The most impatient is my friend, Georges Buis. He says he feels like he's growing roots, and keeps grumbling about turning into a military monument.

Morale has reached an all-time low. The men are already complaining about having to spend the winter in what they call a "god-forsaken hole." For a break, we drive over to one of the

286

clubs behind the lines. The rain never stops. We are prouder of the few miles we cover in a day than of the prisoners we take. Even Captain Déré, who was in Tunisia and is close to retirement, is talking about going back to the *Corps Expéditionnaire*, the task force leaving for Indochina, so he can "see some action." The enthusiasm of the liberation has worn off and the men's spirits are low. It's high time they found us something to do, otherwise, the Second Armored Division is going to be cancelled for lack of interest!

I have just re-read my letter and realize what a dismal picture I have painted. It's really not like that at all. We have fought valiantly since leaving Paris. It must be the weather and the waiting that's getting to me.

I am sitting at a table in the mess hall, writing by the light of a storm lantern, watching the rain through the "window" of the tent. It's getting to even the most even-keeled among us.

Well, it's time I stopped moaning and groaning. I had hoped to feel the warmth of your smile on my face as I wrote. Instead, I feel the darkness pressing down on me and on these lines. Forgive me. Give Charles a kiss for me.

Fondly,
Laurent

In spite of the depression casting a pall over his letter, Laurent was well, but what about François? Why hadn't he written? Léa had gone to the Ministry of War, but they were unable to give her any news of Commander Tavernier.

On November 20, Léa passed her examination, in spite of total disaster on the first aid section, during which the orderly playing the part of a wounded soldier fell off the stretcher. After speeches by Madame de Peyerimhoff, Alix Auboineau, and the doctor who had taught them first aid, Léa put her diploma away carefully.

Three days later, she was sent to Amiens, where the château of Mademoiselle de Guillencourt served as headquarters for the Red Cross. She was immediately put to work helping civilians: children mutilated by land mines, victims from the Front, Belgian and French refugees, people dying from exposure, hunger, and dysentery. At first, she thought that she would never last, but another young woman named Jeanine Ivoy, so tiny that her uniform must have been made specially for her, took Léa under her wing and kept her courage up.

Finally, toward the end of December, Léa received a packet of mail with letters from Sabine, Albertine, Laurent, and François. She ran to the room she shared with Jeanine and tore open François's letter, which was postmarked December 17:

My darling,
I have no idea where my letter will reach you. I talked to Laure on the telephone a few moments ago and she told me that you had been sent to Amiens. She wasn't sure whether you were still there. After my first mission, General de Gaulle gave me another. Now he is sending me ... I can't tell you where, but don't worry, I'll find a way of dropping in on you in Amiens or wherever you are. I miss you terribly. I have this overwhelming desire to take you in my arms and carry you far, far away. When the war is over, I'm going to take you to Brazil. I have friends there. We'll go to the beach and make love and forget the last four years. Take care and don't be angry with me for being so brief. There is a plane waiting for me. Did I tell you that I love you? Well, I do! Kisses and more kisses,
François

François's letter brought the memory of his caresses flooding back, enveloping Léa in waves of pleasure.
I love him, too, she thought.
With a sigh of contentment, she slipped the letter under her uniform, next to her skin.
She opened Sabine's letter.

Dear little sister,
Here in Paris, we are managing thanks to Laure, who is able to get a little coal and food on the black market. She says to say hello and to tell you that she is fine. Ruth has joined us in Paris.

288

You wouldn't recognize her. She has aged terribly and jumps at the slightest sound. We have hired a new lawyer. He has found a good man to look after the vineyards. Come spring, we'll have to decide whether or not to sell Montillac. Laure and I are in favor of selling. It has too many unhappy memories for us. We don't have the money to rebuild and the thought that the house now stands in ruins is too depressing. What should we do?

Pierre is fine; he's into everything. He still only has six teeth and I wonder if that's normal. Charles is too quiet and old for his years. He asks for you often, especially at bedtime. Other than that, he is fine. Aunt Albertine and Aunt Lisa are getting older too, but they are still as good to us as they ever were. My hair is growing back in and pretty soon, I'll be able to go out without a turban. I haven't heard from Otto, but I just know that he is alive. It's awful not having any news or anyone to talk to except Laure sometimes.

As you can imagine, the liberation of Strasbourg was a very emotional moment for Ruth. The purge is still in full swing here. The people who are sentenced aren't always the ones who have done the most harm. Everyone listens to the French broadcasts from Baden-Baden and the familiar voices of Brinon, Déat, Luchaire and company. The other evening, there was a gala for the Resistance at the *Comédie-Française*. Someone read a poem by Claudel in General de Gaulle's honor. It was my first evening out. As I looked around, I saw a few elegant turbans in the audience. A journalist sitting near me told the person sitting next to him that the poem was written in '42, in honor of Marshal Pétain, and touched up.

Monsieur le Maréchal, you hold France in your arms.
You are all it has. It is awakening, calling softly.
France, listen to the old man bending over you,
Speaking to you like a father.

What do you think of that? Laure took me to the bar at *Le Crillon*. There was a huge crowd of women in uniform and English and American officers, vying to outdo each other in elegance. I recognized the former mistress of a German general on the arm of an English colonel. She recognized me and winked as if to say, business is business!

They have finally arrested Petiot. He was a lieutenant or a captain in the F.F.I.!

We are starting to get ready for Christmas with the little ones. We will miss you so much!

Your loving sister,
Sabine

Sabine seemed to be coping quite well. It would be better for her—in more ways than one—if Otto were dead. She was capable of raising Pierre alone. As for Montillac, what did it matter what happened? It was too upsetting for Léa to even think about it. She needed to forget, to turn her back on what had once been her reason for living.

Aunt Albertine's letter contained only advice and the news that Léa would soon be receiving a Christmas parcel with woollen stockings and warm underwear, which she badly needed. The light-weight gabardine uniform was no match for the wind that blew across the flat region.

Léa turned Laurent's letter over and over. At last, she opened it.

Dear Léa,

I hope that you are not suffering from the cold as much as the Second Armored Division. When he saw how cold the men were, General Leclerc ordered lambskin vests made. We are all grateful to him. After the rain and the mud came the snow and ice. This poses as many problems for the vehicles as it does for the men. You have no doubt been following our progress in the papers. After taking Baccarat, we drank champagne out of goblets engraved with a gloved fist. They were to have been for Göring. I have made the acquaintance of Colonel Fabien. He is a Communist and was a member of the International Brigades. He fought with Colonel Rol-Tanguy, who led the French Forces of the Interior on the Île de France during the liberation of Paris. He's a funny sort of man, always dressed in riding breeches with his tunic buttoned right up to the collar. Leading three thousand men, almost all from the suburbs of Paris, he followed the Second Armored Division along with members of the F.F.I. from all over France, including the Janson Group from Sailly. Joining Patton's III Corps, the Paris Brigade has been renamed the *Groupement tactique de Lorraine*. Fabien asked to be part of the French First Army under General de Lattre de Tassigny. On December 10, at Vesoul, the General inspected the troops. A number of the new recruits are barely seventeen years of age; some are having a rough time of it. They find it hard to take orders from some of the officers and noncommissioned officers, especially those wearing brand new uniforms. They're called "mothballs," a nickname which is self-explanatory.

Fabien is an extremely interesting individual. He joined the International Brigades when he was only seventeen and was wounded in action. It was he who killed the German officer at the Barbès-Rochechouart subway station on August 21, 1941. He was arrested and tortured but managed to escape and joined the Underground. His father was shot by the Germans and his wife was deported.

The last few days before the march on Strasbourg were hard on all of us. Buis thinks that the men were on edge because of the bad weather. Leclerc was in a foul mood. He kept pacing the damp rooms of Château de Birkenwald, where de Foucault spent his holidays as a boy. At dawn on November 23, it was pouring rain. The General tapped the floor with his walking stick, knitting his brows, his right cheek twitching, a sign of great agitation. Finally, at half past ten, a messenger pulled up on a motorcycle and came running into the room where all of the officers were gathered. With fingers numb from the cold, he brought out a piece of yellow paper with a message from Rouvillois. *Tissue in iodine.* This meant that Rouvillois had entered Strasbourg. General Leclerc burst out laughing and cried, "Let's go!"

Luckily, we had very few casualties, but there was one death that was a great blow: our chaplain, Father Houchet, had been with Leclerc ever since Chad. When the General found out, he set off for the hospital in the middle of the night. I saw him wipe away a tear as he said goodbye to a man whose faith, humor, generosity, and undying devotion had made him the

291

most loved and respected man of the Division. Two days later, the soldiers who were supposed to act as pallbearers were unable to reach the chapel and so the officers carried his coffin.

On Sunday the 26th, the standard of the Twelfth Cavalry was raised over Place Kléber before a small, silent crowd. There was a long pause. Then, all at once, windows were flung open and flags began to flap in the wind. People started to sing *La Marseillaise*, then fell silent. It wasn't until General Leclerc arrived that the population of Strasbourg would really let themselves go.

Five days later, we left Strasbourg to join up with the French First Army which had recaptured Belfort and Mulhouse. The Germans were now in a pocket, fighting with their backs to the Rhine. I say we "left" Strasbourg, but it would be more accurate to say that we "left like donkeys trying to back up" as my father would say. We did not want to become part of the First Army. The weather was atrocious. Driving rain and snow. It's a good thing the Second Armoured Division is so tough! Even under the worst possible conditions, someone manages to crack a joke. The other day, for example, we took cover in a little train station, the kind that has a sign saying "Departures" on one side and "Arrivals" on the other. Over the tracks came a volley of 88s, which is fairly rare because the Germans don't have much artillery. When it was over, we stood up. Georges Buis brushed off his uniform and pointed to the hole made by the shells, saying to La Horie and me, "Those Germans have no imagination." We burst out laughing: the shells had come in by Arrivals and left by Departures. There was a time when I would have called this sort of remark, sometimes delivered in the thick of the battle "mess hall humor." Now I realize that it helps me not to go crazy thinking about how Camille suffered before she died. Sometimes, when it's too cold to sleep, I see her sweet face bending over me. It's as though she were beckoning to me, saying: "Come, come with me, don't leave me alone."

Forgive me, Léa, for talking like this. I know you loved her too. How is Charles? Maybe you don't know. Maybe you're in some "god-forsaken hole," too. If you are in Paris, tell him about his mother and about me, tell him all about when he was a little boy. It will be Christmas soon. Do you realize that I

292

haven't spent a single Christmas with my son since he was born? Spoil him, Léa. Buy as many sweets and toys and decorations as you can. Tell him that I will be thinking about him especially hard on Christmas Eve.

Love,
Laurent

At the thought of being hundreds of miles away from her family on the first Christmas since the liberation, Léa wept bitterly. Memories of a childhood of indulgence came back to her. Cold, fervent prayers during midnight mass at the basilica in Verdelais or under the medieval arches of Saint-Macaire; wonderment on seeing the creche; the angel that nodded and played the first few notes of *A Child is Born in Bethlehem* when coins were dropped into its plaster urn; joy mixed with fear at the first glimpse of the Christmas tree in the courtyard in front of the house; giggles and squeals of delight as she and Laure and Sabine, their hearts pounding, opened the door of the living room and saw a wondrous pile of multi-colored packages by a roaring fire of vine shoots. After a brief pause, an instant of theatrical surprise, they would rush over to their carefully polished shoes, screaming shrilly. They would tear at the paper and ribbons, jumping with joy, and run to kiss their parents and Ruth, whom they suspected of being in collusion with Father Christmas. Even as they grew older, Christmas was always a wonderful time. Not for anything in the world would they have wanted to be anywhere else. The war had brought an end to all that. It was Léa who tried to keep up the tradition of Christmas during the Occupation; although subdued, they had still been celebrations. This was Léa's first Christmas away from home. Nothing, not the suffering, not the war, not even the loss of her loved ones, seemed more terrible at this moment.

"What's wrong?" asked Jeanine, coming into the room. "Did you get bad news?"

Léa just shook her head.

"Then why are you so upset?"

"It's just that ... it's ... it's Christmas," she blubbered.

Jeanine stared, open-mouthed, at her beautiful friend. Then she, too, began to cry. How hard it is to let go of childhood! They cried, not daring to look at one another, then their eyes met and they burst out laughing, hugging one another

On December 24 they returned late, exhausted after a day spent transporting wounded soldiers to hospitals throughout the region. They climbed the front steps, dragging their feet. The hall was in darkness, but they could see bright lights under the living room door. They could hear laughter and music. What was going on? This was not normally allowed. They opened the living room door and stood gaping at a huge Christmas tree, decorated with strings of lights and bits of cotton batting snow. A fire blazed in the fireplace. A tall man leaned against the mantel, a glass in one hand. He came forward, smiling.

"You're the last ones! Come in and close the door."

Léa slowly closed the door, then turned, gripping the carved handle behind her back so tightly that her hands hurt.

François had some difficulty prying her fingers free. The chatelaine came over to them.

"Mademoiselle Delmas, what's wrong? You're all pale. No doubt, the emotion of seeing your fiancé again."

Her fiancé? What was she talking about?

"Thanks to Commander Tavernier, we're going to have a real Christmas," the old woman continued. "He's brought everything we need! Now, off you go and get changed. You're a sight for sore eyes!"

François leaned slightly forward and said, with his most charming smile:

"If it's quite all right with you, I'd like to accompany Mademoiselle Delmas."

"By all means, Commander. In the meantime, we'll finish setting the table."

Léa followed François out of the room as if in a trance.

"Where is your room?"

"Upstairs."

When they reached her room, he threw his arms around her, covering her with kisses.

She let him kiss her, unable to respond. After a moment he stopped and held her at arm's length.

"I expected a little more enthusiasm."

Something inside her snapped.

"You show up here from God knows where and introduce yourself as my fiancé. Then the moment we're alone, you attack me and . . . what's so funny?"

"That's more like it! I didn't recognize you at first."

Léa blushed and tried to pry herself free.

"Léa, I don't have much time. I risk a court martial for coming here. I'm supposed to be in Colmar."

"Why did you tell her that you were my fiancé?"

"So that no one would question why I was here and so that I could see you alone. Kiss me!"

She was crazy to ask all these questions. She was so happy to see him that she thought she would die. She returned his kisses and pulled him over to one of the beds.

"Come," she said.

They made love as if every second counted, but their bodies adjusted to the quickened pace and pleasure was not long in coming.

Someone knocked softly. Stifling giggles, they straightened their uniforms.

"Come in," called Léa.

Her tiny roommate entered the room.

"Sorry, but I have to get changed," she said, not daring to look at them.

"I'm the one who should apologize for detaining Léa. I'll be downstairs."

The young women got changed without exchanging a word.

The champagne, oysters, and foie gras that François brought made for a very lively Christmas Eve. By the end of the meal, everyone was slightly tipsy. Shortly after midnight, he stood up to take his leave.

"So soon!" they all cried, except Léa, who just bowed her head.

"Alas! I must be back by morning. Please carry on without me. Would you see me to my car, dearest?"

"Good-bye, Commander, and thank you for everything!"

Outside, the snow was blowing in gusts. They found the car under a heavy blanket of snow. François opened the door and pushed Léa inside. His cold hands slid under her skirt.

"Unbutton me," he ordered.

"No," she said, doing as he asked.

They made love fully-dressed, with a violence and brutality that contrasted sharply with their tender words of love. Afterward, in the dim glow of the overhead light, they gazed at each other, silently committing the image of the other to memory. No doubt it was the cold, but Léa thought she saw a tear form in the corner of his eye and lose itself in his hair.

A nearby clock struck two. François stirred and got out of the car.

"I have to go."

He started the engine. Wrapped in a plaid car blanket smelling of gasoline, Léa stood by the door. François left the engine running and took her in his arms.

"Where are you going?" she asked.

"To Alsace."

"Alone?"

"No, my driver is waiting for me nearby. Léa, we won't see each other again for a very long time. When I leave Alsace, I'm going to Russia as an observer for General de Gaulle."

"Why you?"

"Probably because I speak Russian."

He spoke Russian! He had never told her that. There were so many things about him that she did not know—more than a lifetime of telling!

"François—"

"Don't! If you say anything, I won't have the courage to leave you. Remember that I'll always know where to find you. Please say something that will make the wait easier."

"I love you."

"That's what I wanted to hear. You're so stingy with I love you's. Go back inside, you're freezing cold."

"No! Kiss me!"

He kissed her.

"Go!"

He pushed her so hard that she lost her balance. He was about to help her up but stopped himself. The car sent a shower of snow over her, but she did not move.

Noticing that she had not returned, one of her friends came outside and found her huddled on the ground, half-covered by the snow. With the help of the groundskeeper, she carried Léa upstairs and made her drink a hot toddy. Then she put her to bed under a pile of blankets with a hot water bottle.

The next day, she slept until noon.

Chapter Twenty-Nine

On February 6, the day after the signing of the Yalta agreement, two crumpled letters were forwarded to Léa by the Red Cross. One was from Laurent. It was dated January 3.

> Dear Léa,
> As is the custom, I am writing to wish you a Happy New Year. I hope that 1945 brings you happiness. More than anyone I know, you were made for it. You have the strength to overcome the worst hardships. I feel as though I am losing my will to live. I am fighting it, forcing myself to think of Charles, but I cannot help dwelling on the past and feeling that the happiest days of my life are over.
> Here, where all is mud and rain, the passage from life to death is no more extraordinary than breathing in and breathing out. The bravery of men who are ready to die for a cause they believe in is one of the things that has moved me the most since we began fighting. The day before an attack which we know will claim many lives, perhaps our own, there is a feeling of deliberateness about the camp. The men calmly exchange letters, shave with great care, talk in hushed tones. They know, even before the officers do, when there is going to be an attack. They don't need a warning siren. There is something about a man who knows that the next day may be his last. It is as though he fixed his gaze on some point over the horizon, out of himself. This is a very real part of the war, too. Quiet solidarity and dignity, ordinary human beings becoming legends and heroes. Individually, they may not seem important,

298

but through their supreme sacrifice, they enter history alongside those who fought in Year Two, at Austerlitz and on the
Marne.

These words probably come as a surprise to you. They surprise me, too. If I hadn't joined Leclerc and the Second Armored Division, I would still be a pacifist and I would think
very differently. But we cannot stand by while thousands give
up their lives to keep not only France but the entire world
free.

In my last letter, I talked about Colonel Fabien. He and
three of his men were killed by a land mine on December 27. I
can't help thinking about the little daughter he left behind.

If anything should happen to me, remember that Camille
and I want you to look after Charles. I drew up a will before I
left, naming you as his guardian. Tell him about the war, but in
such a way that he grows up hating it. Tell him not to bear a
grudge against the Germans. They were duped. I knew many
Germans before the war. I spoke their language, I listened to
their music, I read their poets, I admired their courage. Many
was the time that I drank to the United States of Europe with
friends from Berlin. After all the horror we have suffered, we
need men and women who believe in this dream and can
make it come true.

Dearest Léa, as the new year begins, I pray God keep you
safe. May He look down on you and bless you.

With what love I have left,
Laurent.

"He's going to die," murmured Léa, suddenly feeling tired.
The second envelope was also covered with postmarks, but
the writing was unfamiliar. At last, she tore it open. When she
saw the name in the left-hand margin of the page of scribbler
paper, she knew.

Without a tear, she began to read:

Dear Mademoiselle Delmas,
No one likes to be the bearer of bad news and yet out of my
friendship for Captain Laurent d'Argilat and because he made
me promise, I must inform you that he died on January 28. Six-
teen officers of the *Groupement Tactique de Lorraine* were

killed, as were Commander Puig and Lieutenant-Colonel Putz, in the assault on Grussenheim. The Second Armored Division suffered heavier losses than in the foothills of the Vosges, Salerno, and Strasbourg combined.

Our objective was to cross the Ill, reach the Rhine, and link up with the Americans in the centre of the Colmar pocket. There were twenty inches of snow on the ground and it was freezing cold. Before us spread a vast, white plain, criss-crossed by hedges, canals, and streams, offering the Horniss's, Jagpanthers, and 88s a perfect target range. The Third Army went first, and captured *Carrefour 177*. The Second pressed forward, with orders to take Grussenheim at all costs. The rest of the regiment waited in the rear, trembling for their comrades and envying them at the same time. The units that were not fighting passed their ammunition forward so that the men in front could reload more quickly. It was during the assault that Laurent was killed. His tank was hit a few yards from mine. In the force of the blast, he was thrown from his tank.

Later, we came back for his body. He looked as though he were sleeping, his face was calm and his body looked untouched. He was buried in the local cemetery awaiting transfer to France. We will all miss him. He marched bravely into the valley of death. Perhaps he wanted to die. If I told you what he did at Hersbsheim, you would believe me only because I was telling you it happened. We court death in an intensely personal way. It is a secret that we take with us to the grave. People—good people—who commit suicide and infringe upon that which is sacred, generally leave a simple note: "Don't try to understand, I don't understand myself." I don't think we really know why we risk our lives at war. We do it because it is expected of us. Laurent did not leave a note. It is better that way. "A good officer," one of the colonels said to me. Coming from him, that was a great compliment. For me, Laurent was more than just a good officer. He was so strong that none of us saw his weaknesses.

Mademoiselle Delmas, I share your pain and your grief.

With my sincere condolences,

Georges Buis.

Now he was with Camille. In spite of her sadness, Léa thought that this was as it should be. Of course there was Charles and, in a way, it was selfish to abandon him with only Léa and her family to look after him, but Laurent had wanted to die.

"Mademoiselle Delmas, we have called you here today to advise you of your next mission. You have been chosen to transport a severely wounded British officer from Brussels to Cannes, where he will be spending a number of weeks convalescing by the sea."

Léa could hardly contain her joy. Her work had become more and more onerous as the days wore on. Driving on roads blown apart by shells was not much fun, but recovering the wounded, not to mention the arms and the legs, administering first aid, hearing the men's screams, seeing their faces as they realized that they had lost limbs, hearing them call their mothers before dying, pulling newborn babies out of the rubble, and being surrounded by mud and blood and pus and filth never lost any of its horror.

The news of Laurent's death revived her nightmares with a vengeance. Not a night passed when she did not see Camille struggling to reach Charles, or the scene on the road at Orléans, or the horrible death of her aunt at Montillac. Death had become her constant companion. She dreaded falling asleep and she dreaded waking up. She might have found it easier to cope had the other women, particularly her new leader, not vented their jealousy and frustration on her. The only exception was Jeanine. Léa was assigned to all the dirtiest jobs: polishing boots, washing ambulances, sweeping offices. At first, she just thought that this was part and parcel of her work, but she quickly realized that she had been singled out. When she objected, she was made to understand that they could manage very well without her. So she was all the more surprised when she learned that she had been given such an important mission.

"You look surprised, Mademoiselle Delmas," the woman continued. "I assure you, you were only chosen because of your knowledge of English. You do speak English well, do you not? That's what it says in your file."

Léa nodded, hoping that her knowledge of the language of the Queen would not be put to the test. She only knew what she had learned at school and that had been several years ago.

"You will leave tomorrow with a convoy going to Belgium. In Brussels, you will contact the Belgian Red Cross. All of the information you will need is in this briefcase, along with your travel papers for Belgium and France. Until then, you are relieved of your duties. Good luck."

"Thank you, Madame. Good-bye."

Léa used her half-day off to have her hair washed and cut at the beauty salon that had been set up in a barracks not far from the chateau. When she emerged, she felt like a new woman, ready to face the future with a faint glimmer of hope. That night, she slept soundly.

The next day, she said her goodbye's and left the north of France without a backward glance.

Chapter Thirty

Had it not been for the servicemen in wheelchairs and the ubiquitous Allied uniforms, it would have been just like a holiday. For nearly a month now, Léa had been living a life of leisure at the side of "her" wounded serviceman.

The man in Léa's care was a colonel in the British army, an eccentric Irishman who preferred whiskey to tea, playing cards to military maps, and big cigars to all of the above. He had an irrepressible sense of humor and was courageous to a fault. He had a keen appreciation of anything in a skirt and was rich to boot. Wounded near Dinan during the Ardennes offensive, Sir George McClintock had come too close to dying not to make the very most of what time he had left. As soon as he was able to get about on crutches, Léa's life became a whirlwind of cocktail parties, garden parties, balls, picnics, trips to the beach, and outings to the countryside. He wanted her at his side at all times, declaring that he knew his life was about to change forever the moment he set eyes on her, with her wild hair, her full lips, and haughty expression. (In spite of her ill-fitting uniform, he guessed the rest). In exchange for a fistful of pounds sterling, he arranged for her to have a room near his at the Hôtel Majestic.

He spent the first few days sleeping, but on the evening of the fifth day, asked to be taken to the dining room. There was a tiny grimace of displeasure as Léa sat down opposite him, dressed in her uniform, with an impeccable blouse, a carefully knotted tie, and spotless oxfords.

"Is that all you have to wear?" he asked in an accent that Léa found delightful at first.

She blushed, feeling ugly.

"Yes. If you're ashamed of me, I can eat in my room."

"My dear, *pardonnez-moi*. I didn't mean to hurt your feelings. It's charming but, how shall I say, *un peu* boring?"

The next day, Léa watched as boxes of dresses and shoes from La Croisette were delivered to her room. At first she refused, but when she saw the black chiffon and the green taffeta and the magnificent Italian pumps of "real" leather, she faltered. And, as the evenings were still a little on the chilly side, McClintock insisted that she also take a silver fox wrap.

Two days later, she accompanied him to a garden party at the American Club. He was thrilled by the response. The officers vied with each other for her attention, bringing her glasses of champagne, juice, and soda, plates of cakes, ice cream, and fruit. Léa just laughed, basking in all the attention.

In early March, McClintock received a dispatch from London ordering him back to England. Dreading the return trip to Amiens, Léa begged him to take her along.

"You still need me," she implored.

"I shall always need you," he replied, suddenly serious.

"There! You see!" she said, teasing.

He smiled and said that there would be all sorts of red tape. Sure enough, obtaining the permission of the Red Cross in Cannes and Paris was no small task: Léa's papers bore an impressive number of stamps.

In spite of the raids and the fear inspired by the V-1s and V-2s, Léa found life in London as frenetic as the weeks she had spent in Cannes. It was as though everyone under the age of thirty were making up for lost time, dancing, romancing, boozing, trying to forget that the war was not over yet...

One morning, tucked between the pot of tea and the bacon and eggs, there was a letter from Mathias. Laure had forwarded it from Paris where it had arrived by way of a very circuitous route that included Switzerland.

It was impossible to make out the date on the envelope and Mathias had forgotten to date the letter.

Dear Léa,

"My honor is my allegiance." This is the inscription over the gates to Camp Wildflecken where I have joined the French *Waffen SS*. I have adopted this motto as my own as I think of you. The camp is in a big park on a mountainside. There are a few small buildings among the trees along spotless paths leading to *Adolf Hitler Platz*. The discipline is very strict and the training is hard. At first, a lot of us couldn't keep up, but now we are all in excellent physical condition. The ones who don't make the grade get transferred to other units. Discipline is the only way to control four to five thousand young men ready for action. It's better this way; it takes my mind off you. In November, two thousand French militiamen arrived. With Darnand and de Degrelle looking on, they swore their allegiance to Hitler on November 12—some reluctantly. The cold was god-awful. With the snow pelting down, members of the L.V.F.— that's the *Légion des volontaires français contre le bolchevisme*—paraded in perfect order. Brigade-führer Krukenberg and Oberführer Puaud inspected the troops. What impressed us the most was our chaplain, Monsignor Mayor de Lupé. With the snow in his face, he sat on his horse in his *Waffen SS* officer's uniform, his cross shining on his chest, talking about the Führer like he was God. His blessing was more like a salute to Hitler. And what a setting! The French tricolor, the flag of the Third Reich, and the black standard of the SS. Three militiamen stepped forward and stood facing an officer holding an unsheathed sword. Then the others raised their arms in the Nazi salute and repeated after them, "I vow to obey Adolf Hitler, Leader of the *Waffen SS* in the fight against bolshevism, and to be a loyal soldier." Some of the men just stood with their arms by their sides.

I'll never forget the day I took my oath. The words were a little different. It was a very solemn ceremony. It took place between two oak trees—that's the custom. Two daggers with our motto were laid in a cross on the ground. An officer stepped forward and took the oath for all of us in German, and we repeated after him in French: "Adolf Hitler, Fuehrer and

Savior of all Europe, I vow to be loyal and courageous. I vow to obey you and the men you choose to lead us until I die, so help me God!" I'll never forget the first time I raised my arm in the Nazi salute. *Heil Hitler!* I felt like I had cut all ties with the past forever.

The officers here do not receive any special treatment. There are no privileges, no officers' hall. We all eat the same food at the same table. If there's a round of schnapps the soldiers get served first and the officers get what's left. The higher your rank, the more work you get. Every week, there's a dinner they call *Kamaradschaft*—sort of like a roast. The lowliest soldier can take pot shots at his superiors. There are heavy penalties for any officer who punishes a soldier for doing it. This is probably what surprises us French the most. We're so used to standing at attention, listening to our superiors, then being sent off to our barracks while they enjoy every luxury. They are turning us into real men! Life at Wildflecken is tough. Up at six, lights out at eight. The training is incredible. Cold shower, roll call, salute, and coffee, then exercises, maneuvers, and marching. The only break we get is the theory on weapons and strategy. At night, I fall into bed. Then they wake us up for night maneuvers. We stumble into our uniforms and brace ourselves against the cold. For the past two weeks, I haven't slept more than four hours at a time. I'm always hungry. Whatever happened to those great meals we used to have at Montillac? Here, it's cabbage soup and potatoes at noon, sausages with a slice of heavy black bread and a dab of margarine at five. It's hard to believe this is enough to keep us strong and alert, yet even the "diehard French" are getting used to it.

It's not all rosy. The atmosphere has started to slide recently, mainly because a lot of the militiamen are having trouble fitting in. Almost every day since the Charlemagne Brigade was formed, French *Waffen SS* have deserted and joined units leaving for the Front, the Wiking Division and the Totenkopf Division.

Our commander is Oberführer Edgar Puaud. He was commander of the L.V.F. in Russia. A few days ago, I became a real SS. Under my left arm, they put a tatoo with my blood group. That way, I have a better chance of surviving if I get wounded—and of being killed if I get taken prisoner! We can't wait to see some fighting. It'll probably only be a matter of days now.

Yesterday, some buddies managed to get their hands on a few bottles of German white wine which they snuck into camp. This is strictly forbidden. Just as we were about to pop the corks, Brigade-führer Krukenberg paid us a surprise visit. I think he knew what was going on because when he went out, he muttered, "Those French!" After he left, we drank a toast in his honor. The wine was a little dry but still pretty good. Not as good as Montillac though! I wonder whether the harvest was a good one.

Where are you now, Léa? I can't picture you anywhere except at Montillac. It's where you belong. If you get this letter— and if you have the patience to read it right to the end—it will be like we had a chat. Remember me, Léa, and remember that you will always be in my heart.

Mathias.

The tea was cold and the orange marmalade had a funny taste. Léa tried to picture Mathias in an SS uniform, but couldn't. It seemed to her that there must have been some terrible mistake. How else could this gentle, sweet boy have become a senseless brute. Yet this was no more absurd than sitting in a cozy old hotel in London with parchment in the place of window panes.

Someone knocked at the door.

"News from home?" inquired McClintock, entering the room.

His cheerful face brought a forlorn smile to her lips.

"What's wrong? Is something the matter?"

"No. No, I'm fine."

"Well, then. Let's go!"

"Where?"

"Germany."

"Germany!"

"Yes, I must rejoin the Second Army."

"But you're barely back on your feet!"

"A doctor friend of mine said I was as right as rain. I can't very well stay here while my friends are getting their heads blown off, can I?"

"What about me? What am I supposed to do, wait here until the war is over? Go back to Amiens or Paris?"

"Not at all. You're coming with me."

"I'm..."

"Yes, one of my friends is the head of the British Red Cross."

"You certainly do have a lot of friends."

"Comes in handy sometimes. I told him how mechanically-minded you were and about your remarkable gift for tending to the sick and wounded."

"He'd better not put me to the test!"

"The woman in charge of drivers here is a friend of Madame de Peyerimhoff's. In a few days' time, you should be receiving a temporary post with our Red Cross people."

Léa leapt out of bed and kissed him on both cheeks.

"You're wonderful, George. How did you know that I wanted to go to Germany?"

"You've talked of nothing else since we got here."

A week later, Léa received her orders and was assigned to Chief Medical Officer Hughes Glyn Hughes of the British Second Army. On the night of April 5, she landed near Duisbourg, thirty miles from the Front.

It was the beginning of a journey down into Hell.

Chapter Thirty-One

Hundreds of miles away, Mathias, too, was living in Hell.

On January 12, 1945, three million well-armed Russian troops, backed up by tanks and planes, marched from the Baltic Sea to Czechoslovakia to crush what remained of the glorious army of the Reich once and for all.

On February 17, the French volunteers, now the *Waffen-Grenadierdivision der SS Charlemagne*, left for the Front. They arrived in Hammerstein, a large town in Pomerania, on February 22. It was very cold, and a bitter wind swept across a landscape dotted with lakes and woods. They stopped at what had once been a *Wehrmacht* camp and was now a prisoner-of-war camp to await the arrival of heavy artillery. In the distance, they could hear cannon.

Mathias and the other men of the 57th Regiment took up quarters in the southeastern section of the city. Immediately upon his arrival, Obersturmführer Feunay went to inspect the positions, accompanied by Mathias and Oberjunker Labourdette. The spring thaw had come, transforming the dirt roads into a quagmire that claimed horses, cases of munitions, and carts laden with heavy matériel. It took dozens of men to extract the carts from the ooze. At nightfall, the roads would freeze up again. All along the road were convoys of refugees fleeing from the Russians. Old men, women, and children trudged through the mud, their faces set and silent. Among them were a few Latvian SS in tattered uniforms, their hands in their pockets, blank expressions on their faces.

The first clash with the enemy took place near Heinrich-swalde. Very quickly, the French *Waffen SS* suffered heavy casualties. Outnumbered ten to one, they were no match for the Russian tanks. Shells and mortars rained down on them. Next to Mathias, one of his buddies bled to death from a leg wound. Feunay gave the order to stand firm.

All night long, new convoys of troops arrived at the station in Hammerstein and went directly to the Front. The men of the 58th Regiment quickly found themselves under heavy fire. At dawn, thousands of Russians descended on them, shouting at the top of their lungs. They repelled the Russians twice, but were destined to be overwhelmed by sheer numbers. The order to retreat was given. The survivors regrouped and waited. Communication had been very poor during the fighting. The Charlemagne Division had taken up positions without a single radio. Couriers had gone from company to company with orders from the commanding officer. By noon, the sound of the tanks was deafening. The 58th dug themselves into foxholes along the edge of the forest. Feunay's men tried to reach them through the woods, but found only a few stunned survivors among the trees, dragging the wounded. That night, they returned to the camp at Hammerstein which they had left that morning. Exhausted, they slept on vermin-infested mattresses in the barracks after consuming a cup of split pea soup.

Of the 4,500 men who had left Wildflecken, 1,500 had either died or gone missing. In two days of fighting, the casualties had been very heavy. The remnants of the Charlemagne Division regrouped at Neustettin, a town of 16,000 inhabitants that was now bursting at the seams with refugees and soldiers. News of the death of Jacques Doriot came as a blow to those he had inspired to enlist. On March 5, they fought valiantly alongside a company of the *Wehrmacht* at Körlin. Not far from Mathias, a German tank exploded. A soldier emerged and ran right in front of Mathias, his uniform in flames. The Division's medical officer threw himself on the man to extinguish the flames. Mathias ran to help him carry the man to safety. He was moaning softly and had lost his helmet. His back was burnt black. Poor bastard, thought Mathias, returning to his post.

Suddenly, he stopped and retraced his steps. Kneeling by the dying man, he cleaned his face with a handful of snow, wiping it with a grimy rag.

"Captain Kramer ... can you hear me?"

At the sound of someone calling his name in French, the man's expression changed. Painfully, he opened his eyes and looked up at the soldier in German uniform, unrecognizable beneath the dirt and grime.

"Captain Kramer, I'm Mathias... from Montillac."

"Montillac ..."

"Yes, Montillac ... Léa ... do you remember now?"

"Sabine ..."

"Yes ..."

"Sabine ... my son ..."

Otto tried to sit up, but collapsed again. His voice grew fainter:

"In my pocket ... papers ... and a letter ... for Sabine. If you get out alive ... give her this. Promise ..."

"I promise."

Mathias reached into Otto's tunic and pulled out a leather wallet carefully wrapped in oilcloth. It reminded him of the kitchen table at Montillac. He put it inside his shirt, next to his skin. The dying man had not taken his gaze off Mathias. He nodded very slowly. The Russians were coming closer. Mathias had to leave. Otto tried to say something. Mathias could not make out the words, but he knew the question:

"What is a Frenchman doing here?"

He shrugged his shoulders. What could he say?

The Brigade-führer gave the order to pull back. Mathias's battalion fled toward the Oder, then to Belgard. The Bassompierre battalion stayed behind to delay the enemy advance.

Hiding by day, inching their way along by the light of the fires that consumed Körlin by night, the 57th Regiment crept past the *popovs*, as they called the Russians. Clashes were brief and bloody. The Regiment was running low on ammunition. The horses had run away or been killed. They survived by stealing food from German houses, where women and girls who had been raped lay weeping. When they could find no food, they ate raw beets which gave them dysentery. They slept huddled together for warmth and awoke, crawling with vermin. The filth accumulated in the folds of their bodies. Some joked that it provided a layer of insulation and kept out the lice. They marched on, faces mask-like with fatigue, eyes feverish and bloodshot. The enemy was everywhere and hounded them relentlessly.

Suddenly, the weather turned warmer and the fields were covered with pale green growth. They stopped in a wood to rest and found themselves walking on a carpet of violets. Mathias lay down, drinking in their delicate fragrance. Discovering the first violets in the protected hollows of the Calvary with Léa had always been a special moment. He would bring her bouquet upon bouquet, until her room was filled with their scent. At first, as he picked the flowers with his calloused hands, the other soldiers looked on, mocking. Then, instinctively, they picked one or two, pressing them between the pages of their identity papers. The violets lifted their spirits. Perhaps spring would bring new hope for them, too.

"We're filthy," said one of them.

They looked at one another. It was true. Not far away, there was a stream. They tore off their uniforms, shaking out huge lice, and dove into the water. It was ice cold! For lack of soap, they washed with handfuls of earth, scrubbing furiously, laughing like little boys. They dried themselves by running naked through the trees. Feunay watched them, pensive. Having worn out their socks long ago, they all wore "Russian socks." These consisted of a square of cloth, one end of which was folded over the toes. The sides were then brought over the instep and the back held firmly in place as the boot was pulled on. The cloth protected their feet admirably.

They arrived on the outskirts of Belgard, which was in flames, at around two in the morning. They crossed the cemetery and disappeared into the city. At around four o'clock, Oberführer Puaud arrived in Belgard with the rest of the Division, about three thousand men. Hidden from view, Russian soldiers greeted them with machine gun fire and mortars. Returning their fire, the *Waffen SS* slipped into the city. Those who crossed the town square, lit only by the flames consuming the houses nearby, had to step over the bodies of hundreds of women, children, and old people.

Now wounded in the shin, Puaud walked as though in a trance, his face redder than usual. In the countryside, the shooting had stopped, replaced by the thunder of engines and the hideous crunching of tracks as the tanks advanced over the plain. The enemy was everywhere. A thick fog rolled in, and when it lifted the next morning, the Charlemagne Division found itself on a vast, featureless expanse, surrounded by Soviet armored vehicles. For a moment, there was not a sound. Time stood still. Then, suddenly, the Russians opened fire. In under two hours, the Charlemagne Division was all but annihilated. The wounded were finished off, and the survivors were marched to prison camps. A few managed to escape into the woods.

The five hundred men in Mathias's battalion arrived at Chateau de Meseritz in pitiful condition. Wounded and weak from the dysentery, they were nevertheless happy and proud that their leaders had found them temporary respite from the inferno. Two days later, clean-shaven and refreshed, their weapons slung over their shoulders, they left under sunny skies for the mouth of the Oder under the command of Krukenberg. With them were two hundred and fifty survivors from the Fifty-Eighth Division, the SS Holstein, a Hungarian Regiment, and the SS Nordland Division. They crossed the Rega south of Treptow and reached Horst, on the Baltic coast, by late afternoon. Wherever they turned, they saw refugees waiting to be taken by boat to Sweden.

At nightfall, Mathias and a handful of other soldiers arrived at Rewahl, a small seaside resort. Like Horst, Rewahl was swarming with refugees and soldiers and in a state of total confusion. The scene was bizarre in the extreme. In full view of grim, listless figures, young women offered themselves to one and all, letting their bodies be caressed by men covered in filth and vermin, drinking schnapps by the tumblerful. Children watched, expressionless, as their parents joined in. The damp sea air mingled with the exhaust fumes, the stench of pus and blood from gaping wounds, the sweet scent of sperm, the stench of excrement and thousands of unwashed bodies, and the pervasive odor of cabbage soup, their only sustenance.

"The Russians are coming!"

Pushing and shoving, men, women, trucks, horses, and tanks collided, flattening anything and anyone that lay in their path. The water's edge was one long procession of damned souls trying to escape the flames. Mothers, half-crazed, clutched lifeless babies, girls threw themselves off the cliffs to escape rape, men pushed their wives into the path of tanks, soldiers murdered truck drivers to take their places ... children screaming ... horses whinnying ... dogs howling ... waves breaking on the shore ... the thunder of the cannon and the shells and the mines ... the sounds of death.

The Charlemagne Division marched on, fighting and drinking whenever they could find wine. Following the hordes of refugees they headed west along the beaches. From time to time, a mortar would land in their midst, hurling sand and bodies skyward. The horde pressed on, oblivious to the screams of the wounded and the moans of the dying.

Late on March 9, they reached the German lines at Dievenow. At dawn the next day, the Russians began shelling, then attacked, but were pushed back. That afternoon, the Charlemagne Division was given access to the German supply depots. They couldn't believe their eyes when they saw automatic rifles that could fire thirty-six rounds of ammunition and new uniforms which they modelled, chain-smoking cigarettes which they didn't want to leave for the enemy.

With Brigade-führer Krukenberg and Obersturmführer Feunay leading the troops, freshly fitted out, they crossed the bridge of boats over the Oder at last, leaving the inferno that had claimed nine-tenths of their numbers.

The next day, a communique from the General Headquarters of the Fuehrer commended the survivors of the

Charlemagne Division for their part in liberating the refugees of Pomerania. Their breasts swelling with pride, they left Swinemünde, singing:

"The ground starts to tremble, Ha, Ha!
Wherever we are, Ha, Ha!
Devil's laughter is with us, Ha, Ha!
Never too far, Ha, Ha! .
The flame is ever pure,
Our allegiance shall endure!"

Two hundred miles from Berlin, in the town of Neustrelitz and in the neighboring villages of Zinow, Karpin, Goldenbaum, and Rödlin, eight hundred of the seven thousand French volunteers from Wildflecken were reunited.

On March 27, Krukenberg, posted this message to the troops:

> *Brothers in Arms,*
> *We have just come through several long days of marching and combat. We fought not as a unit within the German Army but as an autonomous French Divison. It was in Charlemagne's name that the French reputation for courage and strength was reborn. Time and time again, the fierce fighting has united us. Proudly we will recall that south of Bürenwald we stopped the enemy which had penetrated the lines of the Wehrmacht. In less than an hour, around Elsenau and Bärenhutte alone, we destroyed forty J.S. and T34 tanks. At Neustettin, the Flak-Batterie chopped columns of enemy troops to pieces.*
> *We owe our success not only to our fighting spirit, but also to our great discipline.*
> *Let us not forget our SS and L.V.F. comrades who, at Kölberf, were awarded the Order of the Fuehrer for their valor by the Commander of the fortress.*
> *At this very moment, members of our Division are defending the city of Danzig alongside their German brothers in arms. The SS and the L.V.F. have turned back or slowed the Bolshevik*

tide on every front. This valiant struggle has not been without heavy losses. Many of our brothers have been taken prisoner and have yet to rejoin our ranks. Let us hope that Oberführer Puaud is among them and that he and the other heroic warriors will take their rightful places among us once again.

The struggle has made us strong. Our numbers have been reduced by glorious combat but we must push onward, as a single unit, as a single team, crushing anything that stands in the way of Adolf Hitler. Our flag now flies with new glory. We know that every Frenchman fighting for the freedom of our adoptive Fatherland wants a new European order and is watching us proudly.

This is a decisive moment. We are stronger than ever. We will avenge the deaths of our comrades fallen in battle!

The glory of the L.V.F. in the East, the victories of the Sturmbrigade Frankreich in the Karpathians, and the battles waged elsewhere by the militia vindicate the French blood spilled in the name of National Socialism. They shall create a tradition worthy of the revolutionary ideal for which we are fighting.

Our belief in victory is unshakable, though we must fight hard with our German brothers to crush the enemy.

We shall follow the Fuehrer to victory or to death.

Heil Hitler!

We're always the Vanguard, Ha, Ha!
Wherever we are, Ha, Ha!
Devil's laughter is with us, Ha, Ha!
Never too far, Ha, Ha!

We're fighting for freedom, Ha, Ha!
And for Hitler too, Ha, Ha!
The Bolshevik menace, Ha, Ha!
Is dead through and through, Ha, Ha!

Krukenberg summoned his officers and instructed them to retain only those who volunteered for more combat. The others were to form a battalion of workers that would leave Karpin immediately; three hundred men left with a single

316

officer. Those who chose to remain signed a statement in which they swore their loyalty to the Fuehrer until his death.

The Charlemagne Division then fell prey to the ennui and ill humor that afflicts every army waiting to do battle. Men who had been united during the hardships they had just come through, whose courage in the face of the enemy bordered on temerity, were now ready to quarrel on the slightest pretext. Their greatest bone of contention became food. A day's rations consisted of seven ounces of bread, half an ounce of margarine, soup that was either too spicy or too bland, ersatz coffee, and two cigarettes. The strict German military discipline was not enough to contain the querulous French soldiers, who joked about the secret weapons that would save Germany. No one talked about the glory of the Reich anymore.

Morale fell to an all-time low when, in mid-April, four volunteers were shot for pilfering food. After receiving absolution from the little chaplain of the L.V.F. who had replaced Monsignor Mayor de Lupé, now in seclusion in a German monastery, the four went to their deaths without a word of protest.

On April 20, the men received cookies, a blackish substance vaguely resembling chocolate, and three cigarettes in honor of Hitler's fifty-sixth birthday, which they celebrated with songs and wine that Krukenberg had managed to obtain from the supply depot.

There was a film with Zarah Leander whose husky voice reduced them to tears of laughter. After the film, they watched a newsreel. There was a commentary in German as the crowd of Parisians gathered in the square in front of Notre-Dame for the arrival of General de Gaulle began running in all directions to escape the sniper fire—Communist sniper fire, declared the commentator. As the lights went up, the French SS were more convinced than ever that they were all that stood between Europe and the Bolsheviks. Some had visions of a hero's welcome and parades along the Champ-Élysées for the champions of Western civilization. Most had no such illusions: one way or the other they faced a firing squad, or at best, years of incarceration.

During the night of April 23, the Brigade-führer received orders to lead the French SS of the Charlemagne Division to Berlin.

The officers went to the barracks and had their men stand at attention.

"All those who volunteer to go to Berlin, take one step forward!"

All stepped forward.

The next morning, weapons were distributed including grenades, *Sturmgewehr*, and *Panzerfaust*. With bands of cartridges slung across their chests, and grenades hooked on their buttons and belts, the four hundred volunteers had never been so well armed. They climbed into eight trucks supplied by the *Luftwaffe*, proud at the thought of defending the Fuehrer. As they entered the capital singing, Berliners fleeing in the opposite direction stared at them in disbelief.

Chapter Thirty-Two

Under the Franco-Soviet Pact, a certain number of French observers were allowed to accompany the Soviet troops entering Germany. Their mission was to prepare an inventory of weapons that the Germans had taken from French arsenals, a mission which neither party to the pact took terribly seriously. François Tavernier, who was already known to the Soviets, was one of the officers chosen by the French. Before leaving Paris, Professor Joliot-Curie informed him of the real purpose of his mission, something with a little more substance than a list of rusted matériel.

Up until March 15, Commander Tavernier had spent most of his waking hours playing chess, expanding his vocabulary of Russian expletives, and getting drunk on vodka, thereby winning the esteem of Georgi Malenkov, head of the Russian secret service recovering industrial, scientific, and military equipment from Germany. The weeks he had spent at the various army headquarters in Moscow had taxed his patience to the limit.

Appointed by the high command of the First Belorussian Front, François was sent to join the troops at the end of March and there, began waiting again. His only distractions were games of chess and long talks with General Vassiliev, whom he had once met in Algiers where he had been a military attache.

Then, at long last, a massive offensive was launched on Berlin.

At four o'clock in the morning on April 16, Marshal Zhukov gave the order to fire three red flares over the Oder. The sky and the banks of the river glowed purple for what seemed like a very long time. Then, search lights and the headlights of tanks and trucks went on. The beams of anti-aircraft search lights swept the enemy skies. There was a deathly pause. Three green flares were fired, and the earth began to tremble. Twenty thousand cannon spit forth their fire, destroying everything in their path, setting fire to forests, villages, and columns of refugees. The high-pitched scream of *katiouchkas* pierced the air.

The First Belorussian Front under Marshal Zhukov, the Second Belorussian Front under Marshal Rokossovski and the First Ukrainian Front under Marshal Konev began the offensive. One million six hundred thousand men, most driven by the desire to avenge the death of a father, a brother or a friend, swept across the plain. German cities were emptied. Only rubble remained. François understood the hatred of these men from Stalingrad, Smolensk, Leningrad, and Moscow who had marched across Russia to reach the Oder. Of all the European countries, Russia had suffered the heaviest losses. To avenge the suffering of their mothers, wives, and daughters, the entire Red Army wanted an eye for an eye, and a tooth for a tooth. In sheer destructiveness, the Russian campaign was without equal.

François felt drawn to these simple, courageous men who fought with no regard for their personal safety and who shared their meager rations with their prisoners. For the Russians, he was an object of curiosity. He spoke their language, could drink as well as the best of them, and although he didn't fight, was always in the thick of the battle. This earned him a bullet in the thigh.

"Please, you must stay out of trouble," General Vassiliev urged François on a visit to the field hospital where he was having his leg attended to.

"I'd like to see you in my boots," he grumbled. "Not only have I not found any French matériel, but my hands are tied behind my back. What's the point of my being here if I'm not allowed to fight?"

"You know very well that those are the orders. All foreign officers with permission to accompany our armies are in exactly the same situation."

François turned away. He was prepared to die, but not empty-handed. Decidedly, he was not cut out to be a civil servant.

Chapter Thirty-Three

Any doubts that Léa may have had about the need to crush Nazi Germany disappeared forever on April 15, 1945.

McClintock had tried to dissuade her from travelling with the team of doctors and nurses under Doctor Hughes, Chief Medical Officer of the British Second Army, who were on their way to the concentration camp in Bergen-Belsen which had just been liberated. When she protested that they were short-staffed and needed her help, he gave in.

Green fields and pine woods stretched as far as the eye could see. The road climbed toward the steeple high above the houses of Bergen-Belsen with their carefully-tended flower boxes. A sleepy, peaceful town, were it not for the tanks and trucks parking on either side of the road.

Suddenly, at a turn in the road, there was a vast expanse of barbed wire, watchtowers, and row upon row of low dark buildings. Skeleton-like creatures, clothed in striped sacks, wandered aimlessly. Some came up to the barbed wire, holding out putty-colored, stick-like arms. They tried to smile as tears flowed down their sunken cheeks. The smiles horrified the soldiers, who stood rooted to the ground, afraid to go any further. Doctor Hughes had them drink hot coffee. Then they entered the camp.

Still clinging to the barbed wire were the half-naked bodies of men, women and children. On the ground, there were more bodies, naked or in rags, like greying bones on a beach. As they slowly made their way through this nightmarish world, some of the phantoms retreated, raising their arms to protect their faces. Others came forward, hobbling painfully, their footsteps no louder than the rustling of a thousand insects.

Léa walked stiffly, unable to divert her gaze from the hideous faces in shades of blackish-brown, green, grey, and mauve.

The sea of half-dead, half-alive creatures parted as they moved forward, touring the compound first to the left, then to the right. The horror of the camp pressed down on them. Between the buildings, at some distance from the barbed wire, a group of prisoners crouched. Others, lying on the ground, had stopped moving. Doctor Hughes entered one of the buildings, gesturing to the others to wait outside. When he emerged, several moments later, he was horror-stricken and his hands trembled.

"Get them out of there," was all he could say.

McClintock prevented Léa from going in.

"Get your ambulance and ask the others to follow you with the truck that has the blankets."

When Léa returned, dozens of women had been laid on the ground. A nauseating odor rose from their bodies. As their filthy rags were removed, bugs scurried away. The women's tiny bodies, covered in open sores and filth, were wrapped in blankets.

They spent the entire day carrying the women out of the barracks, and washing and feeding them. Almost all had dysentery but were too weak to move away from their excrement. Very quickly, one hundred of them died. All night, the doctors, nurses, and soldiers lifted the prisoners out of the filth. Under the glare of the flood lights, the forty-five barracks looked like a set from a horror movie. The fires cast ghoulish shadows, as the skeleton-like bodies, following the progress of their liberators with huge dilated eyes, wandered through the camp, leaving black, slimy trails behind them.

Doctor Hughes kept pressing the military officers in charge to set up a fourteen thousand bed hospital, saying that he urgently required doctors, nurses, and thousands of tons of medical supplies if he was to try to save the 56,000 prisoners in the camp who were suffering from starvation, gastroenteritis, typhus, typhoid fever, and tuberculosis.

By dawn the next morning, one thousand of the prisoners who had received medical attention the previous day had died. Everything—the sky, the people, the ground, the buildings—was the color of ashes. There was excrement everywhere. Limbs, covered in filthy rags, moved slowly. Men and women died without a murmur. It poured rain.

Accompanied by McClintock, Léa walked to the exit to rest for a moment. They passed a huge open pit, overflowing with bodies, thin as skeletons. Léa stopped and stared. Arms and legs. Faces that had once laughed and loved and cried. It seemed inconceivable to her. There was nothing human about this mound. These could not have been living, breathing beings. She tried desperately to understand. Why? Why this? Why them?

"Come, Léa. Let's take the path through the woods."

She followed him without protesting.

"Oh, my God!" she cried, pointing.

There, among the pine saplings, were hundreds of bodies in rows.

Closely supervised by British soldiers, deathly pale German civilians were bringing more bodies and depositing them on the ground next to the others. Léa and McClintock approached. Not far from where they stood lay the body of a woman whose legs were covered with bruises. Her bones protruded through her skin. The rain made her look like a drowning victim.

"Léa..."

Léa turned to McClintock, but he was now several yards away, talking with one of the soldiers.

"Léa..."

The voice was so faint it seemed to be coming from the

324

ground. Léa looked down. The drowned woman had opened her eyes and was looking at Léa. She was paralyzed with fear.

"Léa. . ."

She wasn't dreaming. The woman had called her name. She forced herself to bend down. Huge eyes, sunken in their orbits, gazed up at her. Who was this woman? Her features meant nothing to Léa. Yet the sunken cheeks, the craters. . . .

"Sarah!"

At the sound of Léa's cry, McClintock and the soldiers turned. The English officer hurried over.

"Léa, what is it?"

"Sarah! That's Sarah!"

"This woman is still alive!" cried one of the soldiers.

McClintock lifted Sarah up and carried her, running, toward the tent that was their makeshift hospital. They laid her on a cot, removed her rags and covered her with a blanket. Léa knelt beside her and held her hand.

"You're alive, Sarah, you're alive! We're going to get you out of here and look after you!"

"None of the detainees are allowed to leave the camp, miss."

"Why not?"

"We have to contain the epidemics. There are many cases of typhus. Not only that, she can't be moved."

"But. . ."

"The doctor's right, Léa. You should get some rest. We'll come back later."

"No, I can't leave her."

"Please, try to be reasonable."

Léa bent over Sarah, kissing the cheeks that would bear the marks of Masuy's cigar forever.

"It's all over now. Try to sleep. I'll come back later."

Léa and McClintock headed for the canteen without exchanging a word. They were served a cup of tea and a piece of cake. Neither could eat. McClintock handed Léa a pack of cigarettes.

"Help me to get her out of here," said Léa.

"You heard what they said. We can't—"

"I don't give a damn what we can or can't do. We have to get Sarah out of here."

"And take her where?"

"To England."

"To—"

"Yes. There has to be a way."

"But—"

"Please, you must find a way!"

"Léa, this is like a nightmare. I feel as though I'm going mad."

"Please, you must help her. Find a plane leaving for England."

"How? And yet. . ."

"What! Tell me!"

"There must be planes airlifting wounded soldiers."

"Yes, that's it! That's an excellent idea. You can have me assigned to accompany one of them."

"It may just work. The hardest part will be getting her out of the camp. Health checks are bound to be stringent exiting the camp."

"We'll find a way. Find out when the next plane is leaving."

"I shall. But promise me you'll rest."

"All right."

"I'll meet you by Sarah's cot later on this afternoon."

Léa did not have time to rest. Just as she was leaving the canteen her superior, Miss Johnson, sent her to help move the sick. It was only much later that evening that she was able to see Sarah. McClintock was already there. Sarah was asleep.

"There you are!" he said. Then, lowering his voice, he added: "There's a flight the day after tomorrow. The commander is a friend of mine—I saved his life. He has agreed to help us. I managed to get the uniform of one of our casualties. Tomorrow night after dark, we'll put it on Sarah and transport her in your ambulance. You will have orders to accompany the wounded to England, where they will be taken to various hospitals.

"But they'll find out that she's a woman."

"One of my friends is a physician to the royal family. He's

326

going to meet the plane and take responsibility for some of the wounded—on His Majesty's orders."

"You're wonderful!"

"Not so fast! The hardest part will be getting her out of here alive."

"What do you mean?"

"Doctor Murray doesn't think she'll live the night."

"I don't believe that," said Léa, bending over Sarah.

Her breathing was very shallow and her thin hands, burning hot. Léa looked at her intently. Slowly, Sarah opened her eyes, recoiling at the face bending so close to her own.

"Don't be frightened. It's only me."

The shadow of a smile crossed Sarah's lips.

"We're going to get you out of here, but you have to help us. You have to get some of your strength back. You have to, do you understand?"

"Please don't tire her out, miss. She must rest."

"Good night, Sarah. I'll be back tomorrow. There, there, I must go."

Léa gently released her fingers from Sarah's grip and went over to the doctor who was examining a child, about ten years of age, who was a survivor of *Revier*, the hospital where the infamous Karl had conducted his experiments.

"Doctor Murray, what's wrong with my friend?"

He gently covered the child with a blanket before turning to Léa. His eyes were filled with anger.

"What's wrong with your friend? What a thought-provoking question! The answer is everything! She hasn't contracted typhus yet, like this little boy who had it injected into him, but she may have been injected with syphilis or smallpox or the plague, or she may have been sterilized or implanted with a chimpanzee embryo."

"Please, stop!"

"Then don't ask me what's wrong with her!"

He turned to examine another patient.

McClintock was waiting for Léa, a short unlit pipe clenched between his teeth.

"Your Doctor Murray is completely crazy."

"Not yet, but there's every chance he will be. What he is see-

327

ing here, he could never have imagined in his wildest dreams. *Doctors* conducted experiments on these people! His entire world has collapsed."

"He'll never let us take Sarah out of here."

"You heard what he said. She doesn't have typhus. I'm going to ask Doctor Hughes to have her transferred to a hospital for non-contagious patients."

"What if he says no?"

"We'll find a way."

And they did. At five o'clock that evening, Colonel McClintock arrived at Doctor Murray's hospital with ten medical personnel.

"This team will stand in for you while you get a bit of rest, Doctor Murray. I'd like you to meet Doctor Colins."

"But, Colonel—"

"Chief Medical Officer's orders, doctor."

"Very well then. Come, Colins. I'll take you 'round to the most critical cases."

By a stroke of luck, Sarah was not among them.

After Doctor Murray left, McClintock kept the relief team occupied while Léa and one of McClintock's aides-de-camp dressed Sarah in the stolen uniform. The other prisoners watched every move with expressionless faces.

Sarah tried to stand up, but Léa and the aide-de-camp had to support her.

"Another of our men who can't take the horror of it all," explained McClintock, stepping between Sarah and Doctor Colins, who had returned.

Léa's mind went completely blank until they were on the landing strip. With the help of a nurse, she put Sarah on a stretcher and carried her to the plane.

Despite the moans and discomfort of the wounded soldiers, the plane was rather like a crowd of vacationers. For most of these young men, the war was over.

Léa held Sarah's hand in hers throughout the entire flight.

Chapter Thirty-Four

Berliners watched silently as the Nordland Division trucks rolled by, carrying the French SS with their red, white, and blue crests. They sang at the top of their lungs, half in German, half in French, pounding the sides of the trucks with their fists.

Tanks and trucks burn, Ha, Ha!
Wherever we are, Ha, Ha!
Devil's laughter is with us, Ha, Ha!
Never too far, Ha, Ha!
The flame is ever pure,
Our allegiance shall endure!

Women dressed in black came forward, holding out a child or a crust of black bread. Young girls blew kisses. Young boys waved, then disappeared back into the rubble as cannon thundered in the distance.

On the night of April 25, Mathias ate a can of asparagus and fell asleep in one of the booths of a pub in the *Hermann Platz*.

That same day, the Soviet Fifth Guards made contact with the United States First Army at Torgau, on the Elbe River.

Wave after wave of Russian planes began bombing Berlin. The explosions wakened the guardians of the city, who reached for their weapons, ready to repel the enemy attack. But the planes did not return. There was only silence.

The next day before dawn, the French SS made their way toward Neuköln City Hall. The sun rose in a clear, blue sky. At last, the order to attack was given.

With the Russian troops firing on them from every direction, they ran from doorway to doorway. With a *Panzerfaust*, Mathias destroyed his first tank.

In the fierce fighting that ensued, twenty French SS were killed. Flames leapt from the buildings, painting the sky red. Soon the dust was so thick that they could barely see two feet in front of them. The roar of the engines and tanks made the ground tremble, drowning out the screams of the dying and wounded.

Struck in the foot, Hauptsturmführer Feunay urged his men on. From Neuköln City Hall, the Charlemagne Division, members of the Hitler Youth, and white-haired veterans fired on the Russian troops, but soon realized that they were surrounded. They could no longer count on the Nordland tanks, which were running out of fuel and ammunition. Their hearts sinking, they watched as the tanks slowly disappeared in a cloud of dust.

Feunay gave the order to evacuate the City Hall and to retreat to *Hermann Platz*.

They spent the night in the basement of the Opera House.

The city was in a state of pandemonium. Preparations for the defense of Berlin were totally inadequate. Ironically, it was the remnants of the foreign divisions of the *Waffen SS*, members of the Hitler Youth, and old men who were left to face hundreds of thousands of Soviet troops.

On the afternoon of April 27, Mathias succeeded in blowing up three T 34 tanks. After being hit in the head, he was taken to the infirmary in Hitler's Bunker. From there, he made his way to Stadtmitte subway station where Brigadeführer Krukenberg had transferred his headquarters. Most of the survivors of the Charlemagne Division had regrouped there. The subway trains, their windows blown out, had been pressed into service as an infirmary, command post, and supply depot. Mathias smoked his first cigarette in two days.

On the platform, the men who had distinguished themselves in the fighting at Neuköln were awarded the Iron Cross. It was a proud moment for Mathias.

At dawn on Saturday, April 28, the Soviet assault resumed. Crouching in doorways and at windows, the French SS waited. As day broke, the tanks moved in.

A *Panzerfaust* caught the first tank. As the flames leapt up, there was a series of small bursts, followed by a huge explosion that hurled pieces of steel into the air. All that remained of the T 34 was a mound of twisted metal and charred bodies. The tanks just kept coming. Mortars whizzed through the air. Mathias, his *Sturmgewehr* on his shoulder, fired on a group of foot soldiers. Five men fell.

"Good work, Fayard," said Captain Feunay, patting him on the back.

Wounded in the shoulder, Mathias was taken to Hotel Adlon, now a hospital. He was released that night or what must have been that night. Daylight had disappeared long ago and they had lost all sense of time.

By some miracle, the building occupied by the French SS was still standing. When the Russians started shelling it, the upper floors collapsed, killing ten of the men. Gasping for breath, his lungs filling with plaster dust, Mathias pulled himself out of the debris. His shoulder was hurting terribly. Flames consumed the buildings all around him.

The survivors managed to take up new positions, dodging the enemy fire and the burning timbers and walls collapsing around them. By dawn, they had been pushed back to the *Puttkammerstrasse.*

That evening, they reached Kockstrasse subway station, the advance defence post of the Chancellery. After resting briefly at the battalion's command post, set up in a huge bookstore that had been totally destroyed, they went back out into the fray.

The next day, April 30, was a continuation of the nightmare into which the French SS had been lured by their dreams and deceptions. They fought on, believing that they were defending the leader to whom they had sworn undying devotion. In fact, they were defending a bunker containing only corpses. Hitler and his new bride, Eva Braun, had committed suicide at half past three that afternoon. After more fierce fighting, the Russians entered the *Reichstag*. Lieutenant Berest and two sergeants hoisted the Soviet flag atop a monument. During the night, General Krebs, commanding officer of the *Wehrmacht*, asked General Zhukov to accept the surrender of Berlin.

On the evening of May 1, the French SS evacuated the bookstore and took refuge in the basement of the Ministry of Security. By the light of candles placed in *Julturm*, earthenware candelabra used to celebrate the winter solstice, Feunay pinned the Iron Cross on their torn, blood-stained uniforms.

A few days later, Mathias was wounded again, this time in the chest and legs. With a few other soldiers, he managed to drag himself to Kaiserhof subway station. They hid him in the rubble at Potsdamerplatz station where he watched as Feunay and six of his comrades were taken prisoner. He was found, burning with a fever, by a German teenager. She and her father hid Mathias in the basement of their apartment building.

Chapter Thirty-Five

Through his friendship with Commander Klimenko, François was able to follow the assault on Berlin at close range, never ceasing to admire the courage of the Russian troops. With them, he shouted with joy as the Hammer and Sickle were hoisted over the *Reichstag*. The monster was dead at last.

On the evening of May 4, he wandered through the streets of Berlin. The warm air was filled with the stench of the bodies decaying under the rubble. The charred ruins stood starkly against the sky. A little girl stumbled out of one of the buildings, her face covered in soot. Rubbing her eyes, she bumped into him.

"Careful!" he said to her in French.

She looked at him, incredulous.

"Sind Sie Franzose?"

"Ja."

"Kommen Sie mit!"[1]

She took him by the hand and led him into the ruins. Climbing over the remains of a wall, they entered a narrow passage. They scrambled down a staircase choked with rubble and into a cellar, lit by a single candle. The room was filled with people. A young woman comforted a crying child; another adjusted a bandage on a little girl's head.

They recoiled at the sight of the Russian uniform, but the girl said a few words that seemed to reassure them, then led

[1] "Are you French?"—"Yes."—"Come with me."

François over to a corner where a man lay, his head propped against a metal cot.

"*Franzose*," she said, pointing to the man.

François approached and bent over the man. He was ill-shaven and glassy-eyed. His chest was crudely wrapped in dirty, blood-soaked bandages. From one of his legs, wrapped in rags, came a rank odor. He was delirious.

"*Er muss ins Krankenhaus*," said the girl.

"*Dazu ist es zu spät, er liegt im Sterben.*"

"*Nein, Sie müssen ihm helfen!*"[2]

"Can you hear me?" François asked the man in French.

The man stopped trembling and nodded his head slowly. "Thirsty."

François turned to the girl, who shrugged her shoulders.

"*Wir haben kein Wasser mehr, mein Vater ist unterwegs um was zu holen.*"[3]

In his condition, a shot of vodka can't do any harm, thought François, pulling a hip flask he had won in a poker game out of his pocket. He poured a few drops on to the dying man's lips.

"Thank you... allegiance... it hurts. ..."

"Don't move, I'm going to get help. The war is over now. You're safe."

"No," replied the man, grasping his sleeve. "The Russians will finish me off."

François gazed at the man intently. Of course, he thought, this must be one of the bastards who fought for the Germans.

"*Waffen SS?*"

"Yes. ... Charlemagne. Charlemagne Division. All of my ... dead. Dying here... crazy... thirsty..."

He choked and began coughing, but the pain in his chest was so great that he cried out, blood spurting from his mouth.

The young girl wiped his face with great tenderness.

"Léa," he murmured.

[2]"We must get him to a hospital."—"It's too late, he's dying."—"No! You must help him!"
[3]"We don't have any water. My father has gone to look for some."

"Ich bin nicht Léa, ich heisse Erika."[4]

"Léa, forgive me."

"What is your name?" demanded François.

"Léa. . . ."

"Er heisst Mathias, seinen Nachnamen kenne ich nicht."[5]

François reached into the inside pocket of the torn tunic and extracted a packet carefully wrapped in oilcloth, secured with an elastic band. It contained two military books. The name on the first was Otto Kramer. The name was vaguely familiar to him.

"Otto Kramer," he said aloud.

"Dead. . . I saw him die. . . a letter. . . for Sabine. . . must give it to her. . . ."

A photograph fell out of the second book. Erika picked it up.

"Wie hübsch die ist!"[6]

François snatched the photograph from her. Léa smiled up at him, her head on the shoulder of a young man who was clearly very proud to have her next to him. On the back, she had written: "Mathias and me at Montillac. August 1939."

François had never known exactly what their relationship had been. He only knew that Mathias had been her closest childhood friend.

Suddenly, there were voices in the stairway. A group of Russian soldiers entered the cellar. The women screamed and stood up, holding their children to their breasts. An N.C.O. came over to François. When he saw the Soviet uniform, he saluted.

"Comrade, who is this man?"

"I don't know, but he must be taken to a hospital, he's badly wounded."

"He won't make it!" the other man laughed.

The soldiers escorted the people out of the cellar. As she was about to leave, the girl looked over her shoulder at

---

[4] My name isn't Léa, it's Erika.
[5] His name is Mathias. I don't know his surname.
[6] "She's beautiful!"

François, her face pleading. Left alone, François looked down at Mathias.

"Léa..."

François realized that he was still holding the photograph. He slipped it and the military books into his pocket and sat down besides Mathias. He lit a cigarette which he placed between Mathias's lips.

"Thanks," he murmured.

They smoked without talking, their thoughts turning to the same woman. From time to time, Mathias moaned. He had to spit out his cigarette to cough. François mopped his brow.

"Write Léa ... her address is in my *Soldbuch* ... tell her my last thoughts were of her."

He tried to sit up, holding François's arm in an iron grip.

"Tell her that I loved her ... that I loved only her ... Léa ... forgive. ..."

His hands slid to his sides. Never again would he see the sundrenched hills of Montillac or the beautiful face that had been his torment and his joy. In death, his expression was that of an astonished child. Gently, François closed his eyes, covered him with a blanket, and left the basement.

Chapter Thirty-Six

On the evening of May 7, François received a telegram informing him that General de Gaulle had chosen General de Lattre de Tassigny to represent France when Germany surrendered, and requesting that François be at the airport to meet him.

He arrived at Tempelhof Airport in a jeep at ten o'clock the next morning and waited in the company of General Sokolovski, who was Marshal Zhukov's adjutant and responsible for greeting the Allied delegations, and a group of Russian officers.

In rows of twelve, rifles touching the shoulders of the soldiers in front, the Guard of Honor paraded back and forth on the tarmac.

At precisely twelve o'clock, escorted by Soviet fighter planes, the DC3 carrying the British delegation touched down. Admiral Burrough and Air Chief Marshal Tedder emerged, followed by three people in uniform, one of whom was a woman. General Sokolovski stepped forward to greet them. Ever the gentleman, he kissed the woman's hand.

After the introductions, the Guard of Honor gave a military salute. Ten minutes later, the DC3 carrying the American delegation landed. Sokolovski took leave of the British delegation to meet the commander of the United States Strategic Air Forces, General Spaatz. Once again, the Guard of Honor paid tribute, while the members of the British delegation left by car

337

for the Berlin suburb of Karlshorst. François watched the English woman, thinking to himself that she was one of the rare few who still looked like a woman in spite of the uniform. There was something familiar about her...

"Commander Tavernier, the French plane is about to land ... Commander, do you hear me?"

François pushed the Soviet soldier aside and began making his way through the crowd toward the British delegation. He arrived at the exit, just as a pair of pretty legs disappeared into a car. It sped off before he was able to catch up.

"Commander..."

François put his hand to his head. I'm beginning to see her everywhere, he thought. What would she be doing in Berlin with the British delegation?

"Commander..."

"I'll be right there."

He just made it back. General de Lattre de Tassigny, escorted by Colonel Demetz and Captain Bondoux, was about to be met by General Sokolovski.

The cars sped through the smoldering ruins of the capital of the Reich. Young Russian women in impeccable uniforms, their bare knees showing over their high boots, directed traffic with tiny red and yellow flags. Everywhere, dazed war-weary civilians lined up at fountains and fire hydrants for a few cupfuls of water.

François listened with only half an ear to what Captain Bondoux was saying. When they reached Karlshorst, the French delegation was taken to a military school that was virtually intact and now served as Marshal Zhukov's headquarters. They were escorted to the officers' quarters. The furnishings were extremely sparse, but the mattresses on the floor with covered with brilliantly white sheets.

General Vassiliev came over to greet General de Lattre de Tassigny, whom he had met in Algiers. The two men shook hands warmly. François chose this moment to slip out in search of the British delegation. He found Air Chief Marshal Tedder and Admiral Burrough, but no trace of the beautiful woman that had accompanied them. To ask them where she was was unthinkable.

The rest of the day was spent making a French flag that could be hoisted with the flags of the Allies in the room where the signing of the surrender was to take place. Eager to help, the Russians fashioned a flag out of a scrap of red cloth cut from a standard, white canvas, and blue serge from a mechanic's overalls. The result was a Dutch flag and they had to start all over again. At last, at eight o'clock, the French tricolor took its place between the Union Jack and the Stars and Stripes, over which had been raised the Hammer and Sickle.

At precisely midnight, Marshal Zhukov, his tunic covered with medals, rose and welcomed the Allied delegations. He then asked that the German delegation be brought in. Field Marshal Keitel entered the room in full military dress, greeting the assembly with his baton in stony silence. No one stood up. His gaze travelled around the room, pausing at the flags, then at General de Lattre de Tassigny.

"Ach! Franzosen sind auch hier! Das hat mir genau noch gefehlt!"[1]

He threw his baton and cap on to the table and sat down. On his right, sat General Stumpf and on his left, Admiral Von Frendenburg. Behind them six German officers, all wearing the Iron Cross, stood at attention. The flashbulbs of the official press delegations went off.

At forty-five minutes after midnight, Field Marshal Keitel left the room. He had just signed the unconditional surrender of Nazi Germany. The six German officers, visibly distressed, fought back tears.

That evening, a banquet was given by Marshal Zhukov in honor of the Allied delegations. The guests did not say their goodbyes until well after seven the next morning. François had not caught another glimpse of the young woman.

At nine o'clock, the Russians accompanied the delegations to the landing strip, decorated in the Soviet colors, where the welcoming ceremony was played in reverse. Tavernier

[1] "Ach! The French are here too! That's all we need!"

learned that the British and American delegations had left immediately after the banquet. He said good-bye to the French delegation and returned to Berlin.

There, he made funeral arrangements for Mathias. One month later, he was called back to Paris.

As soon as he arrived, he went to the apartment in the Rue de l'Université. There was no news of Léa. Her last letter, dated April 30, had been sent from London. At the Red Cross, Madame de Peyerimhoff told him that Léa was in Luneburg, Germany and was, as far as she knew, engaged to an English officer. François gave Sabine Otto's letter and military papers. In a calm voice, she thanked him and went to her room.

> My dearest,
> Tonight, I want to talk to you, to forget the horror all around me, the death of my friends, the destruction of my country, and to think only of the wonderful moments that we had together. Our happiness was cut short by the war, yet you gave me everything a man could ask for. You gave me your love and you gave me a son. I was unable to give him my name, but I want you to raise him with honor and dignity. I want you to teach him to love my ill-fated country and to help rebuild our two nations. At present, we are fighting side-by-side with foreign *Waffen SS* volunteers. I cannot understand why these wretched souls are fighting a battle that is not their own. I dream of being with you once again at Montillac, when the war is over, in the region that I came to love. I dream of you and our baby in the old house and on the terrace, looking out over the vineyards. Go back to Montillac, Sabine. You will find peace there. During the long winter nights, sit at the piano and play the songs that we both loved so much. Music heals the soul.
> My darling, I must say goodbye. The Russians are advancing on the house where we are hiding. I must go back to my tank. These precious moments with you have filled my soul with peace, banishing the anguish of the last few days. I am heading back into battle, armed with our love. Adieu,
>
> Otto.

Chapter Thirty-Seven

After her brief trip to Berlin—François had indeed seen her there—Léa had gone back to the French Red Cross. There had been an empty seat on the British delegation's plane, and she hoped that there might be people who had contacts with the Red Cross in other Allied countries, but arrangements could not be made in time.

Spirited out of Bergen-Belsen, Sarah became the heroine of Marshal Montgomery's officers; they intervened to prevent the Marshal or his superiors from sending her back to Germany. She was placed in quarantine, for fear that she might have typhus, and gradually regained her strength. Nothing remained of the vivacious young woman whom Léa remembered. She was a broken woman, prematurely old, who trembled whenever a voice was raised. She refused to say what had happened to her in the camps, but went over and over her miraculous reunion with Léa with a gratitude that was deeply touching. After she was removed from quarantine, McClintock took her to stay with his family. The British officer confided to Sarah that he intended to marry Léa. In a soft, weary voice, she replied:

"She is not right for you."

Distressed and hurt, McClintock had taken his leave and returned to Germany. From that point on, he watched over Léa constantly. She had changed, becoming more flirtatious yet more tender, spending entire evenings drinking and dancing with young officers. She was surrounded by devoting admirers whom she treated with total indifference. He remarked to her that she wasn't behaving very nicely. In response, she kissed him and told him that he was terribly old-fashioned. Secretly, she thought that he would make the perfect husband. Every so often, her need for peace and quiet made her think that she might marry him.

Léa was sent to Brussels, then to Luneburg, where she was reunited with Jeanine Ivoy and met Claire Mauriac and Mistou Nou de la Houplière. Together, Léa and her friends transported convoys of deportees, to whom their youth and beauty gave new hope. After realizing that their garrison caps reminded the deportees of the concentration camps, Léa and her friends traded them in for round hats. In spite of, or because of, the horror of the camps, the French section was always in an uproar.

They arrived in Berlin in early August and were given quarters at 96 Kurfürstendamm in the British sector. It was one of the few buildings that had not been too badly damaged by the bombs. The French and Belgian Red Cross were the only ones allowed access to the Russian sector in order to search the camps for their nationals. On more than one occasion, they brought English prisoners out in their ambulances, and were rewarded with fuel and food. One of their most painful tasks involving taking children born of French and Belgian fathers away from the Germans. Whenever possible, they spent their evenings dancing at the British Officers' Club or sitting around the pool at the *Blue and White*.

Mistou, Claire, and Léa shared a room at 96 Kurfürstendamm. The other women called it the "whore's boudoir," partly because the three women had tried to spruce it up a bit, and partly because the others were jealous of their beauty. They had only to enter one of the clubs for the men to abandon their partners and step forward to ask for a dance. Mistou's quick laugh and engaging smile met with instant success. The beautiful, melancholy Claire had eyes only for Captain Wiazemsky. He had been liberated by the Russians and had stayed with them until after the war was over, refusing to return to his country of origin. He had since been reassigned to the French army. As for Léa, they had all lost count of the hearts she had broken.

One evening, as she was returning from a particularly gruelling assignment with Claire and Captain Wiazemsky, she bumped into a French officer.

"Pardon me."

Too tired to respond, she continued on her way.

"Léa!"

Just as she had done on Christmas Eve, she froze in her tracks, afraid that if she moved, she might destroy the illusion of happiness.

"Léa!"

Suddenly, he was there, taller than she had remembered. She had forgotten how steady his gaze was and his lips...

Gone the ruins and the thin, obsequious Germans. Gone the walking skeletons and the orphans. No more blood or death or fear. He was there, in her arms, alive and well. Why was he crying? He was crazy to be crying like this. But she was crying, too, and laughing and soon everyone around them joined in.

Mistou blew her nose loudly.

"Love is so beautiful," she murmured.

"Poor McClintock," replied Jeanine.

Claire shook François's hand warmly.

"I've been looking for you everywhere since May," murmured François, burying his face in Léa's hair.

"When I didn't hear from you, I thought you were dead."

"Didn't your sisters tell you that I came to see you in Paris?"

Léa shook her head, sniffling.

Mistou offered her a handkerchief.

"You can't just stand here. If the chief sees you, there'll be hell to pay. He's very strict about house rules. Come and join us at the British Officers' Club later. We're going to have a bath. We stink to high heaven of corpses."

343

"Mistou!" cried Claire.

"Well, it's true, isn't it? You even said that you thought you were coming down with one of your migraines."

"I'd like to see how you'd feel if you got one," said Claire, vexed.

"No thanks, you can keep them! Just thinking about migraines gives me a headache."

"Okay, break it up, you two," said Léa. "Hey! There's Jeanine. Jeanine, do you remember François Tavernier?"

"Do I ever! Thanks to him, I had the best Christmas of my life! Hello, Commander, nice to see you again."

"Hello, mademoiselle."

"All right, girls. Back to work! See you later, Commander!"

When the women had gone, the two men stood looking at one another. Finally, they agreed to meet at eight o'clock at the British Officers' Club.

The men who watched Léa laughing and dancing that night knew that all hope was lost. McClintock watched her too, his heart sinking. Mistou saw the expression on his face and went over to him.

"Come on, Colonel, cheer up. Why don't you ask me to dance?"

When they passed on the dance floor, Léa threw her friend a look of gratitude.

François held her so tightly that she could scarcely breathe, but she would not have dreamed of complaining. They danced without talking, without needing to talk, oblivious to the others, instinctively following the music, changing rhythm effortlessly, dancing in perfect harmony. As they had done at the ball at the German Embassy in Paris, they continued to dance long after the music had stopped. Laughter and applause brought them back to earth. After a few nightcaps, they left the club.

It was a mild evening. They climbed in a jeep parked near the exit, and drove silently through the ruins, crossing the park of Charlottenburg Palace where, in the pale moonlight, the twisted, charred trunks of the trees looked like a forlorn

344

battalion. François stopped on the Charlottenburgerstrasse. The streets and buildings surrounding the Victory Column looked as though they had been eaten away by some dread disease. Perched high above the ruined expanse was the eagle of the Third Reich, golden wings spread defiantly.

Gently, François drew Léa to him. They held each other close, feeling the warmth of their bodies, closing their eyes and savoring a strange new happiness—that of losing oneself in love, of feeling one's heart bursting inside a body that now belongs to someone else. Perhaps for the first time, in this grim setting, their tenderness surfaced. They felt themselves slowly carried away, drowning in happiness, not needing to make love just yet.

The call of a night bird made them both laugh.

"They're returning," said Léa. "That's a good sign."

"Let's go."

As they entered the Kurfürstendamm, they passed a church built in praise of William the Conqueror. Above the four towers, partially destroyed, the central steeple seemed to have been decapitated.

"You're taking me back already!"

"No, my love, only if you want to. When we said goodbye this afternoon, I rented a room with an old woman not far from here."

"How did you manage that? There's nothing for rent."

"I found a way."

They stopped in a narrow street near the Hohenzollerndamm, whose low houses had been spared. Taking out a large key, François opened the door. An oil lamp was burning in the hall. A large cat rubbed itself against their legs. They each took a candle from the table at the entrance and went upstairs, stifling their giggles. The room smelled of faded roses.

By the light of the candles, François began taking off her uniform. He slipped the straps of the pink slip off her shoulders, the whisper of the silk arousing them further. As she stepped out of the slip, he buried his nose in it, drinking in her smell. It was all he could do not to tear off her lace panties. When at last she was naked, he knelt in front of her,

345

gazing upwards. She felt his eyes devouring her, making her body tremble and her knees weak. She shivered as his lips touched the inside of her thighs and began travelling upward. She thrust her body forward to receive his kisses and came, standing up, clinging to his hair to keep her balance. He carried her over to the bed and undressed without taking his eyes off her. Then, very slowly, he penetrated her. She lay back, confident. When she felt her pleasure mounting again, she cried:

"Harder! Harder!"

He took her back to the residence before dawn. She slipped into the "whore's boudoir" without waking her friends.

The next day, they told each other everything that had happened since the Christmas they had spent together near Amiens. François's joy at learning that Sarah was alive and slowly regaining her strength in England was almost enough to make Léa jealous. He was afraid to tell her about Mathias and began instead to talk about Otto and his visit to Sabine.

"Were you there when Otto died?" asked Léa.

"No, I found his papers in the pocket of a French *Waffen SS* who had known him."

Léa closed her eyes.

"And what happened to him?"

"He died too."

François took her in his arms, and continued in a low voice:

"He died calling your name, Léa. He asked you to forgive him. Oh, darling, cry if it helps!"

Léa sobbed bitterly. How hard it is to say goodbye to childhood!

That evening, she asked him to take her to Mathias's grave. On it, she placed a bouquet of flowers from a stand at the corner of the Konstanzerstrasse.

"We can take him back to France, if you'd like."

"No, he died here. This is where he belongs."

"What are you doing?"

346

"I'm taking some earth back to Montillac."

Léa suddenly felt bittersweet happiness.

"Léa, what's wrong?" he asked.

Nothing was wrong. It was just that, for the first time in a long time, she could picture returning to her beloved Montillac. And Mathias had made it possible! She began filling her hat with handfuls of earth. When she straightened up, her face shone with new hope.

François and Léa saw each other every day for a week. Claire and Mistou covered for her as best they could. The work done by the young women of the French Red Cross drew admiration from all quarters. Jeanine, their Section Leader, wrote to Madame de Peyerimhoff:

> As you are no doubt already aware through the progress reports, we are working very hard and have managed to extend our stay in the British sector as a result of our efforts on their behalf. They have been refused permission to enter the Russian sector to look for their MIAs (of which there are approximately 30,000); when we go there on missions, we do for the British what we do for our own. Sometimes we return with hundreds of death certificates and lists of graves from remote villages, all of which have to be sorted by nationality. The paperwork never stops!
>
> Each team has been stripped down to five drivers and one nurse; the British insisted that personnel be cut because supplies are limited.
>
> Deportees from Alsace and Lorraine continue to stream in, and we are only too happy to help repatriate them. These poor people have suffered so! Over a period of ten days, our girls dressed, fed, and cared for seven thousand of them. Their tireless devotion has earned them the admiration of the French and British here.
>
> We are expecting more trainloads of deportees from Alsace and Lorraine (approximately 3,000) any day now, and the British will be calling on us to help. They are in very poor physical condition and we are happy that the French Red Cross is able to provide moral support, as well as food and clothing.

347

General Keller comes from Moscow on a regular basis and tells us when to expect the trains. There are so many of them in the camps in the furthest reaches of Russia.

We are really very fortunate to be able to enter the Russian sector. We have their trust and everywhere we go, we are greeted warmly. When the last train came through, we went to see a very important general for permission to recover those in need of immediate medical attention. He called Moscow right before our eyes. Permission was not granted, but at least he tried. We are very glad that we made the effort; this week, they will be handed over to us, then placed on the evacuation train that has just arrived.

The atmosphere is incredible. I feel very privileged to be working with such fine people, particularly Mademoiselle Mauriac, Mademoiselle Nou de la Houplière, Mademoiselle Delmas, Mademoiselle Farret d'Astier, and Mademoiselle d'Alvery. They are always ready to pitch in and help one another.

François received orders to return to Paris before travelling to the United States. Léa accompanied him to Tempelhof Airport after one last night in their tiny room. When she saw him disappear into the Dakota, she began to tremble. The thought that she might not see him again was more than she could bear.

Her friends redoubled their efforts to distract her. Mistou and Claire did such a good job that Léa managed to find some of her former lightheartedness. With Captain Wiazemsky, they visited the Chancellery and Hitler's Bunker. They emerged from the jumble of telegrams, half-burnt journals, slashed portraits, and defiled medals feeling deeply oppressed.

Chapter Thirty-Eight

In mid-September, Léa received orders to escort a group of children to Paris. She left Berlin and her friends feeling both sad and relieved. There had been too many ruins, too much suffering, too many deaths.

Upon her arrival in Paris, Madame de Peyerimhoff gave her a few days' leave. She rushed to the Rue de l'Université, only to find the door locked. The concierge gave her the keys, saying that the entire family had left for Montillac. Léa was bewildered; she had so looked forward to a few days in the capital.

She left immediately for the Gare d'Austerlitz. The train to Bordeaux was crowded and unpleasant and she spent the night wedged between a soldier with wandering hands and a fat, surly woman. Whenever she dozed off, she heard Aunt Bernadette screaming and Raoul moaning. She wondered how long they would continue to haunt her dreams. She began to think that it was crazy to return to Montillac. What did she hope to find there? After seeing so much destruction, why add another ruin to a list that had grown longer each year? What was the point in going back? Nothing and no one could bring back the dead or the old house.

She arrived in Bordeaux exhausted and determined to take the next train back to Paris but there, on the other platform, was the old train to Langon. Without thinking, she began running. As it pulled out of the station, a hand reached out and helped her on to the train.

The station in Langon was just as she remembered it. Bag in hand, she walked toward the center of the little town. It was market day. Two *gendarmes* stood talking outside the Hôtel Oliver.

"Why! That must be one of the Delmas girls! Mademoiselle!"

Léa turned.

"Don't you remember us? We drove you and your uncle and that poor young woman to La Sifflette's."

Yes, of course she remembered.

"Well, now, you're coming back home, are you? There's been lots happened since you left—some good, some bad. I don't suppose you have your blue bicycle with you. We'll give you a lift. Wouldn't do to leave her standing by the side of the road, would it, Laffont?"

"No indeed, Renault! We won't have it said that chivalry is dead in the *Gendarmerie française!*"

Not knowing how to refuse their kindness, she got into the car.

The two men talked on and on, but she did not hear a word of what they said. She gazed out of the window at the countryside that she loved so dearly and thought she would never see again, overcome with emotion. They agreed to drop her off at La Prioulette. She waited until the car disappeared out of sight before carrying on.

It was one of those wonderful, late summer afternoons when the sun spreads a rosy glow over the vines, announcing the arrival of fall.

The slope seemed longer than she remembered. She slowed her pace. There, behind the trees, was Montillac. Her heart pounding, she stopped at the white gates.

There was a new and unfamiliar smell in the air. It was the smell of freshly sawn wood. Then, familiar noises rushed in, the cackling of hens, the barking of a dog, the cooing of doves, the whinnying of a horse. Beyond the farm buildings stood the blackened timbers of the house. She felt a breeze in her hair. Her legs heavy, she carried on. There was the sound of sawing and hammering, and a man, singing:

"She wore a flower in her hair,
A sign that spring was in the air,
And not just spring, but also hope,
For love and peace of wondrous scope."

Workers were fitting slate tiles into place over fresh roof beams. One side was already covered. The kitchen door was open. She stumbled backwards along the laneway that she and her sisters used to call "the street." From the terrace came the sound of children's voices and laughter. She wanted to run away, but felt herself being drawn toward their voices. The swing swayed gently in the breeze. Suddenly she saw a little girl, hair flying, calling:

"Higher, Mathias! Higher!"

Then the image was gone. The empty swing and the arbor, the rose bushes along the lane and the vines between the rows of cyprus all came into focus again. Far off, a train passed over the viaduct. A church bell sounded the hour. She heard her sisters' voices.

It was as though nothing had changed. As she began walking toward the house, a man holding Charles by the hand came out to meet her.

François!

THE END